Praise for Elizabeth Essex's Reckless Brides series

Almost a Scandal

"Essex will have readers longing to set sail alongside her daring heroine and dashing hero. This wild ride of a high-seas adventure/desire-in-disguise romance has it all: nonstop action, witty repartee, and deft plotting. From the bow to the mast, from battles to ballrooms, Essex delivers another reckless bride and another read to remember." —*RT Book Reviews*

"Elizabeth Essex will dazzle you with her sophisticated blend of vivid historical detail, exquisite characterization, and delicious sexual tension. *Almost a Scandal* is a breathtaking tale of rapturous romance and awe-inspiring adventure!"
—*USA Today* bestselling author Julianne MacLean

"Elizabeth Essex writes the perfect blend of fast-paced adventure and deliciously sexy romance. I couldn't put this book down! *Almost a Scandal* gets a place on my keeper shelf—I will read anything Elizabeth Essex writes!" —*New York Times* bestselling author Celeste Bradley

"The first book in the Reckless Brides Trilogy is a seafarer's delight. Col and Sally's high-stakes adventure is fast-paced and fraught with peril. Well-timed humor punctuates the action and the use of frigate-speak adds authenticity to the shipboard dialogue. The love story teases the reader at first, as Col and Sally struggle to conceal their attraction onboard the *Audacious*. Then things turn desperate when the circumstances of war seem intent on driving them apart. A smartly written, emotional tempest." —*Reader to Reader Reviews*

"Elizabeth Essex has created a fascinating world peopled with fascinating characters. I didn't want this story to end, and with the promise of more books in this series, it doesn't have to. *Almost a Scandal* is a joy to read." —*Fresh Fiction*

"Ms. Essex delivers romance at its finest; adventure-packed, passion-filled, and totally satisfying. Teeming with adventure, passion, sexual tension, secrets, scandal, witty banter, romance, and love, this story is a delight and a definite keeper." —*Romance Junkies*

A Breath of Scandal

"Essex's second Reckless Bride certainly suits the title. The bold heroine easily wins readers' hearts, along with her officer and gentleman hero. Essex brings a breath of fresh and funny air to the Regency while her stylish writing and intelligent characters appeal to hearts and minds. Pure, delicious, sexy pleasure awaits readers." —*RT Book Reviews*

"Creating two very strong-willed characters and a mouthwatering romance, Ms. Essex has penned a deliciously compelling and heartwarming story that will keep the reader glued to the pages until the very end." —Lauren Calder, *Affaire de Coeur Magazine*

Scandal in the Night

"[A] sweeping plot, an over-the-top ballsy heroine, and a villain worthy of an Old Skool romance. This book was fun, barrels of it." —*Smart Bitches, Trashy Books*

"Essex seamlessly shifts the action in the story back and forth between the protagonists' first meeting in India and their reunion in England, and her third exotic, enthralling Reckless Brides historical romance is a potent combination of dangerous intrigue and sexy desire."
—*Booklist*

"*Scandal in the Night* was a story of great talent and beautiful storytelling…The retellings of the India parts left me longing to experience the life and culture of India for myself. Cat and Thomas had a relationship that was combustible and my only wish for this book is that I could have spent more time with these characters…The intrigue and subplot of this book were amazing. This is definitely a must-read book for all of the historical romance novel fanatics out there."
—*Night Owl Reviews* (4½ stars and a Top Pick!)

"Essex has taken her Reckless Brides on some unique adventures, delivering a fresh take on the Regency era. Full of romance, adventure, sensuality and mystery, and set against a lush backdrop, *Scandal in the Night* immerses readers in a nonstop story. Flashbacks enhance the plot, adding depth to the characters and the slowly unfolding mystery until readers are flying through the pages to uncover the truth and see the lovers united."
—*RT Book Reviews* (4½ stars)

Also by
Elizabeth Essex

Almost a Scandal
Breath of Scandal
Scandal in the Night
After the Scandal

Novella

The Scandal Before Christmas

A Scandal
to Remember

ELIZABETH ESSEX

St. Martin's Paperbacks

This is a work of fiction. All of the characters, organizations, and events portrayed in this novel are either products of the author's imagination or are used fictitiously.

A SCANDAL TO REMEMBER

Copyright © 2014 by Elizabeth Essex.

For information address St. Martin's Press, 175 Fifth Avenue, New York, NY 10010.

ISBN: 978-1-250-04458-7

Printed in the United States of America

St. Martin's Paperbacks edition / September 2014

St. Martin's Paperbacks are published by St. Martin's Press, 175 Fifth Avenue, New York, NY 10010.

10 9 8 7 6 5 4 3 2 1

For Hannah,
for her patience and brilliant assistance with plot
points and character names, and for her general
enthusiam for the written word, but most especially
for the delightul trove of sea chanteys she spent
an entire road trip singing for me.
I will cherish that day forever.

May you always be able to find friends and recognize
kindred spirits within the pages of a book.
Weigh hey, roll and go!

Chapter One

Lieutenant Charles Dance was old enough and smart enough to know that some ideas were bad, right from the start. Some choices were no choice at all, especially when fueled by desperation. And some things were enough to drive a man to drink.

Except that his captain was already drunk, reeling about his cabin reeking of gin at ten o'clock in the morning. And they hadn't even left Portsmouth dock.

"Who in the hell are you?"

"Lieutenant Dance, reporting for duty, sir."

The old sot of a captain blinked his rheumy eyes at Dance, and stepped curiously sideways, as if they were in high seas, and the deck were rising up to meet his foot. He squinted upward to try and focus on Dance's rather tall person. "What are you doin' here, man?"

Dance ducked his head to step forward under the beams overhead. He never had fit in a damn frigate. "I've been assigned to *Tenacious,* Captain. I've come to be your first lieutenant, sir." Dance raised his voice slightly, and enunciated his words, in case the man was deaf as well as drunker than a gin whore.

"Damn your eyes. Stand still."

Not deaf then, but most assuredly a grizzled, grumpy old drunk who showed no signs of recognition, or cognizance, much less sobriety.

Dance dug in his old blue uniform coat to produce his written orders, handed to him only that morning. The orders he had been desperate to accept, because he knew damn well he was unlikely to get another posting that seemed such an easy berth.

He had been eight months out of employment, put ashore on half-pay and close rations like most of the fleet. Eight months of watching his chances of getting a better command dwindle to nothing, while better men—men with influence and connections—were deprived of their profession as well.

Now that the navy had won the bloody war, and saved Britain from sure invasion, they were all redundant—a drain on a nation ready to forget the past and be pleased with the future. The trouble was, of course, that after so many years of war, Dance and men like him were unfit for any other gainful profession. Unfit for any other company but their own.

Which might explain why his captain was drunk and alone.

"My orders are to join you for this voyage to the South Seas, sir. An expedition of the Royal Society, is it not? Slated to leave as soon as the ship has finished being made ready?"

Dance had jumped to accept his old friend Will Jellicoe's suggestion that he take the commission aboard *Tenacious*. Such a lengthy expedition looked to provide suitable, easy employment for several years, even without the added bonus of a monetary prize from the Duke of Fenmore for safeguarding the expedition of naturalists under the duke's liberal patronage. One didn't turn down a patron like the Duke of Fenmore, even if it meant signing on with a captain who looked as if he ought to have been put to bed with a cannonball years ago.

Dance might have expected that Captain Muckross be old and less than accomplished. Energetic, successful captains were unlikely to be given such an unimportant—by Admiralty standards—commission as a tame expedition of dull naturalists. But what choice did Dance have? A bad situation was better than no situation at all. He had rather take his chances with a decrepit captain, in a decrepit ship, than sit about in his decrepit lodging house wishing he were anywhere else.

The decrepit old sot of a captain was still trying in vain to focus upon the paper Dance extended toward him, but failed. Instead, he waved his new lieutenant away with an impatient, ill-coordinated sweep of his arm that nearly toppled him into a chair. "Well then, what are you gawping about here, boy? Get your bloody arse topside, and leave me in peace. Be about your damn business."

Dance folded his orders away, and took his arse topside, where there was plenty of damn business to see to. The evidence of the captain's mismanagement was everywhere—the ship was a hovel, about as decrepit and ill-kept as a Royal Navy frigate could be, and still be afloat. Lines were slack and rotting. Hardware and fittings were ill-used, and in bad repair. The entire vessel was filthy and stank like a stale gin mill.

In its present state, *Tenacious* was nothing better than a floating coffin.

It would take a week of work just to sort out the good from the bad, and replace the most pressing of the vessel's rotting needs. And then there was the matter of who might pay for such repairs. Even within the Admiralty, repairs cost hard money. The yards at Portsmouth shipyard only disgorged their stores readily for captains willing and able to pay.

Dance didn't mind spending other men's money—the captain's or the Duke of Fenmore it mattered not—especially if it would keep him from a watery grave. Because in its present state, the ship would see them all drowned before they reached Salvador de Bahia.

Dance ascended the ladder to the quarterdeck slowly, mentally cataloguing everything that needed to be done, and wondering why that very same work wasn't presently *being* done. A very few men idled about, squinting at him without much curiosity, a stranger in their midst. And the quarterdeck, upon which at least one officer should have appeared on duty, was deserted.

"Who has the deck?" Dance asked no one in particular and everyone within earshot, if only to see who would answer.

No one.

Interesting. And disheartening. There was a tension, a holding back that told him *Tenacious* was a distrustful, secretive ship.

"You there." Dance called to the only sailor he could find on the quarterdeck—a fellow lounging near the base of the mizzen mast, whittling carefully away at some piece of knifework. An idle topman from the looks of his once-bright kerchief and gold-ringed ear, with twoscore years to his tattooed hide. "Who has the deck?"

The sailor squinted up at Dance from the comfort of his carving. "No watches in port." And then he added as a sort of afterthought, "Sir."

"The hell you say." Dance had never heard of such idleness. He was no martinet for strict discipline, but in all his years of being at sea, he had never been aboard a Royal Navy vessel that did not keep some sort of watch schedule, even in port. "Who has charge as the senior officer here?"

The idler had the good sense to hear the outrage in Dance's tone, and shuffle to his feet, but the mahogany-skinned tar still looked at Dance as if he feared the new lieutenant had taken a blow to the head, though he tugged his white forelock in belated deference. "Not sure."

Dance had always thought of himself as a patient man. He had never been the hellfire-and-brimstone sort—hellfire and brimstone always took too much energy that could be put to better use. "Let me rephrase. Who is the senior officer who is not currently drunk?"

The tar's wrinkled face creased into a wry smile. "Not currently? Couldn't say for sure, sir. No accounting for officers' tastes." And knowing he had already said too much, the man added, "Begging yer pardon, sir."

Bloody blue fuck. This is what he had come to, amusing men who didn't give a damn if he could have them flogged within an inch of their life. "What is your name, topman?"

"Flanaghan, sir. Topman as you say. Captain of the main."

Irish. Which accounted for both the sunburned skin and the wry humor. But which also meant that Flanaghan was possessed of some skill as well as humor—he was a figure of authority, having been elected by the other men working his mast to lead them. A good man to have on his side.

"Flanaghan." Dance impressed the name and the red face upon his memory, the same as he would need to do with every man jack aboard the ship. "Best to stand to something approaching attention, Flanaghan. I'm sure we'll all be better for the exercise. Who are your officers?"

"Well." The bronzed tar kept up his wry air. "There's you, looks like."

"No points for the easy fruit, Flanaghan. Lieutenant Dance. I'm assigned to be first." Dance did not extend his hand to shake, but took the opportunity to avail himself of Flanaghan's wry honesty. "Who was first before me?"

Flanaghan shook his head. "Haven't had a first in all the time I been with her."

Fuck all. The short hairs on the back of Dance's neck stood up. He'd never heard of a navy ship without a first officer. Perhaps the captain wasn't merely a useless drunk, but an abusive tyrant who couldn't keep officers. "Does *Tenacious* have a sailing master?"

"Old Doc Whitely, sir, be sailing master."

"Doc?"

"Doctor they call him, on account of him having taken holy orders once upon a time in his life back in Norfolk, afore he escaped the preaching and come to sea some thirty years ago."

A strange, gentleman's education for a warrant officer, but Dance was happy enough to have a man of some learning in charge of the education of others—the sailing master being the instructor in navigation for any ship's midshipmen. "Lieutenants and midshipmen?"

"No young gentlemen. Only Lieutenant Lawrence. He be young. Only passed for lieutenant at the end of our last cruise."

"And when was *Tenacious*'s last cruise, Flanaghan?"

"We come into Portsmouth on Michaelmas, sir."

So the ship and what might be left of her crew had been sitting idle for two months, growing barnacles on her hull since September, with no industry under a drunken captain, an elderly master, and a green boy as lieutenant.

"How many men has *Tenacious* lost since then?"

"Couldn't rightly say, sir, as I never learnt my numbers that high."

Another wry joke, Dance was sure, but it soured his gut all the same. This was his lot in life—the dregs from the bottom of the Admiralty's brine-filled barrel. And likely the other remaining inmates of this floating prison were the same—too stupid or too lazy to go elsewhere.

"Pass word for the muster and punishment books to be

brought to me, as well as the watch bills." Although all of the ship's books were under the ultimate authority of the captain, such books about the disposition of the crew—the positions and skills they held—were the responsibility of the first lieutenant. But without a first lieutenant, *Tenacious*'s books must have fallen to the sailing master. "Send the compliments of the deck that Lieutenant Dance wishes to speak to Mr. Whitely."

While he waited for Flanaghan to carry out his order, Dance began making a list in his head of all the tasks for immediate attention, starting with the ramshackle animal pens moldering at the aft end of the quarterdeck. A single goat and a few skinny chickens picked their way through dark piles of straw dank with the ammonia reek of urine. The whole of it would need an unholy holystoning to clear out both the rats that were bound to be nestled in the bedding, and the stink.

But it was going to take more than holystones and lime to make *Tenacious* over into anything resembling a working naval ship. Everywhere he looked was work left undone by a lazy, shiftless crew. Broken ratlines in the shrouds. Loose hardware in the main chains. Slack halyards from the tops.

And he wasn't the only one looking. No. He could feel the touch of the eyes of the men sizing him up, placing him in the rigid hierarchy of the navy by his age and the wear on his lieutenant's uniform. Best to get it over with and let them have an eyeful. They'd find out the sort of man he was soon enough.

Dance stood at the quarterdeck rail and let himself be seen. He could still feel the weight of the crew's curiosity, though they sifted out slowly to have a better look at him, like rats blinking in the watery sunshine, when a large fellow with the greasy look of a well-fed barn cat—not enough of a pet to be altogether civilized—picked his way up the nearby companionway ladder. With one foot over the combing, the man paused and narrowed his face, as if he could scent the particular stench of a superior officer in the air.

Fair enough. Dance's hackles were standing up as well. Instinct honed by years of service told Dance this man was his natural enemy in a way that neither the French nor the Americans had ever been.

But he knew better than to let it show. When Flanaghan returned, shifting his eyes from Dance to the bulky man as if measuring them up, one against the other, Dance simply pretended he hadn't seen.

The bulky man's self-created uniform marked him as a warrant officer, a fact which Flanaghan immediately confirmed when he finally spoke. "Mr. Ransome be bo-sun." The topman said the name quietly, and all but made the sign of the cross, as if he would ward off the evil eye that the bosun surely possessed.

The few men who had ventured out to have a look at Dance moved away from the bosun without a sound, dispersing to quieter, safer corners—rats scuttling back into the comfort of the dark.

So. It was like that.

Bosuns were rarely popular men—it was their job to keep the crew at their work, and to punish those found lagging—but on first impression Dance thought Mr. Ransome was the sort to be rather more hated and feared than he was respected.

Dance would have to think and move quickly to gain the upper hand.

He smiled, and spoke in the instant before the bosun opened his mouth—nothing was as effective as getting in the first word. "Mr. Ransome, I presume. Call all hands."

But Ransome proved to be a devilishly cool customer, with mettle in his backbone. He took a long moment to look at this specimen of a lieutenant, as if he had seen twenty such men before, and found them all lacking. "And who be you?"

"The fellow with white facing on his coat, Mr. Ransome." Dance indicated the sign of his rank, but kept his tone level, giving no room for argument. "Call all hands."

The greasy bastard—and within the last few moments Dance had come to the conclusion that the man was indeed a clever bastard—slid his eyes sideways, and hesitated just long enough to set a quick match to Dance's normally slow-burning temper.

Dance wasn't a man given to ostentatious displays of either valor or displeasure. He did not indulge in fits, or set himself against other men. It wasn't his way—it was too much work and too much excitement for too little return. But for some reason he had no time to fathom, he wanted to take Ransome on.

In less time than it took the big man to narrow his bulbous, round eyes, Dance had snatched the whistle that was the bosun's badge of office from around his neck, and snapped it off its chain in one swift, violent tug. He had the whistle to his mouth and was shrilly piping all hands before the belligerent man had instinctively reached out his hand to grab it back.

Dance pivoted neatly out of the bosun's reach, and looked pointedly at the big ham hock of a hand that hung in the air between them. "Careful, Mr. Ransome," he said in a low voice. "Striking a superior officer is a hanging move." Dance tossed the brass whistle back, and kept his voice low and even—conciliatory almost. "And I would advise you to repair your whistle, so that you are prepared to do your job the next time I might require you to do so."

The bastard was cagey enough to knuckle his forehead. But his greasy smile and sideways glance told Dance that there would be a reckoning.

"Another word of advice, Mr. Ransome." Again, Dance

made his voice conversational, bland even, and he kept his eyes on the men assembling under the waist. "I'm not a bastard for having my way. But I'll expect you to see to your duty, and fulfill your orders when I ask you to. We'll find our feet with each other, Mr. Ransome. And the sooner you understand where my toes start and yours leave off, the better off we'll all be." Dance nodded easily. "And now, with the compliments of the deck, I'll ask you to call your men."

Ransome slid apart from Dance, and started bawling what was necessary, taking his frustrations out on the hapless onlookers, lashing out indiscriminately with his cane. "Look alive there. Look alive." He let a roar down the main hatchway, "Out or down. Out or down. Rouse you out, you grass-combing lubbers."

Within two minutes, Dance counted perhaps sixty men grouped loosely in the waist before him, instead of the one hundred and forty that was the usual complement of a frigate in wartime. Even with allowances for the peace, *Tenacious* was severely undermanned.

And with only two other officers, and no midshipmen—he would have to see to that straightaway.

"Mr. Ransome, I'll have the punishment and muster rolls, if you please." Dance was careful to let Ransome have something of his way, and be seen to have a superior knowledge of the ship's people.

"The rolls? Sir?"

There was enough real confusion in the man that Dance could take his hesitation for something other than insolence. "The books, Mr. Ransom, with the names of the crew and their positions and their allotment into starboard and larboard watches. The muster and punishment rolls."

"Captain Muckross is not one much given to scribblin' nor record keeping."

Again, Dance was no slave to Admiralty regulations, but he had never heard of a ship that didn't at least keep the minimum of records, especially a daily log and the names and wages of its crew. "Mr. Ransome, if you do not know where or by whom they are kept, then kindly find me someone who does know."

"Givens," the mate growled.

Another man, as well padded as the bosun, stepped forward.

Even without an introduction, Dance would have known the man was the purser. He had the nip-cheese look of the profession—the sort of man whose rat-quick eyes were constantly estimating the value of everything he saw.

"Mr. Mathias Givens, purser, at your service, Lieutenant." The man even went so far in currying Dance's favor that he doffed his hat. Dance had met his type before, oily and obsequious in his obvious attempts to please, but secretive and greasy behind one's back.

"Mr. Givens, I require the ship's books, specifically the muster and punishment logs."

"But the punishment . . ." The purser's eye slid back to the bosun.

And well they should, as the bosun was the one who carried out all punishments, and in the absence of a senior officer—at least one sober enough to write down the offense and its consequence in lashes—Dance would have expected a man like Ransome to have kept the books himself. Interesting. Neither man claimed the responsibility.

"Find them. Now." Dance put all the cynical perturbation he could muster into his voice. "Best to sort the bad facts out sooner rather than later. In the meantime—" Dance took out his own hardbound blank book—brought in the now clearly foolish hope that he might write an account of the voyage himself for publication. "But as you will be engaged in finding the existing logs, I will need you to furnish the name of a literate man who can act as a clerk for the interim."

"A clerk?" The purser licked his lips and looked more than flustered. "I'm sure I can do all that's required, sir."

"Not while you're employed in the hunt for those books, Mr. Givens. A name, if you please?"

"If you'll pardon me, sir." One of the younger members of the crew, a wiry boy with a shock of sun-bleached blond hair, stepped forward. "I knows all my letters and numbers, sir. And can read and write."

"Excellent." Here was his first piece of luck, but hopefully not his last. "Your name?"

"Morris, sir."

"Morris, you are hereby promoted to clerk, unless you are one of Flanaghan's men." Dance was careful not to take on the *whole* of the damn ship in this, his first battle. "In which case, your promotion is ad hoc and only for as long as it is necessary. At present, you will assist me in taking down the names of this crew." He would meet each man, find his profession if he had one, his years and his level of skill. And see also what sort of men he was missing.

With Morris situated on an upturned cask, Dance had restored enough of the balance of power in his favor to be able to redress Mr. Ransome. "I'll have the professionals first, Mr. Ransome, followed by the topmen." As the men working the sails would be directly under his command, Dance wanted a good look at them, for their skill and professionalism would be put to the test in rounding the cape of South America, a difficult task in a good ship, and an impossible one in anything less.

"But before we start, I will tell you, one and all, that your hours of leisure are over. From this moment, until the moment we warp over our anchors and proceed down Channel, you will have nothing but unremitting work. Hard work. This ship, in its present state, is unfit for service, and a blight upon the honor of every man jack that belongs to her. You may all be perfectly resigned to sending yourselves to the bottom, but I for one am not. And so we will work, and we will refit this vessel from her loose tops to her rotten bottom."

Dance leaned his arms on the quarterdeck rail and looked down at *Tenacious*'s ragtag people with what he hoped was stoic severity. "We're going to make something of this ship, if it kills us all."

Chapter Two

In the chill November wind of Portsmouth harbor, the unsteady mixture of hope and nerve that had sustained Jane Eliza Burke through long months of clandestine planning and preparation burned away like the morning's fog, leaving her nothing but her naked, shivering ambition. And her determination.

Pray God that her shaky determination held firm.

Because she had only this one chance to make all the years of study and sacrifice come right. It must be now, or it would be never. And never was a very, very long time.

Jane forced a deep, calming breath into her lungs, and told herself that all she had to do was tell the truth. The Bible said the truth would set her free, and so she would make it so. The truth was that she *was* J. E. Burke, the conchologist. She *was* an experienced, knowledgeable naturalist who was more than capable of fulfilling all the needs and requirements of the Royal Society's expedition. She was. She had arranged everything in readiness.

There. She had almost convinced herself.

But the wretched truth was that she was terrified. Terrified that they would not accept her aboard. Terrified that they *would*.

So terrified the pounding of her own blood filled her ears.

Her grip grew hot and clammy on the tiller of her well-packed sailing pinnace, and a cold coil of worry twisted up her insides, until she felt she couldn't breathe. She almost pushed the tiller of the little pinnace hard to port, and headed back across the bay toward Ryde, and home. Almost.

But she didn't. Because it was too late. She was already there—the hull of the big ship loomed above her, and sharp eyes had already detected her presence.

A sailor's shaggy head appeared over the rail. "Whatta you want?"

Jane swallowed against the sudden dryness in her throat, and said the words she had rehearsed all the way across the bay, and longer than that—all through the summer and autumn. "I am J. E. Burke, the conchologist."

The sailor's response was entirely underwhelming. "So?"

Of all the responses she had imagined—from outright hostility to her papa's sort of patronizing dismissal—Jane had never imagined she would generate this sort of idle apathy.

She firmed her quaking voice. "I wish to come aboard."

"No women aboard," the sailor said sourly. "Lieutenant sent all the whores ashore."

Heat burst into her cheeks with such fiery force that Jane thought the brim of her wide felt hat might catch fire. She clamped a hand atop her head just to be sure, and tilted her chin up to speak, so she would be understood. "I am not a wh—" She could not even say the vulgar word. "I am a member of the Royal Society's expedition and—"

The sailor let out a raucous, gull-like cackle of a laugh, and spat over the side. "Sell me another tale, darling."

Jane pulled her thick wool cloak tighter, as if its folds were armor against the sailor's derision. She put all the lofty surety her aunt Celia, the Viscountess Darling, employed when speaking to recalcitrant men. "I assure you, my good man, I am a member of the Royal Society's expedition. And I should like to speak to someone in charge."

"Not worth my hide." The sailor shook his shaggy head, but turned to someone behind him. "Lookit," he called to someone out of Jane's sight. "Have a look at this shorebird."

Another head, this one sporting a gap-toothed grin, now gaped down at her. "Damnedest whore I ever saw. Looks more like a lady parson."

At their loud guffaws, more faces appeared from above, staring down at her. "P'raps it is a lady parson, sent by the lieutenant to preach sobriety to us."

"I tell you what?" The first sailor leaned his elbows over the rail. "Instead o' you comin' aboard, why don't I come down to your little skiff, and you can preach your little sermon to my pri—"

"Mercer." A deep voice cut across the sailor's lewd invitation like a dark wave, drowning him out. "What goes on?"

Jane peered around the edge of her luffing sail to find three other boats riding the choppy waves not more than ten yards off. The vessels were manned with a motley-looking assortment of sailors, scarlet-coated soldiers, and shivering boys. But the voice must have come from the tall, stony-faced officer standing in the stern of the second boat.

The officer whose rock heavy displeasure weighed down upon Jane and the sailor, alike.

The miscreant at the rail above tugged his forelock to the officer. "Lieutenant Dance, sir. Just havin' a bit of fun with some bird—"

"Mercer." The officer's growl carried effortlessly across the water between them, instantly silencing all opposition. And then he turned his displeased attention solely to Jane. "Madam." He touched the brim of his dark beaver hat, but his voice was hard and unwelcoming. "Pray explain yourself."

The look the officer bent upon her was so keen and sharp with intelligence, Jane thought he could cut to the heart of her at a glance. The look he gave her—gave them all, to be fair—was nothing short of intimidating. This man did not have to rehearse his surety. Everything about him was certain and authoritative, even predatory. The wide set of his eyes gave him the look of a night-hunting owl, all pitiless hunter.

And she felt entirely like his prey—a gray mouse of a woman. This morning, she had selected her clothes for ease and practicality, for looking serious and scholarly and scientific. Armor against skepticism. Now, she felt dowdy and insignificant. Unworthy.

But she was not unworthy. She was J. E. Burke, the conchologist and she deserved to be there. Jane fumbled for the packet of letters—her correspondence with Sir Joseph Bank's clerk at the Royal Society—to show him the proof. Yet her hands shook so badly she nearly sent the lot fluttering over the water.

The suffocating heat began in her chest, squeezing the air from her timid lungs.

Oh, God, not now. Not in front of this pitiless man, and all these men staring down at her.

"I . . . Forgive me, I—"

"Forgive me." He touched his dark bicorn hat again, recalled to his manners by her distress. "Lieutenant Dance of *Tenacious* at your service."

He did not look as if he were at her service. He looked as if he were at her inconvenience. As if he were exhausting a very short supply of patience just to speak to her.

Of all the things Jane had imagined—and she had imagined a fantastical assortment of things about this voyage which likely had no basis in reality—she had not imagined handsome, impatient young men. Old, dignified naturalists, yes. Beautiful men, no.

Above her head, the impatient, not-so-beautiful man

Mercer was giving his side of the story. "She said as how she was to come aboard, sir. So I told her you'd already had the whores rousted out."

"Mercer." The deep tone grew more laconic, though the lieutenant's face was as calm and stoic as the sea, grim and unreadable—neither his face nor his voice gave anything away. "Apologies, madam." He directed that dark baritone at her. "I believe you must have mistaken our vessel for another. This is His Majesty's Ship *Tenacious,* bound for the South seas on an expedition of the Royal Philosophical Society. Perhaps I can assist you by directing you elsewhere?"

Jane fought down the urge to take the excuse he so readily offered. To retreat to her soft, predictable, mousy life. To give in gracefully, while she still had the chance.

But if she gave up now without a fuss, she would never know what she was capable of. Never find out who she might have been, or what she might have accomplished if only she had had the nerve. If she did not make the attempt, foolish as it was, she would never know if her detractors—her parents and the local doctor, and any others who said she wasn't capable—were wrong.

She closed her eyes against the sight of the men and the boats and the bright light shining off the water, and drew a long draught of air in through her nose. And again, in and out. She put her hand to her chest and felt the reassuring movement of her ribs in and out. In and out until she could speak.

"I thank you, sir." Jane had to tip her head back in order to look him in the eye. "But my ship is His Majesty's Ship *Tenacious.* I am J. E. Burke, the conchologist. I am a member of the very same expedition."

The raucous silence which greeted her pronouncement nearly unnerved her. Even the gulls across the harbor ceased their endless screeching. The steady slap of the water against the pinnace seemed to fade into nothingness in the still air.

Jane braced herself for the inevitable objection, the hasty judgment and blanket dismissal she had endured every day of her adult life. But she had misjudged him, for when he spoke, there was no hint of any censure or displeasure. "I see. One moment, if you please, ma'am, while we square things away. If you would just lay off a bit, ma'am, we'll lay alongside her and get this sorted out."

No huff of distain. No sneer of disbelief.

Yet Jane did have to work to decipher the officer's naval talk—she could sail a small pinnace, but had never much been around naval men—and attempted to put her boat's luffing sail back into the wind. But in the shelter of the tall hull, and in the constantly shifting space between the boats, she could find no wind, and fumbled as the bobbing pinnace drifted toward, rather than away from him.

She could feel the creeping pressure start up again in her chest, which only made her clumsier, fumbling and bumbling in her attempts to push the tiller in the right direction.

The officer either ran out of patience, or found it—either way, he mercifully intervened. "Mercer, take charge of the lady's boat. Madam?"

And there he was, standing in the stern of his boat as it slid between her vessel and the ship's hull, ready to assist her, impervious to the rise and fall of the boat beneath his feet, holding his bare hand out to her as if he were a perfect, if rough, gentleman, courteously handing her onto a ballroom floor, and not across a crowded boat, and onto a Royal Navy ship.

As if he really were going to assist her aboard.

Jane was too shocked to move. And where on earth in that crowded boat was she to step? Good Lord, did he mean to take her into his arms?

And just as if he had read her overactive mind, he growled, "Give way." In the ship's boat, the sailors slid apart on the thwarts, the sea of blue coats parting at Moses' gruff command.

There was nothing for her to do but gather every ounce of courage she had saved up through years and years of merely dreaming instead of doing, and give the tall officer her hand, and hope that his chivalry would somehow extend to the rest of the assemblage—who would all have a prime view up her lady parson-like skirts if she were to climb up the ladder cut into the side of the hull.

Clearly, the officer felt her hesitation. "Up you go, madam." His voice held something—a knowing hint of laughter that sounded very much like amusement at her expense, but before she could object, his sure hand was at her waist, clasping her securely through the material of her cloak, and boosting her up the ladder as if she weighed nothing more than an empty sea chest.

Jane scrambled upward without knowing how she did so. It was as if her mind had gone completely and utterly blank. No one—not even her family—had ever touched her so familiarly. She had felt the press and span of this stranger's hand all the way to the boning in her stays.

And to make matters worse, once upon the deck she mistimed her step. Or rather, the deck seemed to fall from beneath her foot when it ought it to have risen, whereupon Jane pitched face-first toward the wooden flooring, knocking the wind out of her lungs.

She landed like a fish out of water, stunned and gasping for air. And exposing her boot-clad ankles.

Before she had time to do anything more than feel a hot blush heating her face, a guiding hand came under her arms and hoisted her to her feet. Though his hands were gentle, his voice was all barely restrained amusement. "Careful, madam."

Jane hid her embarrassment by busying herself straightening her skirts, and setting her sturdy hat to rights to save herself the trouble and dismay that would be sure to follow should she look at the men who had but lately mistaken her for a superannuated whore. Now they would think her a clumsy old whore, to boot.

And she'd never seen so many men in her life. Not even at the meetings of the Isle of Wight's Naturalist's Society that met regularly at the assembly rooms over the the Fountain of England Inn in Cowes. Every size and shade of man she could think possible were before her. Small, tall, round, and lanky. Officers and sailors. Young and old. As ugly as a worn old boot and as handsome as the lieutenant.

Not that the lieutenant was handsome, now that she had a closer look at his wide, sharp owl's face. He was too dark for handsome—dark hair and darkened skin from the constant exposure to the sun, and those relentlessly sharp, dark green, wide-set eyes. Much too predatory for handsome. Though he must be a gentleman, since he was an officer, there was something about him—an air of something uncivilized under the smooth covering veneer of his uniform coat.

That barely restrained amusement—that sense that he was laughing at her—she could feel as surely as she had his touch.

A younger, blue-coated officer hurried across the deck. "Mr. Dance, sir," the younger man stammered. "Welcome back aboard."

"Thank you, Mr. Lawrence. Anything to report? Has that anchor cable on the second bower been swapped out yet? But first, let me introduce you."

The tight feeling of alarm eased from her chest. Here were manners she understood. Perhaps this lieutenant was not so very uncivilized after all. Jane lifted her chin, and tried to put her most serene, accomplished expression on her face.

"I've brought us another lieutenant—pending the captain's approval, of course."

The lieutenant put his hands on Jane's shoulders to shift her to the right, away from the ladder—just shifted her right over, as if she were a sea chest, or any other inanimate object in his way.

How lowering. Jane covered her mortification, and the rather alarming feeling of being so casually and continuously touched by a man, by busying herself with scientific observation. Lieutenant Dance was the tallest of the three young officers arrayed before her, as well as the oldest. And he was the most senior in other ways as well—in the commanding, loose-limbed way he held himself, as if he were very much at home on the ship, and within his own skin.

Another officer, this one only slightly younger than Lieutenant Dance, had come up the ladder to be introduced. "Lieutenant Able Simmons is an old shipmate of mine from our days on *Irresistible,* as Captain McAlden renamed the old *Swiftsure* we took at Trafalgar. Able, this is Mr. James Lawrence, who I hope will be glad of the assistance in having another officer to stand watches."

"Very glad, I'm sure." The younger officer, Mr. Lawrence, a thin young man of some one and twenty years, held himself much more stiffly, as he shook hands with the third officer, who appeared to be somewhere between the two others in age, with a lighter, sandy complexion.

"Good." Dark Lieutenant Dance looked pleased, thought he did not actually smile. But his face softened a bit, and somehow it made him look more human, and less of a displeased, stone-carved god. "I've also brought up a half-dozen infant midshipmen the Marine Society has taken fresh from the parish rolls. They've been scrubbed and all but holystoned to free them of passengers. Take them to Mr. Whitely, if you would, and have him find them a berth and put them to making their hammocks."

Passengers? Did he mean pests?

Jane's hands instinctively went to the folds of her cloak to pull it aside, as the boys in question tumbled up the ladder and onto the deck like a pack of untrained puppies.

Lieutenant Dance gave her a wry, amused slice of a smile that almost curved up one side of his mouth. "That's right, ma'am—fleas, lice, and the like. The lads have been scrubbed within an inch of their lives, but best watch your skirts."

He was being deliberately provocative. Testing her out. This was the uncivilized, secretly laughing lieutenant's attempt at humor, for nothing else could have caused his stony façade to crack into that hint of a smile.

Jane decided there and then to disoblige him by making him smile full out. She gave him her own best, most amused smile. "So kind of you, Lieutenant, to assume that I am not carrying any vermin as well."

Oh, that brought his stony gaze straight back to hers, and for just one instant, his eyes widened as if in astonishment, or pleasure, or . . . something. She could not be sure, because in the next instant his dark eyebrow shot upward as he fired off another wry salvo. "To be honest, ma'am, you look as though you've already had a holystoning."

Well. Jane would have admired his wit if she hadn't been its target. She could feel her ears grow hot under the cover of her hat. She had never in her life heard, or been subjected to, such flagrant innuendo. She had never heard such a comment made about her *person*. It made her feel as if she *had* been holystoned—all her fragile delusions scrubbed away. How provoking.

And provocative. "How good of you to notice, Lieutenant."

And that was the moment when he stopped running his eyes over the whole of the ship, and stopped to look at her. Really look at her for more than a moment. As if he had not truly seen her before, but was now trying to see inside her, into the busy workings of her mind.

The effect was unnerving. And his eyes were a very deep green. As green as the South Seas she had dreamed about in her narrow bed at night.

What a strange, unwelcome thought.

Jane might have felt the heat of her mortification return, but the moment passed—the lieutenant had already turned away, back to the business of his ship.

"Take 'em below, Mr. Lawrence," he ordered with a nod at the shivering boys. "And see to making men, if not gentlemen, out of them." Then he turned back to the hubbub of men idling on every side, and roared, "Now get that cutter swayed up. You idlers—lend a hand here." And off he went, supervising as the cutter—the boat Lieutenant Dance and this cargo of boys had come in—was brought up over the side by both ingenious pulleys and brute strength, and swayed inboard.

Right toward her head.

"Oh!" Jane pitched herself flat onto the deck.

"Hold fast. Bloody—" The lieutenant was back to her in a flash, pulling her up and bodily away from the path of the hanging boat. "Handsomely now, ma'am. Miss Burke, was it?"

Oh, how very, very lowering. She was all squashed into his coat, with his arm wrapped around her back to crowd her into his chest so he could drag her away from the rail, and he could not even remember her name.

"Yes, sir. Miss Burke," she answered into the warm wool of his coat. Her voice sounded small and breathless, but her chest didn't feel at all tight. How curious. "The conchologist," she tried again. "J. E. Burke."

"So you said." A deep frown—a scowl almost—etched itself like steel down the middle of the lieutenant's forehead. "I suppose I ought to ask, just what is a conchologist, Miss Burke?"

"Conchology is the study of seashells, of the form of the animal's shell." Back on more familiar ground, both metaphorically and literally, Jane's voice sounded more normal. "I am the author of—"

But the lieutenant did not seem particularly interested in her bona fides. "As you say, ma'am." He touched his hat again and steered her away from the hoist. "If you would be so kind as to stay here at the taffrail, where you're out of the way, until the Royal Society fellows can get you sorted out."

"Yes. Quite." Jane nodded as if she were manhandled by tall, steely, handsome lieutenants quite every other day. As if it hadn't been the strangest, most astonishing occurrence of her rather quiet, parochial life. "I'm rather looking forward to being sorted."

Oh, Lord. The look the lieutenant bent upon her—his incredulous, wide-eyed scowl—told her she had said the very wrong thing.

The corner of the lieutenant's mouth twitched upward into a smile, though he tried to chew down on his lower lip to keep his stony face. But his voice was nigh unto full of that wry amusement. "His Majesty's Royal Navy will do what it can to accommodate you, madam. I'll be damned if it won't."

Oh, Lord. She wasn't going to the South Seas. She'd never make it that far. She was going to go up in a flame of astonishment, singed to an ashy crisp, right there in Portsmouth harbor.

Lieutenant Dance—what a name for a man so tall and imposing that he looked as if he had never danced in his life. His head would have scraped the low ceiling of the Fountain Inn's ancient assembly rooms. And his expression was so carved into his face as to make it seem likely that he never unbent enough to enjoy anything so frivolous as a country dance.

Of course, neither had she. She had always been too

busy with their work, hers and Papa's. Planning and arranging all their collecting. Making sure everything was just so.

But the lieutenant was not in the least similarly affected. He carried on as if he made such saucy quips every day. "If you'll give me a moment before your sorting, Miss Burke—" His attention shifted back to his sailorly business. "Mind that hoist, man. Damn your eyes. You're in Portsmouth harbor, under the eyes of the bloody fleet, man. Have some pride."

Jane had never in her life heard such a load of cursing—her ears felt positively singed. And she was nearly bowled over by two seamen jostling by with crates perched high on their shoulders.

She dodged out of the way, and bumped up into some deck furnishing of some kind.

"Careful, ma'am," the lieutenant said again.

Jane felt all the mortification her clumsiness could bring. "Perhaps it were best if I went somewhere else, so I am not so very much in your way? Perhaps it were best if I spoke to someone else—Sir Richard Smith, or the captain?"

The look on the lieutenant's face turned from wry to sour amusement. "You may try, madam, but I would save your breath to cool your porridge. The captain is . . ."—he heaved in a breath, as if he were trying to give himself time to find the right word—"currently indisposed."

No matter. She had more than enough patience to go around. She had waited what seemed like half of her life to come this far. "Then I will wait until he can see me."

"Be careful what you wish for, Miss Burke." For a moment the stony façade held. But then he shook his head and looked at her directly, and Jane thought she could see something else, something decidedly more direct and honest. And tired. "I do not mean he is busy, madam. I mean he is drunk. So drunk that you will get no satisfactory answer from him no matter what you say. You'd best take your chances with me."

Gracious. How cynical. "And what, if I may ask, are my chances with you?"

Oh, Lord. She had done it once more, because there it was again, that astonishing and almost unnerving awareness that sprang between them like . . . like nothing she had ever known or experienced before.

The lieutenant shook away his rising smile. "Even seas, Miss Burke. I am only commanded to take the Royal Philosophical Society's party of naturalists on this voyage, not to determine who that party of naturalists may be. You'll have to take up your cause with the Royal Society itself." But he could not rid his voice still of that edge of secret amusement.

"But you do not approve?" This she was prepared for— the same condescending disapproval she had weathered in scientific circles all her life.

Yet the lieutenant surprised her again. "It is not my place to approve or disapprove, Miss Burke. It is my place to see to this ship, and her men, and prepare her for this voyage." He squinted out over the harbor. "But to that end, I'll simply warn you—this ship quite literally has no place for a woman. No place for privacy. No place to hide. No place for lies."

The force and acuity of his warning cut away all of her rehearsed argument until there was nothing left but the truth. And the truth was that she was nothing but determination and lies.

But justifiable lies. So though her voice was small and breathless, she made herself face him. "Would you put me off?"

"Again, Miss Burke, it is not my place. My place is only to see that your presence aboard, amongst all these men, does not disrupt the working of my ship."

But he had not put her off. Not yet.

And so she pledged him what she could of the truth. "I shan't disrupt a thing, sir. I promise."

He turned to her with that cynical, amused eye. "Too late, Miss Burke. You already have."

Chapter Three

Fuck all. As if it weren't bad enough taking on a cargo of useless naturalists across the globe on a dilapidated ship, one of them had to turn out to be a pocket-sized lady scientist. With dancing blue eyes.

She was tiny and blond and creamy pink in a way that made him think of wide-eyed woodland creatures—all soft, harmless doe eyes. Except she wasn't harmless. She was Miss Jane Burke, the conchologist, a walking collision course, wreaking havoc each way she turned. Clumsy, inept annihilation. Nothing but wide-eyed trouble.

Dance shifted his gaze over the harbor, narrowing his eyes so he wouldn't look at her. Wouldn't be taken in by her seemingly fragile air. Wouldn't think of her as anything more than cargo. Buttoned-up innocent lady scientist cargo. Who didn't have enough experience of the world to know what she was saying.

Or perhaps, because she was a lady scientist, she *did* know what she was saying.

Dance didn't know which possibility frightened or amused him more. He tried like the devil to keep his voice even. "If you'll be so kind as to stay by the taffrail, ma'am."

He had to restrain himself from putting his hands on her again. Dance had never been one of those men who were categorically and adamantly opposed to women on board—any woman. His time on *Audacious* had taught him that a woman could be as capable as any man. But Miss J. E. Burke was no Sally Kent. Miss Burke appeared to be as small and sheltered and inept and clumsy a sailor as his former shipmate Sally Kent had been tall and experienced and capable.

Unlike Sally Kent, if Miss J. E. Burke the conchologist stayed aboard *Tenacious,* she was going to need to be protected, both for her own sake, and for the sake of order on the ship. He had not imagined the leering eyes of the sailors or the contemptuous look Ransome had given her when she had thrown herself upon the deck. Granted, Ransome seemed contemptuous of just about everyone, but there had something more than usually malignant in his eyes when he looked at Miss Burke.

Or not. Perhaps the randy old bosun was just ogling her trim, white ankles.

But Miss Burke was not Dance's problem to sort out. He would have to leave her to the scrutiny of the party of sober-suited men approaching in watermen's boats, because in the absence of his captain, he had his ship to run. "Mr. Ransome, if you would pipe our guests aboard."

And up they came, one after another, men who looked more like industrious Quakers than eminent naturalists. They gained the deck slowly, and with a great deal more deviation from course, and trouble than even the clumsy but sprightly Miss Burke had occasioned. But at last a scholarly older man in a black worsted coat approached. "Captain Muckross?"

"No, sir." But Dance gave him the courtesy of touching his hat. "Lieutenant Charles Dance, at your service."

"Sir Richard Smith." The man bowed in turn, and introduced his colleagues. "And Mr. Denman, the Reverend Mr. Phelps, and Mr. Parkhurst of the Royal Philosophical Society."

Dance bowed smartly to the group. "Welcome aboard. We've been expecting you. Is this all of your party?"

"All but one, sir. The last, Mr. Burke, was to make his own way from the Isle of Wight, but I should expect him to arrive aboard shortly."

From the Isle of Wight. That explained the trim little pinnace. But it did not explain *her* as opposed to the *him* that Sir Richard clearly expected. At least Dance wasn't the only one caught out flat. "That party has already arrived, sir." Dance ignored the pleasurable stirring of anticipation in his gut as he turned to indicate the dangerous bundle of cloak and science standing off to the side. "Sir Richard Smith, I give you your conchologist, Miss J. E. Burke. Sir Richard, *Miss* Burke. And now, if you'll excuse me, ma'am, sir. I have a ship to see to."

And with that, Dance had done his duty. He touched his hat to her, and forced himself to withdraw to the other side of the quarterdeck from whence he might continue his streaming supervision of the vessel. "Why the hell isn't that cutter stowed? Get after it, man. Handsomely now. Mind that davit. Damn your eyes, man . . ."

Dance tried his level best to keep his own eyes, and that of his crew, on the tasks at hand. "Mercer. See to that line." But the unfortunate truth was that he had no attention for anything but the intriguing confrontation happening on the quarterdeck.

Miss Jane Burke, she of the dancing blue eyes and careful, naïve smile, stood with her sensible dun-colored skirts blowing in the wind like the flag for a gale warning.

"Good afternoon, Sir Richard. As the lieutenant said, I am Miss J. E. Burke." The young woman offered her hand to Sir Richard, the botanist in nominal charge of the expedition, even if he had no authority over the men or the vessel. "A pleasure to make your acquaintance after all our correspondence."

Unlike Dance, Sir Richard did not take the hand she

offered. Wise man. Dance would be careful not to touch her again, after his too-close encounter at the davits. The feel of the surprising soft flair of her back concealed by the voluminous cloak beneath his hands had been enough to wipe the entire contents of his mind momentarily clean.

God's balls. This is what he had come to—lurid imaginings about a wide-eyed, buttoned-up spinster.

Sir Richard was being much more prudent—he was looking at the dangerous girl as if she might harbor the plague. "There must be some mistake. James Burke is a man."

"I imagine he is." Miss Burke kept up her very polite, if very determined smile, and let her empty hand drop. "But my given name is Jane, and I assure you, I *am* J. E. Burke, and I am a conchologist."

"That cannot be."

Miss Burke retained her poise and her smile with some effort—a bloom of high color was streaking across her smooth cheeks. "I assure you, sir. I am she. But to save us from going on in this rather unscientific manner perhaps I might offer you proof? I have the letters of our correspondence here, written in your own hand, and the hand of Sir Joseph Banks's secretary, detailing our agreements and arrangements for the voyage."

Miss Burke fished out a packet of letters—the same letters she had brandished at him in her boat. Then, Dance had thought the stiff breeze had been ruffling the papers, but now in the lee of the rail, he could see that it was her hand that was trembling. Indeed her whole body was nearly shaking with some mixture of indignation and . . . Could it be fright?

Dance took a surreptitious half step toward her. All it would take was for the tiny spinster to collapse in a fit of vapors upon his deck.

But somehow Miss Burke the conchologist rallied—she put her hand to her chest to ease her fright, and hid her tremors by raising both her chin, and the letters of correspondence. "Are these not your letters to me, sir?"

"Yes, but . . ." Sir Richard was clearly discomposed, and losing sea way. "But I had no idea that you were— I was given to understand that J. E. Burke was the son of Lord Thomas Burke, and the grandson of the Duke of Shafton."

"Lord Burke is my grandfather, and His Grace of Shafton my great-grandfather. Both, I am happy to say, enjoy excellent health and correspond with me regularly. And with the Duke of Fenmore, our expedition's patron."

Sir Richard's anxieties were not in the least allayed by Miss Burke's strong connection with her illustrious ancestors. "But there must be some mistake."

"Not on my part, sir." Her voice gained strength, with only the tiniest trace of tremor and trepidation. "Or should you like to quiz me, to prove it so? Shall I fetch my pen and paper from my trunks, and draw you the Mollusca aggregating on the bottom of the hull?" At their blank looks she explained. "The barnacles there—*Lepas balanoides* as classified by Linnaeus in the last century. Which, by the way, I believe may be an incorrect classification, as to my way of observation, the animal shares more characteristics of Crustacea than Mollusca." Miss Burke tipped up that alabaster chin as if she were knocking back a stiff belt of brandy.

Would that he could do the same.

But she was as potent as a belt of brandy just looking at her. Now that she had stolen the wind from Sir Richard's sails, she stood firm, like the calm eye in the center of a hurricane, this tiny little woman, impervious to the havoc that was emanating from her like waves from a storm.

Poor Sir Richard was entirely buffeted back, almost into the arms of the three men who had gathered at his back. The assembled naturalists seemed to have been drawn up to the quarterdeck en masse by the dangerous threat of this small woman's argument. "You believe *the great Linnaeus* to be incorrect?"

"Yes." Miss Burke was undaunted by the man's obvious alarm. "I have been working on the problem for quite some time now, and it seems to me that the necessary identifying and classifying characteristics ought to be——"

"Young woman," Sir Richard cut in, his face ashen with repressed outrage. "I will not debate Linnaean classification with you!"

"Good." Miss Burke was all tiny, unbending resolve. "Then I trust we shall need no further examination of my knowledge before I am allowed to take my place with the expedition."

"It is impossible." Here Sir Richard looked to Dance for confirmation. "See here, Lieutenant. Surely the Royal Navy will not allow this . . ."

Dance declined to partake of the man's outrage—he had troubles enough of his own. "Don't look to the Royal Navy, sir. As I told *Miss* Burke, *Tenacious* is responsible to the Royal Society for your party's transportation to the South Seas, not for the makeup of your party."

"But it is impossible." Sir Richard was as tightly pursed and disapproving as a high church bishop.

"Nothing is impossible to the Royal Navy, sir." The fact that he was going to take this coffin of a ship, and all the souls within it, out to sea as soon as may be was proof enough of both his and the navy's obstinacy. And its idiocy.

Miss Burke nodded as if in complete agreement with the idiot obstinancy, but under the wide brim of her practical felt hat, her fair face had gone white with the strain, though now Dance was sure she would not do anything so missish as succumb to a swoon. Despite her small stature, she clearly wasn't the type. She was clumsy and unworldly, yes, but far too intelligent and determined to ruin her slim chances with a maidenly display of womanly weakness.

Instead, she raised that undaunted chin. "I am not only

possible, Sir Richard, I am *actual.* I *am* here." She swept
her shaky arm out toward the entry post. "That is my
boat, with all of my collecting gear carefully stowed. I am
the conchologist you invited to join this expedition. And I
accepted that invitation. As you well know." She all but
shook the packet of letters in proof.

And despite her obvious trepidation, Miss Burke—
tiny, adamant, intelligent Miss Burke—was now well and
properly angry, though she only gave vent to it in the cut-
tingly precise tone of her voice. And the agitated tremor
in her tightly clenched fist.

She had backbone, Dance would give her that.

And when Sir Richard made her no answer, she tipped
that seemingly delicate chin up another notch, and included the cluster of men behind Sir Richard in the rising
disdain of her gaze. "Your correspondence indicated you
needed a conchologist to fulfill His Grace the Duke of
Fenmore's requirements for a full complement of naturalists on this voyage. And your correspondence furthermore
gave me to understand that I was both your first choice,
and the only conchologist you had invited to join this
expedition."

Sir Richard admitted the truth of her statement with ill
grace, at the same time as he finally admitted the obvious.
"Yes, but while that may be true, I must point out that your
correspondence made no mention of the fact that you are
female."

Despite her tremulous anger, Miss Burke kept a cool
head. "I did not consider the fact of my gender germane to
our correspondence. I am a naturalist and a conchologist
first, and a grown-up woman second. I take no more note
of my own gender than I would of a mollusk's."

"Yet you should!" Sir Richard clung to his argument
like one of the barnacles Miss Burke had described fouling the bottom of *Tenacious*'s hull. "Think of your family.
Think of the scandal."

But Miss Burke was as stubborn as Sir Richard, and hung on just as tenaciously as any barnacle. She raised that honey-dark, disdainful eyebrow. "Scandal? How can there be any scandal in collecting seashells for scientific cataloguing, sir?"

Sir Richard gaped at her, as if the reasons ought to be obvious to anyone with half a brain. "This is a voyage of some duration," he blustered. "You will be away from your family. There will be hardships no doubt too great for you to bear."

But Miss Burke had more than enough brain. Her smile was all intelligent, resolute pity. "As I assured you in my letter when you first wrote me last May, I am well aware of, and indeed I hope properly prepared for, the *hardships,* Sir Richard. I assure you, sir, I have not got to my age and level of experience without understanding both the physical rigor, and the painful sacrifices involved in proving myself both capable and successful. This is *not* my first collecting expedition."

Dance almost admired her cool, intelligent persuasiveness. It was a balm to his cynical soul to watch her discompose Sir Richard so.

"Yes, yes, be that as it may, although you feel properly prepared, *we* do not. We have not planned on a young woman amongst us. I assure you we do not want to be remembered for a scandal." Here Sir Richard made a sweeping gesture to induce the three men at his back.

Miss Burke spoke before any of them had time to concur. "If *we* are any good, we will be remembered for the quality of our science, sir, rather than any imaginary scandal."

"Well said, Miss Burke." The tall, bespectacled younger naturalist at the back of the small pack met Miss Burke's eye, and even touched the brim of his hat in polite greeting. "Miss Burke seems to know her business, Sir Richard." His voice was calm, and his tone measured and

mild, but Sir Richard reacted as if he had been repri-
manded, turning instantly to the fellow with obvious deference. "I, for one, see no reason why she might not join
us if she is so prepared, for she is very clearly conversant
on her subject. And surely she is old enough to make up
her own mind?"

The moment the grave young man spoke, Dance felt
the short hairs at the back of his neck bristle with hostility, much as they had with Ransome. Which was ridiculous. If this naturalist admired Miss Burke, as he so
obviously did, and wanted to be her colleague, it was no
business of Dance's. He had more than enough trouble of
his own without borrowing some from a lady scientist.

He flung his undisciplined mind back into work. "Pass
word for the carpenter. I want a report on those repairs to
the bowsprit."

But his mind wasn't on the bowsprit. It was on the dangerously intelligent Miss Burke. Because at the word of the
bespectacled scholar, and with his own silent agreement,
Tenacious was to be home to this tiny, resolute, pocket-
sized spinster of a lady scientist for the next two years.

And he, Lieutenant Charles Dance, was going to have
to leave her alone.

Damn him to hell. Because he could no more stop
himself from admiring her than he could stop the captain
from taking his drink. His palm instantly conjured up the
feel of the taut curve of her body beneath the layers of
dowdy woolen fabric. And it had not been one-sided—his
fascination. He had not imagined her untutored response
to his nearness. Nor the flare of awareness in her wide blue
eyes.

He would have to take steps to keep her well away from
him.

He turned to one of the men he had collected in Portsmouth—a ginger-haired, one-legged sailor he had known
in his days aboard *Audacious*, and signed on to serve as a

steward to the wardroom. "Punch, have Miss Burke's dunnage stowed in my cabin."

At his command, all of Miss Burke's considerable aplomb vanished—she looked as pale and shocked as a virgin at an orgy. "Sir! I shall most emphatically *not* be sharing any accommodation with you."

Dance did his level best not to let his normally wry sense of humor have its way. Nor did he allow himself to point out that she would be far better off with him than with anyone else, or with taking her chances with the crew.

He made himself touch his hat to her in a respectful manner before he spoke. But even he could hear the cynical amusement in his voice. "Fear not, madam. I mean for you to occupy it quite alone."

Color streaked back into her cheeks, before the embarrassed flush spread downward across the pale neck like a swath of strawberry jam. "Forgive me my misapprehension," she said. She put a gloved hand to her chest in a small attempt to reclaim her veneer of calm, and restore herself to order. "But there is no need to put yourself out, sir. I am sure the accommodations provided for the rest of the society's scholars are more than adequate."

"The accommodations on a frigate of war are never more than inadequate at best, even for men who are used to a life at sea, madam." And for these landsmen from the Royal Society, Dance doubted that the simple, narrow cuddies partitioned off on the berth deck would provide any more comfort than a prison cell. "But I am afraid nothing else will do, madam. Nothing that will let me comport myself as an officer and a gentleman."

No other cabin was as far removed and protected from general congress with the men, save the captain's rooms—and there would certainly be no help from that quarter. But his reasons were not altogether gallant and altruistic—the first lieutenant's cabin was both the largest of the officers' cuddies, and the only one which had its own private head, as the privy was called in a ship. Keeping Miss Burke's toilette entirely private would be best for her and the crew alike. The last thing he needed for the next two years was this little woman having to share her ablutions with fifteen-odd officers and naturalists.

"But where will you go?" she asked with that naïve forthrightness. And then blushed to the roots of her fair hair. "I mean that I should not like to discommode you in any way, Lieutenant. I should have no other accommodation but that which the other members of the expedition have been given."

"Madam, I take leave to advise you that only my cabin will do." He repeated his order to the one-legged old servant. "Punch, please see Miss Burke's trunk stowed in my cabin, and have my dunnage removed to—"

Here Dance faltered for a moment, not wanting to upset the delicate sense of seniority, especially with the entrenched warrant officers, like Ransome, whose cabins were tucked just outside the wardroom on the berth deck. He had allocated all the free cabins for the Royal Society men before he had gone ashore, but now there was Lieutenant Able Simmons as well as himself to find accommodation.

"Just move my bloody dunnage out of Miss Burke's way," he muttered to the steward before he spoke to her. "Punch will take your personal chests to your cabin."

The tiny woman opened her mouth to tax him with something else, when she was saved from the necessity by the tall, solicitous, spectacle-wearing scholar.

"Miss Burke? If I may be so bold? I might press upon Sir Richard for an introduction, but under the circumstances . . ." He smiled charmingly, damn him. "Mr. Jackson Denman, another member of your expedition. I would be happy to show you the way to the wardroom."

So Mr. Jackson Denman knew the way, and knew enough to call the officers' quarters the wardroom. Dance hated him already.

Especially when Miss Burke's cheeks warmed with a new color—a rosy glow that had nothing of embarrassment or indignation.

And Dance's gut twisted with uncalled-for jealousy.

He ought to be rejoicing. He ought to be glad that the scholar had so openly staked his claim to her. Spinster or no, it would wreak havoc among his men were they not to think of her as "taken" or under the protection of some one of the gentlemen. The bespectacled man was just the fellow for the job—just tall and physically imposing enough not to be an easy target for the men.

Not that it mattered to Dance.

Not at all. His job was the care of the ship, and the men. In that order. There was no room for any thoughts of females, spinsterish, blond, pink-cheeked or not.

None of his business at all.

"I thank you, Mr. Denman." Miss Burke took the arm the scholar offered, but then—because fate was not yet done tormenting Dance—she addressed him again. "I should like to settle the stowage of my pinnace and equipment and stores."

"The rest of your dunnage will be stowed below. And the pinnace"—she *would* call the little sailing craft by its proper, precise name—"will be sent in to the dockyard to sell, or be stored to await your return, so long as you are prepared to pay the hefty fees."

"No, if you please." Miss Burke's white forehead pleated up under the brim of that hat, and she dropped Mr. Denman's arm to hurry back to the rail, as if she—this tiny woman—might physically stop any of the crew from removing any of her gear. "My equipment and stores are most exactly stowed, so that there should be no shifting, damage, or wear."

"Everything," she repeated, "is most carefully stowed so that I may transport the whole of it to the shore, and have everything I need at the ready once we reach the South Seas. Oh, no, that crate houses the microscopic lens, which is extremely fragile and—"

And then the confounding little woman actually went over the side, back down the batten ladder on the side of the hull—with a great deal more agility than she had shown on her way up—and started directing the sailor who was unlading the boat. "That lens must stay exactly as I had it. Exactly. The boat must be taken aboard as a whole."

"Madam," Dance called down to her. "Miss Burke—"

But Miss Burke was oblivious, and bending over in the bottom of the boat, delving underneath a tarpaulin, and giving him, despite the cover of her cloak, an absolutely spectacular view of her backside.

And he was not alone in his admiration. Half of the crew was gaping over the rail. A crewman loosed a raucous whistle of a catcall.

It was all Dance could do to keep himself from striking the man. "Damn your eyes, Mercer," he growled. "You're not in a dockside tavern. Keep your eyes inboard. Find work or I'll find it for you."

In any other circumstance, he would have admired her, this buttoned-up lady scientist. Miss Jane Burke might have been just his type—a shapely little pocket Venus of a woman. And as English as a summer rose, with her fair skin and hair, and light blue eyes the color of the sky on a fair day. No matter if she were as naïve and buttoned up as a buttercup. She had backbone.

But he was going to spend the next two years keeping his eyes, and especially his hands, to himself.

Fuck all.

There was nothing he could do but wade into her fray. Dance dropped down into the pinnace. "Miss Burke, kindly leave the disposition of the cargo to me and my crew. You will do yourself an injury here."

"But everything is stowed just so." Her voice had gained insistence. "The microscope and hand lenses are packed in wicker crates with straw," she was explaining with something more than insistence—with a sort of soft, quiet passion. "And the colored india ink as well. I've calculated everything quite precisely."

Well, of course they were. Of course she had. With her mouth pursed up like that she looked the sort to have calculated everything quite precisely.

But above at the rail, Dance could see the men taking snide pleasure in their lieutenant's being confounded by one tiny little woman. Damn their eyes.

And damn his own too. He could not spend the entirety of the afternoon watch dealing with this aggravating spinster naturalist, no matter her dancing wide blue eyes, or enchanting smile. Not if he wanted to keep order upon his ship, and get the bloody expedition put to sea before winter.

"Rest assured that your equipment will be stowed quite carefully in the hull, madam. I don't like to have extra weight at deck level. We can't afford anything that pulls this vessel out of trim." The ship had problems enough with her trim as it was. Though why he was even explaining himself to this bluestocking spinster, and in front of his crew, was beyond him. He might just as well talk to the wind for all the understanding he was like to get from her.

"But I've made calculations," she protested.

To stop her, Dance broke his new-made rule, and simply put his hands upon her slender shoulders, and turned her physically back to the ladder, which he quickly scaled. And before she could say or do anything to stop him, he reached down through the entry port, grasped her wrist, and hauled her topside.

She came as readily as a fish on a line, and he caught her against his chest for a moment before she could gain her own two feet.

"My goodness," she breathed.

Yes, that was the way to deal with her—manhandle her until she was too breathless to speak.

But the moment he put her down, she stymied him again, the damn intelligent girl. She fished around beneath the bloody cloak, and produced a notebook with what appeared to be a full page of mathematical equations for determining the weight of the laden vessel, as well as what appeared to be a diagram of how she had stowed the equipment in the hull of the pinnace. "But I've calculated everything most precisely."

If he weren't so put out at her, he would be impressed. And he couldn't afford to be impressed.

"Miss Burke, I am not about to hoist your boat upon the davits just to test your theoretical calculations. This is a frigate-of-war, madam. No matter our peaceful scientific mission, we carry armament. The weight of guns must be taken into account."

She looked at the thirty-two-pounder carronades lining the quarterdeck. "The pinnace can't possibly weigh as much as even one of your guns."

As if a little pocket Venus of a bluestocking woman knew the first thing about naval armament. The thought shocked whatever gentlemanly sensibilities or instincts he still possessed right out of his system. "And do you know the weight of that thirty-two-pounder carronade, Miss Burke? Or that of the eighteen-pounders lining the gun deck? Over forty-six hundred pounds per gun, Miss Burke. Over fifty-six thousand pounds to be kept in delicate balance. And then you will need to make another calculation to add the weight of the gun carriage, and the weight of the canvas and cordage stowed below and above deck. And the force of the wind that will try to tip this vessel to heel over until her beam ends are awash. Have you made that calculation, Miss Burke?"

"Oh. No, but—"

"I thought not, madam. I shall not presume to tell you anything about whether barnacles are Crustacea or Mollusca, so pray don't try to tell me anything about ships or boats. Be so good as to let me do my job without any interference from you."

Chapter Four

"Yes. Of course. My apologies, sir." With that righteous blast singeing her cheeks, Jane swallowed the dry dust of her embarrassment. For a moment or two she had thought the lieutenant just might be her wry ally, if not her actual friend. But clearly, she had used up whatever goodwill she had at first engendered. "If you would be so kind as to inform me of your final dispensation of my equipment and stores, I would be most obliged."

Thankfully, that took some of the steel out of his cutting tone. But only *some*. "I will. And if you would be so kind as to remove yourself from my quarterdeck, and the risk of any further bodily harm, I will get on with doing just that."

"Of course." Jane could not get away fast enough. But the moment she lifted her foot to step over the combing and move down the ladder, she tripped on the edge of her cloak, and managed to collide with two sailors who happened to be coming upward. "Oh! I beg your pardon." She regained her balance, and collected herself enough to berate herself for being so awkward and so out of place upon the perilously steep stairs.

But the sailors took advantage of the moment, brushing brazenly against her body with their hands. One of them even laughed, "'Tis *our* pardon, miss."

"Carey. Mains. Damn your eyes." The lieutenant's put-upon growl cut across the deck like a lash, yet Lieutenant Dance's hand at her elbow was restrained—gentle even. "Miss Burke, if you would, please?"

The lieutenant's steadying escort took her safely past the men, and downward, farther into the dim depths of the ship, to the foot of a very steep ladder. Jane was nearly out of breath from their swift descent, but the lieutenant was entirely unaffected. "The wardroom is aft, madam. You'll be safer from molestation here, away from the men. Just follow Punch. And of course"—he touched the brim of his hat—"Mr. Denman."

Jane swallowed around the mortifying breathlessness that seemed to happen every time he touched her—which was more often in the past twenty minutes than in the whole twenty and six previous years of her life. "Yes. Thank you."

"Don't thank me yet, Miss Burke. We've a long voyage ahead of us." The lieutenant's dark eyes seemed to settle into her, as if he could see every one of her fears and misgivings writ large across her face. "It's not too late to change your mind."

The gentle gruffness in his voice was almost her undoing. But it wasn't her mind that needed changing. It was her life. The life of managing other people's lives, and other people's dreams. Of being taken for granted, and thought less than nothing.

No. She would not change her mind. She would not go back.

She would cast her own shadow for better or for worse, but she would make her own choice—she would choose to be brave. "I thank you for your concern, Lieutenant. But I have already kept you too long from your ship."

"You have. See that it doesn't happen again." But he smiled as he said it, that wry smile that curved up one side of his face. And with that gently cryptic warning, and a quick tug on his hat, he disappeared back up the ladder to the open part of the deck above, calling his orders as he went. "Hoist those davits. Carey, unstep that mast. Mains, get a line on— Why the devil hasn't that line been replaced? It's as worn as an old shoe and liable to give way. Get me Ransome. I want that pinnace dismasted and swayed up aft, where it will be out of the bloody way. You there—"

The lieutenant strode out of hearing, and was gone.

Jane felt the first cautious easing of the tingling excitement that had stolen into her lungs, and made her breath come short and fast. There. She could breathe now. It was done. She had managed—not elegantly or without trouble, but it was done. She had been brave, and she was come aboard.

Her shortness of breath had everything to do with achieving her long-sought, carefully planned-for goal. It had nothing to do with the lieutenant and his nearness. Nothing.

In front of her, the steward Punch hoisted her large trunk over his shoulder as if it were made of feathers, though he had only one good leg—the other was fashioned of a wooden peg. But he seemed to manage easily enough, leading his hopscotching way into the dark and increasingly dank hull.

Jane was still clutching her packet of letters, her talisman of both her right to come aboard, and her lie. Which wasn't really a lie. She was J. E. Burke. She was a conchologist. She had drawn each and every specimen in the handsome folio edition of *The Conchology of Britain*. Just as she would draw each and every specimen in the book that would result from this voyage. But this time, she would do all the work *and* get all of the credit.

Yes. She could do this. She could adapt and survive two years completely on her own, away from every comfort and every person who cared for her. She could endure the hardships as easily as she had assured Sir Richard she would. She would. Nothing could stop her.

Nothing but the overwhelming smell of men.

It was almost like a living thing, the funk that hovered between the decks. And while they passed along this lower deck, a great number of the crew seemed to have stopped their work to stare at her as she followed the steward aft through the hull. Despite Mr. Denman's presence in front of her, the crewmen actually crowded closer to stare at her openly, as if they had never seen a woman before.

Surely not? Hadn't the sailor Mercer said there had been whores aboard just this morning? But perhaps it were best not to think of that particular incident, though Jane did clutch the folds of her cloak securely in the hopes that she did actually look too superannuated and parson-ish to be taken for a whore.

Oh, heavens. How on earth was she to endure two years of *that*? Surely they should get used to her? Or per-haps it was she who had to get used to them?

"Here y'are, miss." The steward led her and Mr. Denman through a batten door, whereupon he turned up a lamp, and moved toward the end of the line of doors to one side of the neatly organized space.

"Thank you, Mr. Punch," she answered. "And where exactly is here?"

The room was almost entirely fitted out in oak and canvas, with every inch of space carefully allotted. The lantern hung over a table situated in the center of the room and was fitted directly into the backside of one of the great masts that rose up through the decks.

"Oh, not mister," the steward answered. "Just Punch, miss. This be the gunroom, or wardroom, if you like, miss. Officer's quarters. Best there is next to the captain's." He gave her the information as if it were a great compliment, and opened the last small canvas and wood-framed door to show her inside with a flourish like a conjurer's trick. "This be the first lieutenant's cuddy, miss. Bigger'n the rest. If you'll give me a minute, miss. I'll have the lieutenant's dunnage shifted out of your way."

"Thank you." She moved closer so she might have a look inside the place that was to be her home for the next two years, but all she could see was the steward balling up linens to tuck under his arm. "Are you quite all right? May I offer you any help?"

"Bless you, miss, no. I'm spry enough, with me peg. I've had the peg now for longer'n I ever did have the leg." He chuckled. "No trouble for me at all, miss." But then he stopped, and looked up at her. "That is, if it isn't a bother to you, miss. Have you brought someone to do for you, miss?"

"No. I—I haven't." The thought had not occurred to her to have her own personal servant. She had always been the servant, the quiet assistant. She had always planned and arranged and worked for her father. She had been the one to make the measured drawings of each and every specimen. She had been the one who made the precise observations in careful notes. She had arranged each and every collecting expedition, and combed each beach and tidal pool for shells. She had done it all, without one lick of the credit. But that would be changed now.

She had changed it.

Which gave her a convenient answer of sorts. She would use her father's excuse, when he had declared she was too delicate, too prone to asthmatic fits to undertake the voyage. "My assistant was unable to come due to her health."

"Oh, aye." The steward bobbed his gingered head in easy acceptance of her lie. "So you've no one, no servant to fetch and look after you, like?"

She had never had a personal servant to fetch and look after her at home. She had never been attended to. Her mother did have a lady's maid to dress her, but Jane had always been the one to see to everything else. Just as she had always seen to herself.

She had fancied herself to be quite self-sufficient—above the infantizing need for assistance in matters of dress and menial work—but she could see that this steward pitied her for it, and perhaps even thought less of her as a result. "Have all the other members of the expedition brought servants with them?"

"Aye. Most, miss. But if you like, I can do for you—as best I'm able." The splash of darker color chasing up the old man's ruddy cheeks told her that clearly some tasks—the more intimate tasks a maid might perform, like dressing her mistress—were well beyond him. He covered his unease by adding, "I imagine the lieutenant will sort it out. A demon for sorting things out, is the lieutenant."

"Lieutenant Dance?" Jane could not yet tell from his easy tone if the old sailor admired or reviled the lieutenant. For herself, the lieutenant certainly was a demon of some sort, with his green eyes and wry smile. He certainly discomposed her.

But he had not put her off the boat.

And that told her that he was at least a fair-minded man. Not that she knew much about men. If today's experience had taught her anything—beyond her own astonishing ability to lie—it had taught her that she was so very much further out of her depth than she could ever have imagined.

She—who had never so much as gone to a village assembly, or chatted with a young man after church—had now deposited herself in a world made exclusively of men. A world with such sights and smells and looks she knew nothing about.

But she was clever and capable, and she could learn. "How long have you served on *Tenacious*?"

"Just took me on today, the lieutenant did, miss. I'd

been put ashore, you see, for the peace. Found some work in an inn, but . . ." Punch shook his head. "I be right happy to take the lieutenant's shilling, and be back where I belong since it was him doing the asking."

"So you knew the lieutenant by reputation before today?"

"Bless you, yes, miss. Knowed him back in the day, when he were just a young midshipman on *Audacious*. We was in Trafalgar together on *Audacious*. Got the medal to prove it an' all."

So the lieutenant was a veteran of the great battle of Trafalgar. Perhaps the experience of having survived such a battle was what gave him his cynical, barely civilized air. "You are to be congratulated. And thanked. Is that how you lost your leg?"

"Bless me, no, though there were plenty of legs, and arms, and lives as well, gone that day. No, it were years before. That's why I be a steward, see, miss, and not an able seaman. But I know the way of things on ships. You can count on your Punch to see to you."

"Oh, yes, thank you. I see. I hope you do not mind me asking you all these questions, for I most assuredly don't know the way of things on ships."

"Bless me, I don't mind in the least. Happy to do for you, miss. Happy to. Unless the peg puts you off, as it does some people, and you'd rather I found someone else as could do for you?"

"No. Not at all." Jane made sure she smiled to show him that if he did not mind his infirmity, she could certainly have no objection. She was a scientist who found as much beauty and interest in the plainest of shells as the elaborate ones. It was probably the reason she was so interested in the plain but fascinating barnacle. "I'm sure we'll get along swimmingly."

Punch responded with a gap-toothed smile of his own. "Don't know how to swim myself. There, miss, you'll be all right and tight here." He held open the batten-and-canvas door to her small cabin, and knuckled his forehead. "I've cleared away all the lieutenant's things."

"Oh, yes, thank you." The short period of time they had been conversing hardly seemed long enough to clear out all of a man's personal belongings. It had taken her days to secretly sort out which of her own belongings to take with her from home, and many surreptitious hours to arrange and pack them carefully away. It would probably take her an hour or more to unpack and settle herself in. Yet a few minutes had seen the lieutenant's dunnage, as he called it, summarily packed away and into the chest that now rode comfortably on Punch's shoulder. The thought made her inexplicably sad.

And that would never do. Jane cheered her voice. "Thank you, Punch. I am very much obliged."

She stepped tentatively into the small, dim cuddy, and found the room to be as dark, dank, and cramped as the root cellar at home, though it smelled vaguely of tar and oak and spice instead of dust and must. The only furniture besides her trunk were a small washstand with a tin enameled basin and ewer, a small built-in cupboard which the steward had opened in order to remove the lieutenant's clothing, and a rectangular canvas and rope cot hanging suspended from bolts in the ceiling beams overhead.

A very long canvas cot. Tall Lieutenant Dance's cot.

A tingling shiver—that awful feeling of being so out of her element—skittered across her skin. Jane had never slept in any bed but her own. No, not true, she chided herself. She had slept in the guest bed her aunt Celia kept for her at her sunny house in Somerset, and she had twice slept in a bivouac cot when she had gone collecting with her father. But she had certainly never slept in a bed knowing that a man the likes of Lieutenant Dance had slept there before her.

Jane gave the stiff canvas a gentle push and watched it

sway to and fro. The steward had taken away his bed linen, but the lieutenant's particular scent of soap and lime and something else still clung to the canvas. Jane leaned closer to try and identify the spice.

"Miss Burke, are you quite all right?"

Jane leaped back as if scalded, and smacked her back against the curved side of the hull. And perhaps she had somehow been scalded, judging from the heat streaking across her cheeks.

The lieutenant's tall unbending form stood outlined by the lantern light. "Miss Burke?"

No. It was not the lieutenant, but Mr. Denman, who had doffed his round brimmed hat, and stood waiting to speak with her on the other side of the door frame. "Mr. Denman. Please forgive me."

"Not at all. I've been learning from our good man Punch here, as well." He extended his hand, and Jane was pleased to find his grasp firm and friendly. Indeed, everything about Mr. Denman was friendly, from his tousled hair to his warm gray eyes, which wrinkled in easy humor behind his spectacles. Quite unlike the lieutenant. "Are you quite all right?"

"I . . ." There was nothing she could say that would not be ridiculous. "I was just . . . acquainting myself with the accommodations. Everything is so strange and new." The ship was nothing like she could have imagined. But then her expectations had been based on sheer imagination and hopefulness, without any drop of reality to leaven her fantasies.

"New? But I thought you told Sir Richard that you had undertaken previous expeditions?"

"Yes. Indeed." Jane lifted her chin, and made herself smile more confidently. "But never one on a Royal Navy ship. I fear I shall have to rely a great deal on Punch here, to help me along."

From behind Mr. Denman, Jane heard the steward

chuckle. "Don't you worry, miss. I'll see to things. That be why Mr. Dance brought me aboard."

And speaking of tall Mr. Dance. "And now that I have taken his cabin, where, if I may ask, will the lieutenant go?"

"Dunno, miss." Punch scratched his ginger beard. "I'm sure he'll make do. He's that sort of man."

Jane had so little experience of any sort of man, that the lieutenant remained an enigma to her. Unlike the quiet scientist at her door, who seemed much easier to fathom. "Mr. Denman, I must thank you for assistance in convincing Sir Richard to let me come aboard. He certainly seems to value your opinion."

"Oh, I don't know about that." Mr. Denman's modesty was visible in the way he wrung the brim of his hat in his hands.

"I thought it very clear in his deference to your opinion, though Sir Richard has been appointed our leader." Well, thus far Lieutenant Dance had more clearly been the leader, but among the members of the Royal Society's expedition, there was a very clear hierarchy she knew would need to be maintained. But even she, who lived at the edge of nowhere, had heard and read of the famous anatomist Jackson Denman. His lectures at the Royal College of Surgeons in London were famed in scientific circles, and praised as packed affairs with young students cramming into the operating theater to hear and see his work. "Have you known him long?"

"No. We've only just met a few days past. It chanced that we were staying at the same inn in advance of coming aboard this morning."

"And what brings such an august anatomy scholar as yourself on this expedition?"

"Ah. I see my fame—or infamy—depending upon your point of view—"

"Fame, surely, Mr. Denman."

"You are too kind. Suffice it to say that I found myself

in need of a change—in want of a surfeit of life as an antidote to the close study of death. This expedition to sunnier climes seemed a very good opportunity."

His words gave Jane pause. She had been so preoccupied with her own perceived impediments to her career, that she had never considered that even without impediments of gender and lack of opportunity, scientific inquiry came at a mortal cost of its own.

"I see," she finally said, only because she knew she must say something, and she wanted to allay whatever demons had driven Mr. Denman to this point. "That sounds like an excellent plan."

"I mean to make a physiological study of the natives we encounter. Drawings and the like. And I must say that I have seen *your* new monograph, *The Conchology of Britain*, and was impressed by your most exceptional specimen drawings. I'd be interested in speaking with you about your techniques for drawing in the field. I'm always looking for instruction or information to improve my own techniques."

Everything within Jane eased and lifted. This—this lovely feeling of quiet elation—was exactly why she had dared to come aboard, and exactly what she had hoped for. The regard and acknowledgment of her colleagues was everything she wanted—that an accomplished, even famous man such as Mr. Denman should compliment her for her work.

She did not have to force the smile to her lips. "Certainly, Mr. Denman. I should like nothing more. I take it you make specimen drawings as well?"

He smiled, though he looked slightly less comfortable again. "Yes, I do. Well. I'll leave you to settle in then."

"Oh, yes." Jane recalled herself to her manners. "And thank you again"—she extended her hand once more to Mr. Denman—"for your kind interference on my behalf."

He shook her hand cordially. "You are welcome. I am

only sorry that any interference might have been necessary. But I fear we men are a hidebound lot."

Jane could only agree, but it was refreshing to hear a gentleman like Mr. Denman voice such an opinion. "You don't seem particularly hidebound, Mr. Denman. You spoke up for me when others would not." To be fair, the lieutenant had not spoken *against* her. But he certainly had not been entirely supportive.

"Yes. I should like to think I'm a fair-minded man who can weigh the evidence with his own eyes, and not rely upon others to tell me what to think."

Jane could feel a genuine smile cross her lips. "How very scientific of you."

His sober look lightened as she had hoped it would. "Yes, I am nothing if not a man of science. Sometimes I fear to the exclusion of all else. Which is one of the reasons I joined this expedition. To take myself out into the world again."

"Yes. I too." Although she was really going out into the world for the first time. At least the first time entirely on her own. It was both a heady and a terrifying thought. "Sometimes we must stretch ourselves to learn new things, lest we stagnate from staying put without fresh ideas or fresh experiences to prod us along."

"Very well said, Miss Burke. Stagnate. I think you have the right of it."

"Thank you. I hope I do."

"Well." Mr. Denman folded his hands in front of himself, as if he had run out of conversation.

"I'll just settle myself in then."

"Oh, yes. I'll leave you to it." And with that, Mr. Denman ended their mutual awkwardness by raising the hat in his hands in farewell, and exiting into the small cabin right next to hers. How nice. He was sure to make a pleasant, congenial neighbor.

Jane returned to investigating her own little space

without an audience this time. The only light came from the lantern the steward had thoughtfully hooked to the low ceiling beam. Indeed, the ceiling above was so low that Jane could nearly reach the beams that arched up from the side of the ship and held up the ceiling with her upstretched hand. She was quite sure no one as tall as the lieutenant could ever be able to stand in such a small space. Certainly the mirror, tacked to the wall well above her head, was his, hung so high it was of no use to her.

The thought made her uncomfortable again—knowing that it was his, knowing that he hung the mirror close to where the lantern hooked onto the beam so he could shave by its light, his chin tilted high. Uncomfortable because she oughtn't be thinking such intimate thoughts about a man she had just met. A man who was all but a stranger to her.

She would have to ask Punch if there were another hanging cot available for her use. And certainly Mr. Dance would need his own long bed back at some point. Or she might see if Mr. Denman next door might need it. He certainly was tall and would need a long bed. And he certainly didn't smell in a way that was unsettling and disconcerting. Mr. Denman smelled pleasantly of— wax and paper? Oh, she didn't know. It was just that he didn't smell like the lieutenant, that was all.

But she would think of the lieutenant no more. She needed to be practical and quiet and organized and keep herself from his attention, and Sir Richard's attention, at all costs if she were to stay aboard. She would have to be less trouble than anyone else.

What had her aunt Celia always said? That to succeed, she would have to be twice as smart and useful and learned as anyone else. And do her work in half the time. Being twice as smart was going to be difficult at best—for she knew full well that all of the other naturalists on the expedition were first-rate scholars. But since she appeared to be the only conchologist aboard, there was at least no one who could question her abilities.

But useful—useful was going to be very, very difficult indeed. Especially useful enough to please the all-seeing, green-eyed lieutenant.

Chapter Five

Dance awoke before first light to an ache in his neck from sleeping in a chair, and the depressing news that two more men had deserted during the night.

"Gone, sir." Morris delivered the news with the sad-eyed look of a dog who expects to be kicked—his tail was all but tucked between his legs.

"The hell you say." Dance growled his way out of the damned uncomfortable chair, and scrubbed a hand through his short hair, as if he could chafe some better ideas into his tired brain. "How?"

It ought to have been damn near impossible. Both the officers and the marines had been standing regular watches. Dance himself had stood watch on watch for the better part of the night, and had only retreated to a chair in the wardroom at four bells of the middle watch—near two o'clock in the morning—when Mr. Lawrence had finally made his groggy way to the deck. Which meant that the deserters had been gone for at least four hours. Too long ago to make any pursuit feasible.

God's balls. What a fucking mess Dance had gotten himself into—he had never worked so hard in his life for such little good result. This was meant to be an easy, soft posting, not a job where he was like a grave digger—up to his arse in the business with nowhere to turn. "Tell me the worst of it."

"They took the captain's gig, sir," Morris explained. "Some watermen found it abandoned at the sally port and towed it back out. And wanted to be paid for the service, besides."

Despite being a smaller boat, the gig could hold a lot more than just two men—Dance should feel lucky to find that *only* two men had absconded. "Get the necessary coins to pay the watermen from the purser."

"About Givens, sir."

"Yes, Givens." Dance still had a bone to pick with the man, for though the purser had done his duty in seeing all of the Royal Society's party suitably settled, the damn man had still not yet produced the muster rolls or the ship's accounts, despite Dance's insistence. "And send him to me." The man had seemed anxious enough to flatter his way into their guests' good graces, buttering up Sir Richard to no end. But Givens was evidently not that interested in staying in Dance's good graces.

Dance scrubbed his hand across his face. He needed a shave. And a pot of coffee. Perhaps even poured over his head.

"But that's the problem, sir." Morris's voice was full of apology. "It was Givens, sir."

The shave would have to wait. As would everything else. "God's balls." Dance was on his feet and cursing himself for a fool. He hadn't curtailed the purser when he might have—and should have—when he had first sensed the man was less than honest. The man must have simply taken the money and gone. "How long has he been gone? Send Mr. Ransome to me this instant. I want this damn ship turned upside down and inside out for those books. Which one is Givens's cabin?"

"Don't know, sir."

But Dance had already left Morris and the wardroom

behind, opening the doors of the warrant officers' cabins himself, only to find Ransome tearing open his own door, looking much the worse for wear, shading his eyes from the glare of the dim lantern and stinking of sour beer.

"Damn your eyes, man." Was there no one on whom he might count? How in hell was he supposed to keep order and discipline when the men whose duty it was to keep order were drunk or less than honest? "Is there no one on this damned barge who can keep to his feet?"

"No, sir," the bosun stammered, scratching one of his mighty paws across his bristly maw as if he might find his answer there. "'E poisoned me."

It was not the first time Dance had ever heard one warrant officer accuse another, but he had never thought to hear Ransome, of all men, admit to being a victim of any sort. "The devil you say. Who?"

"The devil Givens," the bosun ground out. "He's absconded, damn 'im—" Ransome choked himself off from saying anything more, but Dance had heard enough. The devil was surely at play along *Tenacious*'s decks.

"He's had a head start of four hours." Dance reckoned a man that canny—and clearly the purser had enough brains to take advantage of a drunken, inept captain, put a sleeping powder in the belligerent Ransome's ale, and make away with any ready monies *Tenacious* had possessed— had enough smarts not to wait around Portsmouth, drinking away his ill-gotten gains in a local taproom. But there was something—something in Ransome's frantic manner, a suspicion that nagged at the back of his brain like a Billingsgate fishwife—that made him uneasy about the bosun and the purser. When he had come aboard, he had thought the two were as cozy as a clutch of thieves. "Why would he do such a thing to you?"

"To get off, on his own, din't he?"

Ransome hadn't said, "without me," but that was what Dance heard. Or perhaps he just wanted to hear it. Perhaps he just wanted an excuse to dislike the man more than he already did. "You knew him best, Mr. Ransome. If you had any chance of finding him, where do you reckon he'd be?"

The question—or perhaps the fact that Dance had been the one to ask it—caught the bosun off guard. "Ball and Anch—" He cut himself off with a scowl. "Don't rightly know, sir. But I'll go after him, sir, I will," he amended, and reached back into his cabin for his coat and cane.

"The Ball and Anchor. A very good idea, Mr. Ransome. Well done." Dance knew the dingy taproom on the city's west side well. "I'll report to the captain, and have the port authorities set after Givens, because I can't possibly spare you now. We're better off without him, and will waste no more time on the damn purser, Mr. Ransome, for the tide will turn within the hour, and if we do not make the most of the run of the tide—"

Dance didn't want to think about what would happen with such an ill-trained and ungainly lot of men as were *Tenacious*'s crew if they did not catch the outgoing tide on which to depart Portsmouth harbor. "Pull yourself together and call all hands, Mr. Ransome, ready to up anchor."

"Up anchor?"

"D'ya really mean for us to go?" Beyond Ransome, the berth deck was growing crowded with sailors.

"We are a Royal Navy frigate, not a damn harbor sheer hulk. Of course I mean for us to go."

"Mr. Ransome said as how we won't be ready for months yet."

Dance raised his voice, and pinned the man in question with his most cutting look. "Mr. Ransome says that, does he?"

"No, sir," Ransome stammered.

It was good to know even Ransome's thick hide could be nicked from time to time.

But while Dance waited for Ransome to come up with

the appropriate thing to say, another seaman lent his opinion. "Mr. Ransome's got the right of it." Larsen, one of the bosun's mates, stuck up for his superior. "Best wait."

"Thank you, Larsen. While I value and share Mr. Ransome's opinion of the decrepit state of our vessel and her crew, it were best that this ship's crew resign themselves to proceeding to sea. A good blow in the Channel will make better sailors of all of you."

"True enough." The topman, Flanaghan, spoke— presumably for them all. "But is *she* really staying on, Mr. Dance? For the whole of the voyage?"

There was no need to ask to whom the sailor was referring. "She's not going to swim to Tahiti, Flanaghan." But his attempt at humor was lost on the men.

"Put her in the drink, and see if she can," growled a disgruntled voice from the back of the pack.

Was that the voice of Mercer? Dance couldn't see through the small sea of faces peering up at him in agitation. Damn, but sailors were a credulous, superstitious lot. "I begin to think you're all a lot of old women yourselves. Think of her as one of these sober-suited scientists, and leave it at that."

There were more mutterings from the back, while at the front of the crowd, Flanaghan crossed himself before he tried again to appeal to Dance. "You can't mean to let her stay, Lieutenant?"

Did they think *he* had the authority to change anything about the plan of the voyage? His only responsibility was to man the ship to the best of his and the crew's ability. Past that, they all just had to live with the way things were. "I mean to take the Royal Society's scientists wherever in hell the Admiralty tells me they are to go, Flanaghan. And I mean for this ship's company to do so without complaint."

"But she's a woman, sir," he sputtered.

"That much is obvious, Flanagan. But she could be a

sandpiper for all I care. Put her from your mind, and see to your work."

"Sandpipers be bad luck," another voice griped from the back. "When one crosses in front of you in the tide—"

"That's cats crossing in front of you," one of his mates contradicted.

"Just listen to yourselves," Dance admonished. "Like old fishwives. To my way of thinking, Miss Burke can never be the only woman aboard with you lot around. You bring your own luck upon yourselves. Now get you ladies to your work."

"But how can we see to our work with her aboard?" Flanaghan persisted. "Already things are starting to go wrong—that new foretop we fidded on last dogwatch just won't take right. That's just bad luck, sir. Bad luck."

"That is just poor skills and lazy working habits. This ship has been out of trim and out of practice for far too long. And a few weeks of daily sail and gun drill will knock the collywobbles out of you."

This time there were out-and-out groans from the men. "We can't put to sea with her aboard."

Dance could feel their barely constrained discontent, but he reminded himself that Miss Burke was just a convenient excuse—were she not aboard, they would have made some excuse or trouble about the black-coated, white-collared parson on the expedition, or about the purser's having absconded—which *was* damnable bad luck—and the moment an out-of-repair line wore through, they would have blamed their bad luck on the parson. Or upon Able Simmons for joining on late. Or upon him for bringing the new lieutenant aboard.

Any excuse would do.

Yet, they all stood there gawping at him as if their complaints were as real as the rot in *Tenacious*'s bow timbers. Dance lit the slow match to his temper. "What a load of womanish rubbish. Whether you like it or not, this ship is going down Channel. So look lively, or I'll look lively for you."

The men took their grumbling threat with them and went away. But the bosun had watched his conversation with the men without comment, measuring him out like a short charge of powder.

"Do you have something to add, Mr. Ransome?"

Ransome settled his tarred-straw hat on his head, and took his time in answering. "Worried about the men, I am, sir."

"I thank you for your diligence on their behalf, Mr. Ransome, but the matter is settled."

But Ransome was immune to irony. And tone of voice. He did not know when to leave well enough alone. "It's bad luck, sir, to take a woman over the line."

"Not as much bad luck as disobeying an order, or speaking against a superior officer, or proceeding to sea in a ship that hasn't been properly kept up, Mr. Ransome. Have those lines in the mainmast's larboard blocks and tackles been replaced? Or that new cable for the best bower anchor been bent on?"

"Beggin' yer pardon, sir." Ransome spread his hands before him, all open, excusable innocence. "But you sent Givens to pay for that cable. We've done all we can without fetching more. The cable tier is near to empty now. We've no more to spare."

Fuck all. "Do you mean to tell me that *you* haven't done your job, Mr. Ransome, and seen to it that *Tenacious's* cable locker and boatswain's stores are adequately supplied?" Dance had been over the ship from bilge to masthead, making a long list of fittings, rigging, and canvas that were out of repair. "There was cable enough to see to it that the breeching tackles on the guns could be replaced." He pulled out his book from beneath his coat, and checked for the entry of the bosun's locker.

This was exactly why he wrote such things down—so

thieving bastards like Givens, and perhaps Ransome, couldn't swindle him. "Do you mean to tell me that two hundred twenty-six yards of bloody cable the size of a man's leg have disappeared?" The outrage and menace in his voice could have weighted down an anchor. "Are you suicidal, or just incompetent?"

"No, sir." Ransome spread his big, tar-stained palms out wide, as if he had nothing to hide. "I knows my job. There's cable enough for the guns, sir, just as you say." And the professional pride that had been temporarily vanquished by Givens was back in his rough voice. "But that Givens, sir." He growled the name. "Be selling off things, secret like. And now 'e's made off with all the money."

Fuck, fuck, fuck all.

Every time he thought the situation aboard *Tenacious* could not get any worse, a devious fate took delight in proving him wrong.

All the money, not just the money Dance had allocated for the replacement cables. All. "How long have you known this? And why did you not report it to the captain?"

Not that reporting the theft might have done any good—Dance reported all sorts of things that needed attention to the captain daily, and had yet to receive a satisfactorily coherent response. "And why did you not report it to me?"

Unlike the captain, he would have done something about it. He would have at least kept from giving the man an easy excuse to abscond from the ship.

"Only just figured it out myself, sir." Ransome touched the brim of his hat. "And I couldn't figure if you was in on it or not."

Doubt crept under his skin like an icy dousing. He had never, in the course of sixteen long years in the service of His Majesty's Royal Navy, had his honor called into question. Never. He had always felt his conduct spoke for itself, and was above reproach. He had thought that by running the ship as any normal captain could want, and keeping Captain Muckross's drunkenness as much as possible from the men, he was upholding that honor.

But perhaps he had been wrong.

"What about the boatswain's locker? And the carpenter's stores as well? Did Givens gain access to those?"

"No, sir." Ransome was quick to answer. "I know my job," he said again.

"If you do, Mr. Ransome, you'll be the first one on this bloody ship who does."

Because his own next job was to try and convince the captain to do his. At the entrance to the captain's cabin all looked as it should—a scarlet-coated marine stood at sentry duty in front of the door. But beyond the closed portal Dance knew he would find a shambles to match the rest of the ship.

"Captain Muckross, sir?" Dance didn't wait for the marine to announce him—his polite tap would never be answered. He knocked hard on the door. "Sir?"

Some men idled nearby, looking for a glimpse of their reclusive captain. "See to your work." Dance pulled a selection of tasks from the endless list at the top of his brain. "You men, I want the breeching on every larboard gun inspected. Report the length of cable needed to Mr. Ransome. And the knee at the head on the mess deck needs be recaulked. Pass word for the carpenter to await me when I'm through with the captain."

The mention of Mr. Ransome had the desired effect, which meant that Dance was able to slip into the stern cabin without an audience. "Captain Muckross, sir?" He pitched his voice toward the small sleeping cabin partitioned off from the wide stern gallery. "Sir?"

"Sir, he's sleeping now, sir." Manning, the quiet tar who

served as servant to the captain, appeared in the stern cabin. "Just got him down and away from it this moment."

As if the captain were a suckling child. Perhaps he was. "Down? It's morning, man. Shouldn't he be getting up? And away from what exactly?"

"Why, down from the bottle, sir," the servant said honestly.

"Fuck all." Dance could not even bother to curb his language in the captain's cabin. It was no wonder the ship was in such a state of disrepair if the captain spent so much time drinking each night that he could not climb to the quarterdeck of his own vessel. "How long is he likely to sleep?"

"Couldn't say, sir. It were a powerful lot of gin."

Gin. Not even a gentleman's drink like brandy or claret to add some distinction to his intoxication. "How long has he been like this?"

"Started to drink bad Tuesday last, when you come aboard and started the work, sir."

Another feeling like the douse from a pail of icy water hit Dance, but this time he would defend himself. "He was drunk before I got here."

Manning acknowledged the truth of Dance's assertion. "Well, I suppose he has been at the drink regular like for a while now."

"Years?" Dance gave the steward his barest stare in the hopes that the poor little man's loyalty to his captain was no match to a blunt question from a superior officer.

It wasn't. "Yes."

Fuck all. After such an honest answer, there wasn't much else to say. What a bloody fix. The damn drunkard should have been relieved of his command, or retired to a desk in the dockyard long ago. To someplace where he wouldn't be an embarrassment to the navy. Somewhere where men's, and now women's, lives didn't depend upon him.

But to even suggest such a thing was to flirt with mutiny and treason. The devil would take him then.

"Why do you not keep the drink from him? Why have you not thrown the whole store of it overboard as any sane man ought?"

This time the man shook his head adamantly. "Not my place, sir. I only does for him as he likes."

Dance could feel the exasperation boiling out of him. "Do you not see that it is your duty for the sake of the whole ship to keep him away from spirits?" Dance was appalled that so many people would seem to stand idly by, and let the man drink himself to death.

"Tried it once, sir, under advice from Mr. Reed, who was surgeon a while back, we did." Manning shook his head sorrowfully. "Mr. Reed poured every drop we could find overboard once, and quick as a whore, the cap'n had another out from somewhere only he knows. Cap'n has his ways, an' he can't stop now, sir, even if he tried. Gets the shakes something fierce if'n he doesn't have it. Can't go back on an ebb tide."

No, there was no going back for any of them, damn it all to hell. Orders were orders, not suggestions. "Rouse him out and brace him up as well as you can, because I must speak to him."

Manning looked unhappy, but did as he was bid. "Captain Muckross, sir?" Manning rapped softly upon the batten door to the sleeping cabin. "Captain? You are needed, sir."

"What?" came a groggy voice from inside. "Who's there?"

"Manning, sir. Lieutenant Dance is here to see you, sir."

"What, what?" The sound of fumbling came from the interior.

Before the man could do himself a harm, Manning threw open the door, only to find his captain befuddled and stark raving naked, clutching the back of a chair.

It would have been comical were it not so tragic.

Manning had to catch the man from falling when he wrenched away from the bright light flooding the cabin. "Steady on there, sir."

Manning got the captain into the chair, where the old man sat with no hint of consciousness of his naked state, and instead focused his bleary eyes on Dance. "Who the hell are you? You're not Manning."

"No, sir. I'm Dance. I'm your first lieutenant. And I am in need of your guidance." Though what kind of guidance a grumpy, naked, confused old man could give him was entirely debatable.

"Get me Manning."

"I'm here, sir." The long-suffering servant cast a dark look at Dance, who took the hint, and moved to the other side of the stern cabin to give both the servant and captain some privacy to dress. But he'd be damned if he'd leave for politeness' sake—the old man would be out again in no time, and they'd get no answer. "Manning, when you're done, please fetch coffee for the captain."

"Don't like it, sir. Only takes tea."

"Then brew a bloody pot of tea, Manning. Hot and as strong as you can make it. Immediately." Though Dance feared there was not enough tea in all the gardens of Assam to make Captain Muckross conscious of his duties.

It was very nearly an hour—a full bloody turn of the glass during which time the tide was cresting and beginning its run—for the old man to be made presentable and awake enough to sit at his table, take tea, and receive Dance. But when Manning returned with a steaming pot and poured out a weak mixture—which the captain sucked down thankfully enough—Dance caught the unmistakable astringent whiff of gin billowing from the steaming pot.

Fuck all. Could they not get so much as even a pot of tea into the man without the addition of the gin? At the rate the old man was pouring the happy brew down his gullet, it was a wonder he didn't drop dead in his tracks at any moment.

Whatever the concoction, it had the desired effect of reviving the man sufficiently for Dance's purposes. "Goddamn it. What do you want?"

"I've come to ask after the ship's books, sir. Mr. Givens seems to have absconded in the night, and I am concerned that he has taken funds belonging to the ship, sir."

"The devil you say." But the captain wasn't really attending him. The mad old man's attention had already strayed to the scene outside the stern gallery—the flat calm of Portsmouth's gray harbor. "Why is there a boat out my window?"

It was Miss Burke's little pinnace, hanging on the stern davits, all battened down with her fitted tarpaulin snugly lashed. Just like its mistress. "That is the equipment of the delegation of scientists from the Royal Society, sir." Dance made sure to keep his voice slow and his tone even, and keep his impatience on a tight leash. "The naturalists we are transporting to the South Seas, sir."

"Transporting? I'll have no bloody convicts upon my ship, sir. I tell you that."

Dance prayed for patience, and tried to choose his words more carefully. "Not convicts, sir. Scientists from the Royal Philosophical Society."

"Royal Philosophical Society." The captain's poor opinion of the society was evident in his tone—an opinion prevalent among professional naval men, and one to which Dance himself had lately subscribed. Until, of course, their livelihood had become his own. "Bunch of men with too much time and too little occupation amusing themselves with being important."

"And not just men, sir," Manning cut in meaningfully.

So Manning was another one of the superstitious fish-wives. Dance would have to see to it that they were all too busy with real work—from which there was more than plenty to choose—to have time to complain about a lady scientist. She might be the unknowing bane of his existence, but he would not allow them to make her theirs.

But for better or worse, Captain Muckross did not take the servant's meaning. "Sober-suited Quakers and preachers, the lot of them."

"Yes, sir." Dance tried to steer the conversation back to his purpose, and impress some small aspect of reality on the old man. "I wanted to inquire after the books before we proceed to sea, sir, which we are scheduled to do, as you know, this morning, in order to take advantage of the harvest moon last night. We'll not get such a favorable tide for proceeding down Channel anytime soon."

The captain's face remained slack and blank, as if he had no knowledge of time or tide. Dance felt as if he were bailing water in a typhoon. He didn't mind carrying out the damn orders—he never had, no matter how impossible they seemed—provided he was given the orders in the first place, and provided those orders were the product of a sane mind, but he resented the hell out of not knowing and guessing at what he was supposed to do. Common sense—aim for the South Pacific—could only carry him so far.

"But in advance of that, I have no idea of the ship's accounts, sir, as Mr. Givens seems to have taken not only the money I sent with him to the dockyard for cordage, but the account rolls as well. I have no way of telling without the ship's books, sir."

At the rate the captain's hands had begun to shake with the palsy typical of the afflicted inebriate, Dance doubted the man could hold a thought, much less pen. "Who normally handles your correspondence? Have you no clerk?"

The idea seemed to give the poor man a great deal of

pause before he could supply a name. "Givens. There's the man. Takes care of things."

Of course. "Givens is gone, sir. Jumped ship last night. I've spent a considerable amount of time trying to find the ship's books, as there does not seem to be a complete muster roll, nor any accounting of what moneys *Tenacious* has to her credit. My thinking is that Givens either took them, or destroyed them."

"How should I know?" the old man asked again.

Dance felt his irritability slip its leash. "Because you are the captain, sir. And it is your duty and your responsibility to know." It was damnable how the old man was bleary one moment, and clear the next. "Who is going to know if you don't?"

"I told you. Givens."

Dance could barely enunciate the words for the way he was gritting his teeth. "Givens. Is. Gone. Sir."

"I don't know why you're shouting at me, sirrah. You're the one who let him go. You should have stopped him."

"Yes, sir." There was no point in debating the semantics of blame with Captain Muckross. And if the captain couldn't consistently remember that Givens was gone, the chances that he would remember Dance admitting the purser's disappearance was his fault were slim.

"There is no need for you to have those books, Lieutenant." Muckross's tone was emphatic. So emphatic, it was as if the clouds that hid the captain had parted, and Dance could see the man he had once been, and might yet be, if he would put his mind to it.

But as quickly as the clouds had drifted apart, they drifted back together. "Books. Funds." Muckross's fragile attention had already shifted, his gaze becoming unfocused and weary. "Why are you asking me all of these questions?"

Dance wanted to grind his teeth in frustration. "We are set to sail, sir. And we need to be at the ready."

The captain met Dance's eyes honestly. "Well, I don't know, man. I just don't know."

Fuck all.

That made at least two of them.

Chapter Six

The world was a strange and interesting place, full of strange and interesting and very different people. Who seemed to sleep in chairs.

Jane had been jolted awake in the predawn hours by the sharp sound of a chair clattering over onto the deck just outside her door. She had clambered out of her hanging cot in time to spy the chair—with the lieutenant's coat over the back—on the floor, and see the lieutenant bounding out of the wardroom. And when she stuck her head outside her cabin, she could hear him engaging in a loud conversation—or was it an argument?—with several men on the other side of the wardroom door.

The mention of her name sent her retreating into her cabin to dress herself in her practical buff colored wool gown so that she might meet any challenge to her presence aboard head-on—and at least properly clothed despite the early hour. What could not be avoided ought not be put off, even until breakfast. She had always found it best to tackle unpleasant chores straightaway, before they could become problems.

But when she finally came out into the dim wardroom, what could not be avoided was the strange and interesting sight of the lieutenant in his bare shirtsleeves, divesting himself of the rest of his clothes. He had come back from whatever unpleasant chores had interrupted his—and her—sleep, and was now about to shave himself in preparation for the coming day.

"Oh, my." Heat blossomed under her skin and raced across her chest. Jane hardly knew where to look—a glance around at the closed doors of the other cabins told her it was full early for anyone else of their party to have awoken.

Jane would have retreated into her cabin to allow the man his privacy, had not the lieutenant's voice stopped her.

"Morning, Miss Burke. I trust you slept well." There was something knowing in the lieutenant's tone—he had been right outside her door—some slow insolence, that worked its way under her skin like a splinter, needling her into responding, no matter his scandalous state of undress.

And hadn't she just reminded herself that what could not be avoided ought not be put off? The lieutenant clearly did not want to be avoided, and if he thought he could intimidate her into leaving the expedition by the sight of his shirtsleeves, she should take this earliest opportunity to disabuse him of that notion.

If only she could breathe properly in his presence. He wasn't even touching her and the air felt hot and tight in her chest. She put her hand to the high bodice of her dress to ease the pull of the neckline against her throat. "Good morning, Lieutenant. Have you no cabin yet, sir, within which to wash and dress yourself?"

"No," he answered simply, "I do not." To illustrate his point, he pulled his black silk stock away from his neck with an audible snap, before favoring her with that challenging, cynical half-smile that twitched up one side of his mouth. "Do I shock you, Miss Burke?"

She wanted to meet the challenge in those dark green

eyes, and give him as good as she got. But she could barely breathe. "You are trying to."

Her honesty—and apparent humor—made the smile widen across his lips. "Am I succeeding?"

"A little." Which was a complete lie. Of course he was succeeding. And he knew it.

He advanced on her then, sauntering slowly across the few feet that separated them while he shucked off his waistcoat and tossed it over the back of his chair with his coat.

Jane's shoulders smacked into the door frame at her back, halting any further retreat.

"Then I must try harder." And with that, he used his superior height to lean his hands onto the ceiling beams above Jane's head.

"Lieutenant Dance." Jane hated that she sounded all breathless discomposure even to her own ears. "You needn't do so on my account." The neck of his shirt lay open, and a swath of golden skin was right in front of her eyes. And he smelled of soap and lime and wind.

"But I do, Miss Burke." He was so close, she dared not look up to see him speak, but his voice insinuated itself into her bones, echoing uncomfortably through her body. "Because I believe you have something that belongs to me."

"Do I?" Her voice was no more than a whisper, and she could hear her breath fragment into little gulping pants.

Oh, God. Not now. Not in front of this pitiless, cynical man and his insolent, challenging eyes.

"Yes." He leaned down lower, close to her ear, as if he had a confidence he wished to impart. "My shaving mirror."

And then he reached over her head, and plucked it off the wall. And with a smile that told her he knew exactly what he was doing to her, and was pleased, he ambled back to the wardroom table, and began to soap his face.

"Oh, yes." Jane was determined to overcome this dreadful susceptibility. She would not give in to it—she would not. She would not let him toy with her so. "I thought it must be yours. So very high up."

"Very scientific observation." Dance spoke around the lather he was applying to his face and neck in preparation for shaving. "It reminds me to make my own—still breathing, are you, Miss Burke?"

"Barely." Jane decided honesty was her only weapon at hand. But she hated how breathless and girlish she sounded. Not at all like her usual organized, in-control self. She swallowed down her discomposure and made her tone as tart as she could. "Is there some particular reason you've chosen to toy with me this morning, Lieutenant? Is there some demon plaguing you that you need to exorcize by plaguing me? Or was there something of greater substance than your naked body that you wished to discuss?"

The barb found its mark. He winced up one side of his face to acknowledge the hit. But he was not done vexing her. Not by a very long shot. "I'm not naked yet, Miss Burke. Not nearly." He raised his chin and began to scrape the razor along the long line of his jaw, drawing her gaze to the sinuous musculature of his arms and shoulders.

Oh good Lord, but he was as handsome and fine a specimen as she had ever laid eyes upon. Tall and strong and fit, as if he were made solely for the purpose of hard living alongside the lofty masts and spars. A man in his element.

Unlike her. Who was nothing but determination and deceit.

But she was more than that—she had a mind and a heart of her own. And she would use them.

"Excellent." She kept her tone as dry as her throat. Honesty could be as brutal as innuendo, and two could play at his game. "If you would like to take your shirt off and continue to disrobe, I'm sure I would benefit from the instruction. I have never seen a naked man, and you seem to be rather an intriguing specimen."

Oh, that took him entirely off guard—enough to make him nick his neck with the razor. But he held his composure just as willfully as she, though he did turn to look at her, as if to reassure himself that she was still the same small, harmless female he had thought her not two moments ago. "You've got backbone, Miss Burke, I'll grant you that."

Did he truly mean to be admiring, or was he admiring her in the same facetious way she was ogling him? And she was ogling him, wasn't she? Turnabout *was* fair play.

Jane reached into her cabin and found her magnifying lens on the chair where she had left it, and raised it in front of her, as if it might aid in her examination of him as a scientific specimen. "So do you have a spine, I see. Most instructive. If you would stay there, just like that—posed in such an evocative attitude—I believe I will get my drawing materials out to capture your physique accurately for the benefit of Mr. Denman and the Royal College of Surgeons. I imagine it's not often that they get a specimen of your so particularly imposing physique to study."

Everything within him changed. Every hint of playful challenge disappeared from his face, as if shuttered down. Closing her out. The air in the close room seemed to reverberate with the force of a door slamming shut.

He turned away from her, and quickly shucked the shirt over his head, using the linen to wipe the remains of soap from his face, before he immediately donned a clean shirt, and set about turning himself back into a naval officer. "My apologies, Miss Burke."

What had she said this time? But it didn't matter. She was suddenly ashamed for trying to discompose him as much as he had tried to discompose her. "Lieutenant Dance I—"

He looked at her over his shoulder, his glance still guarded and cool. And she meant to apologize to him as well, to take her share in the blame for the strange changed atmosphere between them. Only there was a patch of soap on the far corner of his jaw, just below his ear. "I'm sorry, but you missed a spot."

He scrubbed a hand along the hard length of his chin, but the soap remained.

"No. There." Jane could not seem to stop herself from pointing out the exact spot. From moving close enough to touch him as if she might rub the offending bit of soap away with the backs of her fingers.

Lieutenant Dance flinched away, as if she were about to nick him with the razor.

His reaction lit a bonfire of mortification in her chest. "I'm sorry," she stammered, and that abominable feeling of choking heat seared up her throat. "I thought you would want to know."

"I suppose I do want to know." His voice was so low, she had to strain upward to hear him. But his eyes. His bright green eyes seemed to burn as hotly as her chest. They bored into her, burning away the last traces of pretense. "But I most assuredly did not want to know that I ought not to play with fire unless I am well and truly prepared to get more than my fingers burnt. Stay away from me, Miss Burke. For your sake as much as mine."

And with that Lieutenant Dance stepped back, shoved his arms into his uniform coat, jammed his hat securely on his head, and bowed. "Good morning, Miss Burke."

Dance thought he was going to incinerate. His skin felt so hot beneath his wool coat that despite the chill November wind, he was like to catch the entire bloody ship on fire.

And it was all his own fault. Miss Buttoned-up Burke had been right—he had let his demons, in the form of Givens and Captain Muckross, goad him into behavior unbecoming an officer and a gentleman.

But there was nothing he could do about it now. He

had already done the only sensible thing when faced with the little scientist's superior gunnery—he had spread his canvas into the wind, and fled topside, whence he could counsel himself that he had made an honest mistake.

One he would not make again.

She had seemed like such an easy target for his misplaced ire, appearing in the wardroom's lamplight, so perfectly buttoned up and battened down, so tidy and neatly arranged in the middle of his untidy and unarrangeable world. And he wanted to teach her what she needed to learn—this ship couldn't, and wouldn't be arranged and made tidy just for her sake. If she wanted to live among them, it was *she* who was going to have to change. It was *she* who was going to have to arrange herself to suit, and not the other way round.

But he had showed her nothing of the kind—it was *she* who had showed him just how paltry his skills at managing a female really were. And that if he were going to have any control over his ship and his men, he was going to have to gain a far greater control over himself.

And the time to test himself had finally arrived. At eight bells of the morning watch, just as the late dawn was lighting the eastern sky, Dance made the order. "Mr. Ransome, pipe all hands to weigh anchor."

Within a minute a shrill whistle rent the air, and the bosun and his mates were turning the men out. "All hands. All hands. Out and down, lads, out and down. All hands to weigh anchor."

The order was not greeted with the energetic rush of feet that Dance had been accustomed to on his other ships, but a slow, fatalistic trudge as the men turned up reluctantly, grumbling and cursing his hide.

But Dance wasn't about to miss the chance to leave Portsmouth harbor on an outgoing tide. Or before most of the fleet was awake. He had his pride. If *Tenacious* were ever to make it out of the Portsmouth roads with any competence, they needed the sweep of the outgoing tide to move them along.

If the men's reluctance promised a bad start, it was only being made worse by the fact that the captain made no appearance on the quarterdeck.

"Mr. Lawrence," he called quietly to the third lieutenant. "Pray convey the compliments of the deck to the captain, and inform him that we are making ready to sail."

It had been one thing for the old man to hide away and leave all the work to his first lieutenant while they were in port, but Dance had never imagined the captain would stay away as his ship proceeded—or tried to proceed—to sea. Dance had a general idea of the vessel's orders—the expedition was bound for the South Seas—but only the captain would have the formal sailing orders, or could set their course.

But what if Muckross were too drunk to set the course? What if he were too drunk to even make his way upon the quarterdeck? Surely the old man had enough sense to know what was required of him—he could retreat to his cabin in liquid solitude once he'd done his bloody duty, set the bloody course and given the goddamned order to proceed to sea.

In the meantime, Dance moved to the quarterdeck rail, away from the young woman who had made her clumsy way on deck the moment the pipes had sounded. He could not allow himself to look at her, or go to her aid when she barked her shin on the hatchway combing, or caromed backward off the sternmost larboard carronade in her attempt to move out of the sailors' way. He could not allow his mind to stray in any way from the tasks at hand.

He kept the men at their work, putting them to the capstan to bring *Tenacious* over her anchor, and sending the topmen aloft to stand in readiness. Below the waist, Punch was at the capstan with his fiddle, and began to scratch out a steady tune, as *Tenacious* began the slow march up to her cable under the eye and cane of Mr. Ransome, who was not perhaps all work and no play, for the bosun started the men to singing a rousing rhythmic chantey to move the work along.

> *I thought I heard the old man say, leave her Johnny, leave her,*
> *Tomorrow ye will get yer pay, and it's time for us to leave her.*
> *Leave her Johnny, leave her, Oh leave her, Johnny leave her.*
> *For the voyage is long and the winds don't blow,*
> *And it's time for us to leave her.*
> *Oh the wind was foul and the sea was high, leave her Johnny, leave her,*
> *She shipped it green and none went by, and it's time for us to leave her.*

The chorus of the song was caught up by the men at the forecastle and in the chains. *"Leave her Johnny, leave her, Oh leave her, Johnny leave her."*

Dance might have let the song continue—it was a common enough song for weighing anchor—if he had not caught the snide look first Ransome, and then others of the crew, sent back toward Miss Burke, who was doing her best to become invisible behind the sternmost carronade. But it was impossible. She was about as invisible as the winds whipping up her skirts and petticoat into a tangle of foam even as she clutched her cloak tight about her, as if it could shield her from their less-than-kind regard. Dance could feel her distress just as surely as he felt the wind.

More and more men joined in at the next verse, and Dance felt the mood turn ugly and snide. *"I hate to sail on this rotten tub. Leave her, Johnny, leave her."*

It was if the crew were openly voicing their feelings about Miss Burke's presence aboard, and their displeasure at him in allowing her to stay. He was not imagining their emphasis, nor the shouting way they joined in the verse. A glance at Miss Burke told him she heard it as well and understood—her rosy face had paled the color of the caulk cliffs up Channel.

"No grog allowed and rotten grub, and it's time for us to leave her."

Dance had had enough. He leaned the force of his displeasure into his voice. "Punch."

The spry old tar had taken a seat high on the hub of the capstan, but he looked up and took the hint from Dance's dark lowered brows readily enough. "Oh, right enough so. Aye, sir, aye." He saluted Dance with his bow, shifted his tune on the ancient old fiddle, and called out to the men. "Lads, here we go."

We are outward bound for Rio town, with a heave ho, haul,
And we'll heave the old wheel round and round.
Good morning, ladies all!

The men plodding around the capstan took up the new cadence.

And when we get to Rio town, heave ho, haul,
It's there we'll drink and sorrow drown.
Good morning, ladies all!

"Up and down. Up and down," came the cry from the crew working the anchor chain at the bows.

This was the moment he liked best, the moment when potential became real, when thoughts were turned into action. When wind filled the sails and a new voyage was begun. But still Dance hesitated, making them all wait in the morning's chill for the old man to put in his appearance, and give them their sailing orders.

The cheerful song went on around them. *"Good morning, ladies all!"*

Mr. Lawrence came back on deck. Alone.

"Well?"

The young officer shrugged his thin shoulders within his new uniform coat. "I gave him your compliments, sir. And he told me to get out."

"Thank you, Mr. Lawrence." Dance tried to sound cool and collected. But it was unheard of that a captain would not bestir himself to see his ship weigh anchor. But it was also unheard of that a ship not heed the Admiralty's explicit orders. Which they had already delayed unconscionably while he had seen the ship repaired.

"Good morning, ladies all!"

Dance could feel the weight of eyes upon him just as he had that first day he had come aboard—weighing him out like short powder. Well, they would not find him lacking today. His way was clear. He would wait no longer. He knew his duty even if the captain did not.

He could feel the ship beneath him as if it were an extension of himself, feel the pulse of her hull riding the tide, feel the taut pull of the cable hard beneath her beak head, and wondered how the captain could not feel the living ship beneath his feet. Could ignore her so coldly?

Dance gave up trying to answer unanswerable questions, and tilted his speaking trumpet to reach the second lieutenant stationed on the forecastle. "Mr. Simmons?"

"Anchor's hove short, sir," Simmons called back.

"Very good." He raised his speaking trumpet to the yards. "Loose headsails."

"Loose heads'ls." At the tops of the masts, canvas began to billow and fill against the sky. "Up anchor. Heave away. Loose tops'ls."

This he knew, the setting of the sails, the smooth order

of tasks to get the vessel under way. He knew his own job, but the only other time he had had to take on another's was in the heat of battle. But they were in another sort of battle now—the whole ship seemed to be a seething battleground of wills and intentions. His versus the captain's and the men's. If this morning's lessons had taught him nothing else, he knew he would have to take care who he set himself against.

"Mr. Whitely?" he asked the quiet sailing master at the helm. "How does she answer?"

"Well enough, sir."

Dance could feel that it was so, as *Tenacious* shuddered to life, like a great sea animal shaking itself awake, answering her helm and beginning to make headway.

But on what course? In the captain's damned absence, Dance made himself think as a captain, not just as a first lieutenant. He broadened his attention to the whole of the ship, not just to his official duties to a portion of it, or they would come to grief right there in Portsmouth roads with the eyes of half the fleet watching him, not to mention the bright blue eyes of the woman at the rail, who watched him just as closely as the men.

Even from the distance of half the quarterdeck, he could see that her eyes were shining with unshed tears. Well damn her for being intelligent enough to understand the crew's barely concealed malice. And damn his own eyes for worrying about her, with the wind whipping up her cloak and skirts, and revealing her stocking-clad ankle to the leering eyes of his men, when he ought to be worried about the ship's course, and the headland of the Isle of Wight off the starboard bow.

The wind that blew up her skirts was easterly, blowing directly down Channel, pointing his way. Dance found his voice. "Lay her two points large on the larboard tack, Mr. Whitely, and set a course to weather the isle." Into the speaking trumpet he shouted, "Courses away."

The cold morning breeze pushed its way into the billowing sails, and shouldered the ship slowly over onto her starboard beam, heeling to the wind as *Tenacious*'s bow breasted the first rolling wave.

"Anchor's secure, sir." Lieutenant Simmons fell aft, soaked from the bow spray.

"See to that forecourse, man." Dance ordered Simmons about. "We're not hanging out the damn laundry." He moved his attention to the main. "Man those braces. Haul over hard, there. Haul, I say," Dance roared to move the landsmen to greater efforts as ropes groaned, and tackles screeched under the strain, and *Tenacious* began to gain headway.

It was, of course, at that moment that the rest of their guests should all choose to come above deck and take to the rail. Sir Richard and his constant shadows, the Reverend Mr. Phelps and the sallow Mr. Pankhurst, took up a station at the larboard gangway, blocking the passage of the men moving to their work.

Damn them for the lubbers they were. "Mr. Lawrence, move those guests to somewhere out of the damn way." They were like old women, hanging on to their hats with one hand and the rail with the other. Entirely out of their element.

So unlike the actual woman, Miss Burke, who quietly tucked herself out of the way braving both the wind and the men's derision. Backbone, he had called it, as if it were something within her, over which she had no control—as if it were not a choice she made to simply be courageous.

Dance wrenched his focus back to the sails where they belonged, only letting his eyes stray to the binnacle to check his compass heading before he allowed himself a cautious breath. The damn ship was still afloat, and was actually sailing fairly well, all things considered. They were proceeding smoothly through the Portsmouth roads. It was as good a showing as he might have hoped for with only himself—and Simmons and Whitely, of course—to rely upon.

Where was the damned captain? He ought to be on his own damned quarterdeck, whether he wished it or not.

Dance flicked his attention to one of the least green of the Marine Society midshipmen. "You there."

"Me, sir?" The lanky boy looked back and forth from his companions to Dance.

"You answer with your name," Dance instructed.

"Rupert, sir."

"Mr. Rupert, take my compliments to the captain, and tell him *Tenacious* is making for the Channel." Perhaps the excitement and confusion of making way was too much for the old man, and he would be glad to come on deck once they were well away from the prying eyes of the fleet. But Dance had more important things to worry about than the captain's pride. "Mr. Lawrence, get a party up to that foretop. I don't like the way the fore topmast is answering. Get the carpenter up there before it comes to grief."

"Aye, sir." Lawrence went pelting forward to hopefully see to the foretop spar before it came raining down upon them before they made the full Channel. But better the damn spar should part now than in the middle of some gale.

"Sir?" The damn young midshipman was still standing there.

Dance only just refrained from swearing out his frustration. "Mr. Rupert, you're meant to do what I ask of you the minute I ask it, damn your young eyes."

"But, sir. My name isn't Mr. Rupert. It's Mr. Honeyman. I'm Rupert Honeyman, sir."

This was what Dance had come to—amusing infant midshipmen. "I beg your pardon, Mr. Honeyman. Now go, Mr. Honeyman, damn your eyes, before I light your damned tail on fire."

Beside him, the sailing master chuckled. "They'll learn,

they'll learn. They are actually a fairly clever group of boys. That one especially. I have high hopes for him."

Dance took a longer look at Mr. Whitely. Actually, he was looking everywhere and anywhere that wasn't the pale blond spinster who was clinging to the larboard rail like a particularly bright-eyed barnacle, but the sailing master was wearing a curiously amused expression that Dance hoped was not indicative of imminent catastrophe. "How does she go, Mr. Whitely?"

The quiet man's smile broadened. "Less and less like a pig, sir."

Dance met the sailing master's cautiously optimistic eye, and felt his own face curve into the first true smile he had enjoyed in months. "That will do for now, Mr. Whitely. That will do."

It was all he would ask for. Anything more would be tempting an already volatile fate.

Chapter Seven

Lieutenant Dance stood as firm, tall, and unmovable in the center of the ship as one of the oaken masts. But Jane knew now he wasn't unmovable. She knew he was just a man—albeit a man who had almost complete control over the world in which she had placed herself. From the front of the quarterdeck—as Punch had told Jane this portion of the ship was called—the tall lieutenant looked over the floating world that was this ship, and gave his steady stream of swift, sure orders. "Fall off two points."

"Fall off two," the order echoed from the sailing master to the helmsman.

"Get some hands to those braces. Mercer, put a hand to that main brace. Carey, you to the fore." He never raised his voice, never wasted his words. He said only what needed to be said. Everything was calm, evenhanded competence.

After her disquieting scene with him in the wardroom, Jane had sought to follow his instruction, and keep herself from his regard. But the moment she had begun to understand the angry catcall from the crew, she had instinctively gone toward him, drawn to that unmovable surety he projected, the way a stray cat cautiously seeks the warmth and shelter of the barn.

And she had not needed to say anything. In his calm,

competent way he had turned the ugly tide. With only one word to Punch, he had somehow changed the entire complexion of the morning.

And when his dark green eyes finally found hers from under the brim of his black hat, she felt she had to speak. "Thank you, Mr. Dance."

"You are welcome, Miss Burke." He touched his hat, and answered without taking his gaze from his sails. "Does this absolve me of my earlier greeting this morning?"

Jane could not hide her relief. "Yes, certainly. Good morning ladies, *all*, indeed. I hope I have not disappointed the men by not running crying to my cabin to escape the derision?"

"I hope you *have* disappointed them. *I* would be disappointed had you not."

The humor in his tone warmed her more completely than her stout cloak in the chill morning air. "I must admit, were it not for the most excellent view this morning, I might have been tempted to do so, and stay there for the rest of the voyage. But I never like to give in to low expectations."

"So I have learned. I can only hope the men will learn as quickly as I do." His answer was as immediate as it was forthright. But then he shook his head—a sharp negative. "Don't ever give in to them. If they see they can make you run, they'll never let up. Never let you out again." His sharp gaze canted sideways to her. "But you look the type who has learned how to stand firm."

That was his second reference to her type. And she was strangely grateful to him for recognizing it. "Thank you, Lieutenant. I'm finding I *am* the type to stand firm." First against her parents, and then Sir Richard and the lieutenant, and now against the derision of the crew. "And I am also finding that there are some men who are kind enough to stand firm on my behalf, for which you have my thanks."

She had said something to the same effect yesterday to

Mr. Denman, when he had spoken for her to Sir Richard. But yesterday she had had her own arguments, her own knowledge of what was right—if not exactly truthful—to add to Mr. Denman's opinions. This morning she had had no other recourse to the chorus of ugly derision rising all around her than the lieutenant. Only he seemed to have any power over the men.

Jane might tell herself all day long that she was J. E. Burke, and that she had a right to be aboard, but only this moment did she understand that in doing so, how completely she had put herself into this single man's power. The entire ship looked only to him. Sir Richard might bluster and say what he liked, but he had no sway over this oaken tower of a man. None of them did.

She would do well to remember that.

"It was not only on your behalf, Miss Burke, but for the good of the ship. If I had given in to their demand to put you off, or allowed the men their show of spite, I would not be doing my job, and would endanger us all."

Oh, heavens. Jane instantly felt her lungs squeeze painfully tight. "They demanded you put me off?" She had thought she only had to overcome the academic objection of Sir Richard and his toadies, but if the truth of the matter was that the vast majority of the men on board objected to her mere presence, not just her scientific qualifications, perhaps she ought to run crying to the sanctuary of her cabin after all.

But Lieutenant Dance was already sweeping her unspoken fears aside. "Do not consider it, Miss Burke. The men's *wants* come a slow second to their *duty*. Their duty is to man this ship as I, and their captain, see fit. But they want to do that with as little work as possible. Their dislike of you is just a convenient and temporary excuse to get out of their work—tomorrow their superstitious objection will be that Mr. Phelps is a black crow of a parson—and that I will not stand."

No, he didn't look like he would stand for much, with that grim, determined look in his relentlessly all-seeing eyes. If the crew's spite kept him probing at them instead of her, perhaps she ought to be relieved.

She was relieved. Off the starboard rail, the Isle of Wight was slipping away into the distance. She had done it. She was aboard her voyage of scientific discovery. She had done exactly as she set out to do, and taken her rightful place without any help or interference from her father.

Not that she had expected any interference from him. Her parents had swallowed her lie, and had waved her off on what she had told them was a long visit to her aunt, with no thought of anything but the inconvenience of having to do without her. They were like dogs—it didn't matter where she was, only that she was not available to be with them. At her aunt's, or on a ship bound for the Pacific—it made no mind to them.

They would know eventually what she had done— yesterday, on the morning of her departure, Jane had posted a letter to her aunt confessing all, but by the time the missive reached Aunt Celia in Somerset, and then Aunt Celia wrote her parents back on the Isle of Wight, it would be too late for any of them to do anything about it. Not that she expected them to do anything—they had for too long counted upon her to manage and arrange everything. Her father had not even had to do so much as sign his name to a letter, nor her mother to argue with the butcher over the price of a haunch, so thoroughly and completely had Jane arranged their lives. Mild, dutiful, organized Jane.

They would find out soon enough that she wasn't so dutiful now.

And the Isle of Wight, and the whole of the coast of England, was slipping away to the stern. Nothing could stop her now. Not Sir Richard, nor the snide derision of the crew. Nor even Lieutenant Dance's strange ability to soothe and discompose her all at the same time.

Perhaps the Bible verse had it wrong—it was not the truth, but her lie that had set her free. The irony could only make her laugh.

"You seem well entertained this morning, Miss Burke." While she had been watching the isle, the lieutenant must have been watching her.

Jane tried to combat the rising heat in her face by turning into the wind. "It has been a most instructional morning."

That twisted-up half-smile threatened to steal across his face. "And have all your—what did you call them?— collecting expeditions been as instructive?"

"If only." But Jane thought it best to say no more on the subject of what she *had* learned. And so she instructed herself to smile more serenely while she prayed that her face did not color with betraying heat. "But I am very much looking forward to learning more."

The lieutenant's sharp, all-seeing glance slid across her face so fast she was surprised it didn't cut her.

Oh, Lord. And there was the suffocating heat. It was a good thing the wind was chilling, or she would be as overheated as a boiled turnip. "I mean, I am very much looking forward to this overseas expedition. I have never collected outside of Britain, nor taken such a *long* expedition before. Two months is hardly the same as two years."

"Yes, hardly the same." His green, green gaze, which had moved on in a constant inspection of all the various and different parts of the ship, came again to rest upon hers. She could feel the pressing weight of his regard as if it were a stack of books sitting upon her chest.

"You do know, Miss Burke, that the Admiralty's estimation of two years is based upon a sort of minimum requirement for getting to the other side of the earth and back?" His gaze spared her for a moment as it swept up the bowsprit. "Two years is the *least* amount of time it could take, barring bad weather and unforeseen circumstances, which, I will scruple to tell you, can be counted upon to plague us every sea mile of the way. The truth is, it will undoubtedly take far longer than two years."

The news jarred the breath from her. She had *not* known, though clearly she should have. She had planned both her stores and her funds for reprovisioning at the standard stops of Madeira, Salvador de Bahia, Rio de Janeiro, and Valparaiso—just saying the exotic names had made her giddy with delight—to last only those two allotted years.

No, she had been careful in her preparation and generous in her funds. And besides, she had provisioned for two people—Papa and her, before he had changed his mind and decided they were not to go—when she would be only one. And those provisions had been a keepsafe—something to go along with the meals she would take sharing the captain's table along with the rest of the expedition, as had been arranged. She would be fine—although she was certainly hesitant, as well as curious, to meet the captain after the lieutenant's cryptic but descriptive comments upon her arrival.

"And if you were asked instead of the Admiralty, Lieutenant, how long would you have said the voyage was to last?"

"I would have said that we will be lucky to see England's shores within five years, Miss Burke, not two. That is, if *Tenacious* lives up to her name, and doesn't sink us all long before that."

Jane absorbed the second blow in silence. She had thought only of what she might accomplish on such a journey, and not of the passage of time. In five years' time she would be one and thirty. She would be the thing she had not wanted to admit to being, the thing that she told herself was not important. Being recognized as a talented, dedicated, scholarly conchologist had been what mattered. But the inescapable truth was that in five years' time, and after having taken herself across the globe and back, she would be irrevocably ruined for marriage. She would be a spinster set firmly upon the shelf.

It was a bitter tonic to swallow at the very start of her triumph. It was almost frightening.

Oh. This time it was she who looked more closely at the grim pleasure on the lieutenant's face. "I see. You mean to frighten me, Lieutenant Dance."

He nodded, all purposeful admittance. "I do, ma'am, I do. I mean for all of you, from Sir Richard on down the Royal Society's muster roll to you, J. E. Burke the conchologist, to be frightened into understanding what might come. Sir Richard spoke of hardships. Make no mistake, Miss Burke, there will undoubtedly be hardships, but there will also be danger—very real, threatening danger. The dislike of the crew, and the resistance of Sir Richard will seem like nothing compared to it."

He meant it, this sharp-eyed, grim-faced man. He believed the truth of every word he spoke. "You're a cynic."

He laughed into the wind. "Assuredly, Miss Burke. But at least I am not a worthless drunk."

His warning chilled her down to her bones, even though she knew he was trying his best to frighten her. But she did not run back to the relative sanctuary of her dark and airless cell in the wardroom. Not when there was such air and such a day to be found above decks.

Because the horizon stretched out before them in all directions. And the sea—the sea that she had seen outside her window every day of her life—looked so different now. So manageable for a man like Lieutenant Dance who seemed to have been at sea all his life, while to her it seemed so wild and untamed. So unknowable. Fathomless.

The word struck her now in a way it never had before, that the distance below her feet was beyond her comprehension. That nothing but the miracle of the wind and buoyancy was keeping them from hurtling straight to the bottom so far below.

But that space, which she had always pictured as so empty, was teeming with life. Even now, the barnacles that she had spotted peppering the lower reaches of the hull—or perhaps *salting* the outside of the hull with their gray and white apertures shining dully in the sun was the better description—were alive and living and breeding and growing. All without any interference from them above. Remarkable.

Punch came on deck, and with a friendly wave in her direction, climbed easily out into the chains off the starboard quarter.

Jane followed, because he looked much more comfortable and nimble than she ever might have guessed, and because an idea was taking shape in her mind. "Punch?"

"Morning, miss. You're out bright and early." He touched his forelock, and returned both hands to playing out line from a rectangular wooden fishing reel.

"Are you fishing?"

"Yes, miss." Punch laughed with good-natured patience at her ignorance. "For our supper, as they say, miss. Good seas for bluefish, miss. Have it as a roasted fillet with a mustard butter."

"Excellent." The sound of such a feast nearly made her stomach grumble in protest—they had not been given any supper last night. But perhaps that was due to the somewhat chaotic circumstances of the Royal Society's party settling in.

Jane stood watching Punch test the tension on the line, which trailed out in the sweep of the ship for some distance. "Is it very difficult?"

"To fish? No, miss. Easy as sitting."

"Excellent. Because I should like a favor from you, but I shouldn't like to interrupt your fishing."

"A favor from me, miss? You've only to ask and I'll do whatever I can for you, miss. You don't need my favor."

"Thank you, Punch. But I only wondered if you might be able to see some barnacles along the side of the hull from where you sit? Along the waterline below you?" she clarified.

The man bent his head to look beneath the deadeyes attached to the thick chain wale where he was seated. "I see some, miss. Though the lieutenant did set the idlers to scraping them off as best they could right before we set to sea."

"Did he?" Jane could easily recall the lieutenant's scowl when she had mentioned the barnacles to Sir Richard—the lieutenant had no doubt taken her words as an indictment of his precious ship. "Yes, he's a very efficient man, your lieutenant."

"Has to be, don't he?" Punch shook his head in sympathy with his superior officer.

"Yes, I suppose he does, Punch. But do you think if I minded your fishing line for a short while, you might be able to scrape off a few of the very low-lying barnacles for my study?"

"What'd you want with them barnacles?" As if he couldn't imagine what anyone would want with such a useless, pestilential thing, and questioned her sanity.

"I'm making a close, scientific study of them. Find out more about where they come from, and why they cling to the bottom of ships, and what damage they do."

"Well, I can tell you that, miss, without any study—get stuck on and make 'er bottom heavy and sluggish through the water. But they ain't so bad as the teredo worms, miss."

"Worms?"

"Swim into the ship they do, and bore holes right through the hull. Turn an oak ship into mush in no time. Got to sail fast to keep off from them worms."

"Does *Tenacious* have a problem, an infestation with these worms?" Is that why the lieutenant was so relentlessly vigilant about the ship—did he fear that they would be turned to mush at any moment? The idea was both frightening and fascinating.

Jane's hands gripped the smooth wood of the rail and gave it a surreptitious shake, as if she could test the stoutness of the hull. "Can you see any of the worms, Punch?"

He squinted along the waterline, but shook his grizzled head. "No. I reckon Mr. Dance keeps us sailing too fast for them to latch on, miss."

That was certainly a relief. Jane relaxed her grip on the rail. "Yes. That is what he would do." Always pushing the crew to trim the sails, and work the helm to get a faster turn of speed out of the vessel—a proverbial rolling stone that would gather no moss, nor worms if the lieutenant had his way. But despite their speed and the lieutenant's vigilance, the hull had collected barnacles. "But do you think you might be able to get a sample of barnacles for me? And then perhaps retrieve something for my study out of my pinnace?"

Punch took another squint-eyed look at the hull beneath him, and stroked his ginger beard in consideration.

"I would of course pay you for your trouble," Jane added to sweeten the pot. "Not much, but something. A few coppers at least, for your trouble."

"No trouble, miss. I'm happy to oblige you."

"Excellent." Jane felt a pleasurable excitement bubble through her—an interesting little thrill of accomplishment at having achieved her object. "I've brought you a small glass vial for the purpose. And a knife." She fished out the small pocket knife she carried with her on expeditions.

"Right so." Punch was nothing if not agreeable. He took the glass but declined the small blade with a laugh, drawing a much larger blade from his waist. "Got my own, don't I, miss. Now if'n you'd mind the line? Just hold it there, firm like, ready should you get a bit of a heavier tug."

Jane felt her mouth spread wide in a grin. "And that is how I shall know there is a fish on the line?"

"That's how you'll know, miss. But you just tell me, and I'll drag it in for you."

"Drag it in?" Jane was envisioning a fish as large as herself, with a tremendous dorsal fin and a long pointed nose spear like the one she had seen mounted on the wall of the fishmonger in Cowes. "How big is a bluefish?"

"Not so big as you can't handle," he answered with a laugh. But Punch had already handed her the long-line reel, and had disappeared back into the chains, so Jane gave the line an experiential tug or two, and reeled the line in a bit to get the feel of the thing.

"Fishing for your supper, are you, Miss Burke?"

What a time for Lieutenant Dance to decide to take notice of her. His gaze washed over her back, and left her shoulder blades itchy with heat. "Indeed, sir." Jane tried to make her voice as breezy and easy as his was dark and difficult. "I'm rather fond of fish."

"There's one blessing. You'll make some fisherman an excellent wife."

Something about the lieutenant's tone of voice conveyed what Jane could only think was cynical amusement, his implication being that she might indeed be a good wife, so long as she were not *his* wife.

As if she would have a man like him. He was nothing she wanted, and everything she disliked in a man. Cynical, ungodly, unlearned. She would make it perfectly clear she *would* make some other man a good wife, so long as that man wasn't him. "Thank you for your kind words on my marital prospects, Lieutenant. I'll be sure to canvass the fisherfolk for unmarried men when we reach our first suitable port."

From his lack of reaction, Jane was unsure if she had succeeded in ruffling the lieutenant's iron-clad feathers or not—two spots of warmth sprouted high on his already high cheekbones, though otherwise he gave no sign. His voice was as measured and detached as ever. "Practical, as always, Miss Burke."

Jane raised her chin and gave as good as she got. "And prepared, sir. Don't forget prepared."

His glance swiveled to hers. "Prepared for what exactly, Miss Burke?"

Jane refused to be made uncomfortable. So she gave him the boring truth. "A study of barnacles, which Mr. Punch has been kind enough to retrieve for me. Ah, there. Thank you, Punch." She turned to accept the small glass vial Punch passed back to her.

"Cap'n." The old steward knuckled his brow in easy respect, and reached to take back his fishing line.

But the lieutenant's response was both instantaneous and furious. "God's balls, Punch. Do you want to get us hanged?" His voice was an irate hiss. "It's lieutenant. Nothing more, nothing less."

The old sailor's face sobered. "Sorry, Mr. Dance, sir. I din't mean nothing by it. I only—"

"I don't care what you meant." The lieutenant's voice was as low and cutting as a lash. "Think before you talk. You'll have us both dancing from a yardarm, talking like that."

The lieutenant's vehemence surprised her, so much that Jane was about to come to the steward's defense, but the lieutenant wasn't done berating Punch. "Just shut your gob, and see to your work, and stop cavorting in the chains, and causing mischief with Miss Burke. And you—" The lieutenant whipped the lash of his displeasure at Jane. "I'll thank you not to bribe and distract my crew."

Gracious. He didn't have to like her, but there was no reason for such unreasonable anger. She had not interfered at all with the running of his precious ship—she was helping to fish for the supper that his ship was contracted to provide.

And as he himself had so cogently advised her before he had decided to take her in such ridiculous dislike, if she did not stand up to him now, she would never find her feet again. "Mr. Dance." Pride pushed her chin up. "I hardly think a few pennies—"

But this morning the lieutenant was as quick as he was unreasonable. "And that is exactly the problem with you, madam. You hardly *think*! If you had, you would never have stepped on board."

Jane's face flamed with uncomfortable, scorching heat. No one—not even her parents—had ever taken her to task so unaccountably, or spoken to her so rudely.

But the lieutenant had still more criticism to go around. "You've been nothing but trouble from the moment you walked upon my deck, madam."

Her only defense was to give him the iciest tone she could manage. "Then I will take care, sir, not to do so again."

Chapter Eight

A new day brought a new dawn. And fresh remorse.

He should not have spoken to Miss Burke that way. Nor spoken about his captain, earlier. Both had been mistakes, violations of his duty to his ship, and his honor as an officer. He should have kept his feelings and his temper under stricter control, and protected both the captain and Miss Burke as long as he could. But something about her—her buttoned-up, lady-scientist practicality, her clear blue gaze, and her refusal to be cowed by anyone or anything—made him want to push her, and tell her the ugly, testing truth. But he'd be damned if he knew why.

But he would likely be damned anyway. Because he could not keep his mind sufficiently on his work while the lady scientist in question gaped over the rail at the few barnacles that remained after he had set the men to scraping them off *Tenacious*'s hoary old hide.

He told himself he watched her out of simple concern that she not do herself—or anyone else—a harm. He told himself he watched so he could drop a boat down to rescue her the moment she disappeared over the side. He told himself all sorts of lies to make up for the simple truth that he liked looking at her very shapely bottom.

As did any number of the men. "Mercer, damn your

eyes. See to that halyard—it's as slack and useless as your mind, you grubby lubber."

Dance forced his own concentration on an assessment of the bowsprit. He didn't like the way *Tenacious's* jibs were drawing—the tack and the luff seemed to fluctuate, almost as if the bowsprit spar itself were moving.

"Mr. Simmons, I'm going to have a look at the bowsprit." He headed forward, only to find Punch clomping unevenly at his heels.

"Lieutenant, sir? That Royal Society fellow sent me."

"Sir Richard?"

"Well, his servant. That West Indies black man come to me."

It wasn't the color of the man's skin that had Punch in a state. Dance knew Punch had been in the navy for far too many years, and served with men of every make and creed, to judge a man on anything other than his character. "What is it, man? Don't tell me our guests are already put out at their less than spacious accommodations?"

They had no right to be put out. Not when he himself had no accommodation. Dance had spent the better part of last night—their first full night at sea—on deck, followed by an uncomfortable hour in a wardroom chair, staring at Miss Burke's door for reasons that he did not want to examine too closely.

"No, sir. And good luck if they are, sir, right, with no cuddies to spare?" Punch chuckled. "But what I came to ask, and I was wondering more, how are the guests to be fed, sir?"

"With food, man. You don't mean for them to starve their way to the South Pacific, do you?" It was nothing more than his usual sarcasm, but the truth was he hadn't the vaguest damn idea.

On a ship of war the officers were responsible for stocking and maintaining their own table. Dance had brought his own supply of foodstuffs aboard, locked safely in the lieutenants' storeroom on the orlop deck, and had purchased shares in both hens and goats—for eggs and milk—from the galley steward. But with the wardroom given over to the party of scientists, he had no idea what had been arranged for their food. "What provision has been made?"

"Beggin' yer pardon, sir, but Mr. Ransome sez as they haven't got their own foodstuffs, they're to eat boiled beef, same as the men. But them Royal Society folk be gentlemen, used to finer food than beef boiled to a pudding."

Dance hadn't taken any meals in the wardroom since the naturalists had come aboard two days ago. He had been too busy to keep to regular mealtimes—standing watch on watch to stay abreast of the constant running list of repairs, which only seemed to get longer in proportion to the distance they had traveled from Portsmouth. "No wonder they're griping. And Miss Burke as well?"

The mention of her name was out of his mouth before he could even question why it had been there in the first place. But Punch was too kind a soul to notice Dance's growing obsession.

"Bless me, no. Not a word from her. But she's brought her own hampers. Hasn't asked a thing of me, nor any of the other servants, sir, though she didn't bring a servant of her own. Seems to be doing for herself."

She would, and deny him the pleasure of thinking ill of her, the efficient, unfairly intelligent little bluestocking. Damn her for being so accommodating.

"Have you asked one of their servants?"

"Beggin' your pardon, sir, but it was one of their servants, that black man, name o' Witness, who come to ask me."

Damn his tired eyes. He'd been on deck for nearly eighteen hours without so much as a mug of coffee. And he wouldn't get it now. "Have they not brought so much as a laying hen with them?"

"Nothing, sir. Far as I can see, they was thinking they

was supposed to share the captain's table. But the captain don't have no table to speak of. Don't think his man has cooked more than a boiled egg for him in years."

Fuck all. Whenever Dance thought his situation simply couldn't get any worse, it invariably did.

He asked the next logical question, even as he damned himself for already guessing the bloody inconvenient answer. "Did they pay the captain money to share his table?"

Punch lowered his voice, and leaned in even nearer. "Near as I can tell, sir, they paid him five hundred pound each."

Holy unmitigated hell. Such a sum. The unease that constantly roiled in his gut coiled into a fist of angry frustration. And Punch was not yet done with the bad news.

"Sir Richard's man says how they met with Mr. Givens and gave the money over to him."

Dance didn't even have the breath to swear. Givens, damn his thieving hide to hell and back, had a lot to answer for.

An easy berth. That's what Will Jellicoe had promised him, along with the benefice of the Duke of Fenmore. The empty promise rolled around his head like the echo from a spent gunshot.

Easy berth be damned. Every time he thought this voyage could not possibly get worse, it did. A drunken captain. An idle and incompetent crew. A lady scientist. No stores. No provisions. No money.

No bloody bed.

Perhaps he should just assume that each and every day he was aboard was going to provide him with a kick in the teeth, and set his mind to accepting it.

And accepting it meant that there was nothing else to be done but open up his own provisions and host the naturalists to dinner. Anything less would be ungentlemanly. And open up the captain and the Admiralty to a charge of

fraud for having let Givens steal so much of the naturalists' money.

Yet Dance was surprised to find he had some friends.
Simmons proved to be an understanding man, and offered
up some of his own provisions to help feed the party from
the Royal Society. "But with five extra mouths . . ." The
young lieutenant let the thought die away.

"We'll be lucky to make it across the Atlantic," Dance
finished for him. Dance thanked whatever lucky star was
still shining on his behalf that he had been able to find such
a competent officer and lure him aboard, or he might be
tearing his hair out now in frustration. As it was . . . Dance
ran a hand through his short-shorn hair as if he might
chafe some better ideas into his head.

Dance had set a course on the northeasterlies blowing
down the edge of the continent so he might take advantage
of the trade winds blowing across the Atlantic toward
South America. He could change course to make port in
Madeira, but that would cost him precious days they would
need later in the voyage in order to round the Cape during
the height of the southern hemisphere's summer, in January. But if they were careful, and hauled on reasonably
tight rations, the food would easily last until they could
make port in South America. By then he would know if
any more repairs would be needed for the leaky sieve of a
ship—the carpenter already reported a steady trickle of
water into the bilges.

But they would make it through at least one dinner before they all drowned.

Thankfully, Punch was an able steward who had seen
his share of blustering lieutenants come and go. He knew
his business, and with a minimum amount of cash, and a
great deal of inventiveness, he secured an additional hen
and a further share of a goat to bolster the table. With the
addition of a fish from time to time, and by watering their

few bottles of claret, the wardroom would be able to lay a respectable, if plain table. They would make do, and make the best of it.

But what he could not make the best of was Miss Burke, who came to the dinner table looking something very much other than buttoned up.

Perhaps it was that Punch had outdone himself by laying a table with glass and silver and china more fit for an admiral's grand day cabin than the wardroom in a leaky sixth rate. Perhaps she had always dressed for dinner at her home on the Isle of Wight. Perhaps he was simply a callow, thoughtless idiot who had not looked at a real, honest-to-goodness woman in far too long.

Because to his eyes, Miss Jane Burke looked not at all like a buttoned-up spinster scientist, but as sweet and edible as a cream puff. The dark felt bonnet and heavy cloak that hid her more obvious assets were gone, and her smooth skin and bright hair shone golden in the warm glow of the lamplight.

She wore a wool gown the color of a creamy rose that even though it was as plain and unadorned as a flower's petal, made her look soft and approachable, and entirely female. And devil take him if the gown didn't fit the curves of her bosom like a well-filled spinnaker, rising below a slice of skin as pale and luminous as a crescent moon. The golden shadow of her collarbones ran toward the hollow at the base of her lovely long neck, and he wanted more than anything—more than food or sleep—to touch her there, and feel the steady beat of her tenacious heart.

Dance had clearly been living in the company of men too long, because he was struck too stupid by her appearance to even think of stepping up to take her arm, and lead her to the table. It was Mr. Denman, damn his spectacled eyes, who was there already, leading her forward and graciously offering her a seat next to him.

Dance forced his brain and body back into action, to play the gracious host. "Sir Richard, if you'll sit here? And Reverend Phelps. Yes, why don't you sit next to Sir Richard?" He tried to keep the older, disapproving men away from Miss Burke. "And Mr. Parkhurst there."

Thankfully, Miss Burke seemed to be doing her best imitation of a polite, well-mannered lady this evening. Those brightly curious blue eyes were demurely downcast as she slipped into the seat Denman held out for her. "Thank you, Mr. Denman. Good evening, Mr. Parkhurst. I hope and trust you've recovered from your earlier fatigue?"

Seasickness was clearly what the spindle-shanked Parkhurst had been suffering, judging by the green tinge around his gills.

But Punch was already ladling out a brown onion soup with the assistance of Sir Richard's and the Reverend Mr. Phelps's servants, and Dance hadn't had a decent meal in days. He had shipped for too long, and had eaten too many cold dinners over the years, to waste time on anything but applying himself to his food while it was still hot. He took up his spoon and set himself to it.

But the Reverend Mr. Phelps's tone told Dance that the parson was quietly shocked at Dance's pagan hunger. "Are we not to say the grace, Lieutenant?"

"Forgive me, Mr. Phelps." Dance set down his spoon and did his best not to feel like a heathen. "If you would be so kind."

All the heads at the table bowed down to pray for God's blessing—even the servants standing at attention behind the chairs. All but his. And Miss Burke's.

Though she sat as silent and docile as a lamb with her hands clasped demurely in her lap, she looked up at him from under her pertly arched brow, and met his eye. And smiled. A very small smile, as if she were trying very hard to subdue it, but could not manage the job, and let this sympathetic, almost mischievous little smile escape.

Dance quickly cast his gaze around the table, but the rest, even Lieutenant Simmons and Mr. Denman, had their eyes closed in grateful prayer.

And then the grace was done, and everyone was reaching for their spoons, and Miss Burke's conspiratorial smile was gone as if he had only imagined it. "You were saying, Mr. Denman?"

"My plan of study is of the anatomical features—"

Dance closed his ears, and forced himself to concentrate on the pleasure of his own hot dinner without trying to mind the conversations at the far side of the table.

It were best if Mr. Denman and Miss Burke formed an attachment, scientific or otherwise. It were best for the ship and for her that she be seen to be his—Mr. Denman's—and under his protection. It were best if he—Dance—concentrated on running his ship and keeping it from falling apart. And keeping the men in line. And eating while there was still food to be had.

In another moment Punch brought out a plate of ham, and Dance's heart sank and his stomach shriveled at the sight of the Royal Society fellows tucking in so enthusiastically. Dance had put by three smoked hams to last him a good long while, but at the rate his tablemates were forking up slices, the first ham wasn't going to last him the evening, much less the week.

He couldn't fault them—they were no doubt as hungry as he for not having eaten a decent meal in two days, and they could have no idea of the state of the officers' larders. Nor did he want them to know. This, at least, he could do to protect his ship and his captain's good name.

Lieutenant Simmons, being a navy man, and understanding the need to make their store of foodstuffs last, took only a small slice of ham. He sent Dance an apologetic glance, and asked Punch for a second helping of the soup instead.

And poor Punch—the look he sent Dance was more

than apologetic. "I'll only put so much on the platter and no more, from now on, sir," he whispered into Dance's ear.

Dance nodded both his agreement and his understanding. "Rest easy, Punch. You've done well."

For a long while there wasn't much in the way of conversation—clearly for all their piety, the naturalists were all as hungry as he—until Sir Richard, with a glance first at Mr. Denman, attempted to engage Miss Burke in conversation. "And how have you fared thus far, Miss Burke, with adapting to our privations?"

Miss Burke offered up that engagingly determined smile. "Quite well, I thank you, Sir Richard."

In another circumstance, Dance would not have been afraid to admire Miss Burke. In fact, he might have done a good deal more than admire her. In the soft lantern light Miss Jane Burke looked a great deal different than she had out on the deck. Without the severe brim of her ruthlessly practical felt hat, her face had a softness and ease that he had not noticed before. She looked . . . comfortable and ready to be pleased. Easy and pliable. Dangerously tempting.

Very dangerous. For a host of reasons, not the least of which was that he knew under that incongruous softness was that spine of tempered steel—he had already tested it more than once. And he knew that no one—no man or woman—voluntarily took themselves to sea without a very great deal of determination. She might appear soft and willing enough, Miss Not-So-Buttoned-up Burke, to bend under pressure, but Dance was willing to bet that she would never break. And anyone who thought her pliable—from Sir Richard to Mr. Denman—was a fool.

Dance might have been many things, but he was no fool.

And he could not afford to admire her.

But the conversation was going on without him.

"Although I am primarily a botanist, as you know"— Sir Richard condescended to remind them all—"I mean to take a close observation of the weather and climate as we journey along. Indeed, the Reverend Mr. Phelps and I were discussing that very idea this afternoon. The society would indeed benefit greatly from such a study."

Miss Burke smiled, and made a comfortable sound of polite encouragement, as did the others. But Dance thought he saw something in her eye, that same struggle to subdue some mischievous thought, as if she were endeavoring to keep her opinion of such officiousness as quiet as he.

Or not perhaps as much.

When he said nothing, Miss Burke raised her pert eyebrow at him before she turned the strength of her clear blue gaze upon Sir Richard. "I expect our naval hosts should be a great help to you there, Sir Richard, as such information is kept quite routinely in the captain's ship's log."

While Dance could only agree with her, the sharp intelligence in her smile alarmed him. "What do you know of ship's logs, Miss Burke?"

She kept her tone firm and neutral, as if reminding both of them of his earlier outburst. "Nothing, sir. Only what I have observed of each of your officers on the watch—is that how it is called?—recording time of day, and wind speed, and the speed of the ship through the water, and the noontime sighting of the sun."

Dance nodded, and relaxed a fraction from his vigilant unease. "Yes. Just so." She was only observant, as a naturalist must no doubt be, and not prying into the affairs of the ship. She could not know that their captain did not appear to keep any log, or notice anything about the running of his ship. Or that Dance was keeping his own log independent of the captain. But what else was he to do?

"But are there recordings of the ambient temperature, and sea temperature, and cloud formation, and wind direction all together?" asked Mr. Parkhurst.

Dance took pity upon the man for the ship's sake, and

made more of an effort to be conciliatory. "Only generally recorded. Wind fair out of the east, for example. So I am quite sure your observations would not go amiss." And anything that would keep them occupied, and out of the ship's company's way for the long length of the voyage, would never go amiss.

"And you, Mr. Denman?" Miss Burke smiled brightly at the reticent man to her right, making sure he had a share in the conversation. "What will occupy your mind as we travel to our destination?"

Your luminous creamy white skin, Dance answered for him. And your soft, pillowed curves.

Mr. Denman was of a more scholarly turn. "While my anatomical studies cannot be undertaken until we encounter native islanders, I am sure that I will find plenty that will occupy my time and talents for the duration."

His answer seemed dull and uninteresting until Dance saw a small sign of some private amusement—the faintest curve on one side of Denman's mouth—that indicated otherwise. Perhaps the myopic Mr. Denman was more farsighted than Dance had given him credit for, and had taken in more of Miss Burke's anatomical offerings than his scholarly bearing let on.

"Yes, I am sure." Sir Richard put a stop to Dance's innuendo-filled wonderings, by taking back control of the conversation. "As I was saying to our esteemed patron and your dear friend, His Grace of Fenmore, when we first met to discuss the proposed expedition—I said to His Grace, Mr. Denman seems particularly well suited to a sea voyage. And he agreed with me, did he not, Mr. Phelps?"

"Oh, yes, indeed," the Reverend Phelps concurred.

"You are very lucky," Sir Richard observed as a compliment, "in your friendship with such a great man."

"Yes." Mr. Denman's tone was almost apologetic. "His Grace has been a very good friend to me these many years. I owe this opportunity to join this expedition entirely to his generosity."

"As do we all." Sir Richard seemed more than happy to be included in the good duke's benefice. "I was most gratified when His Grace sought me out to offer his patronage of the expedition. It removed a very great number of impediments to our voyage."

Not all of them—His Grace had clearly had little influence on the choice of vessel, and its general state of readiness. But this then would account for the deference Sir Richard had shown Mr. Denman. The tall, bespectacled scientist was a substitute for their patron in Sir Richard's eyes. To offend Mr. Denman would be to offend the Duke of Fenmore.

"And you, Miss Burke?" Sir Richard was clearly trying to make up for his chilly original reception of Miss Burke now that Mr. Denman had shown his support. "How shall you pass the time productively? Alas, we are too far from shore for you to collect any shells."

"Indeed, Sir Richard." Miss Burke nodded, all cautious cordiality. "But I thought that I might use this voyage by making a more particular study of the barnacles I mentioned growing on the hull, as I have an idea that they may not be mollusks at all."

Since she did not bring up his ill-mannered encounter with her over those very same barnacles, Dance chose not to take her observation as an indictment of his ill-kept hull—and her study seemed genuine.

But Sir Richard's face immediately puckered up with both displeasure and disapproval. "I hope I need not caution you, Miss Burke," he began, his icy tone clearly indicating the opposite. "But I certainly should not advise an amateur such as yourself, to dare to challenge the wisdom of Linnaeus himself."

The man was working himself into a red-faced lecture, which Miss Burke calmly forestalled by the simple expediency of agreeing with him. "Indeed you are right, Sir Richard. Which is why I shall undertake this small study—if only to confirm once and for all the validity of the Linnaean classification. One may learn as much in failure, as in triumph. Would you not agree?"

"Yes, indeed." Mr. Denman played his position of knight errant nicely, using his influence to defuse any of Sir Richard's anger. "Well said, Miss Burke. Descartes would have us apply reason and skepticism to all fields of learning, no matter from whence, or from whom that learning came."

It was as politic and prevaricating an answer as Dance could ever hope to make in keeping the peace on his own ship. He might have to take a lesson at Mr. Denman's knee. Perhaps the man had so much experience from going on bended knee to his patron? It was an art that Dance would do well to learn.

But while Miss Burke gave Mr. Denman a sunny smile of gratitude and encouragement, she did not emulate Mr. Denman's example of the politic. She would not hide her keen curiosity simply to soothe even Mr. Denman. "And what of you, sir? Are you of the mind that Dr. Linnaeus's classification of human beings with that of the great apes is correct? Or do you stand with those"—here she cast a quick gaze at the Reverend Phelps—"who say that such a conjecture is doctrinally unsound, and must be corrected?"

Though Denman may have looked at Miss Burke with something more of respect for her learning, as well as for her daring and backbone, he still sought the answer least likely to offend. "You are certainly well read on all matters of classification, Miss Burke. Like you, I have read the *Systema Naturae,* but I shall try to approach the classification of the peoples I encounter with exactitude and thoroughness, without reference to either proving or disproving any theories, but to illuminate."

"There," Sir Richard exclaimed, as if what Denman

had said disagreed with Miss Burke, when to Dance's admittedly unscholarly mind he had done no such thing. But Sir Richard was more interested in praising Denman that in scolding Miss Burke. "And there is the brilliance which no doubt brought you to the attention and patronage of the esteemed Duke of Fenmore."

Mr. Denman again demurred. "It was youth that brought us together, sir, and certainly not brilliance. The duke and I were shipmates together—midshipmen—in our youth, on a vessel very much like this one."

"Shipmates?" It was Dance's turn to be intrigued by Denman. "How so?"

"Long before I had even thought of ever becoming a scholar, I was sent to sea as a young midshipman under Captain James Marlow on *Defiant*, back in the year seventeen hundred and ninety-four. But I didn't last long. And although I was never commissioned as a naval surgeon, I should very much like to offer your captain and you—as you are the officer in charge of the dispensation of the crew—my services, as I am a surgeon and physician both by my later education and training."

"But we are a scientific expedition in a time of peace, not war," objected Sir Richard. "I hope for your sake that you will not have the need to perform any surgeries."

"True, Sir Richard," Mr. Denman countered. "But my old captain used to say more men were lost to disease and accident than ever to cannonballs."

"Devil take me if he wasn't right." Here finally was a stroke of pure good luck—the first true good luck Dance had yet encountered on *Tenacious*. "What education and training, sir? Not that I have any idea of the proper education or training of a physician or surgeon, but I can only think that whatever you have done to learn your trade is going to be a vast improvement over letting one or other of the men take to playing apothecary to the rest of the crew." With this crew, they were more apt to poison each other on purpose.

"Trade, sir?" Sir Richard again objected on Denman's behalf. "Mr. Denman is a learned professor, sir. An academic, not a tradesman."

"I take no offense, Sir Richard. For in truth, I find medicine to be both a trade and a scientific discipline. But to satisfy you, I was educated in France and then Oxford, and am now a fellow with the Royal College of Surgeons in London, and a consultant surgeon at the Royal Hospitals in Chelsea and Greenwich."

"Good Lord." Educated in France. Dance thought that he and Denman looked to be of an age, which meant that if his education had been in France before Oxford, he'd had to have been there during the wars. Which made Dance wary. But a fellow of the Royal College of Surgeons was too much of a boon to pass up. "Dare I hope that you know anything of tropical diseases?"

"A little. But that is one of the purposes of this voyage. To make a greater study. And study the physiology of the native peoples we meet."

It was Dance's opinion that there existed in London a greater cross section of the world's peoples and their varied physiology than a man could ever find on a South Seas island, but that was why he was a lowly lieutenant in His Majesty's Navy, and not a learned fellow of the Royal College of Surgeons. He'd best leave the fellow to his business, and get on with his own.

"This is a great relief to me, Mr. Denman. I will gladly take you up on your offer." Dance held out his hand. "Welcome aboard *Tenacious*. I'll add you to the muster rolls for this cruise"—that is, if he ever got the official rolls— "and you can draw pay from the Admiralty while you're making your scientific discoveries. Let me show you down to the surgeon's bay on the orlop platform."

"No need, Mr. Dance, for either the pay, or for the escort. I know my way around a frigate well enough."

Well, damn the man for having such deep pockets that he didn't need the pay. Dance had never been so lucky. But such jealousy was beneath him—beneath them both. Dance could ill afford to dislike such a useful man.

"Then I will leave you to it, and thank you for your offer." Finally a piece of good luck. Perhaps their fortunes had turned.

But Dance could only laugh at himself. Because he knew better than to believe it.

Chapter Nine

If it took a thief to catch a thief, then it took another liar to know one when she saw him. And if Lieutenant Dance was not exactly lying, then he was at the very least covering some very important truth. His brows were furrowed together in a deep frown that was only slightly less combative than his usual scowl.

Unlike her, the lieutenant's lie did not look as if it were setting him free—he looked as if he were being eaten from the inside out.

Perhaps that was why he couldn't eat. But her eyes had told her something else was at play. She had observed the minute, but telling, exchange of glances between Mr. Dance and the other lieutenant—a very gentlemanly young man named Able Simmons. And she had not mistaken their restraint with the ham. As a result Jane had taken none of the meat herself, and kept to the good brown soup and the potatoes, as, she noted, did Mr. Denman. But she could not shake the feeling that there was something she did not understand, a circumstance which was underscored by the fact that the party of naturalists was taking dinner in the wardroom instead of the captain's table as had been agreed upon.

And then there had been his reluctant admission that

Tenacious did not have a surgeon, and his grateful acceptance of Mr. Denman's help. And his bringing on Lieutenant Simmons and the boys from the Marine Society just before they sailed. And his too candid admission that their captain was a drunk.

And his seething, too short temper.

Lieutenant Dance was hiding something. And she meant to find out what—the lieutenant's perpetual scowl notwithstanding.

She immediately sought out Punch, trailing after him as he cleared away the platter of ham that Sir Richard and the other men had just devoured. "Who has paid for our food, Punch?"

The steward only shook his head, and gave no answer.

"Punch?" The man still looked reticent, keeping his gaze turned to the floor, so Jane asked him directly. "Why should it be such a secret? Is Lieutenant Dance trying to make economies and scrimp on the food?"

Punch looked conscious, and glanced around to see if anyone else were listening before he gave his answer. "Perhaps for this meal we did, miss. But it's only as we didn't know it would fall to him to feed you."

"But why did it fall to him? Our dinners were part of our agreement with the captain," Jane countered. "Remitted before we ever set sail. Do the captain's servants not know this?" Perhaps Sir Richard had not made the financial arrangement clear when he had made his inquiries about their missing meals?

"Yes, miss." Punch nodded and agreed, as if he were loath to make any argument. "But the captain don't keep a table. And you lot needed to be fed, so Mr. Dance, he does what Mr. Dance does, and he makes do, and sees to it. He opened up his provisions, and bought more from the others—hen shares and fish, though he don't like it— and Lieutenant Simmons and Doc Whitely done the same, though they ain't told me as I can make entirely free with their foodstuffs the way the lieutenant said. And he give over all his spice."

"Lieutenant Dance? And is that a very expensive thing to do, Punch?"

"Give over his spice, ma'am? Well, it ain't cheap. Though we'll get more in Bahia or Rio, sez he. But I've to get to my work, miss, and not be seen idling. Mr. Ransome be free with his cane, even with the stewards."

"I understand, Punch." She herself had felt the touch of the boatswain's malevolent stare, if not the weight of his cane, enough to understand the steward's misgivings. "I won't keep you."

And since the malevolent Mr. Ransome seemed to be busy patrolling elsewhere, Jane felt free to venture topside, where she was sure to find the scowling lieutenant.

And he was scowling now, where he stood upon the dark quarterdeck, looking up at the sails illuminated like pale slices of the bright moon in the night. He seemed more at home there than anywhere else. Unlike the rest of the crew, whose work and leisure time seemed evenly divided, Lieutenant Dance seemed to spend the greater part of his time standing watch. Indeed, she had not seen him below deck at all before their dinner.

And, though he had somehow and somewhere scraped clean the dark shading of whiskers across his chin before he had come to the table, the dark circles around his deep-set eyes were an indication that he had not yet slept through a night. Because he had given her his cabin.

It was simply not right.

She came only close enough for their conversation to be private from the helmsman and the other few crew members in evidence. "Thank you for the dinner, Lieutenant."

He did not look away from his examination of his sails, keeping his own counsel, but it suited her, this one-sided arrangement—she could look at him without the weight of his probing stare to remind her that she had secrets and lies of her own.

"You are welcome, Miss Burke. Though I noticed you did not partake of the meat. Was the ham not to your liking?"

She could not quite gauge his tone. "The ham was very much to my liking, Lieutenant, but I could not help but feel that it might be in short supply."

Oh, he looked at her then—that swift cut of his eyes, dark and lethal in the night. "You need have no fear on that account, Miss Burke. Your contract with *Tenacious* will be upheld."

It was hard not to react to the clear hostility in his tone—for she felt that she had done nothing to earn it. But she did understand that it might be pride and fear that made him speak so. "You mistake me, sir. My concern is not exactly for the arrangement I made—indeed, we all made—with the captain to share his table, but for the burden it seems to have inadvertently put upon you and your wardroom. While I am grateful that you are upholding our arrangement—for five hundred pounds is a monstrous load of money—my observation of the situation tells me that while the burden of the arrangement has shifted to you, the money has not."

The muscle along the line of his jaw twitched, before his mouth curved into a rueful, cynical smile. "You must be a very good scientist, if you are always this observant. What else do you know?"

She had not expected so blunt a question. "Nothing. I only know there was no dinner yesterday or the day before, and only after Sir Richard made inquiries was the situation remedied, not by the captain, but by you."

"It is my responsibility to act when the captain cannot."

"Cannot? Or will not?"

"The captain finds himself indisposed." He said the word firmly, with a small nod of his head in confirmation.

Just as if he had rehearsed it. "Like a great many men, including our late Admiral Nelson, he finds himself ill each time we set to sea."

"You are not a very good liar, Lieutenant. And however true this tale of seasickness may be, it is still a deception. You said before that he was drunk."

He swore under his breath, and shook his head. "Devil take me. I should not have said so. And you should not have remembered."

"I am, as you said, a scientist, Lieutenant Dance, and a good one. It is my curse always to observe, and see, and remember, and never to forget." And hardly ever to forgive. She could never forgive her father's betrayals—being too prideful to publicly acknowledge her contributions to what ought to have been *their* book. Leaving off all attribution from each and every one of the colored plates in *The Conchology of Britain* that she had spent years and years—happy, fulfilling years, so she had thought—painstakingly hand-tinting. And choosing not to join the Royal Society's expedition, because his daughter's skills would be apparent for all his fellow naturalists to see. All selfishness and pride.

The lieutenant wasn't selfish, even if he had pride to spare—the dinner had just proved that.

But, her conscience reminded her, she ought to judge herself more harshly than she judged the lieutenant. She had denied the truth just as assuredly as her father, in order to justify her own deception.

She was a liar, no matter how justified. What remained for her to find out, was if the lieutenant's lie was justified as well. "What happened to the money—some twenty-five hundred pounds?"

He shook his head, but could not meet her gaze. "You have my word, Miss Burke, that your party will continue to be well fed."

She had not expected such evasion from him, who

seemed so straightforward. "That is not what I asked, Lieutenant. Can you assure me that you are paying for our victuals out of that money?"

"I can assure you only that you will be fed, Miss Burke, to the utmost of my ability. You have my word upon it."

"I believe you. It is not your word that I doubt."

He looked at her again, those dark probing eyes searching her face, trying to gauge what he thought of her, but he did not speak.

They stood in the dark with the sound of the night wind filling the sails, and the hushed rush of the water sluicing down the side of the hull for a long moment of tense, uncomfortable silence before she spoke. "So what shall you do about the captain?" she asked him.

"The same as I am doing now," was his prompt response. "Running the ship, correcting the deficiencies. Keeping the men at their work. Standing watch on watch until it is no longer necessary for me to do so."

She tried to understand what he was not saying, as well as what he was—that he took full responsibility for whatever problems *Tenacious* might have, including her drunken captain. "And if it remains necessary?"

"I will do what is necessary," the lieutenant confirmed. "It is my duty."

Jane absorbed this evidence of the lieutenant's character. And did what little she thought she could do to help him. "I understand you spent almost all of last night on deck?"

He narrowed his eyes then, and gave that quick cynical twist of his lips that told her he was not best pleased to be found out. "Punch should mind his mouth."

"Punch should mind his lieutenant better, and see that his lieutenant gets some sleep."

"I am quite used to sea officer's hours, Miss Burke, I assure you. I can stand watch on watch as necessary, easily enough."

"But for how long, Lieutenant? As you noted, I am a scientist, and although I study the shells of clams and snails, I know that all living beings need rest. For our safety as well as yours, Lieutenant. For if you are all that stands between us and a drunken, incompetent captain, it would seem we have a very great need of you."

Another narrow sideways wince sliced across his face. "I should not have told you that. And must ask that you not spread such news aboard." Another thought seemed to occur to him, for he briefly closed his eyes, as if he were in pain. "Or do all the others of your party already know? What else has Punch said?"

"No. I have said nothing. And Punch has only said that you don't spare yourself, and are doing all the work. The rest I simply observed."

He let out a huff of sarcastic laughter. "Are all naturalists this observant, or is it only you?"

She shrugged her opinion of all other naturalists—for she could not speak for people she did not know. "If they are any good. But I perhaps have something more to the point than the others. I know something of carrying the weight of others upon one's back—of having all the responsibility and none of the authority, Lieutenant. And it rankles. I suspect that under all of your cynical nonchalance, you are too good a man to be taken advantage of in this way."

"You mistake me, Miss Burke. If you ask the men—though frankly, I recommend that you don't, and have no more contact with any of them than absolutely necessary—they will tell you I haven't a good bone in my body. Don't make me into some bloody hero."

Jane wasn't about to let him put her off with such transparent cynicism. "Your giving me your cabin, and feeding us all, was goodness and a kindness, whether it was intentional or not."

"Miss Burke, I vacated my cabin solely to keep the

peace, and keep you in the place where you can cause the least amount of mischief."

Jane felt the fine hairs on her arm bristle up like spines on a sea urchin, despite the fact that she thought the lieutenant meant to put her off again, so she might think ill of him, and keep him at his proper distance. Which was undoubtedly a prudent idea. But clearly, she was rather done with prudence. She rather liked too much this feeling of being right. "Rest assured, Lieutenant, I mean to cause you no mischief."

That brought a full-throated laugh out of the man, and brought that wry smile twisting across his face. "Oh, come now, Miss Burke. You are not a very good liar either." He turned that keen, probing glance upon her, and it was as if he could see straight through her, into the dark heart of her deception. "Surely you're more intelligent than to try to deceive me. Certainly you're more ambitious. You would not have subjected yourself to the discomfort and tedium of such a journey, not to mention the disapproval of men such as Sir Richard, if you were not ambitious."

Jane had never before had someone so easily expose her secret soul. Even her parents had never guessed. "I would never characterize myself as ambitious."

But even as she spoke, Jane could feel her face flame with the lie. As much as she didn't like to admit such grasping, unladylike behavior, the lieutenant had the right of it. She was ambitious. She wanted her own name on the cover of a monograph. She wanted the recognition and respect of her fellow scientists. She wanted the Royal Society's acclaim. She wanted it all.

And the lieutenant knew it. His smile narrowed. "It is not a criticism, Miss Burke. The devil knows I admire ambition in others, if only to make my own ambitions more palatable."

Jane could hear the sharp edge of sarcasm in his voice,

but for the first time, she wondered if the cutting tone was all for himself, and not for her. "And what are you ambitious for, Lieutenant?"

"Same as any navy man—a command of my own that lets me sail. And a fortune to make the living on it as easy and palatable as possible."

Jane heard what he hadn't said just as clearly as what he did admit. "And you haven't that fortune now?"

For a moment Jane thought he might tell her not just the truth, but the whole of the inconvenient truth, so uncomfortable did he look, with one side of his face winced up as if he had the toothache. But all he would admit was, "You and your colleagues will most assuredly get your five hundred pounds' worth, Miss Burke."

"Even if it paupers you?"

"Let us hope it does not come to that, madam."

There it was again—the word *madam* said in such a way as to give her warning that she was treading on dangerous ground. "Which is why I'm trying to thank you. I am not, as you've noted, entirely unintelligent. I know that the comforts I seem to be enjoying have come at some cost to others—namely yourself. And that, as I said, rankles."

"Put it from your mind, Miss Burke. Such privations are merely part and parcel of duty. Nothing more, nothing less."

He was obviously quite determined to keep a prudent, professional distance. His cynicism was like a well-worn old coat—put on only from habit, and having lost all its warmth.

And the conversation seemed to have come to an end, but she wanted—she was determined—to make him think better of her, even if he would not think better of himself.

And, she realized, she was interested in him, this lieutenant. She liked him. He was strange—handsome and off-putting all at the same time, like a spiny combed murex.

Beautiful and dangerous and very, very interesting. And she wanted to catalogue his secrets. "What was your excuse for not saying the grace, Lieutenant?"

He laughed at her abrupt change of topic, but he proved himself to be honest about some things. "I don't believe in God," he stated flatly.

Jane could not stop a gasp from rushing out of her chest. "Truly?"

He shrugged, as if it were just another of his uncomfortable truths, of no more import than having to stand watch on watch. "I long ago gave up praying to a God who certainly had better things to do—and who was obliged to listen to the prayers of my enemies just as closely as he might listen to mine. It didn't seem logical. But what of you, Miss Burke?" He turned the dark probe of his eyes on her. "Scientist or no, you do not seem the type to be atheistic."

There it was again—his mention of her *type*. As if he wanted to figure her out, and catalogue her as a specimen just as much as she wanted to do with him. "I'm not atheistic. I believe in God, rather fervently. I am rather filled with wonder for all His extravagant creation. I just don't care for conspicuous shows of piety. I thought it more appropriate for us all to have said our own private, silent graces—which I already had done when Mr. Phelps made show of it—as not everyone needs must share the same version of piety. Although I am as thankful as the next person—probably more so. But I would rather adhere to the principle that one should do good by stealth, and that God, who sees all and hears all that is done and said and thought in private, will reward one."

"In private?"

"That I cannot answer for. I would be lying if I did not hope my reward in this life, and the one after, will be just and deserving. But I will do all that I can to make sure I deserve whatever rewards God is willing to give me."

But as soon as she said the words, Jane was stricken with the lie.

More than any other thing she had said, this was untrue. However much she might think that she deserved, and had earned her place on the expedition through her own hard work, study, and diligence, the truth was that she had *not* been content with whatever reward, or lack thereof, that God had given her. She had taken matters into her own hands and chosen her own suitable reward.

She had railed against her father and God equally in doing what she had done.

"You astonish me, Miss Burke."

She felt her own face heat, and pleat up into her own version of that wincing smile. "I fancy I astonish myself, Lieutenant."

Within the space of a few days, she had become someone she didn't altogether know. Someone who could see that the world was not so absolute as she might have thought. Someone just a tad more like the cynical lieutenant than she ever might have thought.

The idea was disconcerting. And liberating at the same time.

Because there was no turning back. Even if she had wanted to, it was not possible to turn the ship around in the middle of the black ocean and return her to her life before.

And the truth was, she did not want to return. She had already crossed some invisible line. And there would be no turning back.

Chapter Ten

Out in the open ocean they had more than a week of fine sailing. Dance began to hope that *Tenacious* would spare him any additional gray hairs. Close hauled on the larboard tack to take advantage of the brisk westerly trade winds, the ship stood her canvas well, and gave him a good thirteen knots for several days on end. With the wind at their back, the following sea better suited the flaws in the vessel's construction, and he and Doc Whitely could get a good turn of speed from her sailing with the wind blowing up the ship's skirts from astern.

And other, more picturesque skirts were also blowing in that following wind. Miss Burke was proving herself to be a steady sailor, though she still had moments of clumsiness while traversing the ladders and decks. Dance would not admit it to himself—nor to anyone else who might have asked—but he had been keeping a weather eye on the companionway in anticipation of her arrival. She was always one of the first people on deck, though she mostly kept quietly to herself, tucking down against the rail with her pad of paper, drawing her barnacles, or who knew what.

He told himself he watched for her for the sake of the ship—he had not explicitly asked her to keep her conjectures as to the state of the ship's affairs to herself, and wanted to make sure she did not spread gossip, or add to the constant undercurrent of discontent swirling about the men on the berth deck. He needed time to establish his authority, and to prove himself—to both his crew, and to the naturalists—to demonstrate that he knew his business and was making good on the Admiralty's promises.

But the plain fact of truth was that he watched her simply because he could not stop himself. He could not stop his gut from tightening in pleasurable anticipation of her arrival. He could not stop from hoping she would speak to him again. From wanting more of her interesting, intelligent conversation, and the dangerous pleasure of having her alone to himself, even while he chided himself for wanting the distraction of talking to her.

But what happened today when her dark felt hat appeared above the edge of the combing was that it was accompanied by the tall, bespectacled surgeon. They moved to the taffrail, where she was staring down into the water as if it were telling her secrets. Secrets he wanted to know.

Dance wanted to hate Denman, to cast him into the same void as Givens, and the captain. But he couldn't. The surgeon was far too useful, and far too generous to hate. He had already eased the Reverend Phelps's woes, and physicked a few of the seamen into feeling better about their lot.

Perhaps enough crewmen would fall ill for the surgeon to be so taken up with care that he would have no time for Miss Burke?

No. Dance ruthlessly quashed such an unworthy daydream. It was the last thing he needed, for one of the infant midshipmen he had plucked off the parish rolls to prove pestilential, or rife with a putrid fever. Not even a surgeon educated in the rarefied air of Oxford would be able to help them much then. They would be lucky to make Recife let alone the South Seas in such an instance.

No. Best to let Miss Burke and Mr. Denman be, and let the surgeon work whatever charm he had hidden behind his spectacles to enchant her. And good luck to them all.

But luck was not what they had. Not a bit of it. As soon as the wind eased, *Tenacious* began to pitch and wallow—as Mr. Whitely so cogently predicted—like the veriest pig.

Which brought predictably bad news.

"She's wet again, Mr. Dance," the carpenter reported, as if the ship were an infant in swaddling clothes and not a thousand-ton behemoth. "It's the pine, sir."

"The devil you say." Dance continued to swear fluently in the privacy of his mind, but the truth was he had been expecting such an occurrence. He had understood the first day he had come aboard and inspected the ship, that the iron straps fastening her hull in place of oak lodging knees meant that *Tenacious* had been constructed during the height of the war years, when good strong oak had been scarce, and durability had been sacrificed to speed of construction.

"Don't tell me." Dance knew without even looking. "Water is seeping into the bow with every single pitch and yaw."

"Aye. Works her seams open something chronic in these rollers, sir."

Dance was running short of creative curses. "Yes. If this ship hasn't the devil's own luck." The men's muttering and superstitious warnings would only get louder and harder to ignore at this latest setback.

"Too true, sir," the carpenter agreed. "They're after saying it's the curse of that female we've got on board, but I know better. Always working loose her seams, *Tenacious* is. I been in her since she was launched, and she's always been a wet sailor."

It was only small comfort to know the ship's less than

ideal circumstances could not be laid entirely at Dance's feet. And a comfort that not all of the men seemed to have taken an unreasoning dislike of Miss Burke. Cold comfort, but comfort nonetheless. Dance would take whatever he could get. "What do you typically do to keep her dry and afloat?"

"Don't know about dry, sir—never has been very dry. But typically I'll recaulk them seams afresh, and see what I can do to keep them iron strappings from shifting overmuch. But there's only so much hemp and tar can do to save a seam from opening. What I could use, is more good, well-aged oak in the hold to brace her up. But . . ." The man fingered his dusty beard, and let the thought die away.

Dance understood all the same. "Don't tell me." Dance slapped his hat against his knee in disgust, and pushed his hand through his close-cropped hair to exercise his frustration. "There's no money for oak."

The carpenter shook his head in agreement, looking just as wearied by the ship's constant state of disrepair. "Never was much in the way of money, ever. Always hauling tight, on close rations with Cap'n Muckross."

It was just as Dance had feared. Despite his recent spate of care and repair, *Tenacious* had been kept too long in a state of ill repair, with the monies that ought to have been spent on oak and canvas leeched away from an inattentive captain by a thieving purser. Damn, but Givens certainly had a lot to answer for.

"Do what you can, man," Dance instructed the carpenter. He could all but hear his money—the money he had earned from all those years and years of attentive duty and risky prize taking, money which he had hoped would see him in good stead when establishing his own captaincy—running through his fingers. "I'll do what I can for the oak when we make suitable port."

That would mean constant vigilance across the wide

reach of the Atlantic until they could make port in Recife or Salvador de Bahia, where they could take on food and water, and negotiate with a shipyard for ship's timbers. And whatever else they would need by then.

"Aye, sir. Aye, aye. With some luck, she'll hold."

Dance didn't believe in luck—he believed in preparation and action.

He kept one eye on the glass and another on the weather in momentary expectation of a late-season hurricane to come roaring down upon them from across the Southern Equatorial current. And prayed to a god he no longer believed in.

A god who seemed determined to put Miss Jane Burke in his way.

She approached him alone—a glance to canvass the deck told him Jack Denman must have gone below. Dance schooled his gaze to check the compass heading instead of taking a reading of Miss Burke's snug, sand-colored gown—a color like a warm dune on a sunny day. "How goes your study of the devious barnacle, Miss Burke?"

"Well, I thank you, Lieutenant." Her face was alight with something more powerful and lasting than mere excitement—it was the thrill of accomplishment that put that rosy glow in her cheeks. "I am absolutely sure that there are at least two—and possibly three—different species of barnacles found on *Tenacious*'s hull. The plate arrangement of the carapaces differ significantly—the smaller gray barnacle peppering the hull has both end plates overlapped by side plates, while the other, white species has only one. And what I believe to be a third species has a simple, regular tube-groove arrangement in its side plates. So curious. And so interesting."

Dance hadn't the vaguest idea what she was on about, but she sounded so utterly convinced, and so passionate, he could not resist urging her to keep talking. "That sounds promising."

"Yes." She gave him a marvelous flash of a smile that chased away all his resolve to be reserved with her. "And because of that I must ask you a favor."

"A favor?" Dance's mind leaped to several startling possibilities.

"The only way I am going to be able to identify and document the differences is if I can make a more thorough study under my large, fixed magnifying glass, which is safely stowed, just as I so persistently insisted"—she made a face full of self-deprecating chagrin—"in my pinnace dangling off *Tenacious*'s stern davits. And the water looks dark and unspeakably cold. And I am clumsy, and not an idiot."

That self-deprecating charm annihilated the last reserves of his resolve. "You're not so bad."

She gave him a sunny little smile that peeked from the corners of her mouth, like a warm dawn priming a good day to come. "Am I not? Then why do you always scowl at me?"

Because he was clumsy in his own way. Because he had a run-down ship to keep afloat. And because he *was* an idiot.

"I am trying, for your sake as well as mine, to do what is right and prudent. But that doesn't seem to work around you, Miss Burke, because if you were right and prudent, you never would have undertaken this expedition, nor I think, ever become a scientist at all."

She was such a tidy bundle of contradictions—prim and proper and still somehow daring—that he could not help but be fascinated by her. He could not help but want—

Dance never finished the thought, because overhead, a great shuddering crack rent the air.

The fore topgallant mast—the one he had asked to be refidded, damn it all—had gone, cast forward by the press of the fore topgallant sail, snapping lines and rigging as it shuddered over, taking the fore top royal mast with it.

There was a strangled scream as a man above was pitched through the air, only to be caught in the tangle of the falling lines and the jibs. It was Flanaghan, the captain of the tops. Caught upside down in the tangle of spars and lines. Hanging as limp as a rag, with blood streaming from his head.

"Hove to. Hove to! Mr. Whitely, helm over." Dance was already running forward bawling at the top of his lungs. "Get a man to the fore brace. No! Starboard side, starboard on the fore. Larboard on the mizzen." Hadn't they had sail drill enough for the men to know how to bloody well heave to? "Brace over hard. Hard, I say."

He was across the waist, up onto the forecastle, and at the foot of the foremast with Flanaghan dangling in the air forty feet above. "Get a netting. Rig it beneath." Only the devil knew how long it would take to fish the netting out of the cable tier, but they had to do something for the man.

"Take in the fore course, keep it from fouling." Some of the men were running to obey, while others were frozen in their tracks, staring up at Flanaghan's eerily still form. "Get out from under there, man!" Dance ordered as he pushed crewmen out of the way. "Do you want it to come tumbling down upon you?"

Above, one of the agile topmen began to cautiously shin down the fore jib stay to try and reach Flanaghan.

"Get a line first." Dance tipped back his head to roar at the man. "Get a whip purchase to secure him."

The topman stopped and turned back to his mate on the foretop, while others of his mast mates swarmed up the shrouds to pass and rig the line.

But Dance was already thinking ahead, and ordered the foot of the outer jib to be braced back under the hanging man like a sling. "Cast loose. That's it, man. Handsomely now. Look sharp."

From the quarterdeck—where he should have stayed—

Dance could hear Doc Whitely ordering the helm brought up, and Able Simmons calling for other sails to be braced back as the ship came up into the wind.

It seemed an eternity before the nimble topmen could fasten a line around Flanaghan, and fish his limp body upright. But the sailor was still out cold, and did not yet revive in the other men's arms.

"Lower him down. Handsomely now, handsomely. Take your time." Dance tore his gaze from the scene above on the foremast to the men who stood by with their heads tipped upward. "Rig a litter. And pass word for the surgeon, Mr. Denman."

"I'm here." Denman was coming swiftly across the larboard gangway with his sick bay assistant in tow, and in another moment Flanaghan was lowered down to the waiting canvas litter, and borne away to the surgery by his mates.

And all Dance could think as he watched them carry the topman away past the gaping men, was that the accident was wholly and entirely his damn fault.

His fault that this ship wasn't fit to cross a pond much less an ocean. His fault that he hadn't personally supervised the work he had ordered on the foretop. His fault that he had been flirting with the intriguing and infuriating Miss Jane Burke, and not minding his damned ship and his damned men the way he ought.

Damn, damn, damn his eyes.

And still there was work to be done, and men to put to that work, and a ship rising and falling beneath his feet that needed to be pointed once again southward.

"Get some axes above to cut away that bloody mess." The moment he spoke, Dance thought better of the idea, and countermanded his own order. "No. Avast there. Don't just cut it away and let it go by the boards. We'll have need of everything salvageable." He hated that he sounded as if he didn't know his own mind, or couldn't make his mind up fast enough to suit the circumstances. But his pride could take a cold swim, because the damn fact was, they hadn't any bloody spars to spare. "Bring it down as slow and easy as you can. And get the carpenter's mates up there to do the job properly this time, damn their eyes."

And to show them that he bloody well knew he was as much to blame as anyone else, Dance shucked his coat and his dignity to climb up the bloody shrouds himself and see to the work on the foretop. It wasn't the sort of thing a damned lieutenant who had the command of his vessel ought to do, but there was no one else he could trust to supervise.

They got the foremast properly rerigged even without the fore topgallant or royal masts before the forenoon watch was called, and Dance had *Tenacious* put back before the trade winds with a course south by southwest, bound for the first port he could make on the coast of South America.

And because he had not yet exhausted himself with that work when Mr. Lawrence came to take the deck, Dance took himself below to the sick bay, where Jack Denman was pouring some concoction down Flanaghan's throat after binding the man's arm up in a splint. "How does he fare?"

"Well enough." Denman gestured to the thick bandaging encircling the man's temple. "He came to once the bleeding stopped. Took a gash four inches long. Probably clipped a tackle."

"Will he live?"

Denman looked grave and solemn, and spoke cautiously. "Always hard to say with a head wound. But most likely. I reckon an old tar like him is too tough to die from a little knock on the head."

It had hardly been a little knock—a full quarter of the

mast had given way under pressure. Dance left the orlop deck feeling only slightly more relieved than when he had descended, but his feeling of unease redoubled as he moved through the ship. The men were quiet and grim at their work, casting silent glances and passing quiet words from one to another as they waited to hear how Flanaghan fared.

It was as if a pall had descended over the ship—a pall Dance had foolishly thought he could cast off the vessel with attentiveness and duty and work and repair and decisive action.

Instead of welcoming the work, it seemed to Dance the men welcomed the accident—as if they wanted a reason to be morose and superstitious. He could feel it in the chary glances cast his way, as if he had somehow been responsible for the damn spar giving way. As if his making them work and repair the ship had been the cause, rather than a result of their inattention and idleness.

He heard the mutterings as he moved throughout the hull.

"Never would have happened with the cap'n having his way."

"If the cap'n a had his way, we'd still be safe in Portsmouth harbor, where we belong. Don't know why the cap'n don't put a stop to it."

"It's curst bad luck, the lieutenant being in charge."

He'd give them bloody bad luck.

But as long as they didn't pin their dangerous delusions on Jane Burke, he'd take all the derision they could hand out. He had derision aplenty of his own. Starting with the man responsible for *Tenacious*'s miserable state of repair—the captain who wouldn't captain his own ship.

Dance strode the length of the gun deck all but daring the men to give him the eye, but he couldn't even growl at the poor stupid sods, because the poor stupid sods were smart enough to give him a wide berth as he stomped his way aft, patrolling his ship. Even Jane Burke had sensibly disappeared below.

It promised to be a long miserable night.

At six bells of the middle watch, Able Simmons climbed to the quarterdeck, and came to stand by Dance at the instruments. "She's sailing well, even without the foretop."

"Well enough." Dance had nothing to say that didn't involve a load of self-loathing, so he let the comment pass. "You're up early." The watch didn't change for another hour, at four o'clock in the morning. The night was still and black around them.

"Yes, by design. With all due respect, Mr. Dance, you need some sleep."

Dance would have objected, or made some ridiculous pronouncement about duty and endurance and hardship, but the moment he opened his mouth, all he could seem to do was yawn. And tired men made poor decisions—he stood as proof enough of that. "Damn me, but you're right."

"Go on, then." Simmons nodded his head toward the companionway ladder. "Somehow she's contrived it."

There could be only one she. "Contrived what?"

"She's shifted everyone so you might have a proper cabin to sleep in, as you ought. Can't have the first lieutenant looking like day-old meat from lack of sleep."

"Did she say that?" The revealing question was out before he could wish it back. "Never mind. So long as I don't smell like like day-old meat it doesn't matter." The truth was, he *felt* like day-old meat.

"Go on, sir. I'll take the deck."

There was nothing he could do but concede gracefully. "Thank you, Mr. Simmons."

In the dimly lit wardroom, Punch awaited him at the door to the cuddy he had originally assigned to Mr. Denman. The cuddy next to his own—the cabin normally assigned to the first lieutenant, but now inhabited by Jane Burke. "What's afoot?" he asked Punch. "Where is Denman?"

Punch pointed across the wardroom to the largest of the cabins on the larboard side. "Shifted," was the simple answer. "Miss Burke cleaned out the purser's storeroom, what with it being empty." Punch's scathing tone held a wealth of condemnation of the former purser. "And them two young lieutenants was kind enough not to object to being moved on t'other side of the wardroom door with the warrant officers. Shifted."

Something that ought to have been gratitude, but wasn't, stirred deep in his gut. She had contrived it. For him. Everything had been arranged, just so. But of the arranger, there was no sign. He had only the steward to thank. "Thank you, Punch."

"Nothing to it, sir." The steward held open the door. "I shifted your dunnage back from the storeroom, and she gave back your hanging cot, as none was so long as your former.

She had managed all this. Again, his weary mind shouted, for him.

So he might have a place to lay his head after so many nights of catching his rest in stiff-backed chairs. "Thank you, Punch. I'm sure I'll manage." Dance fished a finger under the edge of his black silk stock and began to tug the neck cloth from around his neck.

"Is everything acceptable?" came a soft, straightforward voice—Miss Burke come to torment him in his waking dreams.

Punch turned to her. "Sorry to wake you, miss."

"It's quite all right, Punch," she claimed, though her

voice was still cottony with sleep, her hair was loose from its normally strict pins. And he could see a foam of soft white lawn peeking out from under the edges of the voluminous, dark cloak she had thrown on for modesty.

But despite her bed-tousled appearance, she was all whispered purpose. "I wanted to make sure everything was arranged as it should be. So you can get some sleep."

Sleep was the farthest thing from his mind. And his body, which had roused itself to an almost painful state of alertness in her soft, sleepy presence.

"I'll just finish changing the linen out for you—" Punch was saying.

"No." Because Dance had already made the mistake of letting his hand slide down upon the pillow. And he fancied the linen was still warm from the heat of her body, where she had laid her head. His hand flexed into the pillowed softness and would not let go.

"Out," was all he could say. His voice was nothing but a hoarse croak.

"But, sir, if I might just—"

"Out." He sounded done in. Because he was.

"Leave him be," she said. "It's quite all right, Punch. The poor man is all but dead on his feet."

Oh, he wasn't dead. Not by a long shot. Not with the heat and scent of her rising from the bedding to wreathe his head and fill his brain with visions of Miss Jane Burke, soft and sleepy, and entirely unbuttoned. Entirely.

Dance shut the door in the steward's face, and shucked his clothing with no thought for its care. All he wanted was to tumble naked into the cot, and let the scent and heat of her lingering in the linen envelop him. Let the soft brushed cotton slide over his skin, and the light scent of white flowers, of jasmine and rose, surround him like a balm for his ills—like an opiate sliding into his veins, carrying him into dreams, hot and powerful.

He would have taken himself in hand had he had any spare energy.

But all he could do was breathe, and dream.

Oh, devil take him, for he was as good as done for. Bloody well smitten. And where the hell would that lead them all?

Chapter Eleven

The Portuguese port of Recife rested on coastal lowland at the confluence of two rivers, where the occurrence of a natural offshore reef protected it from the tempestuous waters of the Atlantic. Despite the treacherous approach to the city through a narrow cut in the reef, the protected port had remained throughout the wars a safe harbor to English ships and trade. Thus there existed more than enough good English merchants who would be happy to take Dance's coin. *Tenacious* would find what she needed—as long as his purse held out.

At least the fine imported Madeira wine could be gotten at a good price, even if the rest of the fresh provisions and timber were bound to cost him the entirety of the fortune it had taken him all these bloody long years to make.

"Bring her up, Mr. Whitely."

The sailing master adjusted his course to make a cautious approach through the reef, where the uneven ocean floor was littered with sharp rocks lurking just below the surface, just waiting to rip the spongy bottom out of his hull.

All around him was sound and motion—the clatter of the pulleys and the creak of the ropes, the shouts of the men on deck and the songs of the topmen above in the yardarms, trimming the sails as *Tenacious* swung itself toward the land and the brightly painted city gleaming out of the jungle.

> *Blow ye winds westerly, blow ye winds blow.*
> *Jolly sou'westerly, steady she goes.*

"Take in the courses." Dance held his speaking trumpet in one hand, but did not use it. He didn't need to. The whole ship was attuned to him, the steady center around which everyone else moved. Everyone was poised to do his bidding.

The feeling was heady and marvelous. And unnerving.

But it was his duty. "Prepare to drop the bower anchor."

"Bower away, sir."

"And the deck is yours, Mr. Simmons. I should expect a boat from the port authorities out within the half hour. In the meantime, I shall be with the captain."

"Aye, sir."

"Mr. Rupert," Dance called to the indignant midshipman. "Pass word for Mr. Denman to join us in the captain's cabin. Mr. Whitely, if you'd care to join me."

Dance had resolved to think more like a captain instead of a lieutenant, and plan ahead. And he had also heard the warning implicit in the men's grumblings, and had resolved to protect himself from any rumors or accusations that he was acting against the captain's wishes—he was, but he was acting in the best interests of the ship and the expedition.

He initiated a formal twice-daily report to the captain, who still could not be persuaded to quit his cabin. But if the captain would not come to the ship, Dance would bring the ship to him. Each day he asked one officer and Mr. Denman, acting both as physician and a representative of the expedition, to accompany him while he made his report.

"Who the hell is he?" The old man squinted at Denman just as he had every day, when they presented themselves in his day cabin. "And who the hell are you?"

"I am Lieutenant Dance," he repeated, just as he always did, "your first lieutenant. And this is the surgeon, Mr. Jackson Denman, sir."

"You don't look like an officer to me," the old man groused as he eyed Denman's black coat.

"That is because I volunteered my services once aboard, sir." Jack Denman was all patience as he answered the question yet again. "I came with the expedition of the Royal Society."

"Are they still here?"

"Yes, sir," Dance responded, and forbade himself the childish pleasure of asking where else the captain thought they would be in the middle of South America. "We'll have them with us for some time yet."

The addled old man turned his back to them in dismissal. "Damn nuisance."

A damn nuisance that was the entire reason for their voyage. A damn nuisance that the captain, and not Dance, had agreed to long before Dance ever came on board.

"Yes, sir. You may have noticed that we have made the port of Recife in the United Kingdom of Portugal, Brazil, and the Algarves, sir."

"Oh." The old man cast only a glance out the stern gallery at the city laid out like a painting before him. "I thought it looked familiar."

"Yes. I chose to make port here for two reasons, sir. First, the provisions for the guests, which ought to have been paid for by the monies stolen by the purser, Givens, must be replenished as the wardroom officers are not sufficiently provisioned for five extra mouths." Dance took a very great risk at such candor in front of Mr. Denman, but trying to conceal *Tenacious*'s troubles had only brought accusations down on his head. And he needed to be as utterly open and honest as he could if he were to keep his head from a court-martial.

"So?" The captain kept his face turned away, as if to say, What business is it of mine?

Dance wanted to bash his own head into the beams overhead at the quavery defiance in the captain's tone—never mind wanting to bash some semblance of understanding and sobriety into the old man himself. "Do I have your permission for the order to purchase victuals for the wardroom?"

"The wardroom buys its own dinners, sir. You'll get no money from me."

"No, sir. I did not seek to." Dance wrote the captain's response all down in his own log. "But I must seek funds for the second reason we have put in at Recife, that *Tenacious* has parted her foremast, and is sailing wet, sir—working open her bows. The carpenter needs better material to shore up the breast hooks with oak, and not iron strapping, sir. We have the longest stretch of the Atlantic, down the coast of South America and around Cape Horn, ahead of us, sir, and I don't want the ship working herself apart."

"Working herself apart," Muckross echoed in a mincing voice. "You sound like a woman."

Dance forced himself to push the insult aside. "If you would like more evidence of this than only my assessment, I have the carpenter outside to give you his report himself, sir. And I would ask you to accompany us to the bows, and see how the timbers have worked themselves loose. The pine simply isn't durable enough, sir. It is not a fit wood for making ships."

"This ship was built in eighteen and twelve in the king's own Chatham Shipyard. Do you think you know better than Admiralty shipwrights, sirrah? Do you think so highly of yourself?"

"No, sir." Dance knew the old man's belligerence was all to keep himself from having to leave his cabin, but still the barbs stung. "I am recording that you chose not to examine the ship, sir."

That got the old man's wandering attention. "What do you mean, recording?"

"My log, sir," Dance repeated once again. "Of the ship's progress at sea, of sailing orders and headings and speed. And the rolls of muster and punishment which must be kept, sir. The noon sighting which must be recorded, along with the time calculations to establish longitude." Every officer kept a log of sorts. Dance had always kept one. He had always paid special attention to taking soundings and charting the seas, while men like Lieutenant Simmons enjoyed charting the land as a cartographer. Dance had no doubt that the sailing master's own logbook dwelt heavily on the calculations for longitude, and his progress at teaching the trigonometry of navigation to the midshipmen.

But of the captain's official log, he had no knowledge. It might contain an account of the quarts of gin consumed, for all Dance knew. He only knew that he had never seen it. And that had to change if he were to protect himself from spurious charges of mutinous conduct.

"The log is the captain's privilege," the old man asserted. The captain put his considerably reddened nose in the air, and attempted to stare down its length at Dance.

But Dance would not allow himself to feel intimidated. He had to act for the good of the ship, as well as his own neck. "Then I would ask you to exercise that privilege, sir. I have been doing it for you, with Mr. Whitely's assistance, since you do not come on deck." Dance held out his book.

Captain Muckross turned to look out the stern gallery windows, but gestured to the table. "Leave it here."

Dance was instantly wary. He looked over at the small portable writing desk shoved to the side, crammed with unorganized papers. If he left his log with the captain, it would disappear into the mess. "Sir. I'm happy to have you or your clerk copy out my entries, but you can have no reason to keep my personal book."

He said the words, even though there could be no excuse for disobeying his superior officer. Except that his superior officer was not acting in a truly superior manner, worthy of obedience—the captain was clearly not in his right mind.

But Muckross had enough presence of mind to understand exactly what Dance was not saying. "By God, sir. I don't need a reason. I am the captain. Do you defy me?"

"No, sir." Dance felt the short hairs at the nape of his neck stand up. "I will do the work here to copy the entries into your log, if you wish, so that *Tenacious's* reports are up to date, but . . ." Dance raked through the weary contents of his brain to think of a way around the captain's obstinance.

Denman tried to intervene. "I'll be happy to make the copy of the lieutenant's observations and navigation into your log, if you have no clerk, sir."

The captain looked back and forth between the two younger men, as if he could not decide which one to vent his spleen upon.

Denman tried again. "I'll make an appointment with you each day, at your convenience, sir. I have acted as the private secretary or amanuensis for the Duke of Fenmore, the patron of our expedition, so I am readily qualified."

Dance waited impatiently for the old man to have the good sense and good grace to bow to the inevitable—if he had any pretense to being the captain, Muckross had to keep a log. Just as Dance himself was going to continue keeping his own log for protection against the vagaries of the captain's mind, if nothing else.

"No, no. I don't need a secretary." He waved Jack off. "No, no."

"Excellent." Dance smiled as if the old man had indeed come to an agreement, happy to bring the infernal interview to a close. "But Manning will need to attend you, sir, as I expect the authorities from the port will make the ship any moment and will want to speak to you."

"Why? I'm not the one who brought us here."

"No, sir. Is it your wish that I speak on your behalf to the port authorities, sir?"

"Do what you like," was the captain's testy answer. "But keep them away from me. Functionaries," he muttered. "They pester a man to death."

"Yes, sir." Dance bowed as if the man had actually given a command. "I will meet with the port authority on your behalf. And then I'll be taking the cutter and a party of men inshore. Do you care to have your gig swayed out, sir, and visit the city yourself?"

All Dance got for the suggestion was a surly growl. "Don't be daft, boy. Don't be daft. Just let me be."

"Yes, sir. As you wish." Dance bowed to his captain, as did Denman at his side. "Thank you. I'll see to everything." Just as he had been doing since Portsmouth.

And the city laid out around him like a bright jewel might as well have been Portsmouth for all the pleasure he could take in it. It mattered not where in the world they were, only that they be able to get the things necessary for them to continue their voyage.

But the naturalists were as enthusiastic as Dance was practical. "And you, Mr. Denman?" he asked the surgeon as they climbed together to the quarterdeck. "Are you looking forward to exploring Recife?"

"Yes. Sir Richard has made arrangements to visit a fellow botanist living here, Mr. John Mawe, who has an exceptional collection of natural specimens, including medicinal herbs and antiscorbutics."

"Anti . . . ?"

"Precautions against scurvy and other wasting diseases."

"That's what the grog is for, man—limes and rum. And

I've no doubt but that we'll take on as much fresh fruit and vegetables as we can store." And afford. Dance could already feel the pinch on his pockets.

"Yes, but I was hoping to make some progress on a prevention that did not include such a large quantity of alcoholic spirits." Here was something of the sober physician Denman looked. "In the present circumstance, I thought it might be helpful to keep the ship clean of alcohol."

Dance moved to the lee rail where the wind would take their conversation across the bay. Still, he lowered his voice. "Do you think it would do any good? Manning says they have already tried to take him off the drink, to no avail. And Mr. Ransome and the captain's steward both say that he cannot go without it. Says he shakes and has fits if we should try to do so."

Now it was Jack Denman's turn to look weary behind his spectacles. "Then he will drink himself to death."

Dance could only agree. "I suppose. And it only remains to see when he will do so." And then he shook off the damp air of fatalism. "But it will likely not be today. And so we must make other plans."

Parties of men were forming along the starboard rail, hoping to be included on the inshore crew.

"Cutter's ready, sir." Ransome was at the quarterdeck rail with his restrained obedience. "I've a party ready to take on water."

"Very good, Mr. Ransome." Dance acknowledged the bosun with a touch of his hat. "But I'm putting Lieutenant Simmons in charge of the party for taking on water. I need you here, guarding the rail to keep anyone else from wandering off into those green hills."

Ransome was too smart a man to let too much show on his broad face. But he couldn't mask his dissatisfaction. "Begging your pardon, sir, but Lieutenant Simmons ain't been with us long enough to know the men, and know who's a good character."

"And that is why I have given him this test, Mr. Ransome," Dance lied. Because he simply wasn't sure about Ransome, unsure about just how much and how far to trust him. The bosun had never been openly disobedient, and he did seem to know his job as well as he had promised. But there was still some disquiet that sat at the back of Dance's brain like a surly fishwife, resisting all attempts to like the man. "Mr. Whitely will have the deck, while you will have the rail. I leave it to your discretion and judgment in allowing locals who might approach in boats, to come on board." Dance could already see the bumboat women with their dories laden with small provisions and other comforts making their way from the quay. Those that stayed on board *Tenacious* would have some fun as well as those that went ashore. Maybe even more, as the men in the cutter would be under the charge of the two lieutenants, and those remaining on board would be under Ransome's more aggressively lenient rule.

Lieutenant Simmons was already in the stern of one of the two cutters bobbing in the jade-green water. Three of the older naturalists were seated in his boat. But not Miss Burke.

She had somehow contrived to be in the other boat. The one that he would take charge of. Anticipation of the pleasure of her company was like the jolt of hot coffee in the morning, cleaning the thoughts of everything else from his mind—she was choosing to be with him.

But of any other preference for his company, she gave no sign—she was as buttoned up and battened down as a hatch cover, with her dress up to her neck, and her sleeves all the way down past her elbows. Although she was wearing a charming straw bonnet in place of her usual stout, wide-brimmed felt hat, everything about her was plainly wrought, without subterfuge or affectation. Unadorned.

The light in her clear blue eyes was adornment enough. And there she was, in his boat.

Or so he thought, until Mr. Denman reappeared at his shoulder. "Ready to embark?"

God's balls. Dance cursed himself for an ass. Of course she could have been waiting for Denman. Of course. Dance jammed his hat down upon his head, and hoped he'd jammed some sense back into it as well. "After you."

Dance saved the rest of his breath to cool his porridge, and said nothing more than was necessary for the length of time it took to row across to the central quay.

Once upon shore the parties separated to their allotted missions. But Miss Burke moved slowly, letting the groups disperse to their different designations around her.

"Miss Burke," Sir Richard called. "Are you not accompanying us to Mr. Mawe's garden? I've been given to understand that there is a magnificent collection of botanicals that can be grown in this mild climate."

"Oh. Well, I hadn't thought . . ." Miss Burke's answer was uncharacteristically vague.

Sir Richard played his trump card. "Mr. Denman will be joining us. The garden contains an impressive collection of medicinal plants and herbs as well."

"How very interesting." She moved closer to Sir Richard, and laid a hand along his arm. "I hope you will forgive me, sir, but I have some shopping of a . . . personal nature to undertake. I hope you will not mind my absence."

Sir Richard was so alarmed by the very idea of what *personal* might include that he drew away. "Oh, certainly." Though he hesitated—clearly he did not like to have Miss Burke out of his oversight. "But will you not be alone in this strange place?"

Miss Burke was not so easily thwarted. "It is Recife, sir, and not a hostile South Pacific island. The steward,

Punch, who has been here before, will accompany me. I feel quite safe."

"A one-legged man is little protection, Miss Burke," Sir Richard cautioned. "I would prefer—"

Before his mouth could consult his brain, Dance spoke. "I'll spare another man, Sir Richard."

"Thank you, Lieutenant," Miss Burke answered. "So there you have it, Sir Richard. I am well looked after." It was only after the other naturalists had turned to walk off across the plaza that she turned and looked Dance in the eye. "And dare I hope that you will be that man, Lieutenant?"

The pleasure that shot through him was like a bolt to the back of the head, rendering him too stupid to think better of it. He felt a smile widen his mouth as he said, "If you like."

The very beginnings of an answering smile brewed along her lips, though she tried very hard to subdue her enthusiasm by chewing on her bottom lip. But he had seen it. And the sight did marvelous things for his equanimity. "I believe I would like."

"Yes." Her unqualified enthusiasm brewed up a heady sensation deep in his gut just at the prospect of walking next to her much less taking her arm. He could not let himself do that. He held out his hand for her to proceed.

She turned toward the market square and began to walk slowly toward the stalls. "Well, that was easy enough. I had feared that you would offer a great deal more resistance."

"Perhaps you have spent too much time with your stubborn barnacles, and think every creature will act in the same way."

She laughed just as he hoped she would. "Goodness, you must have forgiven me, if you are willing to speak of barnacles."

"Forgive you?"

"Yes. I know you were not happy with me for distracting you from your duty before the mast broke—but I have been assured by Mr. Denman that the injured man Flanaghan is going on better and better. And I had thought to try and make up for my mistake by assisting Mr. Denman in his surgery. I have some small skill with still-room work."

He did not want to think about her helping Denman. "Miss Burke, I was not, and am not, angry with you."

"Lieutenant, we have already established that neither of us are very good liars. I may not know much of the world, but I do know when a person is angry. Despite your rather heroic calm in directing the man's rescue, your face was a rather livid shade of crimson, indicative of fury, and your mouth was screwed down into what could only be called a grim line. If I were to teach foreigners the English word for anger, I should show them a drawing of your face, and they would comprehend it instantly."

"If I was angry, it was at myself, and not you. It is my job—my duty—to see to the ship and all the men in her. It is your job to be a conchologist, which you were endeavoring to do when we spoke. The error was mine and not yours."

Miss Burke's milky cheeks pinked in the warm sunlight. "It is very kind of you to say so, Lieutenant. If you are not careful I might discover that there is an actual charming gentleman hiding beneath your impressive naval scowl."

Dance was too happy to think about the reasons for his impressive naval scowl. "Don't tell anyone."

She laughed. "I wouldn't dream of it. Just as I trust that you will not tell anyone that there is a frivolous woman hiding beneath my rather practical scientific exterior."

"Frivolous?" There was nothing wrong with her exterior—it was as gracefully unadorned as its wearer. But he didn't want to share any part of her—frivolous or not—with anyone.

And speaking of Denman— Dance cast a look over his shoulder. Behind him, a trail of men who had been directed to accompany him to the shipyard kept a respectful distance—so respectful, he wondered if Miss Burke was aware of their presence. But of Denman, there was no sign.

"How so frivolous?"

"I am sure everyone else in the world—including you occasionally—must think it entirely frivolous, and mad even, to want to be left alone on a South Seas island so I may draw pictures of shells, if only for the pleasure it will bring me."

Dance nearly stopped walking. He had not thought of leaving her alone on a South Seas island, only of getting her there in one piece. And he didn't like the feeling of powerlessness that came with the thought. If she were alone on an island, she would have nothing and no one to protect her. He didn't like it at all.

And all this talk of pleasure was dangerous. It made him think of other things besides his job. It made him think of the warm blushing softness of her cheek, and the plush invitation of her lips.

Miss Burke continued her amble, oblivious to his less than gentlemanly thoughts. "You are very nice to be around when you are not swearing at me on the deck of your ship."

There was nothing he could say or do, but apologize. "I am occasionally an ass, Miss Burke. For which I hope you will forgive me."

"You were. And still occasionally are. But I do forgive you, for you appear to be doing a very fine job of making up for it."

"Thank you. You are very generous with me."

"You are the one who has been more than generous with us all." She exhaled another long sigh. "And I am six and twenty, Lieutenant. I am too old, and we live in too close confines, to hold grudges for a few sharp words."

Did her voice sound a little wistful? Surely not about him? "Come now. You are not too old. I am eight and twenty. We are of an age, you and I—both in the prime of our lives."

"You may be in the prime of your life, Lieutenant, because you are a man. A woman's age passes more quickly before she is put upon the shelf."

"Nonsense. You are walking in the sunshine in Recife, Brazil, Miss Burke. You are not upon any shelf."

"So I am." Her smile became as broad and sunny as the market plaza, though she shook her head a little ruefully. "And I assure you, I am thanking my lucky stars that I am fortunate enough to be here. But it is not nonsense. It is conventional wisdom."

The reluctant acceptance in her voice told him she was not merely fishing for compliments—she truly believed what she was saying. "Conventional wisdom is an ass. On this I will not be gainsaid."

"And there is that fierce naval scowl."

She was laughing at him, in the kindest way possible, and Dance could feel a smile edging the scowl out of the way. "My apologies."

"Oh, don't apologize. I see now that your scowl is part of who you are—a man with all the responsibility and none of the authority. A man who worries about every sail and spar, every line left in a tangled mess about the deck. Everything that no one else will take the time or energy to be worried about. They say rank has its privileges, but clearly it also has its cost."

Again, she seemed to understand things no one else did. And it was more than a pleasure to feel so . . . understood. But the feeling was also too close to gratitude to be comfortable. "And speaking of cost, I must make for the shipyards. Now, where might I take you for your shopping?"

"Oh, I have no shopping to speak of, other than getting

in some victuals to help the wardroom table. But I have given Punch my money, and put him to getting what is needed, as I thought it best to let him combine our funds to best effect."

Arranging everything just so for others' benefit, just as she had rearranged the sleeping quarters to his benefit. But he could not resist the opportunity to tease her. "So you lied to Sir Richard? Miss Burke, I am shocked."

"No you are not." She laughed. "I should think you are rather vindicated by this obvious show of perfidy in my character. But I have resolved to become a better liar, if only for your amusement."

Oh, he liked her. Damn his eyes, but he did. "You must not reform yourself on my account, Miss Burke."

"Why not? I cannot do so for my own." She smiled as she said it, meaning for the words to be light and joking, but there was something else, an air of melancholy in her tone, that led him to think that she might not be joking.

He repeated her own question. "Why not?"

"Because," she said as they walked along the market stalls in Punch's wake. "I don't know. I suppose I cannot decide if I like the truth."

Here at last was *real* honesty. Dance all but held his breath. "Why not?"

"The truth will set you free, the Bible says. But I have found rather the opposite. Some truths are a cage that keep you in."

"And what is the truth that would cage you?"

She stopped and turned toward him, her eyes sharp and searching as she looked at his face, trying to decide what she would tell him. And then she let it all out in a rush. "I am not really J. E. Burke, the conchologist. I mean, I *am* Jane Eliza Burke, and that makes me J. E. Burke. And I *am* a conchologist. I have studied shells for years and years. But I am not *the* J. E. Burke and *the* conchologist originally sought out by the Royal Philosophical Society."

"I know."

"What do you mean, you know?" After such a heart-felt confession, she was baffled and put out at his nonre-action. "How could you know?"

"Let me rephrase. I suspected."

"Why?"

He gave her the simplest answer. "Because you are a woman."

"You sound exactly like Sir Richard. Why is it so impossible for you to believe that I might actually be as accomplished a conchologist as I claim? That is the truth! I have done all of J. E. Burke's work. I have made all of his drawings and I have arranged—"

"Pax, Miss Burke. Perhaps you will recall that I did not *act* like Sir Richard."

That cooled her pique somewhat. "But if you suspected, why did you not say anything?"

"As I told Sir Richard, it was not my place to say. And as you said you *are* J. E. Burke, and you *are* a conchologist. And I liked you better than the other naturalists. None of them looked forward to being sorted out."

The tease had his desired effect—she blushed a perfect apricot color, like jam smeared across her cheeks. Delicious. "It is ungentlemanly of you to remember that."

"It is not. It is charming. Which is what I was attempting to be before you started in with all your insistence upon the truth."

She looked up at him from the corner of those blue eyes. "Then you don't care about the truth?"

Not today. Not with her. "The truth is a bore, Miss Burke. The truth is bad grub and no money to pay for dinners and a constantly leaking ship badly in need of repair. Let us spend at least this one afternoon as free as possible from the cage of the truth."

"Agreed."

She offered her hand to shake, and he took it, though

he knew he was unprepared for the wash of sensation that engulfed him at the feel of her soft, slender fingers in his palm. Before he knew what he was doing, he bent his head and put his lips to the delicate skin on the back of her hand. Tasting her. Feeling the fragile beat of her pulse under his lips. And knowing then that it was a mistake.

That this one taste of her could never be enough.

But Miss Burke was an innocent. And he could not be kissing her in the public streets of Recife, no matter how prettily she blushed or how hopefully she looked up at him through those shining eyes.

"Forgive me," he said. But he did not let go of her hand.

"Oh, you are forgiven." She was still all honesty now—blushing and pleased and truthful. "If only for your charming conversation."

He was making charming conversation, wasn't he? Devil take him—this had to be a first.

A dangerous, pleasurable first.

Chapter Twelve

Who knew that the stony, sober lieutenant could be so lighthearted? That there was something of the charming scamp behind the worry in his beautiful green eyes?

But the worry was there for a reason—to keep them all safe.

Jane began to feel almost guilty at her own lightness of heart after having unburdened herself of the weight of her secret. The lieutenant was still carrying his. "But as charming as this conversation is and as much as I should like to eschew the truth, I fear I am keeping you from your appointed tasks in the shipyard."

She could see the worry, the weight of responsibility settle upon him like a heavy suit of leaden cloth. "Yes." He swept his gaze toward a small group of blue-clad sailors waiting some twenty paces away. "The carpenter is waiting to accompany me to search and bargain for suitable timber."

"Then I will leave you to your work, and take myself off to make my own purchases."

He looked down the quay toward the shipyard, and then back again at the plaza and the shops ringing its edge as if he were torn between his duty and his desire.

No. She was only fooling herself into thinking that. It

was not desire. Just escape—a momentary diversion that he sought from the cage of truth and responsibility. To keep him to herself any longer would be nothing but selfishness. "You must go, Lieutenant."

"Yes, I must. But I don't like to leave you. I did tell Sir Richard that I would see to your safety."

"I am perfectly safe, Lieutenant. And I do have your stalwart man Punch to assist me."

That narrow frown was back, pleating up his forehead as his gaze found Punch in the crowd. "Yes. But—"

It was clear that the lieutenant did not like to leave off any task he had appointed, or pledged himself to do, even if it was as insignificant as escorting her shopping. And she also suspected that he didn't like to admit to needing help, or that there might be something wrong that he could not fix on his own. So different from her own family, who always wanted help, who always relied upon her to fix everything.

How strange. And almost sad.

But the day was too fine for melancholy. Yet, Jane could think of nothing else to say, so she simply dropped a curtsy and headed toward Punch before the lieutenant could say anything else.

He followed, if only for a moment. "Mind your mistress, Punch," was his only instruction for the steward before he touched his hat, made a short bow, and took himself off.

"Aye, sir. That I will," Punch pledged.

And he did. Punch led her out of the bright plaza through the shaded, cobbled side streets to an English-speaking grocer with fresh produce and poultry. "We'll get another hen, miss, for the coop, and some good dry onions and tatties. And carrots—they'll keep well enough. And turnips . . ."

Jane set herself to the task with confident vigor. This she knew. She was well experienced at bargaining the price down at every chance, insisting on Punch's putting things back if she thought the cost too high, as she had managed such purchases for her small household at home. And it was a pleasure to feel that she had some skill and experience that could help Lieutenant Dance, and alleviate his burden rather than add to it.

She was wading through the stacks of crates when a grubby urchin grabbed at her skirts.

"You there!" the merchant instantly cried. *"Vai plantar batatas!"*

Whatever they meant, the words had the desired effect, for poor child darted away. But not before she had pushed a scrap of paper into Jane's hand.

It was some sort of handbill written entirely in Portuguese, of course, but on the back in small block letters was a note. A threat actually.

If the lady values her life she won't go back to her ship.

Jane stared at it for a full minute before it hit her—a pain, like the quick numbing cut from a knife, sliced into her chest, and choked off her breath. Someone wanted her dead.

The stinging surge of panic bolted through her veins, and she shot up, searching wide-eyed for the child. "Where did she go?"

The merchant made an offhand gesture of good riddance. "Gone, mistress. I'll not have street rats bother you. I've good beetroot as well here, at a very good price."

Bother the beetroot. Nothing mattered but the child. "Punch, we have to find her!"

"The child, miss?" Punch could not comprehend her urgency. "Here now, what's—" Punch took the paper from her nerveless hands, and turned it over, examining it. "What do it say, miss?"

Thank God he could not read. "Nothing." Jane couldn't understand her instinct to keep the threat a secret, but she obeyed it. She snatched back the handbill and crumpled it in her hand. "It's nothing."

" 'Tweren't nothing if it's got you so upset, miss. Here, sit you down." Punch dusted off a crate with his kerchief and gestured her toward it.

"No, I'm fine," she lied. But she wasn't fine. She was the furthest thing from fine. She could feel her breath rising in agitation. Hear her harsh panting intake of the soft morning air.

"There now." Punch took her arm and half pulled, half pushed her to sit on the sturdy crate. And just in time. Because she couldn't seem to feel her legs to make them do as she wanted.

"I'll be quite all right in a moment," she lied again. "I only need to . . ." What was she to do? How on earth was she to obey the threat? Perhaps she could appeal to the grocer—he was an Englishman. Perhaps if she said she needed to lie down, or take a glass of wine, there might be a room where she could hide, or stay.

Jane fumbled for her purse, tucked safely down in the pockets sewn onto her petticoats. She would need money for a passage back to England. She would have to abandon all her dunnage, as Punch would call it. Abandon all of her dreams.

But what else was she to do? End up pitched over the side on some dark cloudless night? It could be anyone on the ship—*anyone*—who wished her gone.

Her mind cast over Sir Richard and Mr. Phelps and Parkhurst. And even Mr. Denman. Perhaps they had—

"She's here, sir," Punch was saying.

Jane looked up to see Lieutenant Dance striding down the street with the grocer's son in tow. Punch must have sent the boy for the lieutenant while she had sat there, frozen with uncharacteristic indecision. Before this voyage, she had always known what to do, always known which road to take. No more. Everything she had known and been sure of—her talent and her ambition, and her absolute right to follow both—was gone, just as surely as if it had fallen over the side and been swept away in the ship's wake.

And here was Dance. Dance who saw everything and let nothing go by. Dance who always did what had to be done. She could rely upon him. She *would* rely upon him.

She thrust the note into his hand.

"Fuck all!" The lieutenant swore magnificently before his narrow, focused scowl bored into her. "Who gave this to you?"

"A child. She's gone now. She was just a messenger, I'll warrant." In his presence, Jane began to breathe easier. With him at her side, she felt less afraid. And more indignant.

How dare they try and stop her.

Jane shook her head and moved, shielding herself from his penetrating scowl with her bonnet. "I'm fine, now. I just took a small faint." She willed her resolve back. "The ground feels a little strange, as if I were still on board *Tenacious.*"

"Fair enough," the lieutenant said. "It's a common enough feeling. But you are still an abominable liar, J. E. Burke. Your face has gone all red and splotchy."

Jane immediately covered her answering smile with her hands. "You are no gentleman to tell me."

He was a gentleman. The best kind. The kind who respected her ambition, and didn't mollycoddle, or try to wrap her in cotton wool, and tell her she was too small and ill and delicate, and ought never to have left home in the first place.

But she had left home, and she hadn't come this far to be frightened off. She was *not* a witless girl. She was a woman grown who had worked hard all her life to take this one chance fate had given her. She would not give up now.

"No, I am no gentleman," Dance agreed with her. "I'm a bloody sailor, and I'm going to take you back to the ship where I can make damn sure no one can bother or accost you. Oh, for fuck's sake, Jane." He stopped and swore under his breath. "It's got to be someone from the ship, hasn't it?"

"Yes." And she ought to be turning her mind to the problem. But the ability to think lucidly was gone. Just gone.

He had called her Jane.

The only thing that registered in her air-starved brain was the fact that his eyes were really the deepest, warmest green. The color of the tropical ocean. And he smelled of soap and lime.

While she was swimming in that lime-green ocean, he took hold of her elbow again, as if he thought she needed to be propped up, even though she did not feel in the least bit faint or breathless. What she felt was his bare hand against the inside of her arm.

His fingers were long, and strong and callused, right there on the edge of his index finger. She could feel the delicious abrasion all the way down her arm to the tips of her tingling fingers.

But the lieutenant was not in the least bit similarly affected. His gaze bored down on her, a heavy weight in contrast to the lightness of his touch. "Goddamn it, Jane. What am I going to do with you?"

Jane felt so light-headed that his oath brought out a sort of giddy humor. "I thought you didn't believe in God."

In response he swore more colorfully.

"I liked it better when you called me Jane."

Until the moment he had spoken she had not known how much she had missed hearing her own name. How she had missed that sense of the familiar and intimate. Of being understood and known.

But even at home, where they had always called her Jane, she hadn't been understood, or really known. They had never understood her needs and her ambition, and neither had she. Not the way the lieutenant did.

"Forgive me." He shook his head, his motion as abrupt

and clipped as his voice. "I did not mean— I was only concerned for your well-being." But he gave lie to the words by the way he tucked her arm over his like the veriest cavalier, giving her his escort as he walked her back through the winding streets to the quay. And by saying "I'm going to take care of you, Jane."

Something more powerful than relief washed through her. For the first time in her life, someone had pledged to take care of her, instead of the other way round.

It was heady. And humbling.

And there was nothing, really, she could do with her arm entwined with his, and the long length of his body pressed against her side but accept his help gratefully. She could only walk with him, and enjoy the feeling for as long as it lasted, and pray that she was doing the right thing.

Miss Burke kept quiet the whole of the cutter ride back out to *Tenacious*. She looked pale and drawn despite the warm southern sun streaming over them and her claim to feeling fine in the face of such an abominable threat.

And her looks did not improve any when they retreated to the wardroom only to find the door to her cabin open, and all the contents strewn about.

As were his. Their cuddies had been ransacked.

There were not sufficient curses to mitigate the feeling of bloody roiling rage ripping through his chest like a loose grenade.

"Get me Ransome," he growled at no one in particular. "Get him now."

The anger in his voice made Jane jump. "Oh, Lord." Her voice was small and thin, and she looked completely done in. "Oh," she cried again, "my barnacles."

She fell to her knees among the messy heaps of clothing and books scattered across the floor. The glass jar in which she had been attempting to keep her barnacles alive had been trod underfoot, and crushed to a shattered, chalk-colored mess.

"It's the barnacles you are worried about?" He would never understand the workings of the female mind, and certainly never understand the workings of this particular female scientist's mind. "There are plenty more where those came from," he said as he drew her to her feet. "And you should be trying to do away with them rather than keep them alive, anyway."

"But the point is that to understand how the creature comes to attach to ships in the first place, one has to understand— Oh." She pushed back a lock of butterscotch hair that had come loose from its pins. "You're just trying to humor and soothe me."

Underneath all that soft butterscotch was sharp intellect. "Is it working?"

"No. Not really." Though she did give him a wan smile, and push the hair out of her face with the back of her wrist. "What an awful mess. All my things—" She hastened to snatch up some article of clothing that looked white and filmy, and was undoubtedly underclothing, judging from the furious blush streaking across her cheeks and down her neck.

And he was a cad, because all he wanted to do was follow that delicious swath like a smear of jam under the high neck of her gown to see where it led.

And he was furious, because someone among his crew had dared to lay their filthy hands upon Jane Burke's private things.

Dance drew in a deep breath, and tried to push aside the stormy, electrical feeling of gathering rage, so he might think more critically. "What could they have been looking for?" Other than the simple chance to run their grimy hands through her delicate things. "Is anything missing?"

Jane began to catalogue her belongings, and Dance ducked his head back into his own cuddy to ascertain that nothing of his seemed to be gone—but he had so few possessions besides his uniform clothing, that it was easy to collect that the ransacking of his cuddy seemed to have been done purely for spite, or to cover up for the more deliberate and far more spiteful mischief done to Jane's cabin.

The topman Flanaghan's face came to mind. He was one of the most vocal of the objectors when Miss Burke had come aboard. But Dance could not imagine that the hardy tar had either the strength or the desire to give in to such small-minded vandalism.

"I can hardly tell," Jane finally answered. "Such mean, willful mischief." And for only the second time in his acquaintance with her, Miss Jane Burke looked as if she might give way to tears—her wide blue eyes were glassy with obscuring liquid. But she brushed the unshed tears away with the back of her hand, and she seemed to notice his cabin for the first time. "Yours as well, I see. Are there any others?"

The closed doors to the other cabins gave no clue. "We'll know presently. The second cutter is returning as we speak."

In the next minutes the wardroom became crowded with the members of the Royal Society's expedition, and their servants, all of whom helped to confirm Dance's suspicions—that Miss Burke, and, to a much lesser degree he, were the targets of a scurrilous invasion of privacy and propriety. Dance wasn't sure which disturbed him more.

But whichever it was, he was going to make someone pay.

"Mr. Dance?" The big bosun had answered Dance's summons with alacrity, but there seemed to be nothing of surprise, no trace of emotion, in the man's face when he stepped into the wardroom and cast his eyes over the chaotic scene. And while it was perfectly possible that someone might have already told the bosun why Dance had sent for him, for some reason, the man's attitude of forbearance bothered him in the extreme.

"Mr. Ransome, you had charge of discipline on the ship while I was ashore. How do you answer for this?"

"I can't say, sir," was the man's cool answer. "Mr. Lawrence had the deck."

"And if Mr. Lawrence had the deck, he could not know what was happening two decks below. Where were you? Did you near nothing?"

"No, sir." Ransome looked Dance right in the eye without blinking, as if he had nothing to hide. And it made Dance want to hate him, for no other reason than he could find no excuse to blame him. "Is anything gone?"

"The point is not if anything is gone, Mr. Ransome, but how this could have happened in the first place."

"Yes, sir," the bosun said. "It's a bad business, sir."

"It is," Dance agreed. Which only fueled the rage within. "I want this ship turned out. Every chest and storeroom. Every locker and cuddy. I want to know what else has been disturbed, and what else might be missing. I want the name of the person responsible for this—this unwarranted intrusion to the goddamned wardroom— and I bloody well want it *now*."

Fuck all. Now he sounded as vulgar as whomever it was he was accusing of this intrusion. So be it. "Muster the men, and turn this ship out."

The ship was duly turned inside out.

And while Dance supervised the slow march through the decks, turning out every hammock and sea chest, and looking into every nook, cranny, and storeroom with every ounce of the angry righteousness he felt, Jane hid herself behind the wardroom's closed doors, putting away her things with shaking hands.

Dance felt fit to murder someone.

But the feeling of righteous rage roiling in his gut vanished the instant the culprit was found, and a drawing ripped from the pages of Miss Burke's sketchbook was found secreted in the dunnage of the young midshipman, Mr. Rupert Honeyman.

Ransome had the squirming, white-faced boy hauled up by his ear in front of Dance. The bosun shook the boy hard, and shoved him forward. "Tell Mr. Dance what you done."

"I ain't—"

The protest earned the child a vicious cuff. "You tell 'im what you took from the lady. You hear me?"

"The paper," the boy stammered, his eyes rolling back to look at Ransome.

"Thank you, Mr. Ransome. That will be all." Dance made his voice as calm and cool as a polar ice floe in defiance of the sick shock he felt at such an unlikely betrayal. "Dismiss the men to their watches. I want all the material brought on board stored, and the cutters properly stowed. And I want it done *this instant*."

And he wanted it done and over before the ship could descend into rumor and innuendo. Damn their eyes and loose tongues, but there would be talk and whispers enough without a public flogging adding the fuel of rumor onto the dry fire.

"Aye, sir." Mr. Ransome flicked a glance to his cane-wielding mates, who moved along, dispersing the men who had gathered with typical morbid curiosity.

When the orlop deck had been cleared of all but the other midshipmen, Dance said. "Give me the paper."

It was a simple drawing, done with concise strokes of black charcoal, showing young Honeyman, with his distinctive head of curls, and another midshipman, taking the sighting of the noonday sun. The paper was ragged along one edge where it had been torn from Miss Burke's book, and was crumpled and smeared from having been shoved down into the bottom of the lad's small sea chest—which the Marine Society had outfitted with only the barest of necessities for each boy. "Mr. Honeyman, explain yourself."

The boy, who by his bold quickness and cleverness was something of a natural leader among the midshipmen, swallowed hard, and skirted a decidedly nervous glance at Mr. Ransome.

Who cuffed him hard on the ear, and growled, "The lieutenant asked you a question. You tell 'im. Or I will."

"That will do, Mr. Ransome." Dance could hear the cutting edge of his own voice, and felt himself poised precariously on the thin blade of his control. "I should like Mr. Honeyman to speak for himself."

"Go ahead," Ransome told the boy anyway with another hard prod.

"I took the paper," the boy blurted.

"Why?"

"Dunno." He shot a wary glance at the drawing Dance held in his hand. "Because."

Dance made his voice calmer by force of will alone. "You took this paper from Miss Burke's possession *because*?" It made him abnormally—monstrously—angry to think of anyone touching *any* of Miss Burke's things. No matter that he had nearly done the same by sleeping in her linen—that was . . . He didn't know what that was. But this—this was an outrage. "Stealing, Mr. Honeyman, is a serious offense."

"Yes, sir."

"An offense which cannot, and will not, be permitted to stand."

The boy swallowed again, his prominent Adam's apple bobbing in the wake of his throat. "What's going to happen to me, sir?"

"You're going to be punished." The thought made

Dance sick to the pit of his stomach, because something—something about the way the boy looked at Ransome, and the way Ransome hovered threateningly over the boy who had become the officers' favorite—struck him as entirely and irrevocably wrong.

But discipline had to be maintained, and the guilty seen to be punished.

And punish he would. He could not be seen favoring the boy. He could not be seen to be lenient and lax when it came to such a public crime. Because he had already been too goddamned lax—he had let cursed purser Givens get away.

It had been a mistake. A giant one.

And he would not willingly make another, no matter how it made him feel. "You will kiss the gunner's daughter, as it were, Mr. Honeyman. You will be bent over a cannon and caned with six strokes."

The pale boy blanched an even paler shade of white. "But, sir—"

"The only reason"—Dance made his voice sharper still—"you are not going to be stripped and seized upon a grating and given the lash, is that you are a volunteer—a junior officer—and so will be treated like the gentleman you ought to be. See it done now."

There was no sense putting it off. The punishment would only grow in the lad's head with the anticipation. Best to have the brutal thing done with.

As there were no guns on the crowded, low-ceilinged orlop deck, Dance pointed to the nearest sea chest. Ransome pushed the boy over the curved top of the chest and directed him, "Hold on to them straps."

And without so much as a blink of an eye, he reared back with the cane and laid into the boy.

By the third hideous whip of the cane, the boy passed out. But Ransome still laid on.

Dance stopped the man's arm in midair. "That is enough, Mr. Ransome."

Ransome pushed on for a second before he caught himself. "Six strokes, you said."

"The boy passed out after the third."

"It's a mercy." Jack Denman appeared right on time, just as if Dance had sent for him. Bless Punch's eyes.

"Take him away, Mr. Denman, and do what you can to ease his way."

"Don't deserve to have his way eased." Ransome shrugged his arm out of Dance's possession.

"Be that as it may, Mr. Ransome, that is my order."

Denman helped the other white-faced midshipmen bear Honeyman away, leaving Dance alone with Ransome.

Dance watched as the man's hand flexed and then retightened on his cane, as if he were not yet through thrashing it, before his grip finally eased, and he tucked it under his arm. "That's that, then sir."

It was said respectfully enough, and not for the first time, Dance wondered whom he could really trust aboard *Tenacious*. Whom he could truly rely upon.

Not the captain, nor most of the Royal Society expedition members, except perhaps Jack Denman. Simmons, and perhaps Flanaghan and Morris. And certainly Jane Burke.

But not many men. Yet for all his distrust of the bosun, Ransome seemed to be holding fast.

Perhaps he had misjudged the man? Perhaps he had let his assumptions and prejudices from the first, when he had seen Given and Ransome together, color his perceptions of the man? Guilt by association, as it were.

And it shamed him. If he were to ever be a captain in name as well as in action, he would have to do better.

"Thank you for your swift attention to the matter, Mr. Ransome. Much appreciated."

"Sir." Ransome tugged briskly on the stiff brim of his tarred hat, and gave Dance the barest hint of his knowing cat's smile. "Just doing my job, Lieutenant. You can always count on me to do exactly that."

Chapter Thirteen

For the second time in her entire life, and the second time within one day, Jane Burke did not know what to do or think. She had never in the whole of her life been so afraid. Or so angry.

Something that had to be frustrated rage simmered under the cold chilling fear, heating her lungs with righteous anger. Fueling her determination.

Her preferred solution to every problem she had ever encountered was to study it until she understood it enough to manage it—to break difficulties down into their component parts so she could organize and arrange everything just so.

And why should she not do so now?

Perhaps she had been going about it—this being a female scientist on an expedition and a ship full of men—all wrong? She had tried to keep herself quiet and out of the way, but clearly, that plan had failed her. Perhaps she ought to simply be herself, and involve herself in their lives, and the life of the ship, until she became a part of the fabric of it, the way Mr. Denman had.

And so, she set out to arrange things more to her liking. Because she didn't like it when little boys got flogged. Because the action demonstrated that Lieutenant Dance was not a fair-minded man—fair-minded men did not wrongfully punish little boys.

Granted, young Mr. Honeyman was not that young, or that little, but she did not believe for a minute that he had taken the drawing, and ransacked her cabin. Not for one single minute.

So she set out to prove it.

She took a pot of sweetened willow bark tea—taken from her own precious stock of herbs and sugar—with her as a posset for young Mr. Honeyman, who lay on his stomach on a flat pallet in the sick bay.

But all her managing and making home remedies for Mama and Papa could not prepare her for the sight of the fearful welts that crossed the width of the boy's thin back, like scratches from some great beast. "Who could do such a thing?" she gasped.

Like Lieutenant Dance, Mr. Denman seemed entirely immune to pity. "The navy. In this case acting in the person of Mr. Ransome. It is the bosun's job to dispense discipline."

"That is not discipline. That is vindictiveness." Jane could not say how she knew, but she did. It was as if she could feel Mr. Ransome's satisfaction in dealing out such blows oozing out of the poor boy's skin. "If this is what he does with a cane, I hope to God I never have to look at what he does with a lash. It's a wonder the man can sleep at night." She might have included both Mr. Denman and Lieutenant Dance in with Ransome until she remembered that the lieutenant already didn't sleep much at night. She heard him tossing and turning in the cabin next door, and arising in the dead of night to see to other men's duty.

"It's not bad, miss," poor Honeyman insisted.

If it wasn't bad, it was because the poor boy couldn't see it. "Here, Mr. Honeyman." She held the warm cup of willow bark tea to his lips.

He took a grateful sip. "Thank you, miss."

"You are welcome. I've also taken the liberty of mixing a tincture of arnica to bathe upon your back, if Mr. Denman approves. It will give you some ease from the pain."

"A very good idea," Mr. Denman agreed. "I didn't judge laudanum appropriate to administer to a boy. But how come you to know about herbs? I thought you were not interested in botany."

"I am a country woman, Mr. Denman. I know as much as any housekeeper who keeps a well-stocked stillroom. But I would be happy to do some still work for you here, and restock and organize these shelves." She could not even look upon the jumbled mess that was the sick bay's shelves without becoming positively itchy with the need to clean and organize and arrange.

She tamped the impulse down. "You look like you could do with some new medicines," she suggested instead.

"I could." Mr. Denman seemed to consider the possibility for the first time. "And I thank you. I have never done any distillate work myself. Surgery is my forte. I leave herbal healing to others."

"I am happy to be that other, Mr. Denman, if it will be to the benefit of your patients."

"I thank you, Miss Burke." Mr. Denman nodded gravely. "Now, if you will excuse me, I should like to check on Flanaghan—excellent man, but I fear he will try to do too much with his injured hand, and the bone will not set properly."

Jane excused him gladly because his absence would give her greater leeway to turn her attentions to young Mr. Honeyman.

The cool bath did wonders for both the boy's back and his spirits. So much so that he felt himself able to sit up, and regard Jane with a rather wondrous equanimity. "Why are you being so nice to me, miss?"

"Why shouldn't I be nice to you, when you have suffered a grievous hurt?"

"But it was a punishment, done for what I took from you. By all rights you should hate me."

"Hate, I have found, is a rather useless emotion, Mr. Honeyman, unless it motivates us to something better. I do not hate you. And I certainly do not feel that the punishment suits the crime." In fact, she did not believe that a crime had been committed at all—at least not by this boy.

She turned to contemplate the shelves. "You know, Mr. Honeyman, I would have given the sketch to you if you had but asked. I have no objection at all to sharing my drawing. I am not so hard or miserly."

"I didn't think you was, miss." The boy was the picture of contrition—every fiber of his being dripped with misery. "I am sorry."

She gave him what she hoped was an encouraging smile. "Then you are forgiven. Have some more tea."

"Just like that, miss?"

"Just like that are you forgiven? Yes. How else is a Christian to act? Do drink some more tea."

The boy took a long draught of the warm brew before he answered. "I don't know, miss. I never thought about it."

"Well, think about it now, Mr. Honeyman." With Mr. Denman gone, Jane could busy herself arranging the jumble of implements to her liking—such a dusty, disordered mess. The shelves cried for a good clean out. "And think as well," Jane went on in as casual and disinterested a voice as she might manage while she began to sort things in an organized fashion, "what you might do to truly earn that forgiveness." She let another long moment pass, before she suggested, "For instance, perhaps you might like to tell me the truth."

If poor Mr. Honeyman had looked miserable before, he

looked acutely so now. He pressed his lips together tightly, and blinked hard to drive away his incipient tears.

"Because I know, you see," she added quietly, "that you haven't told the truth."

Honeyman gave a little hiccup, and rubbed the back of his wrist across his face.

"And do you know how I know, Mr. Honeyman?" Jane asked gently. "Because I think I know your character. I have seen how hard you have worked for Lieutenant Dance and Mr. Whitely. In fact, I have heard the sailing master praise you, and say he has high hopes for you. And I know that if someone as ignorant of the navy and the way of ships as I can see that *Tenacious* is in very great need of another junior lieutenant, then you, who are so quick and smart, must have perceived the lack. And I doubt very much that you would have jeopardized your whole career over a mere drawing."

"It wasn't for the drawing," Honeyman said, and nearly threw himself off the pallet in a movement rife with adolescent overfeeling.

"No?" Jane probed gently. "Then what was it for?"

"He tricked me," the boy blurted. And then he amended his accusation. "No. I let him trick me. It was my fault. I was acting all superior, wasn't I? Thinking I could read and write and he couldn't, and that's why I was going to be a proper officer. But now I've ruined it all."

He turned from her and buried his face in the pallet, and Jane had to curb the impulse to rub his back for comfort. Not in his state. She settled for laying a gentle, reassuring hand on his shoulder, and asking just as gently, "What did he trick you into doing?"

"The writing," Honeyman mumbled. "He got me to write out that note."

Jane would have been shocked to her core if she had any feelings left to spare that day. But as it was, she could feel nothing but the sort of rightness one felt when the last color went into one of her drawings and made it complete, or she hit upon just the right idea or word to describe a specimen—a simple satisfaction of finally knowing she was correct.

But she could not be entirely numb to the significance of Honeyman's confession. However tricked or mistaken he had been, he knew who it was that wanted her kept from the ship.

Her heartbeat kicked up to fill her ears. But she made herself ask calmly, "And who tricked you, Mr. Honeyman? Who got you to write that note warning me away from *Tenacious*?"

"Mr. Ransome."

Any leftover fear faded into that same sense of logical rightness. Who else could it have been? Who else but Mr. Ransome, who never looked at her but to ogle and sneer and amuse himself with her clumsiness? "But why should Mr. Ransome care about me?" Unless he was one of the men Lieutenant Dance had talked about, who didn't like her based solely on the superstitious fear of her sex, as if she were harboring ill luck the way the young midshipmen had once harbored their lice.

"I don't know, miss. Only that he got me to write the words. And then, after he'd sent the note off with one of the bumboat women, he told me that I'd have to be a man, and take what was coming in silence, or I'd be in even more trouble because I wrote the note."

"Mr. Honeyman!" Jane could keep neither the astonishment, nor the pity from her voice. It was monstrous. Absolutely monstrous for Mr. Ransome to have then inflicted that punishment, laying such strips into the boy himself. Monstrous.

The whole ship—the entire voyage—was a monstrous mess of lies and ill-kept secrets and rotting timbers. No wonder the lieutenant didn't sleep at night.

"I'm that sorry, miss. I am."

"I know, Mr. Honeyman, I know. But we're not beat yet, you and I. Well, you have been, but I mean to see that it doesn't happen again."

"Nothing you can do to stop Mr. Ransome, miss. Not even the lieutenant can do so."

"Then you have misjudged the lieutenant's worth just as badly as Mr. Rasome has misjudged mine." There was nothing she hated more than being patronized by a man who felt free to think little of her. And that was what Mr. Ransome had done if he thought he could scare her off so easily. "We'll see about that, Mr. Honeyman. We'll see if I don't. Now drink your tea."

She was a firm believer that a good dish of tea could make almost everything turn out all right. And even if it couldn't solve any of the problems rolling around *Tenacious*'s decks like unexploded grenades, at least a cup of tea couldn't hurt.

The boy did as she asked. "Thank you, miss. Thank you for being so nice to me."

"Of course, Mr. Honeyman."

"Do you think you might call me Rupert, miss, the way my mam did afore she died?"

Jane brushed the damp, tear-wetted hair off the boy's forehead. "Certainly, Rupert. You may safely leave it all to me to arrange things. Just the way they ought."

The first thing she was going to do to make good on her promise to young Mr. Honeyman was to speak to Lieutenant Dance. But though they remained within the shelter of Recife's rivers, the lieutenant returned her note with word that she was to stay in the safe confines of the wardroom, as he had no time to spare to speak to her. The wood for the much needed repairs had been delivered on board, and he had more work than ever, closely supervising the repairs to the foremast, and the bowsprit, and the breastwork knees. The carpenters' hammers began to pound endlessly through the hull.

Jane would have done as Dance asked, and retreated to the wardroom, but she found her way blocked by Mr. Ransome, who loomed out of the dimness of the low orlop passageway like a gruff, dark-haired billy goat, determined not to let her pass.

"Have a good chat, did you, miss?"

In the close confines of the passageway his presence pressed upon her like a weight, the stale smell of sweat and onions choking the breath from the air, but she wouldn't give him the satisfaction of backing away. Though she did sound as breathless and unsure as a debutante, not a grown woman scientist of six and twenty. "A very informative chat, Mr. Ransome." And since she was already out of breath, she decided not to waste what little she had dancing around the issue at hand, and to simply be brave. "Why should you want me to stay away from the boat—which I am sorry to tell you I had no chance of doing, as Lieutenant Dance marched me straight back here."

"It's a *ship*," he growled. But Ransome seemed to have as little desire to dance as she, for he admitted his involvement by asking, "Did he see the note?"

His question made so little sense Jane answered his question with a question of her own. "Did you want him to?"

"Makes no matter. So long as you saw it."

"I most assuredly did. But may I know why?" The bravery seemed to get easier the more she practiced it. "What harm or hurt have I done to you to make you go so far as to beat stripes into that boy?"

Ransome dismissed Rupert Honeyman's fearful welts with a scornful twist of his lips. "Boy don't have nothing to do with it."

"But I do?"

Ransome stepped closer, until she could see clearly the narrow look in his eyes. "Why, it's for your own good, ma'am. I'm that worried about the state of things, I am, and how the men's taken such a dislike to you." For all the odor of onions that came out of his mouth, his tone had a sort of ardent sincerity that made her stop, and listen to him. "Wouldn't want to see you come to any harm, miss, is all. Wouldn't want you to wake up swimming in the night. It's a big empty ocean out there, miss. A little bit like you'd get gobbled up by the sea in no time. No one would ever know you was gone." He shook his head sadly, like a great barn cat tsking over the size of a runty mouse. "Be a shame, that."

"Are you— Are you threatening me?" Jane was ashamed of the way her voice cracked like a broken shell.

"No, miss." Ransome spread his tar-stained hands wide, as if he were as innocent as a milkmaid. "It's for your own good."

"My own good?" And now Jane was well and truly afraid, because she could not for the life of her tell if the big, oniony man were being sincere.

"Aye, miss. And I can help you off with no one the wiser."

"You can?" But why should she want such a thing?

"Aye, miss." He said it as if he were offering her the greatest of favors.

"Miss Burke?" Another voice, from behind Ransome's back. Mr. Dance on his quiet way to find her. "Ah. Mr. Ransome. I've come to fetch Miss Burke for her dinner."

"Yes, I'm just coming." How much had he over heard? He seemed calm enough.

Ransome seemed not to want to linger to find out. "Thank you, miss." Ransome knuckled his forehead and backed quickly out of sight. "You think about that idea now, miss, and you let me know if I can be of any service."

"Service. Yes, I'll do that."

Certainly she would. Just as soon as she figured out who on this godforsaken boat—ship—she could trust.

"Is it true?" Sir Richard was grilling Lieutenant Lawrence when Jane and Dance reached the wardroom door. "That three men jumped ship as soon as it fell dark?"

The young lieutenant hunched his shoulders uncomfortably, but gave them the truth of the matter. "It is," he said. "Slipped out onto the chains and swam to shore, near as we can tell. And they must have bribed the marine on sentry duty into going with them, for Lieutenant Dance found his uniform coat and musket where he abandoned them on the chain wale this evening."

This then accounted not only for Lieutenant Dance's industry, but his fearful demeanor when they stepped into the wardroom. He looked, to put it in language he himself would undoubtedly choose, like hell. His eyes looked red and tired, and whiskers shaded the sharp planes of his cheek. He looked so tired, it would be a wonder if he did not fall asleep in his soup.

Not that she was looking. Indeed, with so many others at the table, it was all she could do to get close enough to whisper, "I went to go see that poor boy this afternoon."

"Spare me your outrage, Miss Burke." His voice was as cutting as it was weary. "It is as wasted on me, as your pity would be on him."

Jane would not let the bite in his tone put her off. "If you mean Mr. Honeyman, Lieutenant, you are wrong."

He turned the green blaze of his eyes on her. "I may be wrong, Miss Burke, but devil take me, I'm in charge. And if you want to get to that South Sea island of yours, then pray let me do my bloody job without any interference from you."

She had weathered the cold blast of his displeasure before. "It is not interference, Dance, it is *help.* And if you want to get me to that South Sea island so you can get me out of your hair, then you might learn to accept others' help when it's bloody well offered."

Oh, that stopped him, and brought that delightfully stony gaze straight to hers. But his fierce scowl migrated from his brow down and around until it was a slow smile curving his lips. "An oath, Miss Burke? Truly, you astonish me."

Jane could not keep herself from basking in the warmth in that small smile. "Truly, I find I no longer astonish myself. And I *can* help you, Lieutenant."

"I liked it better when you called me Dance." He blew out a long, frustrated breath. "But please, don't tempt me so." His voice grew so low she had to lean toward him to catch the words. "Don't tempt a man in hell with such a vision of paradise."

And then hell came to them when the door to the wardroom slammed open, and in stumbled a man who could only be the captain.

Up close, within the confines of the wardroom, he was a distressing specimen—unsteady on his feet, and just shy of being disheveled in his person. His white hair stood up in tufts from his head, as if the wind had just snatched the better part of it away this instant, and he had not yet realized that he was bald. He looked ancient and infantile and utterly vulnerable as he groped his drunken way toward the table, frowning at them all with angry frustration in his cloudy old eyes.

"What is this? A dinner? And am I not to be invited to a dinner on my own ship?"

Lieutenant Dance—who had stood the moment the captain, in his dirty blue coat, had entered—did not falter. He bowed and held out his own chair at the head of the table. "Your place is here, sir."

Lieutenant Dance seated the captain at the place of honor, while Punch quickly fetched a chair for the lieutenant, and tucked it in right next to hers. Jane was shifting over to give Dance room when his glance found hers, sharp and abrupt and raw—naked almost, unclothed by his usual stoically cynical manner.

For the first time in their acquaintance, the granite countenance had cracked, and Lieutenant Dance was entirely himself, exhausted and completely at sea.

It was all such a mess. And the poor man had no one to shoulder it with him.

And what was also entirely interesting was that the lieutenant had most assuredly not exaggerated. The captain was more than drunk—he was a stinking, fall-down, roaring drunk, as pickled as a ginger root and twice as pungent. He stank so much that Jane felt compelled to move the open flame of the candle away from him at the table.

"I want an explanation," the old drunk all but shouted at Dance.

"Dinner, sir." Dance gave almost every appearance of being his normally collected, calm self, though Jane could see and feel the tension emanating from his body, so close to hers. "Another plate for the captain, Punch." He looked across her to Mr. Denman. "You were saying, Jack?"

"Yes." Mr. Denman took his cue, his demeanor as calm and collected as the lieutenant's. "I have been very interested in the long-term health of former sailors, and in making sure that the Royal Hospital at Greenwich is known to be available to them. It's a remarkable facility, although there are times when I think our government would have been better served, and served our veterans of the navy better, had the hospital been located nearer to one of the navy's larger ports, such as Portsmouth or Depford. Have you ever had occasion to visit the hospital, Lieutenant?"

Captain Muckross had no interest in hospitals. "What is this I hear?" he demanded. "Three more good men deserting—driven out by you? What have you to say to that, sirrah?"

"Yes, sir," Lieutenant Dance answered without evasion,

but immediately changed his tack. "That is why the repairs are being made apace, so I might ask for permission to take *Tenacious* back to sea as soon as possible to prevent another such occurrence from happening."

"Out to sea, man?" the captain argued. "The only place this ship should go is back to Portsmouth, where she belongs. Where we all belong."

"But our expedition, sir, is bound for the South Seas," Sir Richard ventured cautiously. "That is the place where we"—he gestured to the assembled naturalists—"belong."

"And who the hell are you?"

"Sir Richard Smith, Captain Muckross. You may recall, we shared some correspondence."

But both Sir Richard and his correspondence had already passed from the old man's rambling mind. "A song!" he commanded. The captain punctuated his abrupt request by slapping his hand against the table hard enough to make the cutlery and glassware dance. "I want a song." He turned the narrow focus of his light blue eyes on young Lieutenant Lawrence. "In my day we liked a bit of song with dinner. Sing, boy."

Young Mr. Lawrence's eyes slid to Lieutenant Dance for permission.

Which only served to rile the old man even more. "Sing," he commanded. "Sing, dammit, sing. 'In Amsterdam.'" He named the song he wanted. "Sing."

"But . . ." Lieutenant Lawrence blushed a vivid shade of scarlet.

"Sing it!" The captain was oblivious to the shocked looks and silence surrounding him. He raised his own scratchy voice, and began to bawl, *"In Amsterdam there lived a jade, an abbess of the whoring trade—'"*

The older men gasped their astonishment and looked wide-eyed at Jane, but it was the lieutenant who stopped the captain's lewd warble.

"I have a song for you, sir. 'Fathom the Bowl.'" Dance

interrupted the old man with the same calm, unperturbable tone as he normally used on the quarterdeck—at least when he wasn't speaking to her. And then the lieutenant leaned back a little in his chair, tipped his head up to the low beamed ceiling, and set himself into a song.

> *Come all you bold heroes, give an ear to my song*
> *And we'll sing of the praise of good brandy and*
> *   rum*
> *There's a clear crystal fountain in England does*
> *   roll,*
> *Give me the punch ladle, I'll fathom the bowl.*

His voice was low and fine, a baritone of warmth and power, but it was his relaxed, easy grace that changed the atmosphere in the room from one of dread to delight. A smile actually curved his lips as he sang.

Heads began to nod with the rhythm, and fingers and toes tapped along in time. The song was obviously well-known to sailors, as the others of the seafaring profession, including the soused old captain, joined Dance in the chorus. *"Give me the punch ladle, I'll fathom the bowl."*

Jane might not have believed the ease of transformation if she hadn't been watching with her own eyes, but Lieutenant Dance was in the space of a few moments once again the charming man of the plaza in Recife. But he was more than merely charming. There was something slightly bashful about the way he put his head back and sang to the ceiling. And something utterly boyish about the smile reluctantly tugging up the corner of his mouth, as if he were trying to be pleased but had forgotten how.

It was remarkable that a man who could so easily ruffle her feathers every time he saw her would go to such obvious lengths to make everyone, including her, comfortable in such an uncomfortable situation. She hadn't thought the lieutenant's rough manners could ever compare favorably to Mr. Denman's always reserved, gentlemanly demeanor, but it had not been the doctor who had kept the dinner from devolving into something far less civilized—something with choruses of abbesses in the whoring trade.

As if on cue, the captain broke the congenial mood of Dance's song. "I want a drink."

Punch stepped forward with the decanter. "Claret, sir?"

"Claret? Claret is the liquor for boys." Captain Muckross misquoted the famous Dr. Samuel Johnson. "You're all boys. In my day we were men, and sang about swiving cunning wenches like men, not sipping punch and claret like women. *'Weigh hey roll and go!'* " he sang for his own amusement and slapped his hand against the table once more. "Like *men*!"

It was too much. Despite all her best intentions to be quiet and invisible, Jane could not hold her tongue. "But not like a gentleman."

Dance spoke into the gasping silence. "Captain, sir." He tried to make his correction as polite as possible. "There is a lady present."

"What?" The blasted old ass lofted his eyebrows like gray jibs in some arcane mixture of drunken outrage and disbelief, before he turned his rheumy squint down the table, raking the face of each of the men until he found her—the lady. "Gad."

Dance spoke to keep Muckross from saying anything more lewd or damning. "During your illness, sir, I was unable to introduce you to our esteemed guests from the Royal Society. Captain Edwin Muckross, I present you to Sir Richard Smith." He went around the table without pause, not wanting the captain to be able to say anything. "The Reverend Mr. William Phelps. Mr. Albert Parkhurst. Mr. Jackson Denman, who has agreed to act as surgeon, you've met. And Miss Jane Burke. Also Lieutenant Able Simmons, a former shipmate of mine, who was able to join us as a cartographer and second lieutenant, is here with young Lieutenant Lawrence, while Mr. Whitely has the deck."

That announcement served to divert the captain's aggressive attention from Miss Burke, just as Dance had intended. "What?" the old man shouted. "What? Hiring a lieutenant? Without my say-so? By God, sir, you go too far!"

Dance felt his collar grow unaccountably tight under his black silk stock. "I consulted with you, sir." Dance bent the truth to serve his lie. "About the need for more officers along with a detachment of marines and midshipmen. We discussed it along with the muster rolls, sir. Some weeks ago now, before we proceeded to sea."

"We did not!" The old man was convinced of it. "I know nothing of this man. Nor any of them." He flung his arm out at the assembled table. "Nothing of these dinners. What have you all been doing here? Plotting, no doubt? Plotting to take my ship from me?"

"No, sir." Dance hated the quick desperate edge he could hear in his own voice. "Not at all. We were discussing the state of the men's health, and Mr. Denman's professional opinion of the services available to veterans—"

"You were discussing nothing of the kind. You were singing! Inveigling the other officers to join in your mutinous schemes with bowls of punch. I'm on to you, sirrah. I am. I ought to have you put to the lash."

Miss Burke gasped. There was nothing else to call the breath of fright and outrage that flew from her mouth, and brought the captain's beady, displeased gaze back to her.

"And a woman!" the old man carried on, oblivious to both the utter senselessness of his tirade, and the deadly seriousness of the charge he laid against Dance. "Who told you you could bring a woman? I won't have your whore in my ship, sir. I won't." Again he slammed the flat of his palm down upon the table, making Miss Burke jump along with the cutlery. "What have you to say for yourself?"

Before he could give voice to the black rage clawing at his chest, Miss Burke spoke. "No one brought me, sir. I brought myself at the invitation of Sir Joseph Banks, and Sir Richard Smith. I am a conchologist, sir. A naturalist the same as these men. You may take my qualification up with the Royal Society, but I believe the time for you to air your objections has long since passed."

Devil take him for admiring her, but she had spine.

She spoke with a shaky voice, but Dance could hear her anger and frustration. This he knew too well. She stood, as if she might remove herself from the table, for fear that no defense would come from Sir Richard, who might take the opportunity to renew his objections.

But she was right. The time for objection was past. Dance tugged her back into her seat. "You signed the correspondence yourself, sir, authorizing Miss Burke to come aboard as part of the delegation from the Royal Society." The damn man had taken their money as well. But the present situation did not seem a good time to bring up the subject of that fraud. It might only make the captain worse.

Next to him, Miss Burke slowly sat back down, but in her agitation, she kept ahold of his hand, as if she needed its reassurance.

Her hand was cool, and soft, and surprisingly strong for such a small woman. "She has been undertaking a study to eliminate the barnacles from our hull."

The inanity served its purpose as a diversion. "The hell you say," was the captain's ridiculous response.

"Indeed, sir." Dance refused to react to the captain's language, and strove to keep his tone as even and mild and patient and factual as if he were talking to one of the infant midshipmen, who were no doubt listening at the keyhole. "Science put to use, sir. Quite remarkable. And quite useful. And here is your fish course, sir."

Punch quickly slid a warmed bowl of fish stew before the captain.

"And perhaps Punch, here, will favor us with a rendition of the old ballad 'The Butcher Boy' while we eat. Punch plays the fiddle, sir."

"Fiddle? I don't have any fiddlers on my ship."

Dance considered that now was perhaps not the best time to tell Captain Muckross that the wardroom steward was another man Dance had hired without the captain's say-so. "What would you like him to sing for you, sir?" And then without waiting for the old man to suggest another lewd and vulgar song like "In Amsterdam," he hastened on. "You'll like 'The Butcher Boy,' sir."

Punch retrieved his fiddle and set himself to a low, slow air, and Dance forced a deep breath into his lungs. But beside him, Miss Burke was still tense and wary, and holding his hand as if he were the only thing keeping her in her seat. And perhaps he was. So he said the only thing he could think, which was the thing he had meant to say for hours and days. Forever. "I'm sorry."

He had pitched his voice low, for her ears only, and her response came back just as quiet. "You are forgiven."

And just like that the tense fear and rage that swilled in his gut like a barrel of brine was gone. The weight of worry and responsibility had pressed down on him like a grating, scoring his flesh, and marking him as an angry, malcontented man. He had to do better. He had to be more equitable.

Because Jane Burke was counting upon him. And she was still holding his hand. And he liked it.

Chapter Fourteen

As abruptly as he had appeared, the captain left. One moment he was spooning fish stew into his mouth, and the next, he wandered out of the wardroom.

Dance bolted to his feet to pursue him—if only to try and prevent any more incidents that might expose his drunkenness to the crew. But the captain's faithful servant was waiting outside the wardroom doors.

Behind Dance, Punch spoke. "I passed word for Manning, sir."

"Well done, Punch." Dance drew in another lungful of air. "Thank you."

"No need, Lieutenant. No need." The banty, one-legged man shook his head in pity. "Didn't know he was that bad."

"No." Dance didn't know what else to say that wouldn't expose the old man. A crew needed to respect their captain. Or at least respect his authority. And it was Dance's job to see that they did. "Do what you can to squelch the gossip, Punch."

"Aye, sir. You're not to worry about that. You've enough on your plate as it is."

What was on his plate was cold. And he'd never acquired

a taste for fish anyway. "I'm for the deck. If you'll heat a bowl, I'll send down Doc Whitely presently."

"You're a good man, Lieutenant. Too good for the likes of him."

Dance could only assume Punch was referring to the captain, and not to their long-suffering sailing master, Mr. Whitely. For if Dance were put upon, so much more so had Whitely been, who had sailed—or sat idle, rotting in port—with the old man for years. But no matter to whom Punch referred, it wouldn't do. "Punch. For the love of God, don't say such things out loud. Don't even think them. We're here to serve *Tenacious,* both you and I, and that's an end to it."

Dance was glad of the quiet solitude of the evening watch. Because the truth was he was poleaxed. He had faced the guns at Trafalgar with a great deal more confidence than he could face the mad old man who was his captain.

And he didn't think he had ever before held hands with a woman like Miss Jane Burke.

She terrified him more than even his captain and all his drunken charges of mutiny. Because he liked her. He admired her. He admired the steel in her spine, and he adored the soft trepidation that made her hold on to his hand for support.

And he wanted to hold more than her hand.

The object of his obsession came up the aft companionway and made her quiet way along the weather rail, a silent ghost of a girl in her light muslin dress made gold in the glowing moonlight.

Below, the hum of Punch's sad Welsh tenor wafted up from the wardroom.

"Rather a different instrument than the low rumble of your baritone, Lieutenant. But it suits my mood, for I find I must thank you again for defending me."

Dance felt the dangerous pleasure of her gratitude and admiration fill his chest. "You seemed to have done well enough on your own. The facts always speak for themselves."

"One might hope they would, but alas . . ." She let the rest die away. And then she said, "I understand your anger at me the other day now. How you have to watch your step. It was frightening enough for me to be the source of the captain's displeasure. But for you . . ."

The pleasure that soaked through him like a warm brandy was only relief at being understood. But that she might also be worried for him was too much. His pride would not allow it. "There are sources enough of his displeasure."

"But to accuse you of mutiny"—she lowered her voice to whisper the word—"when you have clearly been the one holding life and limb together here. Five watches out of six you are the one on deck, working, checking, finding work for idle men."

Dance shook his head, and pitched his own voice lower. "Careful you don't put that abroad, Miss Burke, as it might be seen as evidence *for,* rather than against the captain's claim."

"And has he made such a claim before? Or was that just a drunken rumble?"

"Careful, Miss Burke. I beg you."

"I am not a member of His Majesty's Royal Navy, Lieutenant, I have taken no oath, and I think I may call the man a drunkard based on the evidence of my own eyes. And nose. He stank like a gin mill."

Her outrage somehow soothed the constant coil of worry twisting up his gut. He could feel a smile sliding across his face. "And what would you, Miss J. E. Burke, conchologist and self-professed spinster from the Isle of Wight, know of gin mills?"

His tease amused her enough to thaw away some of her

indignation. "Nothing, I'll grant you." Her smooth cheeks creased with a mischievous dimple. "But I've heard talk. And he certainly did not smell like rum—like the men at their tot of grog—or brandy, which I certainly have smelled, and even tasted before. I must say, he smelled rather strangely antiseptic, like a hedge."

Damn but she was clever. He liked her all the more for the preciseness of her scientific mind. "How observant you are. That's the juniper berries in the flavoring of the gin."

"Ah. Thank you. It's nice to know that even though I am a provincial, self-professed spinster, I can get some things right."

She got a lot of things right. That dimple for starters. And even though he could not afford to like her and keep his head and his commission, he wanted to keep the fragile accord between them. "More than right, Miss Burke. More than right." He checked the compass by the wheel in passing. "How do you progress with the devious barnacle? Has Punch supplied you with fresh subjects?"

"He has. And I have made progress enough. I'm particularly interested in the plates that form the aperture at the top of the creature's carapace. So much more like crustaceans to my way of thinking. So very intriguing."

What was intriguing was the smile that stole slowly across her face. It made Dance feel warm and silly and slightly off-kilter. As if the deck were tilting onto its beam ends instead of staying placidly level in the light breeze.

"It's funny," she said. "I always liked shells for their beauty—the subtle colors, the interesting and fragile curls. But this plain little barnacle is proving entirely fascinating. I never would have thought. But I fear it also means that I shall want to scrape more of them off your hull."

Poor Miss Burke seemed entirely oblivious to the innuendo in her words. But Dance was not. And he very nearly grew hard at the words. As it was, he had to give the stubble rising across his chin a hard rub to keep his countenance. "Miss Burke, you must scrape the barnacles off my hull as much as you like."

She turned that frank open face to his, a pale moon in the low lantern light. "Thank you, sir," she said solemnly. "I think I will."

Very, very soon, he was going to have to kiss her. He did not see how he could not. It was inevitable. And utterly impossible.

Because he had a ship that was falling apart around him, a crew that was on the verge of running amok, and a captain spouting accusations of mutiny. He could not afford even so much as a glance at her invitingly soft pink lips.

But she was so very tempting, as she slipped ever so slightly closer, and lowered her quiet voice even more. "But you have distracted me from the thing I wanted most to say."

Devil take him, but he hoped it was more of the same. More of the pleasurable palaver that held the rest of the world at bay. "And what was that?"

"That I had a quiet chat with Mr. Honeyman." She closed her eyes and gave an almost imperceptible shake of her head—a visible shudder. "He was most fearfully cut up."

She meant to take him to task after all. He straightened, and let his gaze make a check of the compass heading. "It is a harsh world we inhabit, Miss Burke. The navy is not a nursery."

Those blue eyes sparked with more than mere indignation now. "But neither should it be a slaughterhouse."

It certainly had been at times—in his memory, Trafalgar had been nothing so much as a charnel house. But he could not argue with her. That passionate adamance he admired was back in her voice.

"Mr. Ransome laid into that boy for his own pleasure.

And his own guilt. Mr. Honeyman did not take that drawing, and neither did he ransack our rooms. Mr. Ransome only made him take the blame for it."

She could not be right. Hadn't the bosun just pledged his loyalty to Dance and *Tenacious*? She had to have it wrong.

"Miss Burke, you are simply too tenderhearted to be taken in so. The boy would say anything at this point to keep from any greater punishment."

"He said what was liable to get him in even greater trouble if you will not choose to see the truth of it."

"Miss Burke, I know you would like to help, as you said earlier, but you cannot help in matters of ship's discipline. And that is an end to it."

"I spoke to Mr. Ransome, Lieutenant. And he admitted it. Though he said he sent the note to warn me away from the boat for my own good."

Oh, fuck, fuck, fuck all.

Every time he thought he had *Tenacious*'s problems sorted, and knew what was going on, and knew how to handle it, something else came along to prove to him that he was hopelessly and utterly wrong. Wrong, wrong, wrong, damn his eyes.

"Ship," he corrected without thought. "It's a ship."

"Yes, yes, your precious bloody *ship*. But it was Mr. Ransome who sent that note—for my own good, he told me, as he should hate for me to wind up tipped over the side some dark night. It's a big empty ocean out there, he told me, and a little bit like me'd get gobbled up by the sea in no time. No one would ever know I was gone."

Dance could not tell which astonished him more—her swearing again so freely, or her perfect imitation of Ransome's style and cadence of talking. Ransome really had spoken to her.

"And what is more, he appeared everything sincere and concerned. But I cannot like it. The question is not if he is really sincere—for that I don't think I can ever really know—but if he has some ulterior motive in warning me away."

It was near enough to the same question he had asked himself that Dance was brought to a complete standstill. Right there in the middle of the bloody South Atlantic, with the lee shore full of jagged rocks. It was an apt metaphor for his life—there were perils at every turn, and he could not afford to waver. Indecision would put him on the rocks just as surely as the wrong decision would.

Dance wanted to box his own ears to punch some sense into his head, but he already felt as if he had been clouted by a block, and could not think fast enough.

"And which is worse," Jane went on, "he beat that boy to a bloody pulp to cover his own misdeeds, which is disgusting, not to mention a gross misuse of his power."

There was clearly some very great misuse going on here. But to what purpose? And for whose benefit?

Clever, insightful Jane Burke's mind was turning along much the same lines. "What I don't understand is why he should go to such lengths to frighten *me*—which despite my best effort to appear calm and rely upon my friends, he has most assuredly done. I will admit to being very tempted by his offer to see me quietly off without anyone the wiser."

"He offered what?" The hair on Dance's neck bristled in instinctive discomfort, warning him to pay attention.

"Yes." Jane nodded, seeing the connection as clearly as he. "He said he would see me off the *ship* with no one the wiser. Rather like your three deserters of the evening, don't you think?"

"I do think." Fuck all. It was too similar to be a coincidence.

"But why?" Miss Burke was not done examining this specimen of Ransome's perfidy. "Why should he care that the men don't like me? Why should he care if I get off? What purpose could it possibly serve?"

The answer hit Dance like a boarding ax between the eyes—cleaving everything he had thought in more than two bitterly sharp pieces. Because Ransome—damn his canny eyes—was neither suicidal, nor incompetent—he was ambitious. Dance should have seen and understood that.

Ransome and Givens had had near complete control of the ship before Dance had arrived to upset their schemes. And Ransome wanted that back. He wanted his pride.

Jane Burke was just a tool, like Midshipman Honeyman, and perhaps even the captain, for Ransome to use to get at Dance, and undermine his authority. To take back control of the ship. It was all of a piece, Jane Burke and *Tenacious.*

Dance let the hot rage that rose within him burn down to a cold blue flame of purpose. He would see Ransome in chains, damned if he wouldn't. He would disrate the man, or simply put him off, and have done with him, the way he should have in Portsmouth, the moment he had instinctively known Ransome was dirty. There was no room on a ship for such conduct, and it was his responsibility to see justice was done.

But while Dance certainly had all the responsibility, he had very little of the authority—the captain's accusations had made that clear. Dance might disrate Ransome, but the authority to put the man in chains or put him off rested solely with the captain.

But determined, steely, soft Miss Burke who held his hand when she was afraid was now too angry to be dismayed. "I will conquer Mr. Ransome. A man like that, who uses his authority and his cane so freely, has enemies. But more importantly, a man like that has no true friends. I shall have to see what I can do about that, and arrange things differently."

"Not everything can be 'arranged,' Jane. You would be safer, and much better served, to stay as far away from Ransome as possible."

"But it is not possible. You are the one who told me that there would be both hardship and very real danger, Mr. Dance. I believed you then, but I understand you now. And I'll be damned if I will let fear stop me from trying."

She gave him one last look over her shoulder. "And I told you, Dance. I'm very, very good at arranging things."

Jane left Mr. Ransome to be dealt with by Lieutenant Dance, and abandoned her barnacles to concentrate all of her energies upon her new plan—winning both the men and the captain over to her side. Well, more correctly to Lieutenant Dance's side, as the man was doing himself no good of his own. He continued to push the men, keeping them always hammering away at the repairs, and recaulking every seam until the ship resounded with the incessant pounding of mallets, and stank with the heavy smell of tar and pitch.

He certainly did not make any friends when he growled, "You'll be glad of a tight ship when you're rounding the cape."

However true it might be, the men only muttered that they would be best served *not* going around the cape at all, but heading back to England, where they had all been happy rotting in Portsmouth's harbor.

But Lieutenant Dance did not turn them back. He put *Tenacious* to sea—or *proceeded to sea* as Punch told her was the correct nautical phraseology—and pointed her only slightly less leaky bow south down the green coast of the huge continent.

So while Lieutenant Dance concentrated on making his ship sail, she concentrated on making friends by spending every hour she could stand in the close confines of the sick bay, plucking their splinters, binding the bruises, and soothing their burns—hot pitch was a pitiless injurer—and dispensing vast quantities of willow bark tea. And slowly, day after day, it began to work.

Within a few weeks men nodded and smiled and tipped their tarred hats to her when she walked by, armed against detractors with her now-famous medicinal tea, and even her nemesis Mr. Ransome—against whom she had remained especially vigilant—seemed to treat her with new respect. By the end of the month, she was emboldened enough to slip past the dozing marine guarding the captain's stern cabin, and knock on the cabin door.

"What do you want now?" came the querulous answer.

"I want to bring you some tea, sir." Jane let herself through the door, and stepped for the first time into the captain's filthy day cabin. "Goodness, sir. You need a good clean out."

"The hell you say. Who the hell are you?"

Jane had decided upon the same fearlessly straightforward approach she had learned to apply to her crotchety great-grandfather, the Duke of Shafton. "I'm Jane, sir. I've brought you tea."

"I don't like tea. Go away," he ordered before he seemed to think better of it. "Where did you come from?"

"From the Isle of Wight, sir. It's beautiful there. And there is very good tea."

The man made a sound of disbelief, or displeasure—she couldn't tell which because he resolutely turned his back so he could watch the dark Atlantic Ocean pass by the stern windows, as if she were of no account to him.

Or would have, had those windows not been absolutely filthy. "Well, it's no wonder everything is so dim, with the state of these windows." Jane put the teapot and tray before him on the table, and took up the first rag she could find discarded in a messy corner, and immediately began to scrub the accumulated grime off the windows. "I'll just spruce these up for you, sir, so everything will be brighter, and then be on my way."

"What is this?"

Jane glanced over her shoulder, to find the captain sniffing at the steam curling from the spout of the teapot. "Tea, sir." She had brewed up her most aromatic blend and sweetened it strongly in the hopes that it would tempt the older man—as her grandfather had aged, Jane had noticed that he liked things more strongly flavored.

"Hmm."

It was not exactly a sound of approval, but neither was it disapproval, and if nothing else Jane had learned that it was easier to ask forgiveness for something one had already done than to get permission to do it in the first place. "Here, sir. Let me pour that for you."

She did so, and put the cup in his shaky hands. "That's warm, sir. Mind yourself."

"I'll mind myself," the old man groused. "You mind yourself."

"I will, sir." Really, with all his superficial grumbling, he *did* remind her of her great-grandfather. "I'll just have these windows done in half a jiffy, or less than that. And then you'll have more light to see by. And won't that be a better thing?"

He did not comment, but sipped the tea, and watched her progress from pane to pane until she was done.

"There, sir. Isn't that brighter?" Jane also cracked the windows to chase away the stale odor with a whiff of fresh air, which riffled a loose pile of papers sticking out of a portable writing desk set to the side. "That's a lovely light to read your correspondence by."

"I suppose."

Another idea of how she had managed her great-grandfather entered her mind. "And I'll just clear this mess away then, won't I, so you'll have things nice and tidy again." Jane collected a few more of the assorted dirty neck cloths and shirts she found kicked into the corners, but there was no real hope that the place could be made tidy with anything other than a thorough clean out with a scrub brush and a bucket of lye. "There, sir, that's cheerier."

"Is that what you think you're doing, cheering me?"

"Am I, sir? That's nice then. But I thought maybe what I might do was read for you. My father used to want me to read to him of an evening. Books, and sometimes letters, or the Bible if he'd a mind for scripture. And it looks like you've a powerful lot of correspondence here that needs some reading."

"There used to be a man who saw to my correspondence."

"Well, I might not be so good as a *man,* but I did used to manage my father's correspondence. We'll just give it a try, sir." Jane obtained her object with the simple expediency of slipping the first letter off the top of the file. "And you can stop me if I don't read well enough for you, sir."

She was into the fourth letter from a creditor—this from his tailor, Mr. "Old Mel" Meredith in Portsmouth, when the captain's steward interrupted bearing his own pot of tea. But his, Jane noted with a disapproval bordering on disgust, was redolent of the astringent juniper berry that could only denote the presence of gin.

"What's this then?" the steward asked, his voice full of suspicion, like an animal who puffs up his feathers at finding his territory invaded by another species. "The captain doesn't like to be bothered."

The captain made no defense of what he liked or didn't like, so Jane lofted her eyebrow and gave the man a calmer response than his insolence deserved. "It has been no bother. Just a bit of reading. And tea. *Real* tea."

Manning's glance slid to the captain, before he answered in a low voice. "I just bring what I'm asked."

"You shouldn't have to be asked to pick things up, and clean up the place," she answered just as quietly, but she impressed her vehemence upon Manning by her insistence. "You should be ashamed you let it get to such a state. Ashamed. I daresay the insides of those great guns on the deck are cleaner than this day cabin."

Manning's response was a sullen, "I only do as I'm told." And Manning had weapons of his own. "Does Mr. Ransome know you're here?"

Nothing could be so guaranteed to put her on guard. Jane had thought Ransome conquered, but her chin rose along with her trepidation. "I fail to see how what I do with my time is any concern of either yours or Mr. Ransome's."

The steward shook his head. "He won't like it."

An interesting understatement, to be sure. Mr. Ransome seemed to have a rather sharp interest in everything that went on onboard *Tenacious*. "Then I suggest you don't tell him."

"Not worth my life to keep that from him. And he'd find out anyways. Has his ways, Mr. Ransome does."

He certainly did. Underhanded ways. But so did she. "Then you may tell him we are reading."

"Reading?"

"Yes, reading books." Even Ransome could not object to such an innocuous activity. Jane tucked herself comfortably into the stern gallery bench, fished out her copy of Sir Walter Scott's adventures of young Edward Waverley, who was entering into a world which was beautiful because it was new, and raised her voice so the captain could hear her. *"It is then sixty years since Edward Waverly took leave of his family to join the regiment of dragoons in which he had lately obtained a commission."*

The captain said nothing, but since he did not object, Jane took his silence as tacit approval and read on. And as she read the long, picaresque story, she was amused to find her own thoughts wandering from the wild and windswept hills of the Scotland in the story, to the wild, windswept, coast of South America. In the gray light, the wilds off the starboard quarter were less than hospitable; she found them interesting and beautiful all the same in the long, gray, afternoon light.

Jane took a fresher look out the window into the dusk. "Has it gone as late as that?"

"No," the captain insisted. "It's not late. Keep reading."

There was such warm insistence in his voice that she turned to him. And that was when she saw it. With the captain's face illuminated by the flat gray light from the windows, she saw the milky opalescence in his old blue eyes.

There was a reason he had not continued reading on his own. The same reason that he had not paid his bills, or read his correspondence. The reason he liked to stay in the close confines of his own cabin. "Oh, sir. Your eyes."

Chapter Fifteen

Jane sought Dance out immediately after quitting the cabin, and found him on the quarterdeck, where he looked as if he were trying to drive himself to an early grave with his ceaseless work and worrying about the ship. Jane had no idea if her news would aggravate or relieve him, but bad news ought to be told as soon as possible.

Because bad news it was—she felt as if the unrelenting grayness of the ocean and the skies had dripped its way down into her soul.

"Lieutenant Dance? I need to speak to you."

Whatever he heard in her voice sharpened his attention, and he looked at her with that probing singularity of focus that made her so uncomfortable and so pleasantly agitated all at the same time.

"Jane," he asked, not even lowering his voice in front of the others. "What is it?"

It was remarkable how his use of her name undid her with such devastating swiftness. She had to shake her head and brush her eyes with the back of her hand and smile—a polite negation in front of the crew, who seemed to have eyes everywhere.

Jane lowered her voice. "It's about the captain."

His scowl only deepened. "What about the—"

Whatever the lieutenant might have said was cut off when the deck beneath their feet seemed to lift and shudder from the crashing report of a gun. From directly below.

Lieutenant Dance called to Mr. Lawrence, "You have the deck," and was clattering his boots down the ladder to the gun deck, as Mr. Denman came running up from below. Though the ship continued to sail on, rolling up and down the churning waves as a fresh rain squall started to slant across the open waist, the men had all frozen at their work, looking and waiting as Dance followed the sound of the report to the captain's stern cabin.

Jane crowded down the companionway with the others, but she could see little between the men's shoulders.

"Guard the door." That was Dance, speaking to the marine sentry stationed outside the captain's cabin—the same young man who had been dozing in the doorway when she had left the cabin not twenty minutes ago.

From what she could see, the cabin was cloaked in darkness—the lamp she had left burning had been extinguished.

"Get a light," came Dance's order. "Sir? Captain Muckross, sir?"

They could hear nothing. Jane, along with the men congregated in the companionway, pressed closer to the door, listening and looking into the dark doorway.

Which was abruptly filled by the lieutenant, who, if he had looked like hell earlier, now looked five times worse—hollowed out as if he had taken some great blow.

"No one in or out," he instructed the sentry, "except by my order."

"What is it, Lieutenant?" someone asked.

Dance shook his head—a mute, emphatic negative. "Pass word for Manning," was all he said before he shut the door.

In the absence of facts, rumor rose up in its place. "It

was a gunshot," someone in the muttering crowd stated. "I heard it plain as day."

"Who d'ye think he shot?"

"Ransome," was the name muttered under more than one breath.

"What's that?" The crowd turned and edged back from the big, dark bosun, like ninepins moving away from a heavy bowls ball.

Jane ducked behind Mr. Parkhurst's narrow back.

"Nothing, Mr. Ransome," came the quick denial from the crowd, before another, smarter soul thought to change the subject. "There's doings up the captain's cabin."

"I'll see to it," was Ransome's confident assertion as he made his way forward. "Stand aside."

The sentry swallowed so nervously, Jane thought his Adam's apple was going to bounce out of his throat. "Lieutenant said no one out or in, except by his order."

"Well, that doesn't include me," Ransome countered.

The sentry held his ground, but was saved the necessity of challenging Ransome by the appearance of Manning.

"Make way," he cried, as he rushed up from somewhere below.

The sentry knocked the butt of his gun against the door with obvious relief that he had an appropriate excuse to call forth the lieutenant to deal with Ransome. "Manning, sir."

The door opened to admit Manning, but when Ransome tried to follow, the lieutenant blocked his way. "Ransome." Dance all but looked through him. "Pipe all hands to muster in the waist."

Around Jane, there were mutterings about the lashing rain at such an order, and Ransome, perhaps with an eye out for winning favor with the men, tried to change the lieutenant's mind. "Awful bad weather just to muster the men. You can tell us whatever you need to tell us now."

Dance stepped forward out of the doorway until he

loomed over Ransome. But even in the dim light of a single lantern, Jane could see he had shed his coat, and his hands were covered in blood.

Jane felt herself go cold at the sight, as if she had already been doused by the cold rain. Dance's gaze was just as cold, moving slowly from Ransome to the men crowded round. His eyes found hers and paused briefly before they moved on, and back to Ransome. His voice was a rusty scratch. "Muster in the waist."

He led them out into the rain-lashed deck, and then slowly ascended the quarterdeck ladder. Jane hung back under the shelter of the starboard gangway, where Punch somehow found her, and handed her her thick wool cloak. "Thank you," she said, but there was not enough worsted wool in all the world to warm her, or buffer her from the dread of what was to come.

Lieutenant Dance did not mince his words, but gave them the terrible truth straightaway. "Your captain is dead. He killed himself this evening, for reasons unknown to us, and known only to God. We will bury him at dawn, and trust that God will have mercy upon his soul."

Jane tried to pull the edges of her cloak closer to shut out the driving rain, but it did no good, because the cold was from inside—reaching within like the icy fingers of a frost. Pity and horror clamped down her throat, chilling the air with every breath she struggled to take.

And all she could think was that this was wholly and entirely her fault.

Dance stayed on deck for hours, pacing the quarterdeck, up and back, up and back until he could no longer feel the cold cutting rain. Until he was as numb in body as he was in spirit.

But he could not rest. He could not put what he had seen from his mind. He could not.

Dance was no stranger to injury and violence. He had

spent half his youth in the navy that had seen the bitterest fighting of a generation culminate in Trafalgar, and the other half of his young manhood forcibly defending the British peace. He had seen more than his share of death. But he had never, in all his days, seen anyone do such irreparable, violent harm to himself.

And because he had not seen it coming, and had done nothing to ease the old man's distress, he walked.

It was Punch who finally stopped him. Sometime in the dark of the night, the wardroom steward brought him his hat and cloak, and after another few hours of watching Dance try to wear his guilt out on the quarterdeck, Punch planted his pegged leg across his path and simply said, "It's a bad day all right, but that's enough of that, Captain."

The word hit Dance with the force of a wayward cannon shot—he was now the captain in name as well as in responsibility. The authority that he had been trying to assume for all these weeks was well and truly his. And he needed to act accordingly. "Who has the deck?"

"Simmons, sir." Able Simmons stepped away from the shadow of the mizzenmast where he must have been keeping himself out of Dance's way. "I have the deck, Captain."

Captain. It was only a courtesy. It was only temporary. Such an appointment could only be officially made in London—he would have to make a report, and hope to come upon another British ship lying for London. The possibility seemed remote at best.

But in the meantime, he now had full command of his ship and all the souls in her.

Devil take them all.

But he was her commander now, and couldn't let his misgivings show. "Thank you, Mr. Simmons. Carry on."

Instead of proceeding down the second ladder to the berth deck, Punch paused outside the captain's cabin. "I know you gave orders that no one was to go in but Manning and Mr. Denman, sir, but Manning needed help putting things to rights, and him'n Mr. Denman judged I was the man to do it."

"Thank you, Punch. I would not have asked that of you." Dance had long ago learned that there were some things that a man couldn't unsee. Things like Trafalgar, when he had been a sixteen-year-old boy, and the gun captain in his division had been cut in two at his feet— that moment stayed in his mind as fresh as the moment it had happened, though many other memories of that time had long since faded.

"I'm happy to do my duty for you, sir." Punch nodded emphatically, as if to say that was the last he was going to speak on the subject. "Now, we've sewn up the shroud, and put Captain Muckross's body in the sleeping cabin, where Manning said as he'll sit with the body tonight."

There was nothing more to be done. "Thank you, Punch. I'll see myself to the wardroom."

"Cap'n? I've moved most of your dunnage into the day cabin for now, sir, until we bury the man proper, but—"

"No." Dance shook his head, unwilling—or perhaps simply unprepared—to take over the stern cabin at so early a pass. It seemed . . . wrong. As if he were in some ungodly rush to take over for the man. Nothing could be further from the truth. He had simply wanted Captain Muckross to do his job, not to leave it all to him.

Devil take him, but what a coil. And he certainly had no desire to revisit the stern cabin today. "I'll stick with the wardroom as long as I may." Until there was no choice but to assume all aspects of this ill-fated captaincy.

Punch stepped closer, as if he feared being overheard. "But Miss Burke, sir. She said she needed to talk to you. Seemed important. So I let her in to wait for you"—the steward tipped his head to silently indicate the captain's day cabin—"seeing as it's more private than the wardroom."

Funny—all he had wanted for days and days was a chance to be alone with Jane Burke. And now that the moment presented itself, he was dragging his feet. Trying to think of a way to put it off. Because he knew that everything had changed, and that he *had* to be thinking of his men and his ship and the steady push of the contrary westerlies working against *Tenacious*'s bows, instead of taking comfort in Miss Jane Burke.

But she was already waiting. And he was in sore need of comfort.

"Thank you, Punch."

"Right, sir. I'll bring you and the lady a hot brandy to chase away the chill of the deck, as well as hot washing water."

"Thank you." Dance was never more grateful for the man's simple, dutiful competence. It was a small comfort, but a comfort nonetheless.

Dance stripped off his sodden cloak and coat as he entered. The cabin had been restored to order—No. It had in fact been improved upon. In the warm light from the oil lamp, the room looked as if it had been given a thorough scrubbing—as if even the walls had been holystoned. And that change he could not attribute solely to the competence of Punch—and certainly not Manning—but to the exhausted woman curled up in a ball in the far corner of the stern gallery bench.

Dance knew that he ought to wake her, and say something to her, but he had no words, nothing that would give her any comfort, and so kept his quiet, and let her sleep. Because just the sight of her gave him solace. He eased himself down onto the other end of the curved bench seat so he could watch the quick rise and fall of her breath, and the way her apricot lips fell ever so slightly open as she exhaled.

He laced his hands behind his head so he wouldn't be tempted to try and touch her—to test the silken fall of her hair between his fingers—and tried to close his own eyes. He could hear every creak and groan in the vessel, and knew what each one was—the straining of the bowsprit, continuous slow seep of water into the bows, the taut strain of the foretop.

"Dance?"

"Yes." Dance tipped his head to regard her, but kept his voice low—Manning was only a few feet away, behind the batten wall of the sleeping cabin, and sound traveled strangely in a ship.

"Are you—" Jane's soft questions came in fits and starts as she pulled herself up out of sleep. "Is it true?"

"Yes." There was no other answer he could give. "He killed himself."

"Oh, dear God." Her voice cracked with anguish, and she covered her face with her hands. "I'm so sorry. I'm so, so sorry. This is all my fault."

Dance might have expected that there was only one other person in the whole of the ship willing to share that responsibility with him, however wrongly. "Jane, you couldn't possibly arrange for the captain to kill himself."

"Oh, no. Not exactly. But I should have left well enough alone. I should never have said what I said."

Dance was too numb and exhausted for alarm, but he felt his whole body tense as if in preparation for a blow. He unlaced his hands from behind his head, and slowly sat up. "What did you say?"

His question made her cover her face again, and she shook her head. "I didn't mean to cause trouble. I thought I was helping."

"Jane." He could not stop himself from taking her hand in his. "What did you do? What were you trying to help?"

She gripped his hand hard, just as she had at the table that night, when he had first felt the same messy surge of need and protectiveness rise up in him like a rogue wave. "Us. Him. *Tenacious*."

"Jane."

"I read to him, the way I had been used to do for my

grandfather. His correspondence was in as bad a shape as the rest of his cabin—an intolerable mess." She gestured to the now neatened writing desk. "And so I organized it. Sorted it out."

He did not ask how she had gotten the captain to agree to such a thing—that she had a talent for arranging people as well as projects, he did not doubt. "Jane."

She shook her head again, as if she could put off the inevitable moment of truth just a little while longer. "Some of the letters went back years." She left him to go to the writing desk in question, and show him the contents. "But much of it remained unread, and unanswered. Unopened even."

"I know." He had noticed the mess of letters and torn paper when he had made his daily reports—which the captain had simply tossed atop the tottering pile. It seemed the man had taken as little interest in his personal affairs as he had the running of his ship. "What of it? What did you find?"

"You know?" Jane was startled out of guilt and into astonishment. Accusation laced her voice. "If you knew, why did you not do something about it? He had bills and debts that added together must be staggering. It's no wonder he never wanted to leave his ship or even put up sail. He never even read any of these official-looking packets from the Admiralty."

Tenacious's sailing orders, still in their unsealed packets at the bottom of the now neat stack.

Dance took the packet and broke the seal. The Admiralty's detailed plan of sail had never even been read. Dance was relieved to find that he had instinctively followed fairly closely to the orders—they were to have proceeded to sea and made as directly as possible to Rio de Janeiro, and then around the Horn to Valparaiso before turning west for the Samoan Islands navigated by Cook some thirty-five years earlier.

He felt a return of some of his confidence in the easing of his lungs. "Thank you. You didn't by any chance happen to also find his logs? Although I am not altogether sure if he even kept one."

"Oh, yes. They were in his trunks. I persuaded Manning to give me the key so I might pack away his traveling desk, when I saw them."

Of course she had. Of course, she was just that organized and efficient.

She continued to be so, pulling the log out of the trunk placed against the wall, and passing him the book bound in the familiar marbled paper of Waterlow and Sons, the Admiralty's preferred stationer in London. Dance had a store of five such volumes at the bottom of his own trunk.

He opened the pages to find the volume had been begun nearly a year ago, in January of 1815, when *Tenacious* had been on the West Indies Station. Page followed after page of neat daily notations of wind and weather, barometer and temperature readings, noon sightings and calculations of latitude and longitude, as well as the set of the sails and speed of the vessel through the water. And interspersed with those facts were meticulously inked charts of various harbors.

Jane ran her finger along the edge of the drawing. "They are quite good, are they not? Such a loss."

"Yes. He seems to have been a competent captain, and an able officer as little as a year ago."

But the logbook showed the men's physical deterioration graphically, as the notations became gradually less and less legible, until they ceased altogether in September when *Tenacious* had come into Portsmouth harbor.

Dance had never thought of the reasons why the old man might not want to do his duty, only that he hadn't. "You are right. I should have done better. He had entrusted the ship's funds and bills to the purser, who absconded with the money, much as he did with the funds you and the other members of the Royal Society's expedition paid to him to share the captain's table."

Belated understanding lit her face. "Is that what happened? And he—the captain—had no money to feed us, and so you did. Why did you not tell me?"

Dance pushed his free hand through his short-cropped hair and tried to remember the reasons that seemed wholly insufficient now. "Many reasons. Duty to my ship. Loyalty"—such as it was—"to my captain." A selfish loyalty, he could see now. "I suppose he had also entrusted his personal debts to the man." He had only thought of *Tenacious*'s missing funds, and the expense to himself.

"Yes, but did you not ask yourself why? Why would a man who had risen through merit in his profession—for there is no other way to advance in the navy, is there not?"

"Preferment helps, but only to a certain point." It had been one of the banes of his own career that he had no family to help him along, unlike his friend Will Jellicoe, whose father the Earl Sanderson had seen that his son had always benefited from the family connections. To be fair, Will was as brilliant and able as any frigate captain—with the exception of Captain Muckross, who was no longer anything of the kind—and had always been generous in helping his friends.

But not even Will could have foreseen how this voyage would see Dance promoted to his long-sought captaincy.

"But again, why?" Jane persisted. "What made him stop being so competent? What made him stop reading his correspondence and paying his bills?" She came back to the gallery bench, her eyes wide and imploring, asking him to see what he could not. Or would not.

"Gin." It was the most obvious answer. There were enough ruined drunks crawling the gutters of London to prove that the drink was the ruin of many a man, captain or no.

"But what would drive him to the drink in the first place?"

At the moment he did not care about Muckross. Because she was close enough that he could smell the subtle scent of lemons and roses that had clung to her bedding. The same scent he had noticed that very first day she had come aboard, getting underfoot and under his skin.

Dance wanted to shut his eyes, and take a deep breath of her—as intoxicated as if he had taken gin. "Does there need to be a reason?"

"Yes."

He could not miss the passionate insistence in her voice. "Jane, what is it?"

She let out her breath as if she had been holding it in. "It was because he had been slowly going blind. By now, I think he could barely even see."

The grinding gears in Dance's mind fell into place like a trap springing closed. It fit together perfectly—how the captain might have started to rely on Givens. How he might have neglected his correspondence and bills, then his appearance and his cabin, and finally, how he would have turned to the bottle for solace from a world he could no longer control. All because he could no longer see.

And the old man had been helped along his path to blue ruin by an indifferent crew led to idleness by thieving warrant officers. The image of Givens rose like a specter in Dance's mind.

"I should have seen it." Granted, Jane Burke was an extraordinarily observant woman, a scientist trained to look critically at things. But he was a man whose job it was to notice each rope out of place, each slackened line. He should have looked at the old man more closely, beyond the disheveled clothing, and bulbous red nose. He should have asked himself why the old man drank rather than just be irritated that it meant more work for him.

Jane shook her head, but she was just as self-critical. "I

did see. But I should have shut my mouth. I should never have said so to him. He must have thought I would tell everyone. But I didn't tell anyone. It seemed too private, too mortifying to make known abroad."

"I wish you had told me." He would have acted differently. He would have seen the captain's infirmity for what it was, and not just an inconvenience to him.

Or at least he would have liked to think he would. But he'd never know now.

Jane's thoughts were much the same. "I was going to." She turned that wide moon of a face up to him. "I meant to. But it's too late now. I'm too late."

She would have covered her face again if he had not taken her hand. But when he felt the tremor in her hand, and heard the quiet sobs, he pulled her into his arms. Jane—his stalwart, positive Jane—was dissolving in tears.

He pulled her down to sit next to him, hugging her against his damp chest, and hoping that the comfort he might give her would outweigh the impropriety. But there was nothing of propriety about their situation. And if she had been concerned with propriety, she wouldn't have come to his cabin. Indeed, she would never have come aboard *Tenacious* in the first place. She would never have faced down Sir Richard, or braved Mr. Ransome's threats. She would have never tried to befriend the captain.

"It's all my fault," she gasped against his shirtfront.

And because Dance knew what it was to feel such crushing responsibility, he could not bear for her to feel that way. And so he kissed her.

He had been wanting to kiss her for days. Weeks. Since the first moment she had smiled at him, and said she was looking forward to being sorted out.

He had wanted and wanted until it had all but eaten him up inside.

But now he could take. In the face of gruesome death he wanted to cling to wholesome life.

Dance slid his hands upward along the fine line of her jaw, to cradle her face, and thumb the wet tears from her cheeks. "Jane. Don't."

Her lips were soft, and bittersweet with salt tears. Everything easy and forgiving. Everything he wanted. He wanted to breathe in her sweetness and her goodness and her warmth. He wanted to subsume her within him to drive away the cold that had settled deep within his bones. He wanted *her*.

He ached for her, this forthright, innocent woman.

And she was an innocent. She barely knew how to kiss—her eyes were open wide as she clutched his waistcoat front and pressed her mouth to his, but her lips were sealed together in an ardent, battened-down, buttoned-up manner that spoke more for her inexperience than her exuberance.

Dance gave her the only gift he had to give—his patience. He battened down his own need, and took his time, stroking his thumbs along her cheek, tipping her head back gently so he could play, and suck and nip at the plush line of her lower lip until at last she learned to kiss him back. Learned soft sips and sighs, and opened her mouth to allow his tongue to touch and taste her.

Dance heard a sound of encouragement tunnel out of his chest, and hoped it wasn't too much like a groan. Hoped he didn't scare her away.

But she was made of sterner stuff, and pulled herself closer, wrapping those surprisingly strong little arms around his neck and giving her innocence to him like a gift.

It felt like he had waited forever to be kissed like this, by such a woman. And it had been worth the wait. *She* had been worth the wait. Worth every travail and hardship on this misbegotten voyage. Because she tasted like life, and kissed like the end of winter.

He turned her into his arms, pressing her into the upholstered bench, so he could ease his weight into her and appease the aching need that had built and built for weeks and weeks until he felt as if it would consume him.

And she didn't protest. She held him tight, drawing him down upon her, opening herself to him, letting her skirts tangle with his legs, and her lips taste the lobe of his ear. He could feel her breathing fast and hot against the skin of his neck, and knew his own breath was sawing in and out of his chest, as if he had hauled up the anchor cable by himself.

But she was a different sort of anchor, holding him firmly in the world of the warm and living, keeping him off the jagged shore of recrimination and regret. And he would not regret her, he would not. Not until he was old and gray, and cast upon the shore, and she was a distant memory of days gone past.

But she was here now, beneath him, and he could explore her at will, running his hands along the sweet curves of her body, from the trim flare of her waist up the run of her stays until he could cup the drowsy weight of her breast in his palm. She filled his hand completely. Perfectly. So perfectly, he could not stop himself from finding the subtle evidence of her arousal in her tightly budded nipple, and thumbing the peak through the layers of fabric.

The gasp of shock that flew from her lips was enough to remind him anew that she was an innocent, and that he was not only supposed to be the captain, but a gentleman. And she was not only a lady, but a person under his care.

She was sweet and kind and smart and brave and nothing he had a right to.

To take advantage of her grief to ease his own was not the action of a gentleman. Now was not the time, or the place. Not with the captain's dead body lying enshrouded on the other side of the sleeping-cabin wall.

Dance eased his hand away. He rested his forehead against hers, and tried to slow his breath. Tried to listen to the sounds of the ship stirring around them with the change of the watch, and wait for their breathing to return to normal.

Normal. Such an out-of-place word on this ship where nothing was normal. And nothing could be with this woman in his arms. Nor did he want it to be.

But he did not let her go. He could not. He would hold on to her for as long as he possibly could.

"I . . ." She closed her eyes. "I ought to go."

He nodded, but said, "Not just yet."

He held her there, not kissing, not speaking, until the watch had changed and the ship settled once again into creaking quiet. And then he kissed her just once before he set himself away from her.

Because if he didn't set himself away from her now, while good sense still ruled his head, he was like to never let her go.

"You stay," he said. "I'll go." It were better for him to go on deck, than for her to try to make it down to the wardroom unseen. If he stayed on deck all would be well.

Dance shrugged on his coat, and went out into the blistering cold before he could change his mind. It was just as well, devil take him. He'd never sleep anyway, but at least now he had something better to think of—the alarming perfection of Jane Burke's soft, ripe breast in his hand.

Chapter Sixteen

It was a wonder that Jane managed to push herself back up to sitting, because she could not feel her spine. She couldn't feel anything but the heady thrum of wonder pulsing through her veins.

Because Lieutenant Dance had kissed her. And she couldn't feel anything but the breathless wonder that warmed her like the summer sun.

He had kissed her. And it was marvelous. And unexpected, and sweet and messy and undeniably exciting and scary to be the object of such a man. She had no idea kissing would feel like that—like her breath had been pushed from her lungs, but she didn't need to breathe.

And she had not known that a man's face would feel like that under her palm—soft and prickly and endearing. She had not known that his lips would taste tangy and clean and delicious, or be so smooth and yet so strong.

But she knew now.

And she wanted to do it again. As soon as possible. With stony, impassive Lieutenant Dance. Who was not stony or impassive in the least.

And neither was she. She was not the logical, scientific creature she had thought herself.

Her body felt foreign—a new uncharted world she had

never before wanted to explore. Her hands tingled, and her breath came fast, and her legs had gone all rubbery. And her breasts felt full and heavy and aching for the unexpected pleasure of his touch.

Beneath her thick wool gown, her body felt riper for the knowledge—for the fact that she had never felt something she could not control and keep neat and tidy and manageable.

It was messy and bewildering and lovely. Just like him.

"You all right then, miss?" Punch asked when he brought in a hot mug of something steamy and alcoholic.

"Yes, thank you." Jane felt her face flame to the roots of her hair. "The lieutenant went above." She felt she ought to explain herself more, but Punch seemed satisfied. Or perhaps he was simply as embarrassed as she.

"Did he now?" The old tar kept his eyes everywhere but on her. "Good night then, miss."

Jane had never been so mortified in all her life. It was as if the steward expected that she would, and perhaps should stay in Dance's cabin. As if he thought she and Dance had been doing exactly what they had been doing. And that they might be doing more of it.

Jane didn't know which embarrassed her more.

And with that it all came flooding back—the grief and the guilt, the sure knowledge that she had made an irreversible mistake. That she had pushed and prodded and managed a man into his own death. No matter what Lieutenant Dance said, or how he had kissed her, that fact remained unforgivably true.

And would have kept her from sleep that awful night, had she not kept hold of Lieutenant Dance's black silk stock tie. She had taken hold of it somehow when they had kissed, and she never let it go, slipping it into the pocket sewn onto her petticoats.

She took it out now, in the safety of the dark cabin, and let the smooth silk run through her hands, and held it up against her cheek. It still held the lingering scent of lime and soap and cold wind. But it was him. And for that one small moment she could close her eyes and pretend she was still with him, and all was right with the world.

Because even she knew it could not last.

They buried Captain Muckross at dawn, commending his soul to God, and his shrouded body to the cold, dark sea.

Dance spoke only briefly—he asked the Reverend Mr. Phelps to read out the service in his quavery voice. Because no sooner had the body slid beneath the gray waves, than the sea seemed to rise up in protest, and Dance was forced to turn his mind to more important things—to the fate of the living. To the safety of all the souls aboard *Tenacious*.

The serrated landscape of Tierra del Fuego far off the starboard bow was rugged and rocky and littered with ship-wrecking rocks just lurking below the surface ready to rip open the bottom of his hull. Dance had expected worsening weather when *Tenacious* turned into the contrary westerlies at the tip of South America, but he had hoped against hope that they would be spared the kind of blow that howled upon them from the polar south, pushing *Tenacious* relentlessly toward the inhospitable lee shore.

But the looming lee shore wasn't their most pressing problem—the relentless battering of the headwind against the bows was.

"She's opening up again, Captain." The carpenter Pritchard came to him already soaked from the constant spray blowing across the deck, and the wet work to stop the leaking. "I've patched and caulked and shored her up, but the rollers twist her up something fierce, so's I can't stop her working apart at her stem."

Dance gave the order to shorten sail—though he didn't like to send the men aloft in such pitching seas—and set the course farther to the southwest, to take them around the Horn well out to sea, where they would have greater room to maneuver than in the narrow Strait of Magellan, and would not have to tack constantly to make headway.

But farther out to sea, the unpredictable weather of the polar summer forced them all to their duty. He pushed the men as hard as he dared, but he couldn't be everywhere, though he didn't spare himself. Any job he asked the men to do, he turned his hand to as well.

The long days began to blend together, and still the weather did not abate. Nor did the men cease complaining.

"This is the best weather Cape Horn has to offer," he assured them. "This is the height of the southern summer, with the calmest weather and the longest hours of daylight. We can't afford to sit and wait, because it's only bound to get worse."

If the men were disinclined to believe him, Dance kept his curses to himself. Because the life of the ship had to go on—the men had to be fed, and they needed to be led. To that end, Dance made his promotions and his demotions. While the elevation of Lieutenants Simmons and Lawrence could surprise no one, the promotion of young Rupert Honeyman to acting third lieutenant served not only to make up for the lad's mistreatment, but also to enliven the Marine Society midshipmen to renew their efforts to excel under tutelage of the sailing master.

Similarly, the promotion of the topman, Flanaghan, to master's mate, where his years of experience could be useful to Mr. Whitely despite his clipped wing, as he called his broken arm, helped to lessen Ransome's underhanded manipulation of the crew.

And as for Mr. Ransome— Dance spent an inordinate amount of time mulling what to do with Ransome. He was too useful and too powerful a man to strip him of his warrant and turn before the mast—more underhanded skullduggery was likely to ensue.

He settled instead for keeping the man as close as possible to hand, calling upon his personal assistance nearly constantly so the man was kept off balance and too busy to plot.

And Dance kept his eyes and his ears open in a way he never had—and never had had to—before. So the moment he heard even the vaguest of mutterings from Larson, one of Ransome's bosun's mates—"We'd all be better off making back for Rio instead of carting bloody scientists across the seas like a bunch of cooped hens"—he disrated the man and turned him before the mast as an example to Ransome, and replaced him with Morris, who had remained helpful, hardworking, and loyal.

But Ransome was as tenacious as the brutal westerlies. "Don't like it," he muttered day after day, until even mild Doc Whitely began to wonder at Dance's course.

"Do you think we ought to turn back?" The sailing master clamped a hand over his hat as he shouted his doubts over the shrieking winds. "Or seek a more sheltered course?"

"Our orders are for Valparaiso, and to get north we must first go due west." And turning back would do no good. They might find some shelter at a deep bay in the Hermit Islands, but they would find little in the way of materials for repairing the leaking bow. Dance had rounded Cape Horn more than once in his long time in the navy, and it was ever so. Wishing in the face of the relentless westerlies was useless—the wind was not going to stop. They might wait until they were all as old and dead as the captain, and still the wind would not change. "Best to set ourselves to it, and grit it out."

The only one who seemed able to grit it out with any equanimity was the dauntless Miss Jane Burke, who came where none of the other naturalists, and few of the crew would venture, and made an appearance on the treacherous, sloping quarterdeck.

The moment he recognized her dark felt hat coming up the companionway, Dance was at her side, offering her a steadying hand. "Jane. Have a care, the deck is icy and slippery."

They had not spoken in days—not since he had kissed her in his cabin, and they had buried the captain. After such an absence, everything within him warmed at her appearance. She had donned her heavy cloak as protection against the steady stinging spray off the bow, but beneath the enveloping hat, those wide, shining blue eyes greeted him with a steadiness that was like a balm to his misapprehensions. "Lovely weather you seem to have found us, Captain."

"One does one's best, ma'am."

"If this is your best, Captain, I should very much hate to see your worst."

Her wit was the only thing dry within five hundred miles. Heaven help him, but the woman could make him smile. "Would you? I'd think an intelligent girl like you could handle my worst with your eyes closed."

"I'd rather keep my eyes open."

"Yes. I noticed you did."

She colored, that lovely swath of jam spreading down her neck and across her chest.

But she recovered her aplomb far more quickly than he. "Careful, Lieutenant. I might take your little joke as a compliment."

He liked her mistake in calling him lieutenant—it felt more familiar. That warm feeling in his gut was relief, not excitement. "Careful, Miss Burke, I might have meant it as one."

She glanced at him out of the corners of her eyes, as if she were still not quite sure of him, but he could see the mischievous light in her bright blue eyes, and see the smile warming those lovely lips. "You never."

Devil take him, but it was such a pleasure to see if he could make her smile. "Who knows?"

"I shall record this in my diary—on this day, stony Captain Dance has favored me with a joke."

He would favor her with much more than a mere joke if given half a chance. He could prove to her that he wasn't in the least bit stony. At least only where it counted. Damn him, but if they weren't battling the weather at the bottom of the world, he would favor her with kiss after kiss, and spread her out on green grass in the warm sunshine, and kiss her until all her sharp intellect had melted into passion.

But there was no warm sunshine—only endless, raw gray ocean for miles and miles. "I am sorry the weather has put an end to our dinners."

"So am I. Manning is not nearly as cheerful a wardroom steward as Punch."

His alarm was instant. "I hope Punch has not deserted you? He assured me that he would be able to assist you in the wardroom as well as see to the captain's cabin."

"Oh, yes. He has been quite steadfast, and kept us tolerably well in the circumstances."

Another small spate of relief eased the coil in his gut. "Good. I'm glad to hear. Punch is a wonder."

Miss Burke did not agree. "He can't be that much of a wonder if he has let you get like this."

Like this? Dance ran a hand over his jaw to remind himself that he had indeed shaved that day—no matter the weather Punch somehow contrived to get hot washing water, as now that he was captain, Punch had become as insistent as any valet that he look like a gentleman. He had let himself go a bit after his first attempt to shave himself in Miss Burke's wide-eyed presence. "I am sorry my appearance offends you. If anyone or anything is to blame, it is the damn filthy weather and not Punch."

"Your appearance does not offend, Captain. It worries. You can't be eating, and I doubt you've been sleeping. Not that you were much before."

Oh, but it was a pleasure warming his cold bones to think that despite their forced separation, she still noticed anything about him. "Been keeping an eye on me, have you, Miss Burke?"

She blushed a vivid shade of apricot that made him think of jam and sticky fingers. "No, I— That is, one could not help but notice—"

"That you have been keeping an eye on me." It was a pleasure to disconcert and tease her so.

But she had spine as well as a sense of humor. "Well, someone ought to. As I said before, Lieut—Captain. As I said before, as you appear to be the only thing standing between us—this ship—and total ruin, it behooves us to see that you are taken care of. That is all. I meant nothing more." She turned away to try and shore up her pride.

Oh, pride was something he knew about all too well. And he knew it was as useless and unprofitable as sailing into a headwind. "And what if I wanted it to be something more? What if I were glad that someone on this godforsaken ship gave a damn about me? What then, Miss Burke?"

His questions shocked him as much as they seemed to have shocked her. Her hand rose to cover her mouth, as if she were trying to hold back the words she didn't want to say. "Mr. Dance," she whispered. "Captain. I hardly know what to say. I—"

"Miss Burke, ma'am?" Punch poked his head above the companionway combing, dodging the spray. "You'll pardon me, miss, Mr. Denman was asking after that tincture of calendula, and Mr. Phelps was hoping you'd read from the Bible for them."

"Yes, of course." She looked at him then, and he fancied he saw something of resignation—or was it regret?—in her eyes. "I'm sorry. But if you'll excuse me, Captain, it seems I have others that I need to keep an eye on."

And with that, what little warmth there was in the day was gone.

But on he went, driving himself and the ship, day after day with little food, less sleep, and the absence of Miss Burke until Dance thought he would go mad. Until one afternoon for no reason, the wind abated, and after a few hours of relative calm and quiet, he let himself believe that they were finally through the worst of it.

Tenacious held, and they had finally made enough progress to westward, he was able to confidently alter course to the northwest and get some speed out of her.

And for a few daylight hours, he could almost breathe easier, and begin to think of other things. And other people. Of Jane. Almost.

Because with sunset, and the thought of a hot supper, came a shift in the wind.

"Barometer's dropping something sharp, sir." Mr. Whitely shook his white head and looked out at the sea. "Something's brewing, but I can't tell where. Don't like these southern typhoons. Not like Atlantic hurricanes that always come roaring out of the southeastern ocean. Never can tell where they'll come from here, nor where they're likely to blow."

Dance strove for stoic calm. "I doubt we'll get a typhoon, Mr. Whitely. This quadrant of the Pacific is notable for their absence."

Whitely was not convinced. "That may be so, sir, but that doesn't explain the drop in the glass."

A sharp check at the barometric glass showed Dance that the pressure was as low as he had ever seen it, but he was the captain, and it would not do to be seen faltering. "Let us not borrow trouble, Mr. Whitely. Alter the course north toward west, and shake out these sails while the wind remains steady."

Pipes shrilled and topmen scrambled out on the horses to loose the reef points on the course, and set the topsails to let *Tenacious* run before the wind rising out of the south.

"Don't like it, sir." Flanaghan joined Mr. Whitely in frowning at the gray line of the sky. "Shouldn't blow out of the south this time of year."

Dance didn't like it either, but kept his peace instead of worrying aloud like an old soothsayer. But worry he did, especially when it began to blow harder and harder, stronger and stronger, with the winds shifting to come at them out of the southeast like an Atlantic hurricane, pushing the ship westward off course. And with that stormy wind came the following seas that forced him to alter course farther to the west so they could once again run before the wind, or risk working open the ship's bows.

But time and tide, and whatever luck had kept them afloat thus far, were slowly running out. The storm turned into a gale that did not abate upon the storm-washed upper decks, nor in the intrigue-ridden lines on the berth deck. Because below decks, Ransome renewed his campaign of discontent.

"It's as if the sea itself knows that Captain Muckross don't belong," Dance heard as he made his silent way to the bows to check on the state of the hull.

"Wouldn't be surprised if him that calls himself captain did him in. Nobody saw what went on in that room, now, did they?"

"Mr. Denman did," someone protested.

"He's one of them," a different voice scoffed.

And while he was prepared to take whatever insults that were flung his or Jack Denman's way, Dance was entirely unprepared to hear them resume their persecution of Jane.

"This is what comes from having a woman aboard." One low grating voice rose above the others—the unmistakable growl of Ransome.

Dance paused on the orlop deck's fore platform, and motioned the newly promoted bosun, Morris, to silence.

Another voice joined in. "She's the one that done it.

Last one to see the captain alive, she was." Ransome's former mate, the disrated Larson.

"But she's pretty, and nice," another man objected. "She made a poultice that cured me of my itch."

"You just got fleas. Should have put her off at Rio, or left her at the cape. Marooned her there to take her chances, like in the olden days."

"In the olden days they would have taken her for a witch, and drowned her in a sack like a black cat."

The icy fury that poured through his veins was rage, pure and barely controlled. He all but leaped up the ladder. "I'll have the next man that speaks lashed up to a grate myself." He tried to make his voice cutting and controlled, but even he could hear the echo of his roar bounce off the close, curved walls. "If you have no work, then I'll find work for you. Morris, put these men to the pump. Ransome, get your sorry arse topside, where I'm sure I can find plenty of work for you chipping ice off the running tackle."

Ransome refused to be intimidated. He looked Dance dead in the eye and said, "You'll come to regret this, sir. Damned if you won't."

"Ransome, I regret almost everything about this cruise, most especially not putting a bullet in you when I had the chance. Don't tempt me any further. If you want to live, you'll work to keep this ship afloat."

Because the bloody breastworks were quite literally working themselves apart. With every wave that torqued the ship over and up and down all at once, and the force from the wind in the sails—necessary to keep them running before the wind—were pulling the seams of the ship apart.

The ship was dying—committing suicide just as assuredly as the captain had.

Dance sprinted back and forth, from the bows topside. "Take another reef in the main course. And roust anyone not currently employed to pump," he ordered Morris. "Mr. Whitely, what is your opinion?"

"Bad, Captain. The barometer can't get any lower. The storm shows no signs of abating. And I'm afraid we're losing the helm."

Indeed the storm seemed to be strengthening. Dance took the helm from the stoic quartermaster to get a feel for the sea and the ship. The vessel was sluggish and unresponsive.

"Dragging, sir," the helmsman gave his opinion. "As if we were trailing all our anchors at the bow."

Fuck all. The ship was nearly wallowing in the troughs of the rolling swells throwing them up and down, up and over and down. They needed more canvas to pull the hull up and over them, but the more canvas they spread, the greater the force upon the bows, the more the ship would work itself apart.

"Call all hands." He knew the men were exhausted, but there was nothing else to be done. The pumps had to be manned and the sails adjusted. They could not slacken their efforts at all until the danger had passed, and he had done absolutely everything he could. "We haven't used up all our tricks. We're going to fother it. Mr. Whitely, I want an oakum-packed studding sail fothered up, and placed over the exterior of the hull where the bows are working loose, to slow the flooding."

"Ransome." He called to the man he had kept on deck, within his sights at all times. "Get a working party at the bows to pump in rotation. All the lubbers and wasters, starboard and larboard alike, watch on watch. No one is to be spared."

"Not even your Miss Burke?"

"She is not my Miss Burke. She is the Royal Society's Miss Burke, and she has been helping both Mr. Denman, who has also volunteered his services to take care of this crew, and the stewards to see to the men."

But he also took Ransome's words for the warning they were. And set off to find her.

Jane could not sit idle. When the word came that even the party of naturalists were needed to take their turn at manning the pumps, Jane went down to the orlop deck pump room to be counted among them.

But Dance would not hear of it. He came charging down the orlop ladder and carried her bodily up the two flights to the gun deck and the captain's cabin, where he deposited her like a sack of grain on a quay. "Stay here," he growled at her, just as impatiently as he had that very first day she had come aboard, as if he did not know her at all. As if they had not become friends.

She was not a dog to be ordered to sit or stay. She had given up that kind of mindless obedience that had kept her chained to her home and her family for so many years. And she would not take it up now. "Captain, I've been down on the orlop in the sick bay nearly every day."

"No." He rebuffed every argument with a single word. "This is different."

"How? Why may I not be useful?" They had not spoken in days, and now all she got from him was this angry order, as if she had somehow offended him. "I was only trying to help."

"I know. But you'll help me a lot more by staying here. Do some of my work if you need something to do. Only stay out of trouble."

"Trouble?" This was too like the old Dance, the stony lieutenant who had wanted her inconvenient presence off his deck. "Don't be ridiculous. You know I am—"

He cut off her words—and her very air—with his mouth, picking her up and all but driving her into the wall. His kiss was hard and demanding, with a sort of ferocious, mindless hunger that smothered all rational thought. He surrounded her with his hands and his body and his mouth. And she wanted him. Wanted this sign of his care.

Jane's hand stole up his neck. His skin was damp with the chill of the rain, and he tasted cool and fresh. He leaned his weight into her, pressing her back into the wall, pinning her there with the sharp force of his possession.

Jane felt something hot and needy slide beneath her skin. She heard her own breath come faster, felt the harsh warmth of his exhalation against her neck.

He put his thumbs along the edge of her jaw and exerted enough pressure to open her mouth. His tongue swept in and took hers, tangling and knotting her up inside and out. She had to catch at his coat for balance. His big hands cradled her skull, while his tongue ravaged her mouth, giving her solace and incentive all at once.

"Please," he groaned against her ear, his breath ragged and hoarse from shouting orders over the wind, but gentle compared to the rough strength of his hands. She could feel the weight and length of his arousal pressing into her, making heat and something that had to be want pool low in her belly, and between her legs. "For pity's sake, Jane, please stay. Because I cannot afford to worry about you on top of everything else. I will not be able to do my job when all I can think is that I want you safe. Damn your eyes"—he kissed her lids to give lie to the oath—"for once stop trying to manage everything, and do as you're told. If you have an ounce of pity in you, do this for me."

And as if he knew he had said too much, and not enough all at the same time, he kissed her so hard she felt the jolt all the way to her toes.

Then he slammed his way out of the stern cabin until his footfalls were drowned out by the louder noise of the rain streaming onto the open deck in the waist.

And with that she let go of her pride and slid down the

wall to the floor. And was left to contemplate the sight of the monstrous-looking gray-green waves of water that seemed to rise up above the stern gallery windows as if they were about to swallow *Tenacious* whole. Jonah inside the whale.

Chapter Seventeen

There was no respite. The wind picked up another knot if anything, and the amount of icy sleet pouring down upon them was nearly as great as the amount of water pouring through the bow. And it became more and more apparent that they would make it out of the tempest with their lives, only if every man jack of them pulled together and did their jobs.

And if the damn breastworks held.

If the carpenter and the men's incessant work to keep the Pacific Ocean from pouring in through the seams at a rate faster than it could be pumped out was working.

Dance was about to make another trip below, to measure the state of things with his own eyes, when Able Simmons stepped up instead.

"I'll go. You're needed here."

"Thank you, Mr. Simmons." And he had rather keep an eye on the patched foremast, which showed signs of weakening as a result of the incessant strain from the standing rigging of the weakened bowsprit. Though made up of many different, individual component pieces, the ship was only as strong as her weakest part, because it was all tied together into a cohesive whole.

And no sooner had he thought it than a great cracking

sound rent the frozen air, and the whole of the foremast gave way in a splinter of pine. A welter of twisted lines, backstays and halyards, collapsed forward, crashing and tangling with the bowsprit, and carrying it down into the ravenous, clawing waves.

There was no time to even curse. "All hands! Clear away! Get an ax, man," he screamed at a sailor running in the opposite direction, and had to physically shove the man toward the tools locker. "Clear it off. Cut away. Cut away!"

He was at the rail himself, chopping his way through the tangle of fallen rigging, mentally unraveling it like a skein, trying to find the salient line to cut first, to clear the weight dragging over the port forequarter, and making the ship lurch to larboard so that she was taking the pounding of the waves full abeam, pushing them relentlessly into the wall of water on the sides of the troughs.

The pounding rhythm of the axes matched the pounding of his heart, and the relentless pummel of the rain. His arms ached, and still there was more to be done. "Flanaghan, see what you can do to take another reef in the main and mizzen courses and topsails. But send only your best, most experienced men. And tell them to go handsomely."

But the reports started coming in fast and furious.

Ransome came to the quarterdeck at a run, with a look like nothing Dance had ever seen before—wild-eyed and almost as frightened as an infant midshipman and not a twenty-year veteran. "Captain. She's taking on more water than we can pump. The men are in it up to their waists."

Where was Simmons?

"She's settling heavy in the bow," Ransome pleaded. "There's nothing more can be done."

Dance wouldn't believe it. His gaze went immediately to the helmsmen who were all but wrestling the wheel to keep the vessel on course. "Mr. Whitely?"

The sailing master looked older than all his years. "Wallowing like a stuck pig, sir. She's going."

So she was.

For a moment his brain wouldn't believe it. But the cold truth of the matter was that his ship was going down.

Jane.

No. He had more than eighty other souls to think of before Jane Burke—she was safe in his cabin. He had to do what was right for all of them.

But still he could not stop himself. "Send word to Punch to go to the captain's cabin. Mr. Lawrence, keep them clearing away as much as you can. Make preparations to abandon ship—handsomely, quietly—so we can get the davits working, and at least two boats in the water before I call all hands to abandon ship."

He wanted to be sure before he gave the order. He wanted to walk from one end of the ship to the other, looking and taking full account. He wanted to see for himself, and count each man, from Able Simmons in the bows, to the last of the midshipmen working like dogs on the orlop.

Heels clattered on the ladders as the men streamed upward past him, going in the other direction. Down across the waist he went, and down to the berth deck where the floors were awash with a thin but steady steam of water. And farther down, to the orlop platform where the water was up to his knees before he had even reached the bottom of the ladder.

And where Able Simmons was crawling through the wash toward him on hands and knees, with blood streaming from a ghastly gash across the right side of his skull.

"Able!" Dance hauled him up, and slung the lieutenant's arm across his shoulders. "You there," he called upward to the first man he saw. "Mr. Simmons is injured. Get him to Mr. Denman."

"No," Simmons croaked. "Not injured. Struck. There was a claw—a lever—thrown down in the fore peak.

Someone had gone at the bows with it." He strained to get the words out. "Pulled out all the stops and plugs"—he was gasping as his strength failed, and his breathing grew labored—"and caulking that the carpenter had put in. Someone deliberately"—another passing breath—"damaged the hull."

Fuck, fuck, fuck all.

Someone of his crew was deliberately trying to sink his ship. Deliberately trying to kill a superior officer by coshing him over the head, and leaving him to drown at the bottom of the hull. Rage boiled through his blood, making his voice dark with seething anger. "Who?"

"Couldn't— From behind—" Simmons slumped heavily against Dance's chest, out cold from the deadly combination of cold, blood loss, and the blow to his head.

The rage ripping through Dance's chest was such that he was sure he was going to kill the next man who so much as crossed him. Devil take him, but he wanted it to be Ransome. Only Ransome had the bloody, mutinous disrespect to strike a superior officer—hadn't he almost done so the first day Dance had come aboard? And only Ransome had the strength to do such a savagely efficient job of it.

Dance dragged Simmons up the ladder to the berth deck, where he found Denman and his assistants carrying up his boxes of medical supplies. Jack paused, but behind the surgeon the three other naturalists hustled up the aft ladder.

"He'll have to be carried to the boat," Denman judged with one finger at the pulse on Simmons's neck. "I've sent everything that could be carried up already. Is there really nothing more that can be done?"

The deck slid precipitously to larboard, and a wave of frigid water spewed down upon them from the open companionway.

"Nothing." Damn it to hell.

There was really nothing left for Dance to do but gather his necessary things—compass, sextant, log, and Jane—and pray to a God he had long since stopped believing to see them through it safely.

Jane could not do as he asked. Perhaps the habit of obedience had gone out of her, or perhaps she was too tired, taut with exhaustion and the terrible brittle tension of worry, to sit still. And not even the incessant rain could drown out the noises—the creaks and moans of the ship's timbers as she strained and fought against the wind and waves, and the desperate shouted orders and frantic calls from the men.

She could not sit, but neither could she stand—the ship's movements were so fitful, and the deck seemed to slant downward to larboard. Jane braced herself between the stanchion and the batten wall, and waited, though she knew not for what.

And then she knew. She heard Dance's voice through the canvas-covered vent in the ceiling above, low but forceful above the wail of the storm. "—give the order to abandon ship."

Abandon ship. Jane jerked to her feet with the sluggish surge of fear and prickling energy, and the necessity to do something, anything, other than stand there waiting for someone to come and get her. She was J. E. Burke, the conchologist, a scientist and a woman of learning and skill. She was not some drooping damsel. She was not helpless.

She went to the doorway, and found it empty—the sentry had already abandoned his position. And so would she. But the sight of the streaming cold rain and the dark gray water looming outside the stern gallery windows had her heading down to the wardroom to retrieve her hat and cloak. They would at least afford her some protection against the violent weather.

The servant Manning was coming out of the wardroom

with Sir Richard, the Reverend Phelps, and Mr. Parkhurst right behind.

"Miss Burke, we must go," said Sir Richard. "We must go up." His urgent concern and the jittery state of his own fear was evident in his strained voice.

But the naturalists already had their coats and hats. "Yes, I'm coming," she said as she brushed past them. "I'll be right behind you." She did not wait for their say-so, but lunged into her cuddy, to snatch her cloak and hat off the peg on the wall.

Her eyes fell on her sea trunk. It would be the work of a moment to take a few things—some of the foodstuffs she had kept in her personal store. They were only God knew where in the middle of the Pacific Ocean, and very far away from any hope of rescue. They would need every crumb of food they could take.

She threw back the lid to search for the small tin of biscuits and the wheel of hard cheese, along with the dried fruit and nuts she had purchased only weeks ago in the sunny market at Recife.

How long ago that seemed.

But the lamp over the wardroom table was swinging wildly to and fro, and she could not see as well as she would like in order to find the small cotton sack to stuff the foodstuffs into.

The lamplight flickered once more, and then at once the whole of the wardroom was plunged into darkness. "Manning?" she called to still the stab of uneasiness that pierced the roaring black silence.

But there was no answer, and when she turned to grope her way to the door of her cuddy, she found it locked.

Her door was locked. From the outside.

She rattled the handle harder, and then harder still, as disbelief and shock rattled and echoed through her like a clap of thunder.

"Manning." Jane pounded upon the door and then the dividing wall. "Manning!"

Nothing.

Jane fought against the urge to scream. She settled for yelling at the top of her lungs. "Open this door. Please. Manning!" She pounded the flat of her palms against the walls. "Help me. Please." Her voice trailed off into a pitiful howl. "Dance!"

Dance was the last one off the deck. He had left the quarterdeck only to venture to his cabin for Jane, his box of instruments, and his logbook. He took the latter two from his locked sea chest, where he had stored them as a precaution after Jane's allegations concerning Ransome and the ransacking of their cabins. But such things hardly mattered now. He jammed the logbook tightly inside his coat. He wasted a few precious moments looking for Captain Muckross's logs, which he had left out on the table, where he had been studying them, but which were now nowhere to be found.

And neither was Jane.

Punch would have taken her up already. He could rely upon Punch, bless his ginger beard.

"Miss Burke?" the one-legged steward echoed Dance's query, while he tried to hustle him out the door, shoving his sea cloak into his hands, and taking up the box of instruments. "Already up, I should imagine."

"You didn't take her?"

"Already gone, when I came in. She's a clever girl, that lass. We'll find her at the boats."

Dance followed him up to the rail, but he could not but stop, and take one last lingering look around, knowing it would be on his watch and upon his head that the ship had gone down, despite all his work and personal expense to patch up the leaking hull.

All to no avail.

But he had gotten everyone safely off—even injured Lieutenant Simmons, and broken-armed Flanaghan.

But it was still a defeat—his captaincy had not even lasted a fortnight. *Tenacious* was reduced to the large cutter, two workboats, and the captain's gig crammed with eighty-four men and five naturalists.

But he counted only four. Where was she? Where was Jane?

He pushed the rain out of his eyes, and scanned the four boats. "Count heads, Mr. Ransome." Dance felt like he was screeching to be heard above the shriek of the wind and the pummeling din of the rain against the water. "Keep those boats together. Lash those lanterns high so they can be seen," he ordered Morris in the stern of the smaller gig. "I don't want to lose anyone now."

"All accounted for, Mr. Dance." Mr. Ransome stood in the stern of the small gig, with men Dance recognized as loyal to the bosun. He couldn't like the sight of so many of Ransome's cronies crowded together—it boded ill— but he would see to a better distribution of the men as soon as he found . . .

The naturalists were parsed out two in the cutter, and two in one of the workboats, where Denman was hunched over Simmons, trying to shelter the injured man, and wrap a bandage around his head. Damn, but they had their work cut out for them to find their way in such a storm, and keep such a badly wounded man alive.

But his eyes could not find what they were so desperately seeking. "Where is Miss Burke?"

He had directed the question at Punch, who turned to look over the boats in vain until his eye came to rest upon Manning, who was taking shelter behind Ransome's bulk in the stern of the gig.

"Manning," Punch called. "Manning, you said—"

Whatever Manning might have said was drowned out

either by the wind, or by the sound of sheer unmitigated panic that roared out of Dance in a wave of unholy fury.

"Where is she?" He was screaming at the men now. All of them, damn their selfish, cowardly hides.

Because she wasn't there. She wasn't in any of the four boats.

Dance's feet were already taking him back up the sloping deck by the time he understood what it was he was doing. Going back for her. Risking his neck, and the necks of his men, who would be counting upon him to lead them.

Fuck them. One of them had struck Simmons. And one of them might have done the same to his Jane. Nothing mattered but that he find her.

He would jeopardize everything—his men, his career, and his own life to save her. He could do no less. "Jane!"

Only fools rush in where angels fear to tread—he was no angel, so that made him doubly the fool, but he was too full of the rage-fueled rush of blood through his veins to pause and think better of what he was to do.

He fought his way up the slope of the deck and then down the dangerously canted ladder to his cabin. He had told her to stay there—she was a smart girl and would have listened. Should have listened, damn her ears. But she was not there, though he screeched like a frigate bird, shrieking on the wind. "Jane!"

There were only two other places in the ship where she could reliably be found—one was the orlop sick bay. And it was already under water.

Pray God that she had not gone there to get something to assist Mr. Denman.

The image of Simmons, his head dripping in blood, rose before him, and all he could do was picture Jane the same. Whoever had had the bloody hanging temerity to strike an officer would have no hesitation in hitting an easy mark like Jane. She could be lying anywhere, out cold, with the dark wash of water swirling silently about her bloodied head.

But he couldn't search the whole of the ship—half of it was already gone. But the pain—the sheer bloody panic—was like a cutlass across his chest.

Dance flung himself down the aft companionway. The ship had pitched herself downward from the bow, so he still held out hope that the wardroom might be high enough. But by the time he had grappled his way down the ladder, and across the shifting berth deck, Dance knew it was too late. His boots were awash before his head cleared the combing, and he was in it up to his waist before his feet ever made it to the deck below.

But he couldn't stop his feet from surging forward, pushing his way through the icy water, calling all the while he thrashed his way through the wardroom door. "Jane? Jane!"

He paused for a second to try and listen, to hear anything above the rush of water and the cracks and groans of the ship settling ever faster.

It was faint—the barest remnant of desperation. "Please!"

The ship canted hard to starboard, and the rush of water down the companionway was like a wave, pushing him forward. Dance dove into the darkness, half swimming his way aft, pushing against stanchions and doors that were working their way loose as the ship around him died by degrees.

He knocked his head hard against the wardroom table, stunning him for one long, useless moment before he could think enough to move, and fight his way around a floating chair. He thought he saw something—a slick flash of light reflecting off her pale skin. And there it was—her arm reaching through a rip in the batten wall, scrabbling to try and reach the door handle.

Then the ship rolled high on a bow wave, and came

down more heavily, rolling to starboard, tilting around him as the horizon of water within stayed level for only a few seconds before it began sloshing and resounding off the walls, rippling back upon him in irregular waves. And the door before him was lost in the black swirl of water.

Chapter Eighteen

The frigid water fell over her head like an icy black blanket, closing out all sensation and sound for one endless numbing moment.

And the suffocating terror hit her as she went under, and hit again when she tried to rise to the surface, but found only ceiling beams. She scratched and clawed along the long grooves of the seams, but she found no way out. No way to rise farther. No air.

No.

In the frigid darkness she could see nothing but a faint glimmer of light reflecting through the black water, and the hole she had clawed in the tough, painted canvas of the walls. She grabbed at the torn edges again, trying to rip the canvas apart—enough so she might break through and escape. She had to escape. She had to. God couldn't be so cruel as to make her die, cold and alone in the frigid dark.

But her numbed hands slipped. She could get no purchase. Nothing, though she tried and tried again, reaching through the hole to find something to hold on to—something that would help her. Anything.

Anything.

But there was nothing. And she was becoming slower

and clumsier and stupider with each increasingly frantic attempt.

The suffocating pressure in her chest expanded into an ache, and then into a single sharp blade of pain that withered within her as it died out. And then the last flicker of light died. And there was no more.

Her mouth came open because she could not stop it, and the cold salt water rushed in. She swallowed and swallowed, and choked on the harsh rasp of the brine burning down her throat. And then she couldn't swallow any more.

Her mind spoke to her within her head, and said, *It is done. It is over. This is what it is to drown.*

And then there was nothing but pain.

Not in her head, or her heart, or lungs.

But in her arm, wrenched from the socket as her shoulder slammed into the wall. And then another pain as her temple cracked hard against a beam as she was hauled past, borne to the bottom with the pieces of ship wrecking by her.

And then heat. Warmth against her. A body, moving and strong.

Dance.

It had to be Dance. The answer to her prayers. It could be no one else.

But she was past thought, past anything but hideous animal instinct. She scrabbled at him, frantic and clawing as he hauled her upward, trying to push herself above him—push herself to the air and the solidity of his shoulders. His hands closed around her wrists, and held her fast, but she fought him. Fought to push herself upward toward the blessed air.

Their heads broke to the surface, but she could not get the air into her lungs.

His voice came from far away, muffled like an echo from a spent storm rumbling toward her. "I have you. I have you."

Jane did not know how she heard him with the roar of the water, and death groans of the ship cracking and shuddering all around them, and the hissing crackle of the air foaming up the black water, turning it opalescent, like ice.

But her head was above water—she could feel the stark slap of the chill air against her skin. But still she couldn't breathe.

She opened her mouth to draw air in but couldn't, until the painfully sharp pressure of her lungs reasserted itself, and she retched, choking and gasping against the acid rasp in her throat.

God, it burned. It burned, the cold wet air, but she gulped it down gratefully. Greedily. Stupidly.

"I have you."

He did, and she clung to him as he hauled her like a great fish toward the dim glimmer of light. His hat floated by, and she just stared at it, unable to form the words in her head to present to her tongue. She could do nothing but breathe and breathe and hold hard to the sure solidity that was him—that was her Dance.

He had saved her. At least he was trying to.

And he was the one doing all the work. He pulled her up beneath the ventilation hatch in the wardroom ceiling, and wrestled the hatch cover off. And then he was boosting her up, pushing her roughly over the hatch combing.

Her hip landed hard on the lip of wood. She would be bruised everywhere. She felt battered and heavy, sodden from the weight of the water sucking her below. But she was still alive.

For now.

"Come." Dance was beside her, hauling her up by her sodden clothing. "Come on, damn you. Don't you give up on me, now," he roared at her over the din of the rain and wind, blazing away at her with that ferocious scowl.

She had never been so glad to have someone angry at her in her entire life.

Because of him, she was still alive. The pain in her

lungs and the ache in her throat were enough to tell her so, had not the man she clung to been so warm and alive, and so very angry at her for almost dying on his ship.

Which was still sinking.

He half carried, half dragged her up another two sets of ladders, and over to the larboard rail, where the loose lines in empty davits lashed in the wind like whips.

"Morris! Lawrence!" Dance howled into the wind. "Ransome!"

Jane could see nothing beyond the small circle of light that came from a single lamp near the abandoned helm. Above, the few sails that remained flapped uselessly in the wind and rain, the last fluttering gasp of the ship as the wind drove her farther and farther under.

"Ransome," Dance bellowed into the night. "Damn, damn, damn his eyes, where is he?"

Jane followed the line of his gaze but she could see nothing but pitch-black water. Inboard the ship, there wasn't much more to see. The waist was awash with black waves. The vessel had obviously been abandoned, and as they stood clinging to the rail, the forecastle went completely under. A spume of white foam—water and air escaping from the porous old hull—rose across the waist. The ship lurched drunkenly to larboard, tipping the rail down toward the rapidly rising water.

"The damn boats are gone." He was yelling, though she was right there, clinging to his chest like a limpet, as he hauled them up the steeply sloping deck toward the taffrail, where the aft portion of the ship was still above the dark, churning water.

And then she saw it—her pinnace slapping uselessly against the stern. "My boat!" Jane loosed her hold of his coat enough to point. "There," was all she could articulate, as she pointed toward the vessel as it began to be pushed up and outboard by the roiling spume.

"Fuck me. Yes." Dance was reaching for the lines

securing the davit while still keeping his arm clamped securely across her chest like an iron band to keep her from flailing. "Grab hold."

It was everything Jane could do to make her cold, clumsy limbs obey her mind's commands, and let go of him so he could loosen the lines to lower the dangling pinnace into the water.

And then he picked her up, sweeping her into his arms and lofting her over the rail. She shrieked and threw her arms around his neck, afraid to let go again. Afraid of the dark water swallowing her whole again.

"Jump," he instructed. "I'm right behind you."

But she couldn't. She couldn't submit herself to the water again.

Finally he had to let go of her, and pry her arms off, and push her away, his big hand planted solidly between her shoulder blades, propelling her downward.

Jane screamed, and jumped because she had to, flinging herself wildly at the bobbling boat. She landed hard, cracking her ribs against the side. She would be nothing but bruises from head to toe. If she didn't drown. Her legs were in the water, and her skirts and the damn cloak were heavy and pulling her back down into the frigid depths.

She slipped, losing her grip, and her head went under for one awful moment. The water rushed into her ears, shutting everything out, and she could feel herself start to thrash and fight again.

Jane kicked hard, scrambling back up over the side, fighting with every ounce of strength she had left. Which wasn't much. She could feel her will leeching out as the cold water soaked in.

And then Dance's big hand clamped itself into her arm. And then his other hand fisted in the sodden material of her cloak and dragged her up. The two of them landed atop the tarpaulin cover like an ungainly haul of fish.

She lay splayed there helplessly for a few moments like

that ungainly fish, gasping for air, while poor Dance, strong and skilled and thinking, desperately freed the lines.

And then they were free and afloat.

"Unlace the boat cover." He punched a finger at the tight tarpaulin. "You need to move. Move!"

So she did, tearing at the tight lacing that had held the tarpaulin snug and dry, and kept her gear safe and secure.

"Oars?"

She did not bother to attempt to speak, but wormed her way under a corner of the canvas cover, and wiggled her way underneath, groping her way in the darkness to find the oars stacked just where she had left them, atop the railed wooden platform of the well with the rudder board and tiller.

Jane rolled to her knees and handed them up to Dance, and then began to yank down the tarpaulin so he could put the oars to the rowlocks.

"No," he yelled over the screech of the wind. "Only halfway. We'll need the protection."

He was right. If the stormy seas had tossed *Tenacious* about, and filled her decks with running sleet, there would be no escape from the wind and cold without the canvas cover.

Jane did what she could to flatten the tarpaulin so Dance could row them clear of the maw of tangled rigging that swung down toward them, threatening to drag them back under as the ship settled ever farther under the waves.

And somehow he did it. He kept rowing even when they were clear of the ship and in no danger of the swirling vortex of air and waves. Jane kept her eyes upon *Tenacious* until that last lantern hung by the wheel was snuffed out, and blackness of night descended upon them, and she could see nothing. Not even the boat around her. She could feel the floorboards beneath her knees and hands. Feel the smooth, polished wood of the long familiar rail beneath her hands, and the rough rasp of the tarpaulin at her back, but every other sensation was drowned out by the howl of the wind and the engulfing blackness of the night.

She groped out in the empty dark. "Dance?" Her voice sounded battered and torn—unraveling with fright.

"Here," she thought he said. Or maybe he didn't, but his big hand found her, and scooped her toward his chest, and held her there against him in the bottom of the well. She clung to him, this live, human piece of flotsam, holding herself to his warmth, hoping some of the heat that seemed to blaze from him would seep into her.

Which made it difficult for the poor man to see to the boat, but she couldn't seem to let go. He carried on somehow, using his other arm to secure the tarpaulin cover back over the cockpit well to keep as much as possible of the freezing rain and waves out.

"Can you see any light? I need you to look." His voice seemed to come to her through his chest, and she pushed herself up next to him, and tried to scan the black water in the opposite direction from where he was looking, peering hard through the gloom to try and make out some sign of light.

Jane saw nothing. Nothing but the white patch of foamy water where the ship had only moments ago been, and the ebb and flow of the tops of the whitecaps as the waves rose and fell endlessly around them.

"They can't be far," Dance said, as if he were talking to himself as much as her. "I ordered them to hove to, and wait. I think. But they should have done it anyway. Lawrence or Simmons—" His mutter died away for a long moment. "We need to keep the boats together. My damn compass, and instruments were on that bloody fucking gig."

His language, gritted out between clenched teeth, was enough to shock her into action. There ought to have been a compass stored somewhere forward in the little boat's bow. She had packed all such equipment that would be necessary to recording the precise location of each and every shell she had planned to find. But shell collecting seemed a rather far-off, superficial thing now. They needed to stay alive in a small boat at sea.

To that end, Jane made herself detach her arm from around the poor lieutenant's neck, so she might make her blind way under the tarpaulin in search of the instrument box. She had ordered the compass, sextant, and glass through correspondence, and it had come all the way from the famous instrument maker Mr. Josiah Culmer in Wapping, near London. She had stowed it under the curved bench seat on the larboard side, if she recalled correctly, because she had thought that equipment needed to be accessible from the tiller. And there it was. She dragged out the small wicker case.

"Compass," was all she said when she pushed it toward him.

Because she was done being away from him. Her clothes were heavy and sodden and cold, and only he radiated any warmth. She crawled back onto him, like a cat up a familiar tree, sinking into the solid comfort only he could give.

Jane couldn't imagine what the man made of her behavior, but he made no objection, only holding her tighter against him. "I've got you."

"Thank you." Jane didn't think he heard her—she could barely hear herself over the driving hush of the snowy wind. And her throat was so tight it ached from the harsh passage of the cold air. But Jane set herself to endure the pain. She was alive, thanks to Dance. He had come back to find her when no one else would. When another had quite deliberately locked her in.

"It was Manning," she told him, not because he could do anything about it at this point, but because she had to tell someone. And he was the only one. The only one who might even care. "Manning locked me in and left me."

Dance let out a curse so visceral and colorful, Jane was surprised the air around him didn't light up with blue sparks. And his rage was so magnificent and heartfelt, it made her want to cry. Heat built like a bonfire behind her eyes and in her throat.

She felt ravaged. Aching, worn down and numbed by the cold. She could feel the helpless hopelessness creep over her, like a killing frost. Her will was withering away with every toss of the boat beneath her.

"Shh." Dance pulled her closer somehow. "I came back. I wasn't going to let you die."

Jane thought she felt the firm comfort of his lips press against her forehead, and when she looked up at his beautifully harsh face shrouded from her by the dark, she knew that if she were going to die out in the middle of the cold, open ocean, she wasn't going to die without having kissed Charles Dance.

He had kissed her, and given her comfort in the privacy of his cabin, but she wanted to be the one doing the kissing. She wanted to give him comfort, to show him how she felt, and what he meant to her—the gratitude and grace and admiration and respect and need all rolled into one.

So she wrapped her arms around his long neck, and pulled his lips down to hers.

That was almost all she could do, but the taut skin of his lips was warm and giving and comforting, and his hand came round to cradle the back of her head, holding her close. His long fingers seemed to span her skull, and his thumb brushed along her cheek, pushing her sodden hair out of her eyes, and tilting her face up to him so he could draw her lip into his mouth, gently caressing, and pressing warmth and heat into her.

He held her so carefully, stinging heat built again behind her eyes, and threatened to spill down her wet cheeks.

She didn't want careful and courteous. She didn't want soft and sweet. She wanted heat and warmth and needy, hungry life.

Something of her desperation communicated itself to him, or maybe he felt as cold and shattered as she, because his kiss slowly became more. More insistent. More ardent—a fiercer pressure that tipped her head back, and urged her to open her mouth.

His tongue found hers, tangling and tasting until her head spun with the swirling desire, and she felt ravaged and adrift, and saved and secure all at the same time.

This man, this aloof, sarcastic, stony man, was nothing but heat and need and pity.

Oh, God, the pity—this was all they would have of each other now that they were cast adrift to die. She could feel his desperate pity even though he said nothing, but continued to kiss and hold her fast.

"Dance." It was a rebuke and an exhortation. She pressed the word into the raspy skin of his cheek, holding herself fervently into him, wanting to feel everything she could, to hold on to life and love and heat, and be alive while she could. While she still cared that she *was* alive.

Because she was losing hope that it would last. Losing hope that they would live.

And he somehow seemed to understand that.

"Jane." His voice in her ears was the answer to a prayer she had not even known she had prayed—the secret yearning of her silent heart. But to hear her name from his lips, to have it whispered in her ear, was everything she wanted. Everything she needed to push her forward. She could close her mind and pretend, she could cling to the desperate lie that they were fine, that they were anywhere but abandoned in the middle of the ocean.

It was irrational, she knew. A desperate fear lodged so

firmly inside she could not shake it loose. But no amount of self-chiding would silence the need to be in his arms. If she was holding on to him, and could feel the warmth and breadth of his live, living body, then she was alive too. He had rescued her when she could not rescue herself, and so she would not relinquish herself from his care.

But he did not complain. He did not say anything. He merely held on to her as if he knew he had to hold her together like a cracked vase—once the edges slipped apart she would collapse into nothing more than a pile of broken fragments.

But eventually there was nothing more she could do. There was not enough hope left in her to keep kissing him, and she was tired and exhausted from the effort to simply stay alive. So exhausted she didn't even have enough strength to cry.

She clung to him in exhaustion, plastered against his side as if she were one of her precious barnacles stuck fast to his hull. She felt small and nearly weightless, insignificant enough to be blown away by the howling wind. So he kept her tight against him.

And he kissed her, because there was no reason not to anymore. And because he wanted her to live. Because she tasted like cold and salt, and everything sweet and bitter and hopeless. He could feel the will drain out of her, as if she had exhausted all of her powers just to keep herself alive.

And it was nothing short of a miracle that she was still alive, and breathing in painful, shallow pants against his chest. Nothing short of a miracle that she had somehow floated into his arms down there in the flooded wardroom, when he had put his feet against the sides of the batten door, and torn the damn thing off its hinges.

The burning line of stinging pain at the top of his boot, just below his knee, told him that there had been something shoved into the latch to jam it shut—something long and sharp that cut through his breeches and dug into his flesh. Something like a handspike. Something only a sailor would know how to use.

Goddamn their superstitious eyes. Goddamn every last worm-brained one of them who had ever cast an evil glance her way. One of them had locked her in. One of them had left her to drown in the hull of the sinking ship.

Manning, she had said. Damn his eyes, if it were true that mild-mannered, scuttling Manning had tried to kill her. But she had been so sure. He had felt her hopeless rage in her scratching, fighting desperation when he had pulled her out of the water—the frantic clawing that would have sent him under had he not known her panic for what it was, and kept a firm, almost ruthless hold of her.

He would kill Manning. If he survived, he would hunt the skulking little rat of a man down, and choke the life from him, the same way Manning had tried to choke the life out of his Jane.

The thought filled Dance with such a murderous, helpless rage that he had to make himself loose his arms to keep from gripping her too tightly. But she didn't seem to mind—she held him just as tightly, afraid, even in exhausted sleep, to relinquish her hold.

So he cradled her against his chest. Whatever happened, he would not let her be alone in the dark again. He would let her cling to him just as assiduously as he clung to her, the proof that he was a man who could make a choice that went beyond duty.

Because his duty had floated away without him. The four other boats had disappeared into the dark of the night without a trace. Ransome, he reckoned, would have led them away by force of personality. Neither Doc Whitely nor young Lawrence would have been able to withstand his sort of forceful, violent persuasion—not without Able Simmons and Jack Denman, as well as Morris and Flanaghan, to back them up, and Denman likely had all he could handle just trying to tend to the ghastly gash on the back of Simmons's head.

Dance hoped to God that they had been able to stop the bleeding. Except that he didn't believe in God. It was only that he was exhausted, and afraid really, and didn't quite know where to turn. And Jane Burke was counting on him—clinging to him as if he were worth clinging to. As if she had confidence in him.

That made one of them.

He arranged the boat cover so only his head poked out into the dirty weather, and kept searching the dark for the lights from the boats, staring into the darkness until red and yellow spots danced across his vision like demons from the night.

He shut his eyes, and ducked beneath the cover for a momentary respite, shifting his legs so they lay alongside hers, and covered them both with their cloaks. The thick wool was sodden with water, but still it held some warmth, as did his wool uniform coat. Together they might be able to keep the two of them warm.

Together, they just might be able to keep each other alive.

Dance's leg bumped up against the stiff poke of a wicker case, and he remembered then what she had said. *Compass,* she had croaked at him, and shoved the case toward him, as if it were a gift.

He roused himself enough to see, and devil take him if that wasn't exactly what lay within, packed in straw for all these weeks and weeks, just waiting to be made useful.

In the pitch-black of the storm he could barely see the hand in front of his face, but he could make a rough reading of which way was north. They were entirely turned around from where he thought they would be. But with the wind hooking out of the southeast, it was impossible to go east into the wind, toward the mainland of South America, even if he managed to raise the nimble fore and aft sail. And to do so would only serve to expose them to the storm. Best to hunker down beneath the tarpaulin to stay as warm as possible, and let the wind and current take them where it would.

If they were still alive in the morning, he would think of what he ought to do next.

If they were alive and not swallowed whole by the ravenous sea.

Chapter Nineteen

Dance came awake with a jerk, and an ache in his neck, as well as a pain in his leg. All of which told him only one thing—he was alive. Painfully so.

Outside the thin cover of the tarpaulin, the light of dawn was gray and thin, the clouds still hung low over the water, weeping a steady rain that seeped under the tarpaulin cover, and chilled him to the bone.

He shook the creeping lethargy out of his head, and took stock. The wind had died down to a more general roar—enough so that he might sail the boat instead of just letting it float along at the will of the filthy weather.

He let go of Jane long enough to haul out and attach the tiller, but woke her in the noisy process. "How are you? Are you cold?"

Jane shook her head, and disappeared forward, crawling on her hands and knees along the floorboards under the small covered bow. For a moment Dance worried that she had gone off to be quietly sick away from him, but she made no sound, and presently came crawling back, and set about tenting the tarpaulin just so, so that the rainwater collected and ran downward into a collapsable canvas water bag.

Remarkable. Organized and efficient in the middle of nowhere after she had nearly been drowned.

When she had collected enough to drink, she asked, "May I have some?" in a voice so scratchy and dry, he caught himself swallowing in sympathy. "My throat feels as if it were on fire."

No doubt from all the seawater she had swallowed and regurgitated. "Of course."

But she only took a few sips—clearly she already understood the necessity of rationing the drinking water—before she passed it to him. He didn't know why he shouldn't have expected such self-disciplined practicality from her, but it moved him—made him think and admire and ache for her all at the same time. "No. Take as much as you need. But let us collect more."

Dance helped her set up more of her ingenious collapsable canvas pails to collect more fresh water, but in the process they were both exposed to more rain. Within moments Jane began to shiver so violently, and her movements became so uncoordinated, she nearly spilled the entire contents of the canvas pail.

"Let me. Come here." He wasted no time on explanation, but set up the pail, ducked under the cover, set his back to the low bench seat to one side of the cockpit well, and gathered her to him. He ensconced her on his lap, with her back to his chest, so she would be in the lee of his body, sheltered and protected as best he could.

She was stiff with cold and trembling, and he held her tight against him, with his hand wrapped around her middle, doing everything to keep them both warm.

"You're hard," she said, and Dance immediately felt like a guilty schoolboy caught out ogling a young lady, and only when he turned his mind to stripping off his wool uniform coat to wrap around her to keep warm, did he understand what she meant.

"It's my logbook." He had held her pressed against his chest, and therefore the solid bulk of his logbook, stowed securely inside his uniform coat. He had grown accustomed to it.

She looked at the beat-up and now slightly bent book for a long moment before she turned again to crawl forward under the low bow decking to fish out an oilskin pouch with some loose papers in it. "Drawing paper," she explained in her thin, raspy voice, as she drew them out. "But put your book in there, so it will be safe from the wet."

Always thinking, she was, always arranging things for other people's benefit.

He shoved the logbook into the pouch, and sealed it over, but said, "I'd rather keep you safe from the wet."

She nodded mutely, but instead of crawling back into his arms where he wanted her, she began to methodically and neatly stuff the wide sheets of thick rag drawing paper under her clothes as insulation.

It was a remedial, but brilliantly effective idea. Dance followed suit, taking some pages from her, and laying them flat between the still-damp layers of his clothing so the paper might absorb some of the chilling moisture. And when she became too tired and weak to finish smoothing the pages between her bodice and her stays, he took on the job. Only to help her. Not at all because he got an illicit thrill that heated his skin like a warming pan from smoothing his palms along the sweet, luscious curves of her body. Not at all.

But now that his own blood was pumping more enthusiastically through his veins, he got back to the business of warming her up, wrapping her in their cloaks to try and capture the combined heat of their bodies.

But perhaps instead of putting more layers of paper between them, perhaps he ought to take a few away. Perhaps he ought to shuck off his wet waistcoat, and damp linen shirt as well, so the heat of his body could warm her directly? And having her against his skin would assuredly warm him as well, would it not? Which would make it easier to warm and take care of her?

While Dance was talking himself into disrobing for her benefit, another idea that ought to have blistered his cheeks with shame, had not their situation been so desperate, insinuated itself into his lust-filled brain—he could warm her, damn him if he could not. He could warm her through and through.

He set his lips against the soft skin at the side of her pale, white neck, and whispered, "It will be all right, Jane. I promise." He kissed along the cool slide of her soft skin, nosing aside the damp curtain of her hair, while below, beneath the cloak, he set his left hand to making lazy, enticing circles low across her belly.

When she made no protest, he slid the fingers of his right hand through her soft blond hair where it streamed loose over her shoulder. He lifted it away, and indulged his need to taste her by kissing the vulnerable spot at the back of her neck that made her shoulders hunch, and her head roll back over his shoulder.

She was delicious. She tasted of salt and white flowers, still. Of sweet, vulnerable woman.

And with her head turned to the side, he could nuzzle his roughened cheek along the tight, sensitive tendons at the base of her neck, and slide his lips along the soft underside of her jaw. "I'm going to take care of you." He kissed the end of her nose, and tasted the musk-rose-scented warm spot beneath her ear. "Let me take care of you."

He set his teeth gently to the lobe of her ear. "And you'll tell me if you're still cold. You'll tell me if it isn't working."

She lay passively against him, with her eyes closed, but from his vantage point he could see down the front of her bodice, to the sweet valley between her breasts. And he knew he was going to touch them. Knew that even in the middle of the sea—especially in the middle of the sea—she was as close to heaven as he would ever get.

And he meant to take advantage of each and every moment he had with her.

Dance assuaged his guilt by reminding himself that she was cold, and he knew of no better means of warming her in the present circumstances than by arousal. And just the thought of doing so aroused him—his lungs felt tight and full all at the same time, and his skin began to tingle with familiar, anticipatory heat. "Jane."

He said her name like an incantation, a prayer that might save them both.

He ran the backs of his fingers down the exquisite curve of her neck to the hollow at the base where her pulse was gaining strength. "Yes. You'll like this," he promised. "It will make you warm. And sated. And happy."

She nodded against his neck. "Please."

He let his fingers explore farther south along the line of her bodice, barely brushing the ripe swell of her breasts until she shifted in his arms, and it was impossible not to cup the firm roundness in his hand. God, she was exquisite—full and sweet.

"Dance." Her voice held both question and plea.

"Yes," he assured her. He kneaded the plump flesh until a soft flush shaded her neck. And suddenly it wasn't enough to touch her over the barrier of her clothing—he wanted to feel her skin beneath his fingers, and know that his ministrations were doing their job, and heating from the inside out.

His hands went to the practical buttons at the top of her bodice, and undid them one by one until he could peel the edges of the fabric back, and see the thin white lawn of her shift peeking out from under her practical front-lacing stays. He loosed the tie of her shift, and tugged the edges down to expose the tops of her perfectly white breasts.

The sight of the creamy swells alone brought him to

full and aching erection. But when he peeled back the fabric to reveal the delicate pink tips, his own breath grew hot and unruly within his chest, and he had to shift beneath her to ease his arousal. She was so beautiful, pale and fragile, like a porcelain that needed to be handled with delicate, careful care, that he wanted to protect her with his body as well as his love.

So he touched her perfect pink breasts carefully, almost reverently, gently thumbing and tweaking her nipples into tight constriction, until her breath shivered out of her on an uneven sigh of pleasure.

His own sigh was the breath rushing from his body, as the pleasure that was almost a pain, from holding back his own desire, broke across him like a wave.

Her torso began to move restlessly beneath his hands, rising to counter the gentle pressure of his palms and fingers as he worked to arouse her, trying to give her the same pleasure that he got just by looking at her. Slowly, as if she were waking from a deep, troubled sleep, she began to undulate, the movement flowing sinuously through her body so there was no mistaking what she wanted, even if she did not yet know what that was.

He reached down to get a handful of her skirts, and fist up the long wet length of fabric, drawing the damp ends of skirts, petticoats, and shift up over the junction of her soft, cool thighs.

He pushed aside the damp fabric, concentrated all of his energy and remaining intelligence on getting it right. On touching her gently and carefully as he circled his thumbs on the vulnerable skin of her inner thighs. On readying her by trailing his fingers over the soft downy hair covering her mons. On waiting until she sighed and shifted restlessly within his arms, and eased her legs apart before he parted her folds and eased his finger within.

Her body was soft and warm and welcoming. And for a long moment, the painful pleasure of his own arousal was sharpened by the incandescent bliss of touching her so intimately.

"You're tight," he whispered into her ear, and wondered how he was going to control himself. But she was weak and exhausted, and struggling to stay alive, and only the basest of men would take advantage. And he was not the basest of men. He was an officer and a gentleman, and he could bottle up every ounce of heat and aching, frustrated passion he had to until the time was right.

"I'm sorry." He could hear the embarrassed confusion in the smallness of her voice.

"Don't be, Jane," he assured her. He turned his head to murmur into her ear, so she could feel the words hum through her, all the way down to where his fingers played upon her body. So they could feel the echoes of need and desire together, almost as one. "It's lovely. You're lovely. Perfect."

He slipped his finger inside her, touching her deeply, stroking lightly within her sweetly tight passage until her hips arced up into his hand. A wordless sound of breathless want and discovery flew from her mouth, and her breath started to come in heated gasps that blew warm against his cheek. Dance's own pulse was roaring in his ears as he slid another curious, questing finger alongside the first, and twisted his wrist so his thumb could graze ever so slightly against the hidden pearl just beneath her folds.

"Dance." Her eyes flew open, as did her mouth, forming a perfect O of shock and surprise, and her hand clamped upon his wrist, holding him still. "Dance."

"Shh," he murmured as he took her bottom lip, and sucked it tenderly between his own. "Too much, or not enough?"

"Too—" But her hips were moving, arcing into his hand, bringing his hand back into fleeting contact with her pearl.

"Yes," he assured her, as best he could, but his voice was tight and drawn, and his own breathing was just as fractured and gasping as hers, as if he had run up the shrouds.

"Yes. Just enough, Just—" And he moved his hand so that just the very tip of his callused finger brushed against her, and her body convulsed against him, and she was gone.

Jane came awake to daylight, and gray, overcast skies, warmer air, and the nearly overwhelming memory of Dance bringing her to ecstasy with his fingers.

Her body heated and tingled just at the thought, and she pushed herself upright. She had been sleeping on top of the starboard bench seat, where presumably Dance had placed her.

The object of her thoughts was standing in his shirt-sleeves in the middle of the boat putting up the small mast.

"Hello," he said, as if he were a casual acquaintance, and not the man who now had an intimate knowledge of her body.

"Hello," she answered, because she hadn't anything else to say. "Where are we?"

"That has yet to be determined. Can you by any chance do complicated mathematics in your head?"

Of course. She was a spinster scientist. She could do complicated sums in her sleep—at least she thought she could if she weren't being brought to shattering climax at the same time.

Another wash of heat scalding her skin had her turning away from the deep green intensity of his eyes to the flat gray expanse of the ocean stretching in every direction around them. There was nothing. But at least it wasn't sleeting or raining, although they might miss the water soon enough. "Some."

"Excellent. I do better with a bit of paper. Can't carry

figures in my head. I use a page in the back of my log normally, but though I've got the book, I made the mistake of not bringing pen and ink while the ship was sinking."

He had other talents that more than made up for this slight deficit. "But I have pens and ink, as well as paper. I packed a great supply for my drawing in waterproofed folding cases." She had ordered them made to her specification by the chandler in Cowes.

Jane pulled back the edge of the tarpaulin where it was still draped over the small covered bow and began her search. "It should be right . . . here. I packed everything—"

"Just so," he finished for her. "And so you did. For which"—he took the paper and uncut pencil from her hand, and put it on the bench seat while he went back to attaching the sails—"I remain eternally grateful. What else have you got in there?"

"Equipment. Collecting gear. Pails and nets. More paper and pen and ink. And a great many folded tarpaulins."

"Any food?"

"Some. Tinned biscuits. Salt. Flour. I'm afraid I left more food on the ship. I had gone to my cabin to get it."

"I wondered why you hadn't stayed put." He looked away out over the sea and back to her, as if assuring himself that she was still there. But mercifully, he did not rebuke her for not staying in his cabin as he had asked. Perhaps he knew she had already paid a very steep price for her disobedience.

"I should have known you would be so prepared and efficient," he said instead, almost praising her. "I have never been so glad that I violated all navy protocol in leaving your boat on the davits." He smiled at her—a genuine smile that gave her the first inkling of hope.

"So am I. We should have drowned otherwise."

"We didn't." His tone was emphatic, leaving no room for the slightest intrusion of argument. "So let's not think about it at the moment."

But the scowl etched between his brows as he scanned the endless gray horizon told her that was exactly what he was doing—thinking about the treachery of Manning, and the others who had not kept their boats nearby until Dance had brought her up to the deck.

He might want to find them and have his men near, but Jane was happier thinking them hundreds of miles away, or better yet, at the bottom of the gray brooding ocean where they belonged, God rot their souls.

But she kept her opinion to herself, as did he while he finished rigging the main sheet on the foot of the boom, and sat at the tiller to put the vessel into the wind.

"So if we don't know where we are," she asked, "how do we decide where we are going?"

"I do have some idea of where we are—vaguely. We are in the Southern Pacific. And judging from the air and water temperature, I should reckon we're somewhere above forty degrees of latitude, but that is only my guess, based on . . . dead reckoning. On instinct. And years of naval service."

But Jane couldn't seem to share his confidence. She didn't like looking out at the endless gray. She had much rather look at him instead. At the granite-hard line of his jaw. At the implacable surety that he projected from every inch of his taut body. "Seems sensible enough," she made herself say, though the words stuck in her throat. Mostly because her throat was dry and sore.

She scrubbed her tangled hair off her face, and tried not to think about wanting a drink of the precious water they had diligently collected through the storm. "How long do you think it will take for us to get . . . anywhere?"

He squinted at the horizon. "A month, to be safe. Take a drink of water."

Jane felt her heart plummet to her still damp shoes. "I don't think we have enough water for a whole month. Not unless it rains again."

"And it will. The air is heavy with moisture. So we will collect more water, and you can take a drink now." He spoke with that confidence, that surety that she wanted to lean on to keep her shaky hopes propped up.

While she took a few grateful gulps of the life-saving rainwater, he adjusted the sails. "But the consequence of the rain will be that without the sun to take a noon reading for the longitude . . . I can't yet make a plan." He sat, and Jane slid over, so he might have adequate room on the cockpit bench. "And so we sit."

But there didn't seem to be much else to say. "But as soon as we have sun you will be able to fix our position?"

"I will. As long as there is sun at noon. And you will do the mathematics just to be sure I get it right. At noon." He dug a watch out of the pocket of his waistcoat, and held it up to his ear before he opened it to check the mechanism. "And if this watch did not get too waterlogged and can still keep time. It was in my pocket, when we were . . . in the water."

"Do you mean while I was drowning?"

He heard the self-pitying despair she could not manage to keep from her voice, and spoke to counter it. "Yes."

He reached out to take her hand and held it, much as she had done in the wardroom that first time. When his mere presence had given her a comfort and reassurance she could not entirely feel now. "But you did not drown. You are alive. We are alive and together. Don't despair."

He put his arm around her shoulder and pulled her up next to him as if they were an old married couple— though she had never seen her father do that to her mother. But he meant it as a companionable, comforting gesture, she supposed.

Though she had to admit it was not nearly so comforting as the gesture he had made on the previous afternoon.

Heat swept across her skin and up to her hairline so visibly, that he looked at her with some concern, and put the back of his hand to her forehead. "Are you feverish?"

Yes. That was certainly a much more acceptable explanation than the fact that she seemed to have turned into a trollop who thought of nothing but a man's touch. "No. I'm fine. I'm just . . . feeling a little helpless, I suppose, while you do everything. What can I help with?"

"You can recover your strength. You slept a great deal yesterday."

And there was the heat again, spreading from her face down her neck. "Yes. But I meant something more actively helpful, like scanning the horizon for ships."

"And there you have it."

She was saved from the necessity of saying anything more by the arrival of raindrops, mercifully falling to cool her face.

Together, she and Dance rigged one of the rectangular tarpaulins over the bottom of the boom to make a sort of a tent over the well of the cockpit, and set out their canvas buckets to collect more rainwater. But in the process they both got wet, and so to prevent either of them from becoming chilled again, Dance took the precaution of sitting down very close to her in the bottom of the well, and wrapping his arm around her for comfort.

It was strange and nice and unnerving how he managed to do so much without letting go of her. It was a strange dance they did together—a nautical waltz.

But so long as he touched her, or she could lean against him, or feel the heat of his body surrounding her, Jane felt that she would be all right. She would eventually get out of this misadventure she had willed upon herself with her vanity and her pride and her overweaning ambition. She would cling to him and his warmth and pray incessantly to stay alive.

Because the alternatives—death, or worse, Dance's death—were simply, utterly, entirely unpalatable.

Chapter Twenty

Dance was in hell.

He wanted her so badly his eyes ached from looking at her, but she fell asleep on him again. Literally, the moment Dance settled her head against his chest, she fell asleep, before he could even so much as formulate a plan to kiss her. And despite her saying otherwise, Dance was convinced that she was in fact ill.

Her breathing was strained, and her brow seemed warmer. He'd seen it before—men pulled from the water, saved from drowning, only to have the sea claim them by somehow filling up their lungs with water and drowning them on dry land.

They weren't on dry land, but he would have given her all of the water they had collected before he took another sip if it would help to flush the salt out of her lungs. So he let her sleep, and collected the rainwater that pattered against the tarpaulin, and when the breeze picked up, he let the wind push them to the northwest.

And tried to think of anything but the fragile girl in his arms. So he thought of his ship, and his men—of Able Simmons with his head bashed in, and Rupert Honeyman herding the midshipmen together in the cutter, proud of his newfound responsibilities, and mindful of where his loyalties lay. And of others less loyal—of openly defiant Ransome, and the silently treacherous Manning.

The serrated gash at the top of his shin began to heal now that the air was warmer, and he could leave off his boots, and move about the small craft barefoot. But his real concern was for Jane. Who coughed and slept, and showed absolutely no interest in a return to their previous intimacy. Indeed, it seemed to him that she took pains to keep her normally straightforward gaze averted from his. And though she showed no aversion to his touch when he brought her to rest against him in the cool of the evenings, neither did she do anything to advance or enhance their closeness.

Or it could have been that she was really sick.

And she knew it. Her lips moved in a constant silent litany of prayer.

And so the nights and days took on an endless repetitive cycle as their little craft sailed onward—they collected water, and he made her drink it. She watched the horizon, and he watched their course. He gathered her to his side every evening, and spent the night trying to think only of the treachery of his crew to keep his mind from the soft fall of her hair against her shoulder, and the sweet curve of her breasts where they pressed against his chest.

Dance lost count of the days. Sunsets were set apart from sunrise because the twilight to the west was streaked with fiery yellows, and the dawns from the east were painted lurid shades of pink and purple. But the one color they never saw was blue. The sky remained an ominous, overcast gray that reflected itself onto the ocean day after brooding day, and made it nigh unto impossible to take the reading of the zenith of the sun. And with the difficulty in fixing the sun, neither could he calculate with any true degree of accuracy if his watch was still keeping time, or if the salt water from his dunking in the wreck had eaten its way into the mechanism.

And so he stayed wide awake each night, and tried to find the stars, and tired not to think too much. About how it was a big wide ocean. About how many days they had been alone on the sea. About how a miscalculation of only a few degrees could keep them from sighting land.

Jane had packed quite a lot into the little pinnace—the pails that kept them in rainwater, and the tins of potted meat, and biscuits and marmalade they rationed carefully—but she had packed no maps or references, and Dance had only his memory of reading Captain Cook's accounts of his voyage to rely upon in choosing his course.

He tried to tell himself that he had as good a chance as any man of finding what he sought—a speck of dry land—and better than most. But the consequences of missing were enormous. As enormous as the sea itself.

And he was haunted by thoughts of what might have become of the others. Eighty-four men and four naturalists under his command were adrift somewhere else upon the sea, and he was responsible for them even if they had seemingly forsaken him, and left him to go down with Jane in his ship.

And he had seen no other ships or boats, though he had watched the horizon incessantly, and set Jane to doing the same. The waters far to the northeast, off the west coast of South America, were the familiar whaling grounds for Yankee ships out of New England, good sailors and fairminded, hardworking men. But of those wide-hulled ships, and smoking stacks, he had seen no sign.

Easier to look at Jane. Easier to suspend his thoughts by letting his idle fingers play with her hair. Even windblown, it was soft, and it soothed him to run the silken strands across the backs of his fingers. Just as it quieted his doubts to trace the smooth line of her jaw—so often tipped up in the air, so resolute—and the plush line of her lower lip, now beginning to crack and chap.

When he looked at Jane, his mind could come to rest.

Her beauty—that indefinable quality that was a combination of both her person and her personality—gave him a focus, a duty. He would do whatever it would take to keep her alive. He would close his mind to everything but her.

But he could not close his mind to the sound that rolled low across the water. There was a gathering dull roar that did not come from his head. It came from somewhere out there, out on the sea.

Dance stopped, and tried to make his sleep-deprived and thirsty mind concentrate, to test if his imagination was getting the better of his senses. The wind had also picked up at a good clip, whistling past his ears, and the sound of the hull slicing through the water lulled him with its rhythm.

But still, he could not ignore the prod of instinct—that bristling pressure at the nape of his neck, pressing down on him, warning him to pay attention. Dance eased Jane out of his arms, and stood up.

And saw before him in the silver glint of dim moonlight, the shadowy loom of what looked like land—a low, irregular hump of darkness that rose out of the sea with a line of white surf demarking where the water gave way to the sand. It was real. He had not imagined it.

A raw mixture of hope and fear and excitement shot through his veins like uncut rum.

"Jane." His voice was tight and dry from disuse. "Jane, wake up. I think I've found it."

He had aimed by sheer instinct and dead reckoning at the easternmost of the Pitcairn Islands, knowing that English people—or formerly English people—lived there, and that the Royal Navy made frequent trips to the vicinity. But by the time he realized that the low hump could not be the mountainous Pitcairn, and that the line of white was *not* the pearlescent sand of a beach, but the foaming churn of surf crashing across a low reef that surrounded the island, they were upon it.

Dance flung the tiller over hard to fall off the wind and

come about, but the fast little pinnace was already career-ing over the razor-sharp rocks. The vessel shuddered and splintered beneath their feet as the waves pounded the hull into the reef.

"Fuck all." As if it weren't enough for him to have wrecked a Royal Navy frigate, he had just done the same to a blasted boat. Even he might have to start to believe in bad luck.

But the same surge of surf that pushed the pinnace onto the reef carried it over, and into the calmer water of a wide lagoon. Which they now had to cross if they were to reach the low hump of land.

Dance hauled in the main sheet, and readjusted the sail to get them moving through the water again. "Check the floorboards for water," he instructed Jane, his voice a dry bark. "Tell me how much is coming in."

Jane dropped to her hands and knees to feel her way in the darkness. "Only a little. But it's a steady trickle," she reported, her own voice just as dry and reedy. "There's a hump in the ceiling boards. I think the keel may have been damaged."

"We'll make it." He was determined. He had brought them this far—he would not falter at the last. "It's not too far. Another minute," he assured her. It was harder to tell the distance in the dim moonlight reflecting off the high clouds, but it could not have been more than a mile across the wide stretch of the lagoon. And at least the water was calm and smooth within the reef. Small comfort, but in a leaking boat with a damaged keel, he would take all the comfort he could get.

Dance trimmed the sail again to get as much speed as possible from the wind shifting around the landmass, and stared through the darkness as the low hump of land slowly took shape out of the gloom. It was not one single piece of land, but several small separate islands with one larger one, strung along the ring of the reef.

He altered course, and aimed for the second largest of the isles for no other reason than twelve-odd years of instinct. And because it was closer, and the dim strip of beach seemed slightly wider, and he thought he had seen the wraithlike shadow of a reef shark glide by the side of the pinnace. After everything that Jane had been through, he would do everything he could to spare her that additional terror of sinking into shark-infested waters.

And then the sand was rushing at them as he ran the pinnace hard up onto the beach, where it shuddered to an ungainly stop. He let go of the tiller and the sheet, and for one very long moment, felt for the first time in months the welcome but unaccustomed feeling of stillness. For a full minute nothing, absolutely nothing save the waves at the foot of the beach, moved.

"Are we there?"

Wherever the hell *there* was.

"Yes." He made himself sound confident. He made himself ignore the rush of fresh worries that rose up like an imaginary fog from the unknown dark of the island before him. He went to Jane where she was crouched in the well, pressing her hand down upon the fractured keel, as if she might, through sheer will, have held the little boat together.

"You can let it go now." He reached to take her hand, for his own comfort as much as for hers. He felt old and tired—weary from exhaustion and the knowledge that he had both saved and still failed her all at the same time. "We've made land."

"Where are we?"

They were not on Pitcairn. The low atoll he had grounded them on resembled nothing of the descriptions of the island from Admiralty records. "It doesn't matter," he lied. "We've reached some land, and that is enough for now."

He gathered her in his arms both so he could give himself the calming assurance of holding her, and to carry her out of the boat.

But his feet were too unsteady—the sand shifted under his feet, and made him feel off balance, and unsure. Dance was forced to set her down in the fine white sand that seemed to suck at his feet, and sap his strength.

And he had to tend to the broken boat. He had to drag it higher up the slight slope of the beach to a spot above the high-tide mark, where it would be safe. Broken or not, it was all they had.

But when he had done so, his strength was gone, sapped by the effort, and by the constant vigilance of staying up for days and nights at a time. It was all he could do to go to her, and find a spot under a tree where he could finally lay himself down to stop the world from spinning around him.

"Dance," she said, though her voice seemed to come from very far away, high up at the top of the tree.

"Come down here with me," he said, and tugged her down beside him so he didn't have to look up. So he could pull her into his arms, snug against his chest, and close his eyes. And finally let the black oblivion of exhaustion overtake him.

Dance awoke to the terrifying feeling that he was alone. Empty and depleted.

Jane was gone.

The clawing pressure building in his chest might have felt like panic, if he allowed it to be. He lurched to his feet, only to find himself unsteady. He raised his hand to shield his eyes from the glare of the watery gray sunlight.

The yellowish cast to the western sky that had obscured the sun for days still made him feel uneasy. He'd been at sea for more years than he liked to count, and sailed the Pacific twice before, and he'd never seen the like.

But the truth of the matter was that his unease was not due to the strange weather, but from the fact that Jane

Burke, who had clung to him as tenaciously as one of her precious barnacles for uncounted nights, was gone.

She was nowhere nearby. She was not within his sight.

"Jane." He staggered toward the boat, hoping that she had taken shelter within its familiar confines. But the pinnace was empty. More than empty—items were missing. The line that had been the main sheet, controlling the sail, was gone, as were many of the tightly packed supplies. "Jane!" he bellowed.

That *was* panic, cracking his voice wide open like a boarding ax.

"Dance!"

Dance turned a full circle to see her running—tearing up the beach at him as if a tribe of spinster-scientist-eating cannibals were after her.

No. There were no cannibals. And she was smiling.

She was running easily, as if she hadn't just spent however many days it had been in a small boat in the middle of the Pacific Ocean. Her feet were bare in the sand. He could see her small toes, and her white, white ankles and shins where she had tied her skirts up to keep them out of the water. Her hair was streaming loose on the breeze.

Everything that had heretofore seemed so buttoned up and battened down was coming gloriously undone. The drawn, coughing girl of the boat was gone, and left this glowing creature in her place.

When she reached him she held out her hand and offered him a handful of shells, as if she were giving him rubies and pearls, or manna from heaven. Or better yet, carpentry tools with which he might fix the broken boat.

He looked again at the contents of her outstretched palm. Shells. But she was beaming at him as if she were ecstatically happy.

Happy. Shipwrecked only God knew where in the middle of the ocean.

"It's unbelievable." She was breathless with her joy. "You won't believe what I found. *Tridacna gigas.* Giant bivalves. Clams as big as a breadbasket." She spread her arms to indicate the monstrous size. "And more than that. A Venus comb murex, *Murex pecten,* and another murex, I think, but that I've never seen before but it's definitely a gastropod mollusk with a very wide operculum. And this whelk of the *Triton* type that I've never seen anywhere but is definitely some sort of *Cabestana.* Oh, Dance. It's—"

Dance thought her face would split in two with the width of her smile.

And then she hurtled herself into his arms, wrapping her arms around his back, and sighing into his chest. "Oh, Dance. It's heaven."

Heaven.

Impossible. At least highly improbable.

Or that is what he would have thought if she had not been in his arms. Because the feeling of her pulled tight against his chest was a thrill of something tight and right that stilled all his worry.

Happiness radiated off her like the warmth of the sun, this girl who had been a pale, clinging shadow in the boat. "There are so many shells right here within this lagoon that have never ever been found or categorized or described. Right here." She spread her arms again to encompass the whole of the lagoon. "Just waiting for me."

She looked at him as if he had done it on purpose. As if he had quite purposefully found her this particular speck of palms in the middle of the sea to present to her like a gift. "Thank you. I don't know how you did it, but thank you."

"You're welcome," he said, because he could say nothing else. Because she was looking at him as if he were the answer to all those fervent prayers she had mouthed through dry, fever-cracked lips. As if this being marooned with a broken boat on little more than an overgrown reef had been exactly what she had asked of her God.

But her lips didn't look dry now. They were wide and smiling at him.

"Oh, Lord, what am I thinking. You'll still be as dry as a bone."

He must have been staring at her like a demented man, because she put a hand to his shirtsleeve, and steered him toward the palm trees lining the edge of the beach.

"I've found fresh water. There's a stream that flows right down onto the beach from the hill beyond into the lagoon. And I managed to open up a coconut by smashing it on a rock. We could not have chosen a better spot."

As if there had been a plethora of islands to choose from. As if this speck of land in the middle of the ocean had not been the only speck of land in the middle of the damn ocean he had seen. As if she were actually enthusiastic about the prospect of their being quite effectively marooned there until such time as they recovered themselves—and repaired the boat sufficiently to move on.

But she was pressing the canvas pail, heavy with water, into his hands.

It was everything he could do to simply drink, and not deluge himself in the bliss of clean water. He gulped it down, astonished at the fresh taste and soft texture—the almost voluptuous feel of it against his lips, running down his chin and chest where he spilled it in his clumsy thirst. It tasted like a kiss.

And he wanted to kiss her. He wanted to have her back flush against his body so he knew where she was. He wanted her slight weight and her warmth and the surety of knowing that they were in this together.

Because when he had awoken alone, he had felt lost.

With her, he was found.

So he kissed her. He kissed her because they were alive, and because he did not know what else to do. He kissed her lips and her nose and her ear because she was in his arms and happy.

It was nothing like the bittersweet press of her lips in the rain in the boat. This kiss was soft and slippery and sweet. So, so sweet. Like happiness condensed into a drop of sunshine.

Dance's arms tightened themselves around her supple back, and stole up the sweet curve of her spine to cradle her skull, and hold her still, and fill the void within him with her simple sweetness. He wrapped his hand around the back of her neck and pulled her to him, taking her mouth with the same thirst he had for the water. And she was like water, cool and crisp and sweet. She was warm and melting against him like honey in the sun—deliciously, dangerously sticky.

And she didn't seem to care that his clothes were stiff with salt, and that he had the dark growth of a two-week beard rasping against the soft skin of her cheek. She smiled even as she kissed. Her eyes were open, and looking at him, cataloguing his scowls and bristles like the spiny protrusions on one of her shells, and he wanted nothing more than to lay himself down before her, and let her examine him from stem to stern, masthead to jib. But she had other ideas.

She blushed and laughed and pushed him away, and straightened her salt-stained skirts. "Drink."

He did, if only because his brain couldn't seem to think of anything else to do when he could not be kissing her.

She caught up his hand, leading him down the beach toward the tip of their small island. "Come see. Come see what I've found, and what I've done."

"What have you found?"

"Fresh water first of all, but not here. There." She pointed across the lagoon toward the largest of the green group of islands. "I found that the tide varies by a total of about three feet, so that when it is lowest, as it was this morning, it is possible to walk down the sandy edge of the reef to the larger island. Which is where I found the water.

The spring comes out of the side of the hill and flows into the lagoon—there." She pointed to a low spot on the larger island. "And there are trees that bear fruits besides coconuts. I have a book on edible fruits in with my things in the boat. But I couldn't carry it all out, though I did take a few things back to set up there, as that side of the island seems to be protected from the prevailing winds. But I rather thought I ought to at least consult with your first, to see if you agreed."

She looked up at him in full expectation that he would agree, as if he would be quite stupid and wrong not to do so.

"Yes. But . . ." He tried to make his brain function at at least half the speed of hers. All that time he had slept like a dead man, she—this girl he had thought fragile and helpless—had worked and explored and fended for herself. She had done all of the things he ought to have done. "I'll have to have a look round, and see if it's safe."

"Safe from what?" She laughed at his ridiculous attempt to salvage his pride. She shaded her face with her hand to look back over the island. "I am quite sure that if native islanders lived here, they would have seen us long before we saw them. And I haven't smelled any other cooking fires."

Other? He had always admired her spine, but now he had to stop to take stock of her intelligence. And sniff the breeze. He caught a whiff of cooking fire.

Devil take her. Was there nothing she could not do?

Dance cast about for something—anything—he could do. He looked toward the larger island across the lagoon—which did have a higher elevation from which he could watch for passing ships. "I could put a signal fire on that promontory."

"Certainly," she agreed. "Very good idea." She gave him that sunny, pleased smile. "But we won't need that for quite some time."

Dance could feel his scowl etching itself into his face, slowly building like clouds before a summer thunderstorm. "What do you mean?"

"I mean that we are fine as we are for a very long while at least. We have water and fruit and a very great number of fishes and crustaceans to choose from in the lagoon. It is as perfect for my purposes as I could hope for."

"Perfect?" She was mad. There was something in the water that had turned her brain, like the lotus blossoms that waylaid travelers in the old Greek myths.

"Yes. The only thing lacking from the ideal is the presence of the good ship *Tenacious* sitting at anchor outside the reef. But this is better," she insisted, "for if *Tenacious* were anchored outside the reef, you would be there, and I would be here alone." She gave him the gift of that wondrously pleased smile. "I like this so much better."

"You are *happy* that we have washed up here?"

She corrected him, with a laugh. "I am *elated* to be here. Look around you—we are in paradise. There are more than sufficient murexes alone in this lagoon to keep me occupied drawing for months without wandering any farther afield. Which I can't wait to do."

"Months?" The word turned his gut as tight as a purser's fist. What in the hell was he supposed to do for months while she collected enough information to take the Royal Society by storm? He would run mad without a ship, or any useful employment for his time.

But her smile was so wide and glorious it nearly blinded him with its brilliance. "Months!" Her joyously open grin was transformative—everything about her that had ever seemed severe and restricted broke loose the moment she smiled like that. As if she had been drowning, and was finally taking a full breath of air.

But she had almost drowned. And she was breathing fully now. It was almost a miracle. Or maybe it was the soft island air.

"But I think it best we wait for the low tide again tomorrow to move all of our things over to that island. In the meantime, while you were having a much-needed sleep—you let me sleep, but I know you haven't slept in days and days—I've got us a bit of supper."

She took his hand again, and led him on from the point at the north end of the little island, and down the lee side of the beach to where a small fire set within a circle of rocks crackled under a slightly rusty cast-iron pot.

And behind that, just off the sand at the tree line, a tarpaulin had been set up to form a tent.

Dance stared at it for a long moment, trying to get his brain to catch up with his eyes. It was a tent. A canvas tent. "Where did that come from?"

She beamed as if she had conjured it out of magic. "I tried to rig it the same way you did making the shade over the well of the boat. I had to give it several tries, but eventually I got it right."

She had done all this. She had emptied the boat, and taken the main sheet. She had set up the hearth, and lighted the fire. She had found whatever it was that was in the steaming pot. Dance felt rather like someone from his childhood fairy tales who wakes from an enchanted sleep to find that the world has changed around him.

Jane was unfazed by her feats of near-magic. "I had several in the boat, you see? I had planned on setting up just such a camp for myself once we had arrived in the islands, and begun our various studies. But this is nicer, to have you with me."

That was the second time she had said that. And he had never thought of what she would do when *Tenacious* arrived at its destination. He had thought only of his part, of the transportation and the navigation and the many and different pieces of work necessary for him to get the party of naturalists to their destination, not of what they might do once they got there.

But *there* appeared to be *here*.

"Dance, are you all to rights?"

He was not. He was staggered. By her. By this tiny, resolute, tenacious woman. "No. I'm stuck on a deserted island in the middle of the ocean with a beautiful woman, and she turns out to be as able as Alexander Selkirk and Robinson Crusoe combined. And I adore her."

It took a very long moment for her to understand what he was saying. Her face stayed blank while Dance felt as if he were exposed and hung out on a yardarm, flapping in the breeze for all the world to see. His throat went dry, and he swallowed, and tried to think of some retort that would deflect her rejection, or her pity, or whatever was coming next.

What came next was that she kissed him. Simply and directly. She tipped up that resolute chin, and kissed him, and her mouth was there, just across the gap. If he angled his head, and leaned in, the soft suppleness of her lips would brush against his.

His hand was already stroking along the fine edge of her jaw, tugging her fractionally closer, testing to see if she wanted to be kissed anywhere near as much as he wanted to kiss her. And he wanted to kiss her with every breath of his body.

He wanted her surety. He wanted her joy. He wanted her to smile at him in the way that pushed all doubts from his mind, and made him forget for just a little while that he had sunk his first and only command, and that if they ever made it back across the oceans to their former lives, he would face a court-martial for the catastrophic loss of his ship.

But Jane broke the lifeline of her lips. "Come, you'll feel much better when you've had something fresh to eat. You have your own knife, of course, but I have an extra fork—I have two of everything. I had packed for the two of us originally, before I ever thought to come alone."

"The two of us?" His mind was still racing to catch up with hers.

"My father, the real J. E. Burke. No." She shook her head—an emphatic denial. "The *other* J. E. Burke. I am the *real* one. I did the work. And I am here. This is real."

She moved back to the fire and the iron pot at the boil. "And we have real, fresh food," she said as she fished him out the ugliest, spiniest creature he had ever seen.

"What is that?"

"A lobster." She waited a moment for the creature to cool, and then twisted off its tail, and presented it to him in an tin enameled bowl.

He had heard of them—particularly in the West Indies—but had never eaten one himself. And though he had never before turned down a meal in all his years in the navy—he had even eaten rats—this creature was . . . unsettling. "What kind of lobster?"

"The kind that comes from the sea. The kind that someone else was kind enough to catch and cook for you."

"You caught this?"

She looked at him as if she feared he had taken a blow to the head in the landing of the boat. "There is no one else here, and I assure you it did not willingly leap out of the water, and conveniently throw itself into my pot."

"No. Of course not." He shifted his weight to his other foot. "It's just that I don't particularly like things that come from the sea, like fish."

She fell into a sort of overtired laughter. "And you a sailor. There's more than irony there. Well, Captain Dance, you'll learn to like it, or you'll go hungry this evening. Your choice."

He felt his pride catch fire in his chest. "Are you mocking me?"

Her smile gentled, but her look was arch under her brows. "I do believe I am. At least until you start providing me with dinner."

His pride welled stronger. But Dance knew it wasn't just the damn creature that was unsettling, it was her—doing all these things, being so bloody competent. It made him feel devilishly stupid and incompetent. Entirely unnecessary.

He cast his gaze back at the forested hill across the lagoon. "Surely there's some game I could shoot."

"And how many bullets do you have to hand, Captain? I have several dozen cartridges for the fowling piece I packed—although it is dismantled and in its case—but I have no intention of hunting with it. What would become of us if we needed it for defense? And besides, I've seen no sign of indigenous mammals on the island. And the birds don't look particularly appetizing."

Devil take him. And his stomach was growling—in another minute it would be loud enough for her to hear.

There was nothing else to do—his pride would have to be the first course.

Dance swallowed it down, and sat himself in the sand next to her. "You have this all thought out, have you?"

"Yes. I should hope so." Her look was frank but cautious. "I thought it all out for well over a year. And planned everything just—"

"So," he finished, on a sharp sigh. He should not have expected anything less.

"Yes." She drew back a little, unsure of his tone, as if it were her pride now that stung. "I had thought it out for a particularly long time. I have been planning this expedition ever since my father and I concluded our last one to Cornwall, some four years ago."

"Devil take me, Jane. I'm sorry. I didn't mean—" It was only that *his* considerable pride *had* been stung. More than stung—trussed up and made useless, while this glorious, tiny Amazon of a woman had rendered him redundant.

But if he did not thank his lucky stars for her competence, he was a fool. And though he was many things—hungry among them—he was no fool.

"You should have been in the army or the navy," he groused companionably. "We could use quartermasters and pursers like you." His ship could have used somebody who cared about her work as much as she. "You'd have done much better for *Tenacious*. You wouldn't have run off with other people's money, or let the ship go to rot, or let the captain drink himself into a stupor. You'd have figured it all out. You did figure it all out." Dance ran his hand through his hair as if he could rub the idea more firmly into his brain. "You're bloody incredible."

Her smile came back, slow and beautiful. "Careful, Captain, I might take that as a compliment."

For the first time in what felt like forever, Dance felt his chapped lips curve into a true smile. "Careful, Miss Burke. I might actually mean it as one."

Chapter Twenty-one

And he knew without a shadow of a doubt that he was going to make love to her. Right here on this sand. Slowly and carefully. With attention to detail, just as she so richly deserved.

The only question was when?

His answer was as soon as possible.

And with that thought, his stomach let out a fearsome grumble. "And so I must eat lobster?"

"You really must," she confirmed. "It is very nutritious. The Americans, I'm told, eat it all the time."

"And there you have all of my objections put into one. I should hate to be taken for an American."

She laughed as he had hoped she would. "Dance," she began. "Or perhaps, given the circumstances, we had best be Jane and Charles now?"

"Absolutely not. You may be Jane all you like, but I refuse to be Charles. You may call me Dance, which is bad enough. But Charles—" He shuddered overdramatically, like a dog that needs to shed cold water, uncomfortable for the moment in its skin.

He was rewarded for his troubles by a glow that owed nothing to the strange sky, but seemed to light her from within. "Dance then."

"Yes." And he would eat this hot supper she had caught and cooked for him. "I thank you, Jane."

They ate in companionable silence as the long daylight waned into purple night. "Rather remarkable, is it not?" She was looking at the strange western sky.

But he was looking at her. "Yes. You especially. I could never have hoped to be shipwrecked so comfortably."

She laughed, a happy relaxed sound. The sort of sound he wanted to grow accustomed to hearing. Every day. For the rest of his life. "I'm glad you're comfortable," she said. "Poor Ransome. I am quite sure he can have no idea how much I am enjoying this."

"No." Everything that had been relaxed and easy in Dance drew into a low fist of loathing. He turned from her, lest she see the damning mark of hatred on his face. "I imagine he thinks us both at the bottom of the sea. I know Manning meant for you to be."

The easy happiness that had lit her face dimmed. "Yes."

But he could not hold it all in—all the vicious vengeful thoughts that had been on a slow boil at the back of his mind for days now. He flung himself up off the sand—if such a thing were possible. And it was, if only because that is exactly what he did—he threw himself into movement, to keep from spouting a filthy host of obscenities. She deserved better than to be sworn at. "There was no reason why we should not have been able to find them. There is no reason they should have put their lanterns out. No reason why we should not have seen them, except that they did not want to be seen."

"Yes." She stared across the darkening expanse of the lagoon. "They must have taken themselves away in an indecent hurry."

"Indecent." He nearly spat the word out. "Disobedient and mutinous more like." But thinking of justice—for that was a more palatable way of thinking than revenge— clarified his way forward, and sheathed the sharp end of his temper. "Which is why I need to get a decent reading so I can fix our position, and then I need to repair the pinnace, and see what I can do to find a ship."

Jane showed no signs of well-deserved temper herself, but concentrated on eating her lobster before she spoke. "It seems to me we'd have much better luck finding a boat from here—a place with fresh water."

"A ship," he corrected automatically. "We need to look for a ship."

"A ship," she acknowledged. "But the hill"—she pointed across the lagoon to the largest of the islands—"will afford a higher, and better, vantage point from which to search, than a boat upon the water, will it not? And only on land could you build that signal fire you mentioned. I should think the smoke from such a fire would be easier to spot from a ship than a small boat would. I'm sure you will have your own opinion, but I really do think we had best stay here."

"Yes. But . . ." He had no rebuttal. Her suggestion made very good sense. But he was a man of the sea, a man for action—the idea of just standing on a hill, looking out to sea for what might be months, terrified him in a way that facing enemy cannon never had.

He wanted to do something. He wanted to find his men. Of the officers in the boats, only Mr. Whitely and perhaps Able Simmons might have been reliably counted upon to have taken their instruments for navigation, but Simmons was injured—

No. Simmons had been struck by someone of his crew. Which was a hanging offense.

He wanted to find them, not wait to be found.

"You really ought to eat, Dance," she urged. "It's very tasty. Granted, it would be more so swimming in a sauce of butter that Punch could have concocted, but I shall count us lucky to be able to eat, and keep ourselves alive with so little work as wading across some rocks."

The image arose unbidden again, of her with her skirts hiked up to keep from the water, and her shapely white legs bare in the sea. It was erotic and enticing and so very not conducive to sitting down next to her in the sand and eating supper like any kind of gentleman.

But maybe he didn't want to be a gentleman. He was shipwrecked and marooned on an island with a beautiful young woman who seemed to think it all the greatest of good fortune. Why should he not take advantage of that? Why should he not make it fully the paradise it could be?

But if he wanted to do that, he had best keep both his wits and his strength about him. And so he sat, and put the fresh food she had so cleverly provided for him into his mouth, and thought about how he might make his fantasy a reality.

By complimenting her. "Thank you. Both for the food, and for making a remarkable go of our extraordinary circumstance. I am sorry if I sounded ungrateful. I should be kissing your rather lovely bare feet in thanks."

She extended one elegantly pointed foot in front of her. "Go ahead."

He would have done so—he wanted to do so, to start kissing the delicate arch and ankles, and work his way up the pale slide of her legs until he was kissing all of her, until—

The blood that ought to have stayed in his brain flew south for the winter—he was almost instantly hard. So hard he could not move up from his place on the sand. He was poleaxed by lust, riveted by the mental image that sprang before his eyes of what those breasts might look like, pale and full and pink tipped and—

He closed his eyes to shut the thought away, but the image rose, and grew to include more and more of her—pale, pink shadowed skin under her breasts tapering down to her waist, and flaring again over the smooth, round curve of her hips down across her soft belly.

She must have read his intent in his face, because by the time he opened his eyes, Jane had colored a vivid shade of sunset pink that painted a swath across her cheeks and neck, and she had pulled her foot back under the cover of her skirts. "No. Never mind that. Finish your supper before it gets cold."

It was surprisingly good. Meaty and smoky tasting from the fire. Much better than he had thought. Which brought another thought about something he had overlooked—the fire. "How did you start the fire?"

"I packed a tinderbox with a fire steel and flint," she said as if it would have been unthinkable for her to do otherwise. "I had planned to do this—to stay put in a camp to work and collect my shells while the rest of the expedition moved about, making maps and charts and finding new islands with new peoples and fauna to study."

Again, he had not thought of the particulars of the expedition's study. But it was clear that she had thought of little else. Remarkable.

He ran another compliment up her masthead. "You are taking this all remarkably well. I don't know another lady who would be so sanguine about being shipwrecked on a deserted island with me."

"Oh, you're not so bad, now that you've stopped being all disgruntled, sea captainy. Unprepared as you are, I expect you'll prove to be a smart, handy fellow to have around." Her eyes sparkled with mischievous pleasure. "I reckon, once you find your feet, you'll do well enough."

She was teasing him. And doing a very good job of it.

He turned to survey the small but well-defined area of her temporary camp—and it was clearly *her* camp. He had had nothing to do with its provision, its location, or its construction—he had bloody well *slept* while she had done it all. It was as neat and tidy and organized as she had made the captain's day cabin. "Damn my eyes, but you really ought to have been a quartermaster—I am quite in awe of your practical planning abilities."

"Well, I did not think of everything. I packed a great deal of things for shade, but not very much for warmth. I had thought that once we got to the islands that it would be a great deal warmer."

"So had I." He looked up at the deep purple sky. While the temperature was certainly warmer than it had been rounding Cape Horn, it was certainly much cooler than he might have thought. "I can only think that I've made an error in my navigation, and that we are much farther south than I had thought."

But that still didn't explain the strangely overcast skies. "In all my years of sailing I've made two trips into the Pacific, and I've never seen the like. It's as if we've brought the weather from England with us."

"Yes. And though I did pack good English wool in my trunks, with the exception of my cloak and what I am wearing, what little I had in the way of warm clothes went down with the ship. Which is why I thought it best to remove ourselves to that much more protected spot on the larger island."

"Yes, we'll do that tomorrow." It was too late in the evening now to think of such an undertaking. And though he had slept the day through like a newborn baby, he felt as if he were sailing against the tide. And she, who had clearly toiled all through the day while he slept, was tiring as night darkened everything but the small circle of light around her fire.

But her talk of being cold gave him at least one task he could do for her. "Speaking of your cloak, I'll collect it, if it's still in the pinnace with mine. I want to have another look at the boat while there is still some light, and I'll collect more fuel for the fire."

"Yes, thank you."

There had been some scattered bits of driftwood at the

high-tide mark all along the beach, and there was bound to be some fallen timber of a sort in the scrub covering the low hump of the island. But what he really needed was to move, to feel like he was doing something to contribute to their upkeep.

He headed back for the boat, dragging it higher on the sand, well above the high-tide mark, and retrieving his coat and logbook, and her cloak, all the while cursing himself for feeling so entirely out of sorts in the face of Jane's enormous competence.

Her flint. Her fire. Her tarpaulins. Her lobster for dinner.

Not for the first time in his life, Dance felt entirely extraneous. And he didn't like it one bit. But he did what he always did—he carried on. He moved a few more small, well-packed crates from the pinnace. He thought about ways to repair the cracked keel. He made an unobtrusive pallet on the sand from a tarpaulin and his uniform coat, and their cloaks. And he waited for her to fall asleep.

Because he had known what he was doing when she had been in his arms. He had felt useful and strong then. He had slept better when he had been touching her, when he could personally account for her safety. But with her sitting in the sand on the other side of the small fire, he was everything on watch, alert and searching the endless dark around them for dangers.

But he didn't like to be away from her for too long. And when he returned to her camp with his last load of driftwood, she had already nodded off in front of the fire, with her head on her knees, asleep where she sat. "Jane? Are you asleep?"

"No." She almost opened her eyes.

"Yes," he countered gently, and eased her into his arms, and settled them on the soft pallet, with his back propped against the horizontal trunk of a palm tree, and her settled firmly against his chest.

And thought that perhaps she was right. Perhaps this place was Eden, because this—holding this woman in his arms—was indeed bliss.

Jane awoke to find herself wrapped in the woolen warmth of her cloak, and held securely against Dance's chest, as tucked in and warm as if she were still in her bed at home. But her bed at home had never contained a man. But sleeping with Dance was a marvelous improvement on her years of being alone in her narrow bed. He radiated lulling warmth, and his chest was a marvelously comfortable place to be. And since his arms were wrapped tight around her, it appeared he thought it a marvelous thing as well.

In fact, one of his arms was around her waist, his hand pressed flat against her belly, while the other hand was curved along her rib cage, just under her breast.

The moment she made the realization, awareness swept through her, unleashing a flood of dark, forbidden thoughts. He had held her like this in the boat, and warmed her then with his clever fingers and erotic murmurings.

Beneath the salt-stiffened confines of her clothing, her nipples contracted into tight, needy buds. She knew what it was, this awareness, this want. She was six and twenty, and not some wide-eyed young girl fresh from the schoolroom. She had lain awake at night in her narrow bed at home feeling the pulsating hum and rhythm of her body, and wondering what it would feel like—a lover's touch.

And now she knew—it was almost bliss.

It had been bliss, before, in the boat. And she wanted those feelings, that glorious bliss again. But she could not bring herself to tell him so, though it was ridiculous to feel awkward with Dance—she had slept for nights and nights upon his shoulder. And chest. And because he had brought her to unimagined ecstasy. And because he had held her as if she were precious.

It had seemed natural then—something he did in order

to help her survive the shipwreck, and the trial of staying alive in the boat. It was only natural that they should have clung to each other in that situation.

But things were different now. There was fruit and water and a fire on which they could cook their food. Their survival was assured—for the short term anyway. Yet there was only the two of them, alone together at what felt like the end of the world. So why should she not take comfort in his presence? Why should she not learn what it was like to fully be a woman?

She could not keep herself from moving to try and ease the discomfort of her strange and inappropriate arousal. But doing so made his hands tighten around her. His palm flexed and pressed against the slight swell of her belly, but she felt the motion deep inside. The pang of want spread until she had to close her eyes to hold it in.

She indulged herself in the heady luxury of being held safe in his arms, without contemplating how she had arrived there, or when, or how she was going to extricate herself before she went up in flames.

She drew in a long, deep breath to savor the lime and salt scent of him. Her movement didn't wake him, but it disturbed him enough so that he shifted, taking her with him as he rolled onto his side, snugging up tight to her from behind. He pulled her back against his chest and his thighs. He was everywhere around her, enveloping her in warmth, protecting her with his body.

And doing other things as well. His fingers flexed lightly against her belly as if he were still truly asleep, and simply making himself comfortable. But he was making her something more than comfortable—his sleepy, offhand caress was sending wave after gentle wave of pleasure lapping through her body, until she could think of nothing else. Until all her concentration was centered on the next fraction of an inch his fingers might stray to left or right. Or up or down.

Oh, sweet heaven. Down.

And as if he had actually heard her most secret longings, his fingers fanned out, low across her belly, kindling a low fire within, before his hand swept higher, skimming across the bones of her stays before it came to rest on her breast.

Jane wanted to look at him, to be able to gaze and marvel at his rugged handsomeness like a schoolgirl while he was still asleep, and could not scowl at her with his own stony, probing gaze. She shifted slowly, so as not to disturb him, but when she had turned, she found him wide awake, though those green eyes were slitty with sleep. And pleasure. "Kiss me."

"Dance." She gave herself willingly to the irresistible lure of his lips, to the voluptuous pleasure of his sweet, lazy kisses, sending her tongue to swirl and waltz with his, sucking lightly at his taut lower lip, and feeling the pleasure blossom up from deep within her.

And she wanted more. She wanted to touch him. To run her hand up the corded tendons at the side of his neck, and slide her fingers through his short-cropped hair. She wanted to feel the warm bliss of his skin against hers.

She slipped her hand inside the open neck of his shirt to press her palm flat against his chest, and he made a sound of acquiescence and encouragement that soothed and enflamed, and made her all the more curious. So she kissed the corner of his mouth, and the rough line of his jaw, and the smoother side of his cheek above his rough beard. She put her lips to the hollow of his throat, and tasted the salt on his skin, and felt the strong steady beat of the pulse pumping through his veins.

He was everything sure and steady. Everything she could depend upon. Everything she could love.

And he kissed her back, pressing his clever lips to places she had never thought about—the corner of her shoulder, the thin, sensitive skin over her breast bone. His hand flexed and the tips of his fingers flared low between her hip bones, and her insides clenched into a tight needy burst of pure, instinctive want, sending a shivery sensation rippling across the surface of her skin despite his warmth.

"Shh." It was more of a sound than a word—the whispered reassurance hummed in her ear. But his hand retreated. And then moved higher. And all trace of lazy sleepiness was gone when his hand took possession of her breast with unmistakeable intent.

"Yes," she said, in case he should be in any doubt, and think to take his hand away.

"Yes," he affirmed, and rewarded her boldness by fondling her more firmly, brushing his callused fingers back and forth across the fabric of her bodice until her nipple had budded into a tight, needy peak.

Oh, heaven. It was glorious. It was bliss.

It was not nearly enough.

"You have no idea how long I've been waiting to do this," he whispered as he played his lips along the sensitive skin at the side of her neck.

"You have no idea how long I have wanted you to."

Her whispered words seemed to prompt him into greater action. He rolled her onto her back, and rose above her, pulling her bodice down so he could take the pale pink flesh of her nipple between his lips and suck and lave her until she thought she would float away on the flood of pleasurable need.

Jane closed her eyes, and surrendered to the pleasure arcing through her, making her arch her back, and press herself into the sweet pressure of his clever, clever hands and mouth. Showing him what she wanted. Hoping he would do more. Bring her more of the delicious, needy pleasure.

He made another low sound of encouragement and approval that hummed and insinuated itself under her heated skin, and fed the sly hunger that only seemed to grow instead of being appeased. He turned his attention to her other breast, lavishing her with his attention, taking her aching nipple between his strong white teeth and biting down ever so gently.

Her breathing fractured into a gasp, and Jane could not stop the sound of inarticulate longing that flew from her lips, but she was rewarded by the low hum of satisfaction that came from his as he wound her higher and higher with every delicious stroke of his tongue across her heated skin.

And then his clever fingers were at the buttons at the back of her worn, salt-stained gown.

"Yes." She twisted away from him to give him access and help the process along.

And when he peeled the gown over her head, she immediately turned her attention to loosening her front lacing stays. She wanted to be rid of them, free and unbound. She wanted to feel his skin—his golden, glowing, warm skin—flush against hers.

"How practical you are." His voice was a teasing growl while his clever fingers helped pull the laces away.

She didn't care if he were teasing her. "Very," she breathed. It was true—she had always valued practicality over fashion so she could dress herself without assistance. And she didn't need any assistance now, quickly unlacing the short stays, and pushing them away so Dance could practice more of the practical magic of his mouth and hands.

He did not disappoint. He kissed down her neck and over the sensitive skin that covered her collarbone, stroking her through the thin lawn fabric of her chemise, until she felt the heat and hungry intent within him soak down through her to her bones.

But she did not want to be passive and idle. She wanted

his skin next to hers, his weight pressing down into her—nothing between them but pleasure.

She had to push his hands away to get at the half-undone buttons at the neck of his linen shirt, but he kept his mouth busy nipping down the sensitive side of her neck, pulling her thoughts away from her chore, wrecking her concentration while he let his hands play upon her body.

"Stop that," she begged. She wanted to be able to do the same to him, to touch and arouse him just as he was doing to her.

"Stop this?" His clever hands brushed aside her chemise, and found the peaks of her nipples, rolling them gently between his thumb and forefinger. "Or this?" His mouth followed his hands, and his clever lips nipped and laved her breast until she abandoned his shirtsleeves, and concentrated on arching herself into the decadent pleasure of his even cleverer mouth.

"Or stop this?" While his mouth was busy, his hands had begun to gather up the long hems of her chemise and petticoat, sliding them higher and higher over her bare legs until she felt the cool morning air against her most private skin.

She could only watch through wide-open eyes, fascinated and undeniably aroused by the sight of him looking at her, at her body, and by the exquisite feeling of his dark, masculine hands stroking her pale white flesh. By the bliss burning low under the surface of her skin and spreading like wildfire throughout her body, turning her to needy licking flame from her fingertips to deep within her core.

"Oh, Jane." His fingers stilled, and he drew back to look at her. The scowl was back, etching itself into two sharp vertical lines between his thunderously straight brows, and his voice was low, and full of anger and pity. "You're *covered* in bruises."

"I'm sorry," she said, because she didn't know what to say, and because she was angry too. Angry for all the reasons she had gotten those bruises—for being almost drowned and battered about. She was angry and she was frustrated, because she didn't want his pity. She wanted his hands at her breasts, and his lips on her mouth, making her forget that she had ever been so abused. "They don't matter," she insisted. Scalding heat was pooling behind her eyes, and she squeezed her lids tight to shut the tears out. "Don't let them matter."

"But they do matter," he said in a voice that was calmer, though no less insistent. "They mean I haven't been taking proper care of you. I haven't paid enough attention to all of you. A deficiency I mean to correct. Immediately."

He braced himself on his arms above her, and slowly lowered his lips to her breasts.

Oh, clever, clever man. It was as if he knew the pull of his lips on her nipples created a tight, needy heat between her legs, because his broad, warm palm pressed low against her belly, letting her learn the gentle feel of his hands, teaching her to want him to touch her more intimately.

His kisses moved to the side of her face, pressing soft encouragement along her temple and down to that astonishing spot at the edge of her jaw. And she did the same to him, kissing across the prickly line of his strong jaw, brushing her fingers into the short crop of his dark hair, stroking her hands across the strong planes of his cheeks. Her fingers burned where they touched his skin, pain and pleasure mixing like an elixir in her palms.

And he had his own elixir. He circled his thumbs on the soft, vulnerable skin of her inner thighs, readying her, making her wait until the soft rush of sensation broke over her like a wave, spinning her round and lifting her up, until anticipation and want were tumbled together into a heady, breathless mixture as his darkly possessive gaze ran slowly down her body.

Jane twisted her legs together, trying in vain to stem the flood of embarrassment and want that pooled within. "Don't," was all he said, before he stirred his fingers lazily through the curls at the juncture of her thighs.

Her body drew even more taut, and more ready, impatient for the touch that would send her over the edge of simple pleasure and headlong into bliss.

"I want to kiss you."

She wanted to kiss him too—she opened her mouth to him, hungry for the taste of his lips upon hers.

But he kissed her there. There, where heat and need had become almost painful anticipation.

Jane could feel him push her legs wider, opening her to his gaze and his touch, and her mouth stayed open, shocked and pleased and wanting. Oh, yes. There.

He parted her folds with his thumbs, and blew a soft, warm preparatory breath across her. "You're beautiful."

Jane felt a thrill of forbidden pleasure at his words. And for the first time in her life, she felt entirely beautiful, and entirely free. Free to choose, free to make love to this extraordinary man. Her skin prickled with bright heat as his sea-roughened hands slid closer to the tight heat at the junction of her thighs, and his thumbs pushed her soft flesh gently apart.

The warmth of his mouth was both arousing and soothing, lulling her into desire gently, until with one precise application of friction, he licked her in a spot that sent silver bursts of shivers coursing over her skin, shaking her to her core, loosening and tightening the tense heat within her.

And then he did it again, only differently, his tongue swirling in the opposite direction, pulling her deeper and deeper into the vortex of her own desire.

But she was not alone. He felt it too somehow, this unholy need, this compulsion to touch and be touched, because he slipped a finger inside her, touching her deeply, stroking lightly and strongly all at the same time, until a burst of bliss radiated out from her belly, warming her through and through so her breath felt light and hot, so she was mouthing inarticulate words of yearning.

But he heard and understood. He fed the need, and threw tinder upon the flame of her need by sliding another finger along with the first. She felt full and yet drawn tight, inflamed by the enormity of her desire.

And then his tongue flicked over her one more time, and she could no longer hold herself together. She could no longer do anything but give herself over to the crashing wave of bliss and let it take her into oblivion.

Chapter Twenty-two

Dance watched Jane's breathing slowly subside, and resisted the urge to finish what she had started in undressing him. But he could not keep from easing his own need by lying down on top of her, and settling the weight of his body fully upon her. It gave him some semblance of control, made him understand his body's power and strength and size, and made him more aware than ever of his responsibility to her. To them both.

A sharp stab of conscience rose like a specter in the back of his mind, but he was too full of the glorious sight and intoxicating scent and exquisite feel of her to become prudent now.

Instead he lowered his ear to her breast bone so he could be closer to her, and listen to the quieting beat of her heart, and rest his head between her pillowed breasts. But that pleasure was a torture of its own, for he could not simply lie there and not touch, not taste.

Her skin was unutterably soft beneath his callused, questing fingers. Incredibly responsive—quick to react. And in arousing himself with the tight budded perfection of her breasts, he had aroused her as well.

"My turn." Her fingers were back at his buttons, swiftly undoing them in a clumsy manner that said more for her enthusiasm than her experience. But he let her. He rolled away, onto his back, and spread his arms wide in open supplication and surrender.

She rolled with him, straddling his lap, tugging his shirt free of his waistband, before she went for his breeches. Dance lifted his hips to assist her, clearing his arse off the ground, but pressing up into the soft heat of her in the process.

The look of astonished pleasure that widened her eyes, and had her gasping openmouthed for breath, had him doing it again, slower, and more completely. Thrusting his hips powerfully beneath her. And she reacted more completely, rolling her hips down into him as he pressed up, closing her eyes against the wave of pleasure.

But she opened those bright, inquisitive eyes soon enough, raking them over him, finding exactly what she wanted. She urged him to sit so she could haul his shirt off over his head. And her hands, her delicate, organizing hands sorted out all his pertinent parts, learning quickly the contours of his shoulders and neck, and taking great delight in finding that his flat nipples were nearly as sensitive as hers.

She was scientific in her approach, God bless her, meticulous in her attention to detail. He could feel his chest expand and flex under her delightfully curious fingers, and he took the opportunity to pull her more fully into his lap, and divest her of her remaining clothes just as she had divested him. Because he wanted nothing more than to make her lose all that intelligent, scientific aplomb. He wanted her naked and laughing and shrieking with unscientific pleasure.

In a minute. After he had unglued the lids of his eyes, and could see again, so blinded was he by the ravenous want that consumed him the moment Jane slid her hands into his breeches, and took hold of his cock.

He nearly came right then, so long had it been since he had indulged himself with a woman's touch.

But she wasn't just a woman. She was his steadfast, prepared, curious, scientific Jane, who was experimenting with her grip, and bringing him to the very edge of unspeakable bliss with her untutored touch. It was more than mere physical pleasure. It was a hunger for more than her body.

He wanted *her*. All of her.

He wanted her naked soul laid bare before him, just as he wanted to lay himself bare before her.

Dance shifted her off his lap, lifting her up onto her knees so he could peel off the last of her petticoat and chemise, shuck his breeches and kick them away so there was only the two of them, skin to skin, naked in Eden just as nature had made them.

He pulled her tight against him, so she could feel his arousal jutting between them. So she could know exactly what she was getting herself into.

She responded by wrapping her arms around his neck, and pressing her naked self to him from stem to stern, capturing his mouth in a kiss that left no doubt in his mind as to what she wanted.

"Jane," he began, wanting to be absolutely positive.

"Yes." She kissed the corner of his mouth, and set her teeth against the edge of his ear. "For Lord's sake, don't think to stop now. Please."

It was everything he wanted to hear. He didn't have anything more of patience within him—he felt pulled apart by the inexorable force of his desire for her. Right from the start, since the moment he had first laid eyes upon her, he had wanted her like this.

His. And his alone.

He rolled her onto her back beneath him, and came swiftly into her. He was nothing but impulse, giving way to the crashing force of need and primitive possessiveness. This woman—her face open and honest, her skin almost luminous in the pink and yellow cast of the morning sun—was his, and he would make her so in the most basic way possible.

He twined his hands with hers, and pushed them up over her head. He wanted nothing to interfere, nothing to stop him from taking possession of her beautiful, supple body.

She drew in a tight breath, full of wariness, and clutched at his hands where they pinioned her over her head.

"Jane." He kissed her mouth, and down the slide of her neck to the hollow at the base of her collarbones, to ease her worry, and to ease himself into her taut, tight body. He pressed the head of his cock into her soft, slick heat, nudging his way forward, rocking her bit by bit as he made his way. "It will get better—easier. I promise. I'll make it better."

"I'm fine. It's—"

He took her at her word, and let go of her hands, levering himself back a bit trying to give her room to breathe, but he felt as if he were looming over her, looking down at her body, pale and laid out before him on the beach like a pagan sacrifice.

She tried to cover her breasts with her hands, but he stopped her, pushing them over her head again. "You don't need to hide from me. I want to see you. I want to see everything from the golden pink of your nipples to the gold hair that covers your sex."

She shifted restlessly beneath him, her body rising in response to his words, and he held her wrists in one hand while he stilled her hips with his other, holding her as he took full possession of her tight, lush, inexperienced body.

She made a harsh, anguished sound, a sharp exhalation of pain that tore at him, but he could not stop.

"Oh, God. You liar." His voice was as fractured as his mind. "You're not fine."

"Now you believe in God." Her voice was strained, but her smile was a revelation—breathless and wicked and lovely and yes, yes, if she would look at him like that he would do everything he could to believe in God, because he obviously didn't deserve her.

"I believe in you. In your smile. And in your beauty. In your lov—" He stopped himself before he made an idiot of himself. "And in your perfect breasts and in your sweet little arse, and in your lush little passage." He suited his actions to his words, and touched her, cupping her beautiful breasts, and rounding her luscious bottom, and sweeping his hand around to delve into her soft hair where their bodies were fused together.

He could only swallow her pain on his kiss and murmur his assurances into her ear. "You gorgeous, terrible liar. But I won't lie to you. I'll make it good, Jane. I promise you."

He promised her with his mouth and his hands and his body and his single-minded attention. Watching her, waiting for her body to ease into acceptance. Waiting for acceptance to grow into desire.

When she opened her eyes to look up at him, he smiled and kissed her, and let go of her hands so she could hold and stroke him. Her fingers reached the curve of his face, and he found himself turning his head, rubbing the bristles of his unshaven cheek into her soft palm, tamed to her hand like a dog at her command.

Her fingers found their way to his nape, and then up, raking through his hair, petting him, and encouraging him without words, with only the evocative language of her lush body.

Lust overtook him then—dark and fierce and unstoppable. He pushed himself deeper within her, losing himself to the pull of her exquisite flesh, and the sinuous rhythm of her body as she began to move beneath him.

Her name became a chant in his head—Jane, Jane, Jane—filling his ears with a roar, and pushing him on when she arched beneath him. Dance drove himself on the rhythm, pulsing within her, until he lost himself to the hot slippery friction of her body beneath him, and his release washed through him and pulled him under.

Jane took to living on the island even more fully than even she might have wished—and she had wished and prayed a very great deal through all the hours that she had written and prepared and arranged. Yet not even she could have planned the joy she felt at the start of each new day, or the perfect suitability of their island to her purposes.

It was something of a trial that she could not always share her happiness with Dance, who fretted about how to repair the boat without tools, and worried about his crew and his ship and his future, and climbed the hill to make a signal fire and scan the endlessly gray horizon. She could only kiss the scowl from his brow and immerse herself in the joy of her work.

She set up a schedule that followed the tides so that she could make as thorough a survey of the reef as possible, but without the pinnace, a full circle of the islands clustered on the ring of reef was not possible.

But still, as she had told Dance that first day, there were shells aplenty to keep her busy from each yellow-tinged dawn through the slightly less gray, warming days to each purple sunset.

This morning the sun shone bright enough for her to spot a dark pink, scrolled cone shell of a sort she had never seen before, but she felt sure to be an undiscovered species of the genus *Textilia*. She was hurrying back to their little camp so she might get to mixing the colors before the shell might begin to fade out of the water, when Dance came striding along the sand from the other direction with that near permanent scowl etching an even deeper line into his brow than usual.

"What is wrong?" she asked immediately. He had been up to his lookout position on the hill, and might have sighted a ship far out to sea that she couldn't see.

But his mind was on something entirely different from potentially passing ships. "Good God. What are you wearing?"

Jane looked down at herself clad in little more than her chemise, and a canvas apron. With the sun peeking through the curtain of cloud, the day had proved too hot for the wool of her only gown. "My collecting apron. I devised it to protect my clothing when I'm out collecting. The seawater tends to be rather harsh on clothes, as you have no doubt noticed."

But he did not take notice. He bent one of his stony looks on her. "You're practically . . . I mean, I can see your bare legs."

It was something of a pleasure to nettle him so. Jane made her voice as bland and easy as the breeze. "Can you? Oh, good Lord. Yes, there my legs are, at the end of my feet."

"Jane." His voice held a note of warning she blithely ignored.

"Why, Captain, I had no idea you were such a puritan."

"Jane." His eyes grew a stormier green.

"You will recall we've lost all our other clothing." She decided upon an instructional tone. "And we are quite, quite alone. And if any of the natives do come along, chances are that they will be quite naked, so all in all, I'm feeling quite sanguine about my sartorial choices."

"Sanguine," he repeated before he closed his eyes, as if the very sight of her pained him. And she was sure it did. She had endeavored to make it so. "How can you have no idea what you do to me? How can a woman so learned and so clever have absolutely no clue that the sight of her rather magnificent bosom pressed so innocently against the plain cotton of her chemise leaves me eaten up with lust and longing for her?"

"Dance." He was teasing her, even as he sounded so put out.

"No. You've left off your stays, and a moment ago, when you turned to face the wind to push your hair out of your eyes, your rosy pink nipples peaked into visible buds against the fabric of that chemise."

She had no resistance when he looked at her like that. As if nothing mattered to him but her. As if he could see into the needy selfish depths of her soul, and wanted her anyway. "I know."

"You know?"

Jane all but stopped breathing. There was heat and even pain that became pleasure in her chest where his words rumbled down inside her. "Yes." The word sounded breathless and sure and frightened all at the same time, but he slowly began to smile, and she had nothing left of fright, only sureness and want. "I know."

He took her hand, and without another word led her back along the sand line of the beach to their camp, and carefully placed her beautiful shell—which was one day in the near future going to be christened *Textilia fenmora* after the expedition's patron, or even perhaps, if she dared, *Textilia burkesana*—in her specimen bucket.

And then he loosed the ties of her apron, and set that carefully aside, just as he did her chemise, until she was well and thoroughly naked. And then he made love to her with his hands and his mouth and his tongue and his body, until she could think no more of shells, or patrons, or tomorrow, and could only think from each heady moment to the next. And wait for the bliss that was his gift to her to explode within, and leave her sated, and thinking about how next she might seduce him.

For the first time in as long as he could remember, Dance felt himself begin to relax. Jane had already awoken, and had quietly eased herself off his chest and away before he was sufficiently alert enough to hold her back. So he did what he had never done—never in all his years of being in the navy, not even before that, as far back as he could remember—he lazed about his pallet bed in the soft morning air.

In a little while he would begin his day with his usual walk up to the top of the promontory at the north end of the small island to check the horizon for ships. If he had been left to his own choices, he would have made their camp there so that the moment a ship was sighted he could light the signal fire without having to leave her, and sprint up the hill.

But Jane had been right—the promontory was the most exposed place on the island, and it was far more comfortable and convenient and practical for them to camp nearer the drinking water and fruit trees down the side of the hill. And the walk gave him something to do.

But on a day like today, when the sun was strong enough to shine through the strange atmospheric gloom, he gave himself the pleasure of watching Jane instead. She had taken to their primitive life as if she were born to it—as if she had spent years happily cracking coconuts open on sharp rocks and wearing next to nothing. When the sun shone down, and made her hair and skin golden and glowing, it was hard for him to remember her as that buttoned-up lady scientist of Portsmouth harbor.

But lady scientist she was, now more than ever. And when she took up her pails and her nets and set off up the beach for the most accessible part of the reef, Dance shook off his lethargy and set himself to his chores, collecting water, and gathering fruit and firewood before he went up the hill.

This was his job—this was what he spent nearly every minute that he was with her in the comfortable camp thinking about—looking for ships. And looking for signs of *Tenacious*'s boats.

They had to have come somewhere near. They had to have been subject to the same forces of wind and current as he. Doc Whitely ought to have been as aware as he of their position at the time of the storm, and the location of the nearest land. The Pitcairn Islands had been on Royal Navy charts for nearly thirty years. They had had only an hour's advantage on Dance and Jane, if at all.

They must be nearby.

Unless they had been rescued by a ship—the southern ocean off the northwest coast of South America was winter whaling grounds for Yankee whalers. It was more than conceivable that the small flotilla of *Tenacious*'s boats—if they had stayed together—might have been visible to the eyes of a larger ship in a way that their small pinnace might not. And certainly any whaler, with its churning stacks sending inky plumes of smoke high into the sky, would have drawn the boats' attention.

Dance shaded his eyes against the sudden glare as a few fitful rays of light broke through the gray to dapple the lagoon, and surveyed the horizon one more time, searching, always searching. He had to employ the trick he had learned long ago as a midshipman of not looking for anything but water, so the moment there was anything different out there on the horizon, his eye would pick it up.

But he was no topman. Picking a ship out of a thousand miles of water had never been his strong suit. Just what his strong suit was, was moot these days. And with every day that went by, it seemed to matter less and less.

With every day, he grew more accustomed to the idea that they might never leave.

He turned full circle, surveying the horizon in all directions, when a movement on the beach below caught his eye—Jane walking barefoot along the sandy ridge of beach at the outer edge of the reef. Her long blond hair was blowing out of her braid, and the wind was pressing her sun-bleached chemise against her legs, and making the ragged hems flutter in the breeze.

She carried one of her canvas buckets, and a long thin pole, suitable for poking and prodding snails and other creatures. She was on with the business of her day—collecting—wearing only her chemise and that strangely erotic canvas apron that made her look like she was naked beneath it.

And then she was naked. Because she was peeling the apron and chemise off, and leaving them in a neat, organized little stack on the sand, and wading deeper and deeper into the lagoon. Entirely and thoroughly naked.

Dance's feet, which appeared to be far more instinctively intelligent than the rest of his body, were carrying him down the path before he had even properly formed an excuse for going to her. But here he was, rushing down a hillside as if that canvas apron were on fire. He rather thought it was he who was on fire.

He broke out onto the beach near their camp just as she disappeared under the surface. An instinct he could not stop, and could not direct to better use, had him speeding to a run, splashing his way down the curved line of the beach onto the reef, and across the ankle-deep water.

"Jane!"

She surfaced a dozen yards from him with a gasp and a smile as wide as the lagoon. "Dance. It's all right. The water doesn't bother me at all like I thought it would. Because I've located those *Tridacna gigas* I saw that first day—bivalves the size of a breadbasket. Four of them. Come see."

What he saw was the neat pile of her clothes on the rock outcropping. And what he saw through the clear blue water not a bivalve clam, but the unmistakable outline of her naked body, the pink crests of her breasts, and the darker whorl of dark blond hair at the apex of her thighs.

His eyes had not deceived him. "You really are completely naked, aren't you?"

She stared at him for a long moment, her body moving to and fro as she treaded water, before she answered. "Not completely. I am wearing a knife."

Lust, pure, clean, and unadulterated by anything like gentlemanly manners or caution, sliced through him as if she had cut away his clothes with that knife. Every fiber and sinew in his body came alive with awareness. Awareness of her golden body dappled in the fitful sunlight, her arms and hair glinting and glistening in the sun. Awareness of his own body, his chest expanding with something more heady than air, and his cock swelling in arousal.

"Jane." He could hear the strain in his voice as he waded in until the water came up to his calves. "I want to see you."

It took her only a moment to answer. "Then I want to see you." She looked up at him, those wide, forthright blue eyes shining at him. "All of you."

Dance backed himself out of the water until he was completely on the beach, and began to take off his clothes. He went slowly, methodically, giving her time to say something, or protest, or swim away.

But she didn't. She watched him undoing each and every button at the neck of his shirt before he drew it slowly over his head. And folded it neatly and placed it next to hers. He heeled off his worn-down boots, stooping to pull the heavy leather off his feet, all the while watching her, making sure she felt the brush of his gaze against her wet skin.

Making her part her lips, her delicate nostrils flare, and her skin pebble up in anticipation.

He moved his hands even more slowly to unbutton the flap on his breeches. He shucked the breeches and small clothes in one fluid motion. And he was naked before her. Tall, erect, and proud, not hiding.

She swam forward slowly, stroking the water in a languid, deliberate fashion without ever once taking her eyes from his, until she was only fifteen feet away from him. And then she stood. And the water lapped against the very peaks of her breasts.

Dance dove into the water, letting the cool liquid slide of the lagoon wash over his skin. He surfaced within reach of her, but didn't touch her. Jane had turned toward him, her hair trailing out like kelp.

He swam out farther, circling around her, so he could dive down below the surface and see the weightless liquid grace of her body underwater. The pale slide of her long limbs, the dark slash of the belt holding her collecting knife, slung from one shoulder and across her chest. The suspended sway of her long blond hair, the erotic contrast of the darker curls at the apex of her thighs.

He surfaced next to her, and a bead of water at the corner of her mouth drew him in. He took her in his arms and kissed her, the cool of the lagoon contrasting with the surprising heat of her mouth, and making him think of other surprising, heated places on her body that he wanted to explore and discover.

She wrapped her hands around his back, molding her soft supple body to his chest, felt the pillowed push of her breasts against the taut skin of his chest. He let them sink with their mouths and tongues enmeshed, but she thrashed away from him.

She shot to the surface and he came up next to her, to hear her gasping for air. He reached for her to steady her and buoy her up, but she mastered her fear and her memories. "I want something different," she said. "Something new."

And he thought she meant that she wanted to erase the memories of the shipwreck and the dark water closing over her with a newer, better experience of the water, but something just as lasting.

"I've got you." He kissed her again. "I'll hold you up." He cupped one hand beneath her nape, and the other across the small of her back, until she tipped her head back into his hand and floated upon her back, a pale, erotic lotus blossom upon the surface of the water.

She half closed eyes that had gone wide and dark with arousal, but his gaze had already strayed because the pink tips of her breasts were tightened into buds, pointing skyward, begging for his kiss.

He covered her with his mouth, tonguing and sucking until her back arched and her hips rose to the surface— the pale topography of her another island he wanted to explore. His own body tightened and stretched in response, his erection curving away from his body. He slipped behind her and floated up underneath, his hands cradling and teasing her breasts, his fingers rolling and tweaking the furled sensitive peaks. The slight weight of her body above his assuaged his savage need to have contact with her only a little. Not enough. Not nearly enough.

He pulled them back toward the sand, towing her slowly, taking his time. Kissing her ears and nose and eyes and lips, until his thighs were out of the water, and he sat, waist deep in the shallows, with water lapping across their bodies. Out of the water her breasts took on a pleasant gravity in his hands, full and round. He fitted her snug against him, with her back against his chest. His rampant erection assuaged by the heat and friction between their bodies, the caress of skin against skin. His cock held between the taut globes of her sweet arse.

He kissed the side of her neck, and worked his way down along the long slide of sensitive tendon to the delicate line of her collarbone. Wrapped his legs with hers and teased her thighs open. He could see the soft tangle of hair covering her sex. Splayed his dark hand across the taut white flesh of her belly, sliding lower, scooping his thumbs across the erotic little hollows at the top of her thighs. Placed his hands on the inside of her thighs and pulled them wide apart, so he could look down over her shoulder and see her. So she could look down and see his hands on her body, and watch what he did to her.

Because he knew he was already aroused beyond all expectation and all experience. Nothing could compare to the feel of this woman in his arms. Nothing could compare to making love to her out of doors in the broad daylight, where there was no mistaking the flush of her skin and the heated response of her heightened breathing.

It was new and different and supremely, extraordinarily erotic.

Making love out of doors. Living with a man, with her lover, sharing everything that she had and everything that she was, as openly and honestly as the first man and the first woman in the Garden of Eden. It was all new and different and absolutely marvelous.

She felt as if she were discovering who she really was beneath the layers and years of duty and arranging things just so. She was emerging like a snail from within its shell to find that she was beautiful.

Because she could see that she was beautiful in his eyes.

Just as he was in hers.

And she wanted to see him. She wanted to meet him eye to eye, lip to talented, taut lip. She turned in his arms, and crawled atop him, straddling his waist, clasping her heels together behind his back to snug herself up tight, and press the wanton part of her body against him.

She liked that she could look at him, and kiss him, and be an equal to him in this new dance they did together. All she had to do was whisper his name into his ear, and he was there, his mouth on hers, warm and firm. She did as he did, and learned from him, taking his lip carefully between her teeth, and worrying at it for a long, sweet moment before she bit down enough to show him that she wanted him at least as much as he wanted her.

She liked that she could wrap her arms around him, and hold him close, and run her fingers through his short, wet hair. She liked that he could close his big strong hand around the back of her neck, and pull her close, and hold her face still before him to kiss her tenderly. And then not so tenderly, but with heat and need and hunger.

She liked the warm sound of abandonment that flew up from her throat, and the answering sound of possessiveness that came from his.

And then he did the thing that she liked best—he looked into her eyes, and held himself perfectly, absolutely still, and looked at her. As if she mattered to him. As if she were the only thing in the whole of the world that mattered.

And he said the words that he knew would enflame her. "I want you, Jane. I want to put myself in you, and feel the sweet heat of your body."

And what she heard, and what she saw when he spoke so, and looked at her with those relentless, unfathomable green eyes, was that he cared for her, and would care for her as long as possible.

And she knew that she loved him.

And knew she would go on loving him until the end of her days.

When she was old and gray and nodding in her armchair before a warm fire at home on the Isle of Wight, this was what she was going to remember. This moment with this man looking at her as if she were the rarest creature in creation. Looking at her with admiration. Making her love herself. Sharing the most extraordinary time of her life.

"Thank you," she whispered in his ear.

"You are welcome." He smiled and kissed her and raised her up just enough so that he could find her entrance before he lowered her slowly upon him.

She could not look at him then, could not bear the erotic weight of his gaze without flying into a hundred pieces. She ducked her head, and set lips to the pulse in his throat. She could feel the hectic beat of the blood in his veins, and taste the salt tang of his skin. She did as he had done, and plied her teeth along the strong tendon at the side of his neck, nipping her way back toward his mouth.

And when she kissed him, he took her bottom lip between his teeth and bit down, just enough, just enough to arouse her and mark her as his.

Her breathing fractured, and her eyes slid shut against the liquid silver glare of the water. Her breasts rose, and fell against his chest in blissful torturous friction, each breath sending a tongue of flame licking deeper, and deeper still.

And he felt it too. His head went back, and his eyes clamped shut in an attitude of blissful agony. "Jane, Jane, Jane."

And she answered with her body pressing in time to his, following the cadence and the gentle lap of the waves against her back. And then there was nothing else but him. Nothing but his heat and his care and his passion. Nothing but the bliss he gave her like a gift.

A groan of pure uncensored pleasure shuddered out of him and into her, and he began to stroke in and out of her—long languid thrusts she felt from the pebbled tips of her breasts all the way down the tender insides of her thighs and on to the toes that dug into the coarse, wet sand for purchase. It was too much and not enough. It was everything.

And then his hand slicked down through the water between them to find the very center of her being and touch her just so, sending her careering over the edge. Losing herself to him, and finding herself all at the same glorious moment in time.

Chapter Twenty-three

"We can't stay here forever, you know."

Jane looked across the low burning fire at Dance, who stared into the glowing coals as if they might foretell the future. After the few blissful days of sun, the wind had shifted to the southwest, and brought back the yellow-streaked, dismal dawns. In the face of such foreboding gloom, the warmth of the fire had seemed comforting.

"I know," she hedged. "But it seems silly to think about it until the boat is repaired."

He had gone at it with a vengeance the afternoon before, dragging woods of various kinds down from the hill, and fashioning a sort of mallet with some of her collecting tools.

"What is the great hurry?"

He looked at her then, and it was as if he were suddenly standing twenty feet off instead of two, so great was the distance in his gaze. "You are a naturalist, Jane. Surely you know the natural consequence of our copulation."

The word itself was a slap. "Copulation?" As if they were animals and had not chosen this physical intimacy, this spiritual bond with one another of their own accord and free will. As if he had not treated her with infinite care. "Don't be deliberately cruel."

"I'm not trying to be cruel." He ran his hand through his hair in a well-recognized gesture of frustration. "I'm trying to be a realist. You could be with child. Or you will be shortly if we keep on the way we've started." His scowl was small and tight to cover the rising color in his cheeks. "It's inevitable."

"Not so inevitable as all that." They had never discussed such an intimate thing before. Indeed, she had never discussed such an intimate thing with *anyone* before. She had never discussed with anyone that her courses were irregular at best, and that they had stopped months ago at the start of the voyage, long before she had ever even dreamt of physical intimacy with him. "I have no reason to think that I am fertile. Indeed, I have reason to think the opposite."

"Jane." He shook his head, and suddenly there was no distance between them, because he had come to her, and had put his arms around her and was holding her tight. "We can't stay here forever. We can't. Sooner or later we will need to leave. Or someone—anyone, friend or foe— could find us. We have to be prepared."

The practical part of her—the part that made lists and weighed possibilities and arranged everything just so— agreed. "I know it can't be forever. But why can it not be for now? Why can we not enjoy this time while we are here?"

He laughed, a rueful sound full of self-rebuke. "Devil take me, Jane. If I enjoy you any more, I'd be a cad."

She would not accept such one-sided logic. "How can you be a cad if I enjoy you as much."

"Do you really?"

"How could you have any doubt?" He was looking at her in a way that made her feel rather like she was the specimen being examined. Rather like he was taking note of each and every movement or muscular twitch, or the variations in her coloring.

But he could not be. He wasn't like her. He wasn't a scientist. He wasn't observant. He was just a man with nothing better to do now that he was beached like a whale upon the sand. He was frustrated and out of sorts, without any real employment for his talents. And resentful that she did.

"Surely someone else must be missing you?" He would not let the matter drop. "Your family? The other J. E. Burke?"

"I don't know." She gave him the bitter truth. "I don't think so. I honestly have no idea if they would even take me back after what I've done, were I to try and go home."

"Won't you? Where else would you go?"

The question was like another slap, stinging her face with unexpected heat. "I don't know." She let the terrible silence stretch out horribly between them, hurt that he could not, or would not see what she had thought so obvious—that they would somehow be together. That their time together meant something more. That she meant something more than a temporary mistr—

She could not even think the word.

"Were I you," he finally said, "I would not be so quick to abandon my family."

"But I have. And it is done." And then it occurred to her—that she knew nothing of Dance beyond her own experience of the man. She knew he was kind and loyal and brave and steadfast—almost to a fault. But she had no idea—she had never asked—if there were others in *his* life. A family, or God forbid, a wife.

No. No, he could not be so cruel.

But fate had been cruel before.

That truth made her feel light-headed and dizzy, as if she were still at sea in the bobbing little pinnace. But she gathered her courage like fistfuls of sand, and asked. "What of you? What of your family?"

He looked at her, and his expression was so bleak, her heart felt as if it had been torn into ragged tatters. "I have no family."

Jane had braced herself for a blow that didn't come. "No family? Surely there is—was—someone?" People had to come from somewhere and someone.

"My mother passed away some years ago. While I was at sea."

The hollowness in his voice rebuked her. "I'm so sorry."

He tried to be philosophical. "It was years ago. After Trafalgar." He rested his elbows on his drawn-up knees. "I didn't know it until quite some time after. I was posted to a new ship in the aftermath of the battle and the hurricane that nearly did for us what the French and Spanish never could. But the letter from the parish vicar finally reached me nearly a year after she had died. And by then . . ." He shifted his shoulders uncomfortably. "I had been away for six years by then, and had already ceased thinking of her very much."

Jane suddenly thought of her own mother. She had never thought that her mother would not be there when she came back. She *had* worried that someone so concerned with appearances would not welcome her back into her home, but she had never thought that she might be dead. It was a sobering thought.

"And what of your father?"

He blew out a breath as if he had been holding it in expectation of the question. Dance turned to look at her. "I have no father."

Again, Jane had to stifle the urge to point out the scientific impossibility of such an occurrence, but he amended that statement on his own. "At least I never met him."

He waited while the cold hard truth of the matter settled into her mind. "Oh. You mean—"

"Yes. The truth that I have never shared with another person on this earth is that I never knew the man, and have no idea if he is living or dead. I only know that sixteen-odd years ago, when I was twelve years old, he paid for my position as a midshipman in the Royal Navy, and that was the first and the last that I have ever heard of him. I can only assume I am the natural son of some man of consequence who felt he could discharge his duty to me and my mother by starting me in a profession, and leaving it at that."

"Did your mother never say?"

"No. She did not. Never. I had thought she might, once, just before I had first shipped out with the navy. But she had held her peace."

"And she left no record? No indication?" How someone could omit recording a fact of such importance to a young man, Jane could not fathom.

"No. Not that I know of. But I never went back."

"Back to where?"

"Our home. Her home, I suppose, for she lived there longer without me than we had ever lived there together. But I hadn't lived there for almost seven years by the time I found out she had died. It didn't seem important to go back."

"Not even to find out who your father was?"

"If she had wanted to tell me, she would have. The cold truth of the matter, Jane, is that I am a bastard, and no better than I should be. I have advanced thus far in my career only through hard work, but I will, as soon as we are either rescued, or I can repair the pinnace and we can rejoin the rest of the civilized world, be court-martialed for my loss of *Tenacious*."

"But you did everything to save the ship. You alone—"

"The Admiralty will decide that for themselves. So think very carefully before you— I am a bastard, Jane, with nothing and no one to recommend me except my conduct, and that too will be called into question. I have nothing to offer."

She made a cautious but heartfelt reply. "You have yourself. Just as I have myself." She would show him how she felt about him, so he would be left in no doubt. "I am all I have to offer. But offer myself I do."

"Jane." When he said her name like that, it was as if he had touched her, as if he played some secret chord within that only he knew. "So you see why we must go back? Sooner rather than later. The sooner I can clear my name—Without doing so, I have no chance."

It didn't make sense to her. They could stay right where they were indefinitely, where problems of court-martials and dubious ancestry meant nothing. "Can we not stay long enough for me to finish my catalogue?"

He looked away, out over the lagoon. "How much longer do you need to fill those precious notebooks of yours?" he asked.

Months, she wanted to say. Another month at the least, was on the tip of her tongue. But she had already found and recorded at least three new species—more than enough to see her made famous for her discoveries. More than enough to publish her own monograph of conchology under the aegis of the Royal Society. More than enough, even though she felt as if she had barely catalogued the first two sections of the reef.

But more than that would be selfish. "I'd like to make one last check of the northern tip of the island after that change in the wind last week." She ought not be greedy. He had his reasons for needing to return. So even though she had rather stay for the rest of her life alone on the island instead of face the sea in a boat again, she said, "If I have to choose a limit, one more week should be enough. Please. Promise me you'll wait another week."

"Then one week you shall have. I promise. But after that I'll light the signal fire and keep it burning until such time as we sight a ship."

Dance left her to her shells and her snails and her disquiet, and headed up the hill, ignoring his instinctive need to take her in his arms and kiss her until they both forgot there was anything else in the world besides the two of them. Because she wasn't likely to have him now, was she, now that he'd told her all?

But the telling had left that sour feeling in his gut as if he'd swallowed a barrel of brine. He felt betrayed, even though he had been the one to betray himself.

But it were better for her that he had told her. Better that she knew exactly what he was. Unfit for the grand-daughter of a lord, and the great-granddaughter of a duke.

She deserved better.

The only problem being that he didn't want her to have better—he wanted to have her himself. He wanted to have her and hold her until death did them part.

But he could not have her until he cleared his name. And he could not clear his name if he did not get them off this island.

And so on he tromped up the hill with leaden feet, until he came to his well-stacked pyre, laid with layers of dry tinder and brush to catch easily and burn dirty, throwing up as much smoke as possible into the sky. Everything was in readiness for the moment when he would light it, and keep it lit day and night to draw someone—anyone at this point—to the island.

It was another flat, gray day, with the wind out of the southwest, and the sea stretching pale and colorless in every direction. Not very promising.

But he had nothing else to do, so he kept himself busy by taking out her telescopic glass—*her* telescopic glass. He didn't even have his own bloody, beat-up glass—it was on the cutter somewhere, hopefully being employed to better purpose by Punch or one of the officers. If they had survived.

That grim thought pushed him back to scanning the horizon, back to his usual three-hundred-and-sixty-degree rotation, checking the seas in all directions. He made a full turn of the compass, when something, some irritant, like an eyelash stuck in his eye, made him look again east by south.

The sea was flat and placid, and with the wind out of the southwest, any ship from the east would have to take a more northerly heading—Dance's mind wandered to the ordering and setting of sails, as if he needed to come up with the correct trim for answering a question before the lieutenants' board of examination.

But there it was again—the thin shadow, as fine as an eyelash, a darker tick above the surface of the sea.

Dance steadied his suddenly slick palms on the cool brass of the glass, and tried to control the surge of blood pounding in his ears. Steady on, man. This was no different than sighting another ship at sea from the quarterdeck of *Tenacious.* Except that it was.

He tamped his excited impatience down as if it were an exuberant midshipman, and kept his eye steady on the dark tick mark, willing it to evolve into the high crosstree of a foremast top. And there, the wide slash of flat color from a rectangular sail beneath.

He waited another full minute for the tiny bits of shape and color to resolve themselves into something more, something that would prove that the sight was not a product of his imagination—a hallucination he had conjured out of demented will—something that he could distinguish as a number of masts or a particular set of sails to work out its identity.

And then that single tick mark shifted, and changed, presenting three clear mast heads, leading away. The vessel was changing course to the south. Away from them.

Dance abandoned his glass and leaped to the pyre, falling to his knees to fumble with the tinderbox and flint. Striking over and over, until he could calm himself enough for the dry tinder to finally catch a spark. He fed the fire, blowing gently to tease the licking fingers of fire into flame. It seemed so monstrously slow that he moved to the other side of the pyre, and pulled away some of the brush so that the steady southwesterly wind could fan the flame.

Finally, finally inky gray smoke from the green brush began to curl into the air.

He kept at it, feeding the growing fire, replacing the green brush from the stack he had made nearby to keep the smoke billowing into a column, checking over his shoulder to see if the ship had gone over the horizon, or if it had altered course.

He took up the glass again, scanning the area where he had last seen it, squinted down the length of the telescopic lenses until his head began to ache. And still he could not find it. There was nothing.

It was gone.

He had failed. He had lost his chance to take Jane back to civilization.

Jane. She would not be upset by his failure. She would be relieved, the strange girl.

But Dance could not shake that sour feeling that still swilled around his gut like a keg of stale, vinegared wine. The feeling that told him the longer he was away, the harder it was going to be to reclaim his life and his profession. The feeling that told him Ransome was out there, alive, and doing them both, he and Jane, ill.

Fuck all. Dance gave in to the roil of frustration and anger and kicked the nearest log with his threadbare boots. Sparks danced into the atmosphere and faded away. Just the way he would if he could not get them off the island.

Forget what he had promised Jane. Time was of the essence—he could feel it in his bones. He would keep the fire burning from this moment on, even if he had to chop the whole of the island down to do so.

Normally, Jane filled her notebooks with detailed lists of each shell's dimensions—volume and measurements—and characteristics, as well as informal sketches of her shells, drawing them from different perspectives, and working out the exact colors she wanted to record or highlight in the formal drawing. There was an unwritten code to scientific drawing. The perspective was always precisely from above. The proportions were exactly to scale, and the colors had to be as true to life as possible—something that was often difficult with shells, as their colors changed and faded when out of the water.

Which was why Jane took such great care to keep her subjects as alive as possible when drawing them. Her treasure of the morning was the murex comb. She had delineated the outline on a loose page before starting on the formal drawing in her book.

She bent over her drawing board in concentration, relaxed and happy, clothed only in the simple cover of her shift and petticoats, comfortable as the morning warmed slowly. Jane was already deep into articulating the finely wrought arms of the spiny murex comb, wanting to get the delicate colors exactly right, when the hair on her arm stood up, as if from an ill wind.

And she smelled the fire that Dance had promised her he would not light.

Well, damn his eyes.

Jane threw down her pen—no, she stopped herself from throwing it, though she wanted to. But the ink would stain the drawing, or obliterate the detailed notes, and where would she be for her fit of pique? Instead, she wiped the pen dry, and took up one of her collapsible pails to march down the beach to get more cool lagoon water to cover the murex, and perhaps she could find another one of the *Triton* whelks, in a smaller, more juvenile size.

And out at the edge of the beach, where the larger island tapered into the thin line of reef, she could look up and see the dark plume of smoke Dance was sending high into the sky. Just as he had so earnestly promised her he would not. Why would he do that?

Only if he needed to.

Her selfish indignation faded into something more acute.

Jane turned and looked out to sea, at the flat gray expanse stretching in every direction, following the long line of the reef as it circled around them. And there, at the far south side of the atoll, was a ship riding to anchor.

A Royal Navy ship, judging from the pennant flying at the masthead. Just as he had wanted. Just as he had told her it must be.

She heard the clanging roll of the bower cable as the ship let go its anchor, and came to moor outside the reef. A ship's boat immediately appeared over the side.

And there she was, exposed on the slip of beach in nothing more than a chemise and a scrap of canvas apron. Oh, God, what would they think?

Jane hunkered down and scuttled behind a rock, trying to gauge the distance back to the camp where her only gown hung on a line beside the tented tarpaulin. Pray God Dance was watching and had seen—both her and the boat—and would head down to the beachhead on the south side. He had brought them here—he could go greet them.

She abandoned the shelter of her rock for a low run down the length of the beach, trying as soon as she reached the tree line to stay in the shelter of the deeper shade, where she might pass unseen. Because all she could think of was the row of officers on the quarterdeck of that ship, with their array of brass telescopic glasses all trained on the island.

All peering at her as she tugged the worn wool dress and stays off the line, and ducked behind the cover of the shade tent. Heat and shame took a chokehold of her throat, and built into stinging pain behind her eyes.

Because as she hastily laced up her stays, and threw

the dress over her head, she was full of childish, angry resentment. They had come, and ruined it all. Damn their intrusive eyes.

"Well," growled a voice she had hoped never to hear again. "Isn't this cozy?"

Jane whipped around, and there was Ransome.

Chapter Twenty-four

Goddamned Ransome, the ill wind that blew nobody any good, standing not ten feet away from her on her beach.

She hated him. Hated him. His presence seemed to still the breeze and suck the air from her lungs. She had to fight for breath.

But where were the others? And where was Dance? How could Ransome be here alone, sneering at her?

"Shoulda known you'd land on yer feet, like a cat in the cream."

Cats never put their feet in cream if they could help it, so neither would Jane. She saved her breath to cool her porridge. Or scream for Dance if need be. Because Ransome did not look as if he were weak from enduring the privations of days and days at sea. And he had not taken the oiled canvas water bag down from its place hanging in the tree and slake his thirst, or try to shove coconut meat into his wide, leering mouth.

Instead he came into the neatly organized confines of their camp, and looked until he found Dance's cloak. "So you both got out. Damned if he hasn't the devil's own luck."

Jane held her tongue. They hadn't drowned, no thanks to him, and it clearly had him madder and meaner than ever. His wide leering smile was the same, though his clothes were new—likely given to him from the stores of his new ship.

Where were the others from his ship?

And more importantly, where was Dance?

"You were always a mouthy little thing, talking back to the captain." Ransome's laugh was as mirthless as ever it had been—too full of his own surly pleasure. "Cat got your tongue now?"

"What do you want?" Jane took a step toward him, but also toward her drawing area, where she could take surreptitious hold of the small but sharp knife she kept for sharpening her pencils.

"I want my own back. What he took from me." Ransome took out his frustration with Dance on nearby inanimate objects, ripping the water bag down from the tree, and kicking it about as a way of showing her that she would soon be treated the exact same way if she did not give him what he wanted. "Where is it? Where's the damn log?"

The logbook from *Tenacious?* The one that Dance had kept under his coat, and that she had stowed safely away in the oilskin pouch? How could a book give him his "own back"?

Her knowledge of the book must have shown on her face, because Ransome advanced toward her slowly, as if he were savoring the moment before he throttled her to death.

Where was Dance?

"It's here somewhere." Jane feigned looking around as she backed away, picking up the small work board on which she drew, and carrying it with her, keeping it carefully between them. Ready to cosh him if she could.

Except that she didn't know if she could really cosh him, because the fear was like a vise around her lungs, cutting off the air—she could hear her breath start to come in little gasping pants.

"That's it," he agreed on a raspy laugh. "Be afraid. You'll

think better when you're afraid, and you'll do as yer told. Where is it?"

Despite her best intentions to lie and prevaricate and do whatever else she could think of to stall Ransome until Dance got there, the image of the very book Ransome sought—the dark marbled paper on the thick cover—rose in her mind, and her glance strayed toward the small stack of oilcloth pouches where she had placed it last.

And Ransome saw it on her face. "Where is it? Or so help me I'll gut you from stem to stern and leave you bleeding for the seagulls to pick to pieces." He pulled out a knife that looked bigger than her foot for emphasis.

Jane was more than convinced of his sincerity. Her heart was pounding in her ears, filling her up with the rush of fear. But even afraid, she had to be smarter than Ransome. She had to think of something, anything to keep him until Dance could get here. Dance would know what to do. Dance would stop him.

But Dance wasn't there. She was.

And she was J. E. Burke, conchologist, and she was going to handle Ransome. She was going to manage him. Somehow. "I'll get it for you—I'll get it, if you'll just put that knife away."

Ransome had his own ideas of bargaining. "I'll not put the knife away until you hand it to me."

"I'll get it for you, I will. Just"—she made her face the picture of weak, feminine distress—"don't hurt me."

Ransome smiled, and lowered his knife slightly to show he would do as she asked. But his smile—his smile held all the single-minded meanness of a great feral tom-cat who likes to toy with its mouse before he devours it. The moment she gave him what he wanted, he would turn on her with that knife.

And where was Dance? Dance who in the past month had hardly ever been so far away as out of the reach of her hand. Strong, loving, protective Dance.

Where was he?

Where was he while she was alone with Ransome?

She couldn't give Ransome what he wanted—but she couldn't *not* give him what he wanted. She had to *pretend* to do so.

She sidled around him toward the small stack of identical notebooks, neatly arranged in their protective pouches, just as she had stacked them. Efficient, organized, meticulous Jane.

"Did you want the captain's old log, or Dance's new one?" she lied. "Or the copy of the old one?" She meant to page through the books, as if they were the ones she was looking for. Stalling until he realized they were not, in fact, logbooks.

"Fuck me blind," the greasy bastard muttered. "I thought I'd taken the damn thing."

Jane tucked that piece of information away in her brain, and refrained from answering. And Ransome's question was purely rhetorical—not that he would know what that meant. Because another idea had popped into her brain—if Ransome had taken the logbook, why did he not know he had? Or had Ransome been unable to tell one book from the other?

He had needed young Honeyman to write that note for him, hadn't he?

She reached for the stack of oilskin parcels, and took the first one off the stack, but her hands were shaking so hard, she dropped it to her feet in the sand, opening so he would see that it was not the logbook he sought. And if he couldn't see that—if he really couldn't read—she would simply tell him that she had the wrong book, and would go on to the next. And then the next. Stalling for time.

But Ransome either didn't see or didn't care. He rushed forward to snatch the book she had dropped out of Jane's hands, and immediately throw it, oilcloth bag and all, straight into the cooking fire. The oils embedded in the canvas to make it waterproof quickly caught fire, sending up an inky smoke.

And then he grabbed the rest of the small stack and tumbled them all into the fire after.

"No!" Jane started toward the fire, as if she could do something—kick sand over the flames to smother them out, or simply snatch the precious volumes out of the flames— and save the books.

And save herself.

But Ransome was as quick as he was ignorant, and he hauled her back, wrenching her arm behind her back, and holding her helpless to do anything but watch the books go up in licking flames.

"No." Jane struggled vainly against his strength. "No. Those aren't—"

"Jane!" Dance came striding around the bend in the beach, and into view with a host of others—a blue-coated officer and a party of red-clad marines. Dance's face was animated and pleased, sure of their deliverance, until the moment he saw Ransome. "Let her go this instant."

But Ransome—Ransome had his own ideas and ambitions, and had his lies at the ready. "I've caught her trying to destroy his log," he said to the blue-coated naval officer. "But I was too late." He must have judged the books sufficiently destroyed because he shoved her away from him.

"No!" She fell to her knees in front of the fire, maniacally shoveling handfuls of sand onto the burning remains, desperately trying to smother the flames sufficiently so she could grasp the singed corner of a cover, and pull it out. But the book was still so hot it burned the ends of her fingers.

She dropped it upon her knees where the sparks popped, and embedded themselves in the wool of her dress.

Dance was there in another moment, pulling her up so

that the book fell to the sand, batting away at her skirts to extinguish the burning embers. Her dress was peppered with a dozen blackened holes. "Jane," Dance said again, as if she were a child, and could not understand what was happening. "Jane, it's all right. We've been saved."

Perhaps he had been saved. But she had just been ruined.

Ransome smiled as if he had heard the words in her head. "And there *he* is." He pointed his rough-whiskered chin at Dance. "There's the man I told you about—the man who killed Captain Muckross. Take him."

For a very long moment no one moved. No one so much as shifted in the sand before the rage that he had been keeping clamped in irons roared free, and Dance launched himself at Ransome. "You lying bastard."

Ransome tried to duck behind a scarlet-faced, sweating marine, which only served to further enrage Dance, who came on like a gale, and struck hard, clamping onto Ransome's throat.

He was going to throttle the life out of the bastard here and now for both his lie and whatever it was he had done to put that look—that devasted, hopeless look—upon Jane's face.

And then there was a red wave of marines swarming over them, pulling him off his former bosun. Dance let them, and shook himself back to reason within their grip.

"That will do." The blue-coated naval lieutenant drew his sword. "I'll see the next man who moves flogged."

Dance stilled in the arms of the two marines who flanked him, but he did not take his eyes from Ransome. "Mr. Ransome has a very convenient way of twisting the truth to suit his own needs."

Ransome smiled, and muttered low, "The truth will be as I say. And you can't say otherwise."

Of course he could. And would. And there was no

court-martial in the world that would convict him of the murder of Captain Muckross. Not even if Jane was the only other witness left. But she had been on deck with him at the time. She had even thought it *her* fault.

Lieutenant Gibbs of HMS *Centaur* sheathed his sword, and looked from Dance to Ransome and back, clearly not knowing whom he ought to trust. So instead of relying on trust, he fell back on duty. "Escort both Captain Dance and Mr. Ransome back to the boats."

Dance acted as if they hadn't just effectively put him under armed guard. "Thank you, Lieutenant. As I was saying to you before Mr. Ransome accosted Miss Burke, Miss Burke is a conchologist with the Royal Society's expedition, and is under my protection. And if we are to remove to your ship, she has various equipment and material that will need to be carefully transported back to the ship."

The lieutenant frowned at Dance in confusion, but gave his order without even looking at the small encampment. "Have this gear packed up and taken to the boats." He turned to regard Jane with something just less than respect, and Dance saw his error—he had just exposed her to the censure of all of these men by stating that she was not married, but under his protection. His mistress, they would all think.

Jane was still staring at the fire, and picking at the charred remains.

Dance lowered his voice, and addressed Lieutenant Gibbs again. "Miss Burke is my betrothed, sir, and as such I expect the navy's courtesy to be extended fully to her."

This time Gibbs looked from Dance to Jane and back, weighing this new information much as he had the last, and just like the last, he fell back on duty. "I will see to Miss Burke personally, sir, if you will go with my men."

Dance took one last look at Jane, hoping that she would

look at him and understand, hoping he would be able to tell her good-bye. But she was pulling charred books from the sand, and did not look at him. And so he did the only thing a king's officer could do—he did his duty, and obeyed.

Immediately upon their arrival upon the deck of the third rate HMS *Centaur,* Dance was escorted—which was a very polite way of saying compelled under guard—to the captain.

Captain Sir David Douglas was a man Dance knew by reputation only—a veteran of twenty years' seniority, and a frigate captain of some renown before being elevated to the position of Commodore of the Fleet working out of the Valparaiso station and promoted to the third rate. He had a reputation as a hard man who made up his mind quickly, and never looked back.

When Lieutenant Gibbs announced him as Captain Dance, he decided that discretion was probably the better part of valor with such a formidable commander, and corrected Gibbs. "Lieutenant Charles Dance, sir. Lieutenant Commanding."

"Lieutenant Dance." Sir David Douglas made his own correction. "You have given me a rather extraordinary amount of trouble these past days. I have been fishing what is left of your crew out of the Pacific."

"My thanks, sir. How many of *Tenacious*' s men did you recover?"

"*Centaur* has encountered only one boat thus far, with a single man, but I judged it best to search these waters for more. We were, of course, forced to alter our course to answer your signal."

"Again, I thank you, sir."

"Mr. Ransome, your bosun, provided your name. And the fact that *Tenacious* was lost."

"Yes, sir, at approximately forty-one degrees latitude,

and one hundred and eight longitude. Driven off the cape by a polar gale."

"Ah. I see," Sir David said, though his tone indicated the opposite—that he did not care to see or hear Dance's account of the loss. "That is what this Ransome character said. But also that you had gone down with your ship."

"It may have appeared so, sir, as I went back to save one of my passengers, my betrothed, Miss Burke, who is a naturalist—a conchologist—and a member of the Royal Society's expedition. One of my crew had quite deliberately locked her in, and left her to drown."

"Miss Jane Burke? Of the Devon Burkes?"

"I—" Dance was embarrassed to find he had no idea—only that her great-grandfather was the Duke of Shafton, wherever that was. He had never asked.

Sir David's reaction was only slightly less than scathing. "Do you mean to tell me you do not know the family of your betrothed, sir?"

The accusation stung, and Dance felt his unshaven cheeks grow hot. "Miss Burke's grandfather is Lord Thomas Burke, the son of the Duke of Shafton."

"Of course he is—the Devon Burkes," he reiterated. "Well, Lieutenant, you seem to have landed yourself in it."

"Sir?"

"First losing your ship—your *ship,* sir—and now, ruining the reputation—for that is clearly what you have done to get yourself betrothed to the Duke of Shafton's relation."

Dance said the only thing he could think to say. "I did all I felt I could do to save the ship, sir." The other, he would not venture to speak of, because the baronet was correct.

"Did you?" Sir David looked down the very great length of his nose at Dance. "But that is yet to be determined."

Despite the fact that he had been expecting just such an outcome since the moment he had given the order to abandon ship, Dance felt his gut tighten into a knot. No matter that a formal inquiry was standard procedure after a ship was lost, it still felt as if his competence, as well as his integrity, were being questioned.

And it was. The captain looked hard at Dance, as if he were trying to assess his character at a glance.

Dance straightened his shoulders. "I welcome any inquiry, sir. My conduct will speak for itself."

"Will it? A ship has been lost. Your former captain is dead. Accusations have been made."

"By whom?" Dance belatedly tried to amend the vehement heat in his tone. "If I may ask, sir?"

"By your former crew."

There was only the one. "I take it you refer to Mr. Ransome."

"I do. A man with some twenty-six years of experience in His Majesty's service, and who spoke very highly of his former captain, Captain Muckross."

"While Captain Muckross was indeed a fine man, before his death by his own hand, Captain Muckross did not concern himself with any aspect of running his ship."

Sir David Douglas pushed himself away from his table, and slowly sat back in his seat. "That is an alarming accusation."

"It is not accusation, it is fact. Duly noted by both the officers, and many members of the crew." Devil take him, here he was, already lying to save his salt-tanned hide. While it was true the officers, especially Mr. Whitely, knew of Muckross's drunkenness, Dance had very deliberately tried to keep the fact from the crew.

"A fact which cannot be substantiated, as only one man of your crew has survived. The other are all, we must presume, lost. As are all the records of your ship. Mr. Ransome says he makes his accusations in the memory of his lost shipmates, and to right a very great wrong."

It was on the tip of Dance's tongue to correct Sir David's misinformation, but something—something that was bloody, damn well angry at being brought back to the ship by marines, and being kept from Jane—held him back. He had the log—it was surely in all of the gear that Jane would see was stowed carefully aboard.

Unless Ransome knew something he didn't.

Dance's mind flashed back to the fire, and Jane sifting through the ashes. And Ransome's triumphant look. Had he burned the log?

Fuck all.

There was nothing he could do but rely on sixteen hard years of training, and brazen it out. "I am sure that recounting suits Mr. Ransome's version of events. Mine is, however, quite different."

He would speak to Jane at the first opportunity that presented itself—which he hoped was immediately after the conclusion of this interview. He missed her already. His hands felt empty, and his heart off kilter. And his head—he needed to keep his head and his wits about him for the present interview.

"I had no doubt it would be." Sir David merely lifted his eyebrows. "Ransome's version of events, as you call it, includes an accusation of both incompetence and gross misconduct on your part."

Dance looked Sir David in the eye. "I have no doubt that Mr. Ransome feels that he should have made a better commander of *Tenacious* than I. But as first lieutenant, that responsibility fell to me. And I executed those duties in the manner I saw fit, in accordance with our official orders, which were to conduct a scientific survey of the greatest number possible of Pacific islands. Orders, I might add, I was not privy to until the death of the captain."

"What do you mean? Do you mean that Captain Muckross did not tell you, the first lieutenant, the sailing orders, even when, as you allege, he did not concern himself with the day-to-day work of his ship?"

"Yes. sir. That is correct."

Sir David pushed back his chair. "Extraordinary."

Extraordinary was actually a tame word for the events of the past few months. Dance had never spent so much toil for so little return, except in the rather extraordinary reward of Miss Jane Burke.

The captain's mind was running down the same stream. "And you say you saved this Miss Burke from the wreck?"

"Miss J. E. Burke. A conchologist with the Royal Society's expedition. A rather extraordinary, and extraordinarily resourceful individual. And my betrothed." He said it again, as if mere repetition of the word could convince Sir David.

Who regarded Dance with decided disfavor, his lips in an elegant curl. "You were alone with her for quite some time?"

"Forty-seven days, sir, from the moment I pulled her out of the shipwreck, where I will again remind you, some member of my crew maliciously locked her below decks, either so she might drown, or so I would in trying to save her."

At last Sir David's arches rose in perfect horror. "Captain Dance, you astonish me."

"It has been an astonishing cruise, sir. An extraordinarily astonishing expedition."

Chapter Twenty-five

The ship set sail as soon as she was brought aboard with the charred remains of all her work. Of Dance, she saw nothing, and heard less. Not in the hour after she was given a comfortable cabin just forward of the large stern cabin. Not in the afternoon when she was sent tea on a tray by a tight-lipped servant. And not the following day, when she forced herself to spend her time sewing herself proper clothes made from the bright calico of the purser's slops rather than go crazy staring at the walls and worrying about what they had done to Dance.

If she looked like a strange version of a bright-shirted topman, it did not matter—there was no one to see her. She was kept most carefully to herself until she was finally called before the captain.

"Miss Burke." Captain Sir David Douglas stood and did her the courtesy of bowing over her hand, after he deigned to invite her to take a dish of tea with him one afternoon after they had been at sea more than a few days. "I knew your grandfather. We were briefly at school together before I came into the navy. And I have a great regard for His Grace, your great-grandfather."

So much for the relative anonymity of being J. E. Burke,

conchologist. "Thank you, Sir David. But my concern is all for Captain Dance. I am anxious to see him."

"Best not, Miss Burke. Best not," he informed her over the top of his gold-rimmed spectacles. "Young Dance is in quite serious trouble, which I feel certain His Grace of Shafton should want you to be kept clear of."

"What sort of trouble?"

If Sir David found her tone pert, he only elevated that prodigious nose and looked down upon her from it. "The sort of trouble a captain earns when he loses one of His Majesty's vessels."

Jane raised her own chin a notch. "I feel certain His Majesty would approve of the way Captain Dance fought to keep that vessel afloat."

"Fought?"

"Yes, fought. Worked, as you navy men call it, watch on watch when others wouldn't or couldn't. When Captain Muckross was too blind and drunk to do his duty."

"I will do my best to forget that you said that, Miss Burke. I feel certain your grandfather would want you to forget such a sentiment as well."

"It is not a sentiment, Sir David. It is the plain truth of the matter. A truth I will swear to, if need be."

"And how do you think that would look, Miss Burke? A young, unmarried woman, who had been so rash as to take herself out upon the seas in a ship full of men, and who was stranded upon an island with a man she was not married to."

Jane felt her face flame as hot and red as if she had been sunburned. "Captain Dance was a perfect gentleman."

"Be that as it may, no one will believe you. A man with no family. I will not scruple to tell you, Miss Burke, what Dance assuredly did not. He is a nobody—a talented officer, perhaps—but he has no family, no name. He is the bastard son of God knows who. And if he knows, he is not saying. No, for your family's sake, I will not allow you to make a scandal of yourself."

Jane found herself propelled to her feet. "Captain Dance was kind enough to inform me of his ancestry, which I assure you troubles me not in the least. And if I should want to associate with him, that is for me to choose, sir, and not you."

"You are quite wrong, my dear girl. It is for me to choose. I am the captain, and what I say goes. It shall be as I say. Keep yourself quiet, and put Captain Dance completely from your mind."

In due time, all of which was spent in the close confines of her own small cabin, or in the superintending presence of the captain, *Centaur* was brought into Valparaiso, and Jane was whisked off the ship in the captain's gig, and taken to the palatial home of a British merchant who lived halfway up the sloping hillside of the city where the Pacific breezes were said to cool the air.

"Mr. Balfour, of the merchant house Balfour Williamson, is an esteemed friend, and happy to make himself useful both to me and to His Grace of Shafton. And he is a man whose discretion I can trust."

Sir David showed her through the doors of an imposing stone mansion overlooking a fountain plaza, and immediately withdrew himself, pleading Admiralty business. Jane was conducted above, and shown into a beautifully furnished soft green room that was astonishing in its opulence after her travels and travails.

Shown in, being a polite way of saying *shut in*. She heard the lock turn behind her with no instruction of what she was to expect, and no invitation to join the family, or view the house's public rooms. She was quite effectively cut off, just as Captain Sir David Douglas had, no doubt, intended. There was not so much as a piece of writing paper in the ornamental desk set before the tall windows.

But she did have an excellent view of the plaza and fountain. Jane tossed her much abused cloak on the desk chair, and pushed the heavy wooden shutters wide. She refused to be entirely closeted away like a naughty child, all because she had chosen to take a scientific journey on her own, and been shipwrecked with a man who might not prove to be a gentleman.

No. Jane rejected the thought, just as she had rejected Sir David's directive to put Dance from her mind. It was impossible. He was everything she thought of, everything she wanted—every comfort and joy. Every need. And nothing, not even the loss of all her other dreams, could compare to the hole in her heart—her very soul—without Dance.

No. She firmed her resolve. She would not be so disloyal.

But there was precious little she could do short of climbing out the window—though the drop did look formidable.

Jane retreated to the velvet-upholstered desk chair, and sat, listening as snatches of chatter in Spanish and Portuguese and English, as well as several other, unrecognizable languages, fluttered up from the street—the clatter and calls of maids as they shook out rugs and emptied pails, or hurried with their baskets toward what looked to be a market at the very far end of the street.

A snippet of a song filtered up from the cobbles, and echoed around the high, painted ceiling—such a large lovely room within which to be jailed. *"But stout and strong cider are England's control—"*

"Give me the punch ladle," Jane found herself humming along, *"I'll fathom the—"*

Dear God. She would know that Welsh tenor anywhere. "Punch!"

She bolted for the window and levered herself out over the sill, scanning the street for the familiar ginger beard. There, on the corner. "Punch!"

The one-legged old tar immediately raised his hand in silent greeting, as if he weren't in the least bit surprised to see her. He hop-skipped his way under the window, and asked in a low voice, "Can you come out?"

"No." She shook her head as she mouthed the word, and then, because he was right beneath her, and she had never been so glad to see an old friend in all of her life, and because she had no better idea of what to do, Jane took a deep breath to hide the hard hammering of her heart, and climbed straight out the window.

Punch wasn't fazed in the least. "Get that railing there, miss," he instructed. "And see if you can hang down from it there. That's it. We've got you."

Stout hands grasped her by the waist and lowered her down, but the moment her feet hit the pavement, Punch was hustling her across the plaza and out of sight down a winding street.

"Are you all to rights then, miss?" Punch took in her strange calico dress.

"Yes, now that you've found me. And how did you find me?"

"Had my ear to the ground, so to speak. And the chatter up the market there was that good Mr. Balfour had some duke's granddaughter at his house. And knowing that the cap'n would have taken good care of you, and hoping it might be you, I came to see for myself. But them being mighty high in the instep"—he hooked his thumb over his shoulder at the house across the plaza—"they wouldn't tell me, nor take a note in to you. So Flanaghan here suggested a song."

Jane looked behind her to find the former topman, who tugged his forelock. "Mistress."

His choice of words made Jane flush with heat to the roots of her hair, but he meant it kindly enough.

"Come to fetch you, we have."

"Thank you," she said, even though she seemed to have

fetched herself out the window. "I'm so glad you did. How did you get here? How did you survive? Who survived?"

"All that stuck together, miss." Punch answered the last question first. "Mr. Whitely and Mr. Simmons, when he recovered himself, headed us out of the gale and found us a Yankee whaling ship that brung us here safe enough."

"And Mr. Whitely, and Mr. Simmons and Mr. Denman? Where are they?"

"Inn not too far from here." Punch pointed down the road. "Been taking their time reporting to the Admiralty, letting Mr. Simmons recover hisself a little better."

"Oh, thank God. Let us go to them this instant."

"And the captain?" Punch asked, as he looked back at the house across the plaza. "Where is he?"

"Oh, Lord. I was hoping you knew. They won't tell me anything. Captain Sir David Douglas, who brought me here, said he was to be brought before a court-martial for the loss of *Tenacious*. And Mr. Ransome has accused Dance of murdering Captain Muckross."

"God's balls," said Punch.

"Exactly, Punch. My sentiments exactly."

Dance was brought to court-martial for the loss of *Tenacious* with alarming swiftness. Immediately upon their arrival in the port of Valparaiso, a board of three post captains was convened upon *Centaur* under the authority of Captain Sir David Douglas, who as senior, acted as both president and judge-advocate.

The deck was cleared forward of the stern cabin to admit the number of people necessary—Admiralty clerks and personal servants to the sitting captains, as well as the witnesses, who were kept out of Dance's sight in the wardroom below.

But the gathering was surprisingly small. When Sir David saw Dance's gaze taking account of the smallness, he growled, "I want the senior services' dirty laundry aired to as few people as possible. I want this over and done with quickly."

Dance could only hope the baronet's speed would not involve a rush to judgment against him, but there was nothing he could do but stand as documents and orders were shuffled, clerks put pens to ink, and the charges were read against him.

"In the matter of the loss of His Majesty's Ship *Tenacious,* frigate, sixth rate." Sir David looked up from the document in front of him. "Lieutenant Charles Dance, acting captain, by the death of Captain Muckross. By storm, was it, Lieutenant?"

Dance couldn't read the intention in Captain Douglas's careful voice. "By storm, and neglect, sir."

"Neglect, sir? Do you accuse yourself?"

Dance swallowed his oath and set his course. "Partly, sir," he admitted, and hoped to hell he hadn't damned himself. But the truth would out one way or another. But he had to go carefully. Any hint of disloyalty, or accusing a senior captain who was no longer there to defend himself, would not sit well with such post captains as were seated to judge him. Best to take the responsibility upon himself, and hope the truth would out. "I had thought I did all I could to see *Tenacious* brought into a state of readiness and repair, but I understand now that I could have done more as her lieutenant. But I failed then in my duty to convince Captain Muckross of the seriousness of the vessel's state of disrepair."

One of the other captains—a middle-aged man Dance had never encountered before—asked, "When did you come to this ship?"

Dance answered the question factually, and there was a little back-and-forth among the panel as to his particulars and record of service, before Dance thought it would behoove him to mention, "*Tenacious* was a Leda-class frigate, sir, built of pine using Mr. Josiah Brindley's patent method of construction, without lodging and hanging knees, using instead iron fastenings and iron knees."

That information had all the effect he might have liked, for the captains' expressions turned sour in commiseration—it was well-known that pine rotted much more quickly than oak.

"And you say that it was under your orders that the ship was put to repairs?"

"Under my orders, and under considerable weight to my own purse. Upon a week of my arrival, the purser, Mr. Givens, absconded with *Tenacious*'s accounts."

"The devil," Lord Douglas murmured as he flipped the papers in front of him. "This fact has not yet been mentioned."

The more vocal member of the panel spoke up. "Clearly there is a great deal more to this affair than has been mentioned—there is an accusation of murder."

Dance forced his face to impassivity—he had known that Ransome was his enemy, and had accused him of the murder before, in front of Lieutenant Gibbs. But Dance had held out hopes that the bosun would think better of fabricating such a lie. Because it was a hanging offense, and it was a blow that knocked the wind from his lungs to hear it spoken so plainly.

"May I hear that charge, sir?"

Lord Douglas made a swift gesture of consent, and the clerk read out the charge. "Lieutenant Charles Dance stands accused of neglect of duty, abandonment of his post, and conspiring treason and murder against his captain, both as first lieutenant of the ship *Tenacious,* and acting as her captain."

He asked even though he knew the answer. "Who makes this charge?"

"The boatswain, George Ransome," answered the clerk.

It was all as predictable as a Covent Garden broadsheet.

Ransome was called, and rolled in looking chastened and concerned and deeply respectful of the impaneled officers. He knuckled his forehead to each of them in turn, and acted almost reluctant to speak against Dance.

"I take no pleasure in it, your lordship."

"Yes, Mr. Ransome." Sir David was both pleased and impatient at this show of servility. "So you said. But I should like for the benefit of my fellow adjutants, if you would repeat for the court the accusations you lodged against your superior officer, Mr. Dance."

Ransome laid it out meticulously, accusation after accusation—Dance's preempting of the captain's will to hire his own men, Dance's setting sail against the captain's advice, his captain's accusations of treason, Dance's insistence that no one see the captain's body, and his command, against the advice of all others, to take them into the teeth of the storm. It was all there, fact after fact. And yet none of it was the truth.

"He'll say different." Ransome pushed his chin toward Dance. "I'll be bound he does. But there's no one left as can say otherwise. He's got rid of them all. Wrecked or killed. And he destroyed his logbook in the fire when we found him. So's there wouldn't be any evidence against him."

Dance was both astonished at the man's audacity, and enraged at his cleverness in arranging it all so damningly. There was only one thing he could say that would not feed into the half-truths and innuendo that the bastard had set up. "I did not destroy my logbook, sir. I was with Lieutenant Gibbs at the time, and whatever was destroyed, I do not believe it was my log, which is with the rest of the material that Mr. Gibbs had packed up from our time on the island."

"Our?" The post captain to the right of Sir David narrowed his eyes. "Were you not alone when *Centaur* found you?"

Ransome made a snide sound of delight, but before the bosun could say anything derogatory about Jane, Sir David cut him off with a withering eye, and a firm command. "Pass word for Lieutenant Gibbs to search for that logbook. Now." He refocused his gaze upon Dance. "How long were you in command of *Tenacious* before she was lost? With nearly all souls, I might add."

"I was in command for twelve days, as captain, sir, though I had all the responsibilities of the command from the moment of weighing anchor in Portsmouth. To my knowledge the captain only came out of his cabin once during all of the time I was aboard."

"That's a lie," Ransome countered.

"It is the truth." Dance kept his voice calm, but it sounded more weary than he had intended. But in for a penny, in for a bloody pound. "The captain had been going slowly blind. His eyesight had deteriorated to the point where he could barely see. I believe this was the reason that he killed himself, because he was found out."

"Blind?" Sir David was something between astonished and angry at such an inconvenient charge.

The shrewd post captain to Sir David's right sat back in his chair. "So we have the opposing word of two men, one an officer and the other a warrant, and no other way to verify either of their testimony?"

"I am sure that my log will confirm the truth of my testimony," Dance averred.

"There is no log," Ransome repeated.

"But the loss of the vessel—" Sir David began.

"Pine-built, Leda-class. I wouldn't have wanted to go round the Lizard"—the sharp post captain waved his arm in referring to the legendary rock of the south coast of England—"much less round the Horn. And you effected repairs on a lieutenant's pay?" He looked to Dance to answer.

"And what I had saved in prize money, sir."

"And you spent how much?"

Dance swallowed over the uncomfortable reminder. "All I had, sir. Or nearly all of some eight thousand pounds. I have not had a letter from my banker since I signed for oak in Recife. But I suspect he will be displeased."

The post captain was rifling through the pages in front of him. "You were in what vessels before *Tenacious*?"

Dance gave his bona fides. "Midshipman in *Audacious*, sir, under Captain McAlden, who promoted me to *Swiftsure* with him as third lieutenant, and then with Captain Colyear, again in *Audacious* as second, before being promoted to first lieutenant back with Captain McAlden in *Irresistible*, as *Swiftsure* was renamed."

"Which meant that you were made lieutenant when?"

"At Trafalgar, sir. In the year oh-five." Dance took a very great risk bringing up that battle, as he knew Sir David had not been a part of it, and might resent the reminder.

But the sharp post captain sat back in his chair, and gave a satisfied nod. "Your captains must have valued you to promote you back and forth amongst themselves."

"I hope I served them well, sir."

But Sir David was not as impressed by Dance's record. "Mr. Ransome here is a twenty-year veteran, as well, and has no marks against his service."

"So two men, with two exemplary records—"

"I don't know that I would say that Lieutenant Dance's record is exemplary," Sir David opined.

"I would," the post captain responded shortly. "Not all of us share your insistence upon family and lineage, Captain Douglas." The use of his rank rather than his title brought the point home. "Service and merit is what matters."

The older captain on the other side of Sir David spoke up for the first time. "And we have two men, of unequal rank, with fine records of service from which we must choose, and weigh one man's word against the other."

"No," said a quiet voice from the back of the room. "There is more."

Jane had forced her way into the proceedings by the simple expediency of lying, and saying that she had been sent for by Sir David. Who did not look best pleased to find her interrupting his court.

"Young woman." His eyes blazed at her over the top of his spectacles. "I have advised you that this is not the place for you. You ought to have taken that advice, for your family's sake, if not your own."

"My family, sir, would want me to do my duty in seeing justice served."

"And who are you?" asked one of the captains sitting in judgment behind the table.

Jane tipped up her chin. "I am J. E. Burke, the conchologist."

"And how are you concerned in this matter?"

"I was a member of the Royal Society's expedition aboard *Tenacious*. And I come in support of the lieutenant. As do these officers." She turned and indicated the empty space behind her, knowing full well that Lieutenants Simmons and Lawrence, as well as Mr. Whitely and Mr. Denman, had all been denied entry at the door, as potential witnesses were kept apart from the proceedings until they were called, while Jane had presumably been admitted on the grounds that she could not possibly be of any use, being both female and small. She was taking great pleasure in disabusing them of that notion.

And she did so, by going to the doors, and pushing them open to admit *Tenacous*'s officers. "These gentlemen come to testify in the lieutenant's support as well."

But Sir David was not done teaching her a lesson. "You were shipwrecked with the lieutenant, were you not? Alone on an island? Who is to say that your sensibilities were not turned by him? Especially in such harrowing, and forgive me, intimate circumstances."

Jane could feel heat scalding her cheeks, and the hot pressure wrapping like a hand around her throat, threatening to choke off her air.

No. No. She would not succumb to it. She had outgrown such childish panic. And Dance was much more important than any threat of scandal—his very life was at stake.

She drew breath by force of will alone. If Sir David wanted a scandal, she would give him one to remember. "Intimate? What do you allege, sir? Surely your lordships can see that I am not the *type* of woman to have my sensibilities turned. I am not a green girl, my lord. I am a conchologist and a scholar. And Lieutenant Dance is a gentleman. But I do not invite you to take my word for it. I have brought you the evidence of the lieutenant's log."

It was a vast deal of time later before Dance's pulse returned to normal. The adjutants had taken a great amount of time deliberating over the logbooks—Doc Whitely, Able Simmons, and Jack Denman all produced theirs, taken with each of them during the shipwreck—and closely questioning all those men.

"Do you mean, sir," the sharp post captain probed Lieutenant Simmons' testimony, "that both you, and the bow works, were deliberately attacked?"

"I do, sir. And I believe it was that man"—Simmons pointed his finger at Ransome—"who did so. I accuse him."

Sir David's straightforward case was going up in flames around him.

"It was Manning," Ransome countered. "He's the one. Locked Miss Burke in too. Wanted revenge on her for finding out about the captain."

Sir David passed a hand before his eyes. "Finding out what, exactly?"

"That he were blind. And broke—" Ransome bit his answer off.

"And so the captain *was* blind, and did *not* take part in commanding his ship?"

"I never said—" Ransome began.

"Yes," Dance countered in a stronger voice. "Yes. And while both Miss Burke and I can testify that Manning was indeed the one who locked her in, I find it curious that he should have tried to damage the ship and strike a superior officer. Especially as he is not here to defend himself. What happened to Manning, Mr. Ransome?"

"What happened to all the men in your gig, Mr. Ransome," added Able Simmons, "when you quite deliberately ignored Mr. Whitely's orders and took your boat apart from all the others?"

"Ignored orders?" Not even Sir David could overcome such an offense. "And who is this Manning?" He consulted the papers spread out before him.

"Steward to Captain Muckross," Dance clarified. "I believe he took the captain's suicide quite hard."

Ransome leaped upon the idea. "Devoted to him, he were—as were we all—and crazed with grief. That's why he coshed Mr. Simmons over the head with that lever, and locked in herself. Crazed."

"And where is this Manning now?"

"Dead," spat Ransome. "Devil take his soul."

"And how did he die?" the quiet judge asked.

Ransome blinked, and put his tongue out to lick his lips before speaking. "In the boat. From exposure and thirst. He weren't a strong man."

"And yet you allege that he was strong enough to pull out repairs—extensive repairs made by the carpenter— and attack a fit man such as Lieutenant Simmons?"

Ransome would not give up. "Crazed he was, I tell you."

"Mr. Ransome." The sharp post captain leaned forward over the table. "I must warn you that your answers stink strongly of lies."

"I've heard quite enough." Sir David rose in order to stop the spilling over of so much dirty laundry. "Gentlemen." He addressed his fellow adjutants. "If you will follow me."

The men filed out of the room to consult, and a heavy hush descended upon them. No one spoke. And Dance could only look at Jane, and hope that his thanks, and more, was visible upon his face. Because there was no time or opportunity for anything else. The panel of judges was already back.

And in less time than they had taken to deliberate, Captain Sir David Douglas took up his charge.

Everything that was within Dance contracted into a single tight knot. He felt almost dizzy, as if the blood were being squeezed out of him—his palms pricked and tingled as Sir David adjusted his spectacles and took his blasted time finding his place on the paper before him.

Get on with it, man, Dance wanted to shout.

Sir David cleared his throat. "The court having maturely and deliberately considered the evidence, finds these charges against Lieutenant Charles Dance not proved." He paused and looked over his spectacles. "Lieutenant Dance, do you wish to accuse the bosun, George Ransome, of neglect of duty and willful misconduct, as well as false testimony?"

Blood and air and gratitude pounded back into Dance's lungs all at once. He heard the murmured approval of his officers, and Jane's sharp intake of breath, but had to steady himself before he could say, "I do."

"So you have." Sir David leveled his steely gaze at Ransome. "It is the judgment of this court that you, George

Ransome, be reproved for the false witness you have given this day. You are stripped of your warrant, and are hereby dismissed from the service. Let some merchant take you off the service's hands, but you will not find employment among honest men."

And so it was done.

But not to Ransome. He turned on Dance. "You couldn't leave well enough alone, could you? You couldn't let things be easy as they were. You had to meddle and prod and go where you weren't wanted."

Dance drew himself up. "What I did, Mr. Ransome, was my duty." And so he had.

"Duty!" Ransome spat on the deck timbers at the judges' feet. "Duty can hang. What has duty ever got for men like me? Twenty years in the king's service, and put ashore for the peace with nothing to show but the clothes on my back. I was only after taking what was mine. What I earned for twenty years of backbreaking work of saving my bloody country."

Ransome's words hung in the air for a long stunned moment before Sir David spoke. "It is your good fortune that you have been dismissed from the service, Ransome, as duty would not have hanged, but you most assuredly would. Now get this man from my sight, and put him off my ship."

And so it really was done. Ransome was taken up by the marines, and dragged, cursing, from the ship.

Despite his acquittal, Dance felt like he had been keel-hauled and flogged round the fleet. Even his brain felt tender and sore as he shook hands with Sir David and the other adjutant captains, and endured the hearty congratulations of Denman, Whitely, and Simmons.

But there was only one person he wanted to see, and she was slipping out of the cabin, and headed for the entry port.

"Jane!" He ran after her, and took her arm in a firm

grip. He had thought he had lost her twice before, and he was not going to let go of her now. "Where do you think you are going?"

She looked up at him with her honest blue eyes and said. "I hardly know."

"I do." He was all serious, impulsive decision. "We are going to get married. Right now."

Jane looked up at him with those marvelously bright eyes, and smiled that smile that warmed him like nothing else. And then she looked down at her strange calico dress. "Right this moment?"

"Yes." He took her other hand just in case she did not understand him. "I refuse to spend another day apart from you."

"Do you?" She looked at him from under her brows, the mischievous warmth lighting her eyes. "And in what manner have I given you to think that I would marry a man like you, with no fortune and no name?"

He refused to think that she was doing anything but flirting with him. He refused to be intimidated, though her great-grandfather was the Duke of Shafton, and she did deserve better. So did he—he deserved *her*. He had earned her. "My dear Miss Burke. I cannot possibly make a list of such things in public."

Her smile was like the sun on a cloudy day, breaking through all his unspoken doubts. "Might you be persuaded to make such a list in private?"

"Most emphatically. But we cannot easily be private until you have married me." It was all he could think of— all he had thought of for days. He had been delivered from his accusers by her hand, and that hand he would make his own.

But she was not so impetuous. "And this is your proposal?"

He stared at her. "Yes."

She looked at him with those forthright eyes. "It is a very

bad one. You haven't at all arranged things in the proper manner."

"Jane. Nothing we have done, from one end of this voyage to the other, has been done in the proper manner. What on earth makes you think I am about to start doing so now?"

"Well," she objected. "You have done a few things in the proper manner, I suppose. A very few things."

Few?

"Jane." He tried to invest his voice with a wealth of warning, but she was his Jane, and she was not in the least intimidated by this captain growl.

"If I marry you, and go on your ships with you, will you promise to let me have access to all your barnacles?"

He thought he was going to expire on the spot. "Oh, yes, Miss Burke. Oh, yes. You will have free and unlimited access to each and every one."

She gave him her very sunniest smile. "Then yes, Captain Dance. I will."

Epilogue

They were married on a rare sunny day by the Reverend Mr. Phelps who was not best pleased to find himself after the fact, but as the typhoon that had separated Dance and Jane from the others was an act of God, their being thrown together on the island was also an act of God, and who was he to object to the Almighty's sovereign will?

The ceremony in the *Centaur*'s wide stern cabin—Sir David not wanting to pass up an opportunity of making himself useful to the Duke of Shafton—was entirely private, consisting of only the reverend, and themselves, and Sir Richard and Mr. Parkhurst—who, with all their precise interest in the strange weather, had determined its cause to be an ash cloud from an explosion of the volcano Mount Tambora in the Lesser Sunda Islands of the Dutch East Indies, where they were now bound to investigate—as well as Jack Denman. And *Tenacious*'s officers, of course, and Captain Sir David Douglas as official witnesses. And Punch, who was kind enough to give her away. And a few sailors who proved remarkably sentimental about a shipwrecked bride—they passed her various trinkets and pieces of carved ivory, and bid her hold them for good luck.

But Jane did not need good luck. She had Dance, and he was all the luck she would need.

If Jane had ever dreamed of something grander than the quiet words said in borrowed clothes, she forgot it, and learned to fill her dreams with other things.

Because Dance had made plans.

As soon as the Reverend Mr. Phelps had finished reading out the words, and made a written record of the event in his logbook—and Dance had made the august notation in his—her husband let her be kissed by her friends, and then ushered her into a boat.

Though Jane would rather have done almost anything than get into another boat, she tried for patience. "Where are we going?"

"You'll see." He smiled though he did not look at her.

In fact, Jane thought, he smiled and would not *let* himself look at her, lest he tell all. "Dance?" she wheedled. "Tell me."

"We are going there." He pointed across the water to a trim schooner anchored some distance off.

His answer was not at all as she had expected. "I thought you said they had posted you to a frigate."

"They have. But not quite yet."

"Not quite? Dance?"

"Patience," was all he would say, until the gig slid alongside the low, sleek hull and Dance stood—impervious to the motion of the sea—and handed her aboard. "Up you go, madam."

The flush-decked, two-masted ship was beautiful in and of herself, with her polished wood and brass gleaming in the sunlight. Her husband—her husband, hers and hers alone—made a quick inspection of the vessel, until he finally asked, "What do you think of her?"

He was wearing that strange little half-smile of his—the cynical-looking one, that she had not seen in quite some time. It worried her. "I hardly know what to think. She is a very beautiful vessel. Very American, I should think, with this efficient fore and aft rig. But hardly a suitable command for a post captain."

"But she is my command. At least temporarily." And now his smile spread full across his face as if he could no longer contain it—as if he no longer *wanted* to contain it. "Sir David Douglas has gifted her to us for a honeymoon."

And now Jane could not contain her smile. "How thoughtful." It would be wonderful to have someplace private to be together at long last. Somewhere they could touch and hold hands and sleep curled against each other. "It will be heaven."

"Exactly," Dance confirmed. "Because that is where we shall be going. But I shall need your help to make sure everything is packed in readiness, and arranged just so."

For a moment Jane's face burned with the thought that he was speaking metaphorically, and that he thought to return them to that state of connubial bliss they had enjoyed on the island, but the look in those green eyes of his was too open, too literal—

"Dance? Do you mean—" Jane squashed her hand over her mouth to keep the words in. She could hardly dare hope.

"For your honeymoon, Mrs. Dance, I mean to take you to a very private place I know of at approximately twenty-four degrees latitude and one-hundred twenty-four longitude."

"We're going *back* to the island?"

"We are, and you are going to find those giant bivavles, and tritons, and cone shells and whatever else were going to make you the most famous conchologist and discoverer of shells the Royal Society has ever known, so you can replace each and every one of the drawings that Ransome destroyed."

"Dance." Her voice had gone all hot and soft, and her vision of him was clouded by an astonishing press of hot tears. "I can't—"

"What do you mean you can't? I thought— Jane. What is the matter? Why are you crying?"

"Because I'm happy."

He looked at her with that stunned, uncomprehending expression she so loved. "Now you cry because you are happy? You who have endured more hardships than even Sir Richard might have imagined—superstition, near drowning, and shipwreck, not to mention the loss of your book, which I know you feel more keenly—without so much as a single tear?"

"Yes." Once she had started she could not seem to stop.

So many things, so many hardships and changes—the tears flowed until she knew her cheeks were wet and her eyes had gone red from the stinging tears. Because she wouldn't change a thing. "Because I would endure it all again this instant if it would bring me you. Nothing, no shell taxonomy, nor mention by the Royal Society, will ever mean as much to me as you."

Dance took her face between his big hands, and thumbed away her tears, and pressed a single, solitary kiss upon her forehead. "I don't know what I have ever done in my life to deserve you."

"You saved me from drowning, for one thing—and that counts a very, very great deal with me. But you know you could have stopped me that morning. You know you could have simply shaken your head, and told me to be off, and never let me board, and I would have slunk home across the Solent in my pinnace, and none of this ever would have happened. But it did, all thanks to you. Because you said yes."

"I never actually said yes."

"Dance. Shut up. You are ruining a perfectly good, sentimentally heartfelt speech."

"Good. I deplore sentiment. And I have a much better way of shutting up your mouth, my dear Mrs. Dance. Just the way you like it." He looked at her then, in that way that made her feel as if she were the only person in the entirety of the world—as if they were the only two people in creation, and they had all the time in creation to simply be together, in love.

She took firm hold of his hand. "Do you, Captain?"

And so he kissed her, to end all doubt. Firmly and tenderly and with hunger. Just the way she liked it.

FIC
ESSEX

A scandal to
remember.

DATE			

BAKER & TAYLOR